FUSE
OF ARMAGEDDON

FUSE

OF ARMAGEDDON

SIGMUND BROUWER
HANK HANEGRAAFF

TYNDALE HOUSE PUBLISHERS, INC., CAROL STREAM, ILLINOIS

Visit Tyndale's exciting Web site at www.tyndale.com

TYNDALE and Tyndale's quill logo are registered trademarks of Tyndale House Publishers, Inc.

Fuse of Armageddon

Library of Congress Cataloging-in-Publication Data

Hanegraaff, Hank.
    Fuse of Armageddon / Hank Hanegraaff, Sigmund Brouwer.
        p. cm.
    ISBN-13: 978-1-4143-1025-1
    ISBN-10: 1-4143-1025-0
    ISBN-13: 978-1-4143-1027-5 (pbk.)
    ISBN-10: 1-4143-1027-7 (pbk.)
    1. Qubbat al-Sakhrah (Mosque : Jerusalem)—Fiction.   2. Jerusalem—Fiction.   3. Terrorism—Fiction.   I. Brouwer, Sigmund, date.   II. Title.
    PS3608.A714F87 2008
    813'.6—dc22   2007008868

Printed in the United States of America

13 12 11 10 09 08 07
 7   6   5   4   3   2   1

To Stephen Ross,
with appreciation for your commitment
to reading the Bible for all its worth.
Hank

O,

*Thanks for the help with military matters, your continued
encouragement, and the enjoyable discussions.*

". . . the Lobby's campaign to squelch debate about Israel is unhealthy for democracy. Silencing skeptics by organizing blacklists and boycotts—or by suggesting that critics are anti-Semites—violates the principle of open debate upon which democracy depends. The inability of the U.S. Congress to conduct a genuine debate on these vital issues paralyzes the entire process of democratic deliberation. Israel's backers should be free to make their case and to challenge those who disagree with them. But efforts to stifle debate by intimidation must be roundly condemned by those who believe in free speech and open discussion of important public issues."

JOHN J. MEARSHEIMER (University of Chicago) and STEPHEN M. WALT (Harvard University), "The Israel Lobby"

"[Dispensationalists once] sat high in the bleachers on history's fifty-yard line, watching as various teams took their positions on the playing field below and explaining to everyone who would listen how the game was going to end. For the first one hundred years of their movement, then, they were observers, not shapers, of events. But all that changed after Israel reclaimed its place in Palestine and expanded its borders. For the first time, dispensationalists believed that it was necessary to leave the bleachers and get onto the playing field to make sure the game ended according to the divine script."

Historian TIMOTHY WEBER, On the Road to Armageddon

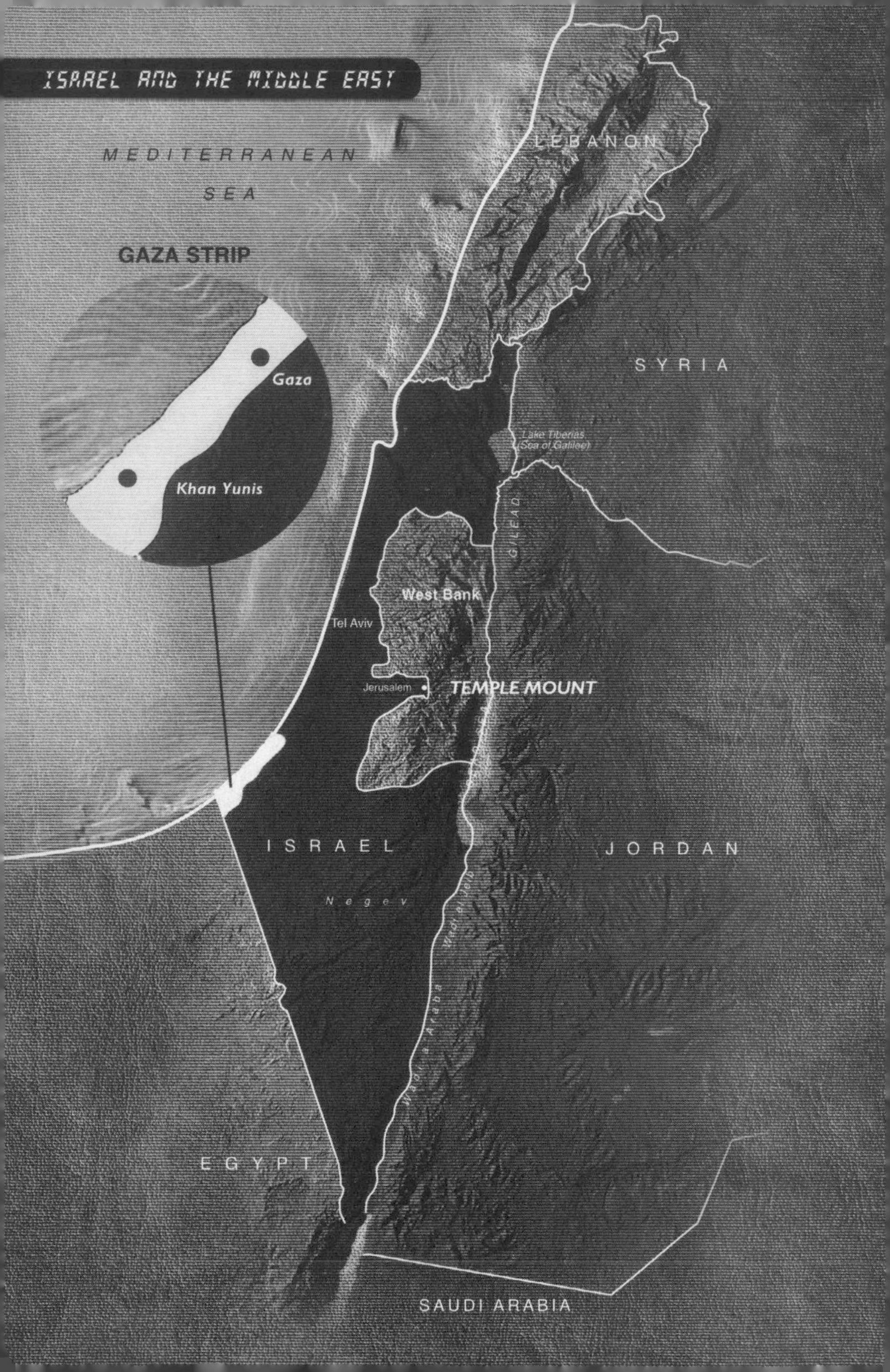
ISRAEL AND THE MIDDLE EAST
MEDITERRANEAN SEA
GAZA STRIP
Gaza
Khan Yunis
LEBANON
SYRIA
Lake Tiberias (Sea of Galilee)
GILEAD
West Bank
Tel Aviv
Jerusalem
TEMPLE MOUNT
ISRAEL
JORDAN
Negev
EGYPT
SAUDI ARABIA

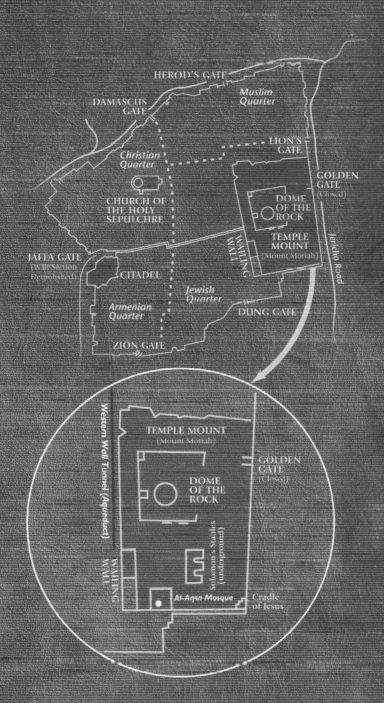

HEROD'S GATE

DAMASCUS
GATE

*Muslim
Quarter*

*Christian
Quarter*

LION'S
GATE

GOLDEN
GATE
(Closed)

CHURCH OF
THE HOLY
SEPULCHRE

DOME
OF THE
ROCK

WAILING WALL

TEMPLE
MOUNT
(Mount Moriah)

Jericho Road

JAFFA GATE
(Wall Section
Demolished)

CITADEL

*Jewish
Quarter*

DUNG GATE

*Armenian
Quarter*

ZION GATE

Western Wall Tunnel (Aqueduct)

TEMPLE MOUNT
(Mount Moriah)

GOLDEN
GATE
(Closed)

DOME
OF THE
ROCK

WAILING
WALL

Solomon's Stables
(underground)

Al-Aqsa Mosque

Cradle
of Jesus

PROLOGUE

With dusk falling on a windless and cloudless autumn day in West Virginia, a veiled man in a black sweater and black pants stepped into the hunting cabin owned by Four-Star General Anthony William Underwood.

Underwood was big, with no sloppiness in his body, even at age fifty-nine. He wore a flannel shirt and was unshaven. There was no electricity in the cabin, and a hissing lantern hung from the ceiling, throwing out light that seemed to grow brighter as night approached, casting shadows on the square face beneath Underwood's equally square crew cut.

He sat at a small dining room table, with a Colt .45 beside an open Bible in front of him. Sometimes a person needed more than God's Word. Underwood had expected the visitor but not the black veil that revealed only the man's eyes. He picked up the Colt and leveled it at the veiled man's chest. "I'm waiting," he said. His idea. Password protection was as old as mankind. Underwood liked things that didn't lose effectiveness in the face of computer technology. The Colt was another good example.

"Armageddon," the visitor complied.

This was the man then. Spooky, all in black like this—someone ensuring he would be invisible when he left the cabin. Even his shoulder bag was black.

Underwood set the pistol back on the table beside the Bible—within easy reach—and made no apology for the implication of its continued presence.

Underwood had been there in the hills at his lakeside cabin for two days. Alone. Hunting during daylight. His staff knew the retreat had been planned. There was nothing unusual about his stay at the cabin.

That made it the perfect site for this meeting. His staff did not know about the visitor, who, as required by the conditions the general had set for this meeting, had parked five miles away and walked the rest of the way, using a GPS locator to find the cabin.

"I don't like the veil," Underwood said. "Looks like what a Muslim woman wears."

"Niqab," the visitor said.

When Underwood frowned with obvious incomprehension, the visitor repeated the word. "Niqab. It's what Muslims call a face veil."

"Call it what you want. I don't like it. Muslims are the reason I agreed to this meeting. That veil is a mockery."

"Think of it as irony. Using something so fundamentally Muslim against them . . . if you'll pardon the pun."

"A hood is more American," Underwood said. *American.* Unlike his visitor's accent. British?

"Easier to breathe beneath a niqab," the visitor said.

Yes. Underwood decided the accent was English. Not Cockney, but what was it called? It came to him. Posh.

"More efficient for vision than eye holes in a hood," the visitor continued.

"Don't wear a nabasco then," Underwood said, deliberately mangling the word. "Or a hood."

"I'm afraid it's quite necessary. If you don't know me, we're both protected."

"Could be you are one of the Muslims. There's lots of them in London, right?" Underwood was fishing for a clue to the man's identity. "What do they call it now? Londonistan?"

"Think of all the effort it took to set this up and who set it up for you," the visitor said with those cultured vowel inflections. "You really believe I'm Muslim?"

Underwood grunted.

"If it makes you feel better," the man said, "call me Smith. A good, clean, American name." As he spoke, the veiled visitor set his shoulder bag on the floor.

"Smith," Underwood said. "Get started. If you know anything about me, you know I don't like wasting time."

"Let me show you a terrorist's greatest weapon," Smith said. He stooped to reach into the bag.

"Hold it right there." Underwood had the pistol in his hand again, now pointed at the face veil. "The agreement was no weapons."

Smith froze with his hand inside the shoulder bag, eyes on the Colt. "An agreement I see you had no trouble breaking."

"My cabin," Underwood said. "My rules to break. Tell me what you've got in there."

"A laptop."

Underwood's cabin had other rules—no computers, no cell phones, and no electronics. Normally the general would have barked out a command to leave it in the bag. But this was a meeting with many exceptions already. Including the absolute secrecy.

Underwood set his pistol on the table again as Smith pulled out the laptop. He hadn't been too worried that Smith would try anything dangerous. He'd just wanted to make a point. He left the pistol near his right hand, happy to continue making the point. "Laptop? You'll notice my Colt is more effective."

"The Internet gives terrorists more reach," Smith said.

"You have to have access to have reach," Underwood said. "If you're depending on a connection here, you've wasted a lot of time and effort to meet with me."

"You're right; without my satellite link, this would have been a waste. But you need to see what we are capable of." Smith turned the laptop slightly to give the general a view of the screen. The browser had already begun to link to a Web site, and images began to fill the screen: pieces of Monet's art.

It looked like a page of a university site. Underwood noted the Web address and memorized it. He was known for this ability, and it intimidated his staff.

Without hesitation, Smith clicked on the painting in the lower right-hand corner. It was titled *The Saint-Lazare Station*. While available online as a digital image, the painting itself was displayed in the Musée d'Orsay, Paris.

Smith spoke as if he were lecturing. Internet. Digital download. Encryption. Anonymous chat rooms. In the third millennium, this was a new battleground. Al-Qaeda had shown how. Web sites devoted to training. Chat rooms where suicide bombers encouraged each other. Servers switched daily. It was a world where warriors could gather without crossing borders.

Yes, a brave new world.

An image of the Monet painting opened, and Smith saved it.

Then he brought up the Web site for the Musée d'Orsay and found another copy of *The Saint-Lazare Station*. Smith saved this image too. Side by side, both copies of *The Saint-Lazare Station* were now on his screen, intricate blurs of pale color in Monet's style.

Smith's eyes shifted from the laptop to Underwood. It was eerie for Underwood, seeing only eyes and the pale outline of flesh against the black veil and sweater.

"I'm going to use an encryption program that will analyze the files and compare the differences of both images' binary code," Smith said.

"Binary code." Underwood thought of his boyhood on a Wisconsin farm, when the telephone had been rotary dial, connected by a party line. Then it was typewriters, carbon copies, and slide rules. Now? Satellites provided GPS locations for things as trivial as giving golfers the exact distance to the middle of the green.

"Every pixel in the image is represented by three colors—red, green, or blue. Each color has a binary value—a string of numbers composed of zeros or ones—for computer recognition. I explain this because I want you to know how difficult it has become to stop terrorists."

The explanation continued in that sophisticated accent, as if Smith were an Oxford professor. A pure red pixel, he said, was 1111 0000 0000, which computer software translated into 100 percent red, 0 percent green, and 0 percent blue. By altering the binary code slightly and adding one bit—one binary digit—of information to the blue segment, the binary code became 1111 0000 0001, a color change imperceptible to the human eye.

Although it was only the addition of a single bit, given the millions of bits in a digital image, there was enough room to hide a message that counterterrorist programs would never discover. Intercepting an embedded message would take knowledge of the suspected sender or recipient and access to the suspected computers and e-mail accounts.

"This is why terrorists have no fear of being caught," Smith said. "Nor should you when you use this method to communicate with me."

"Assuming you come up with a good enough reason," Underwood said. He decided if there *was* a good reason, he'd still insist on seeing the man's face. In this light, the man's eyes were brown. Colored contact lenses?

"Keep watching," Smith said. The black veil appeared seamless with his shoulders.

The cryptology program analyzed the differences and assembled the hidden bits into words.

```
Opimgt terb lkajerlkj

kljltkjeppoit l;ol tp29 m,/.,ad/.
```

"Not much of a message for all the work it took to get it," Underwood said.

"Wait." Without closing this program, Smith opened another, then copied and pasted the gibberish. His hands were the only exposed skin. Not the hands of a young man. No visible scars. No wedding band, but a groove worn into that finger. The general was trying to absorb as much about the man as possible.

The computer disk continued to whir. Moments later, both men were looking at an e-mail account and password generated from encryption.

Back in his browser, Smith entered this new information with deft movements of his thick fingers and was given immediate access to the new e-mail server. In the account, he clicked on an e-mail draft marked "Underwood."

"Extra security," Smith said. "This e-mail is saved on the server in draft form. Since it is never sent and we're reading it directly from the server, there is no possibility it would ever be intercepted by any counterterrorist program. It's a terrorist technique that's totally secure and totally anonymous."

Attached to the e-mail draft was a read-only spreadsheet file and some satellite photographs. Smith opened both.

The general leaned forward and began reading with the same intensity he brought to weekly staff meetings.

The message began with this: *Iony, for the sake of America, strongly consider what this man has to tell you.*

After a minute, the general stopped and stared into the eyes of the veiled man. "These documents are from yesterday's White House meeting between the president and the secretary of defense. Those satellite photos are highly classified. Nobody else was at that meeting."

"Exactly," Smith said. "You know then that one of the two of them sent it to me and has suggested you join. You'll understand why I don't reveal which one."

"Join what? Some kind of conspiracy?"

"Consider it a conspiracy of one," came the voice from below the veil. "There's only one link here: me. Just like I'm the only link to one of those two in the White House. To an equivalent person of power in the Israeli government. To some in the Mossad. Another in MI5. A Supreme Court justice. And so on. Not a wide web across the world. But men in positions of great influence to discreetly change what needs to be changed."

"And you want to recruit me, too."

"You've just seen how you and I can communicate, using the terrorists' own techniques against them. Anytime, from anywhere in the world. With utterly no chance of our communications leaking. Let me emphasize: You are not linked to the others. Nor them to you. It's just you and me. Total safety."

Underwood took a few moments to think about it.

The veiled visitor misinterpreted his silence. "You've been in the military for forty years," Smith said. "You are very familiar with how difficult it is to infiltrate and break an enemy composed of cell groups. Now imagine being on the other side. Protected by the same cell structure that you and every other military man find impossible to defeat."

"I'm a general," Underwood said. "I don't have an imagination."

"Of course. In an ideal world, you don't need imagination when you have unstoppable military machinery. But you can't unleash the dogs of war against this enemy. The irony of it must be extremely frustrating. Your weapons are mightier than the ones used by any other general in history, yet you live in a country and age when public opinion is more powerful than your machines."

Underwood grunted, a mixture of agreement and disgust.

"Maybe then imagination should be in your arsenal," the veiled man continued. "I'm here to supply it."

"You're here only because the man who set up this meeting is a man I trust with my life." Underwood was not using the phrase as a metaphorical cliché. Men in the military knew the value of life and trust.

"Precisely," the veiled visitor said. "You have his word that I can be trusted, and I have his word that you can be trusted."

"Wonderful," Underwood said. He felt edgy and knew his sarcasm was a result of it. "Now we know we can buy and sell used cars to each other."

"Sure. If that's what we really wanted." Smith paused. "God will bless those who bless Israel but curse those who curse Israel."

Underwood studied the man's eyes.

"I understand your deep faith," the man said. "That's one of the reasons you have been approached. Also because I know what you want when it comes to the military. A way to unleash the dogs of war. What is the borrowed phrase you are publicly so fond of? 'Drain the swamp.'"

"Donald Rumsfeld called it correctly." Thinking of the time he'd recently spent in Iraq, Underwood couldn't escape an emotional reaction at the futility he'd experienced there. The way he'd been handcuffed in a war against terrorists. "You don't fight the mosquitoes. You drain the swamp."

"For the record," Smith said, "and because it is relevant to this conversation, Rumsfeld borrowed the phrase from an Israeli general, Yehoshafat Harkabi. This is relevant because you and I believe God's mandate that the land must not be divided."

Man against man, Underwood's soldiers could destroy the enemy as easily as squashing a mosquito. But in his camp in Iraq, Underwood had been like a man sitting on his front porch, staring at a swamp through a swarm of mosquitoes around his head. Like a man who owned a bulldozer that could clear the swamp in hours but was shackled by legislation and environmental do-gooders who insisted on protecting the swamp, even though mosquitoes invaded his house every day.

"Gutless liberals," Underwood said. "All through history, war meant war. Romans knew how to do it. Carrot and stick. Offer the king a chance to join the empire. Destroy and loot if the king refused." He snorted. "Embedded media. Think Julius Caesar had to deal with this? *Embedded*—that's a word you use for bloodsucking ticks."

"Terrorists are experts at using the media. You have jets, guided missiles, tanks, the best-trained soldiers in history. . . . Terrorists have homemade bombs and the media. Who is winning?"

Underwood said nothing.

"Let me suggest again to use terrorist weapons against them. The Internet. Cell-group structure. The media."

"What are you trying to sell me?"

"God will bless those who bless Israel but curse those who curse Israel. The men helping me want what you and I want—to drain the swamp. With help from you."

"What exactly do you want from me?" Underwood said.

"Your next tour is Afghanistan."

Although this was still classified information, Underwood wasn't surprised his visitor knew.

"I need intel in Afghanistan," Smith said. "Some units there are ready to do the dirty work that you can't. They don't have to worry about embedded media."

"Units of mercenaries?" Underwood asked.

"Crusaders. Men who are doing it because they believe in it."

"That's ambiguous."

"Like this niqab, ambiguity protects you. But first let me tell you what the fighters there need."

"Go ahead."

"Not only intel. They need for you to look the other way during your tour. Give them a chance to clean up before you send in legitimate U.S. military a day or two after every engagement."

"That won't drain the swamp," Underwood said.

"It would be a beginning."

"I'd need to know more about the end if you want me in at the beginning."

"Eventually, you will be in a position to drain the swamp. To lead and win the greatest battle in history." A significant pause. Direct eye contact. "As a five-star."

"Sure." Underwood snorted. He was a religious man, and he knew of only one battle like that. The password that the man had chosen to identify himself. "Armageddon."

"What else would you call open war between two of the most important civilizations on the globe until every Muslim country is forced to submit or be destroyed?"

"You're serious."

"You mentioned Londonistan," the veiled man said. "And you're right. Europe is already in trouble. Within fifty years, radical Islam is going to dominate the world. It needs to be stopped now, especially Iran. The West has the technology and military might to do it. But it lacks the willpower. With your help, within a year that will all change."

"How will it change?"

"Not knowing is your protection. You have seen enough tonight to know there are others like you, dedicated to saving Western civilization, all with enough power and connections to make it happen."

Another pause from beneath the veil. "You're a devout evangelical. You believe Armageddon is almost upon the world. Perhaps this is God's destiny for you."

"If I say yes?" Underwood leaned back, his hands behind his head.

"I ask you to send something. By Internet. Something that proves you are willing to be part of this. I'll ask for more as required."

Underwood gave it more thought. Entering the service, he'd sworn not to betray his country. While his beliefs put God ahead of his country, was this a time and place to put God ahead of that oath? Had he been asked to worship a beast? ordered to do something morally wrong that would justify turning his back on the military he'd served his entire life?

Underwood made his decision. "No. Flawed as our system is, and much as I hate liberals, it's democracy that makes America great. I won't support any form of anarchy against it."

"No? Remember your faith. God blesses those who bless Israel. The swamp must be drained."

"No." Underwood was military, not covert ops. "God doesn't fight His battles like a terrorist. He doesn't need to."

The veiled man snapped the laptop shut. "I won't embarrass you by trying to convince you otherwise. You are a strong-willed man." He stood and moved away from the dining table, leaving the laptop in place.

"You are a man of honor. Too few men are willing to take a stand and speak their minds." He pulled off his veil and gave Underwood a genuine smile. "I owe you this at least."

"I know you," Underwood said, staring into the face above him. He was too surprised to consider the significance of the removed veil. "I met you once. Arafat was there too."

"You impressed me then," the visitor said. His English accent had disappeared. "You impress me now." Smith extended his hand.

Underwood stood, leaving the gun at the table. He accepted the handshake, then winced at the man's firm grip and a stab of pain. Underwood pulled his hand away and stared at it. Blood dribbled from a small puncture wound.

He looked back at his visitor.

"Old spy trick, General," Smith said. He opened his hand, revealing his palm and the ring with a small spike, gleaming with a trace of blood that looked black in the light of the lantern. "Take my advice. Sit down and make yourself comfortable."

Underwood felt numbness going up his right arm. "What—?"

"You've had a couple of close military friends die of heart attacks in the last month, haven't you?" The visitor smiled grimly. "It wasn't coincidence."

"You're telling me that you met with them, too?"

"I'm sorry, General. We can't take the chance that you'll tell someone about the offer you refused. The paralysis acts quickly. Don't fight it. In about thirty seconds, your diaphragm will begin to freeze. Suffocation will not be pleasant, but you will have enough time to pray and put your soul in order."

His visitor guided him to the couch at the side of the cabin. Barely able to walk, Underwood was powerless to shake off the visitor's help.

"I . . . trusted . . ."

"The stakes are too high. The friend you trusted with your life knows that. He thought that you could be recruited but was prepared to risk that he was wrong. He believes, as I do, that sacrifices have to be made now if the war is to be won later."

Smith settled Underwood against the back of the couch.

"An . . . autopsy . . ." It was a struggle to speak. Underwood felt as though a giant hand had gripped his chest.

"Will point to murder? I'm afraid not. You have no idea of the power and reach involved here."

"This . . . is . . . unbelievable." Underwood's eyelids fluttered.

"Our crusaders will get help one way or another." The visitor shook his head, as if chastising a child. "It could have been you. Blessed, not cursed."

66 DAYS BEFORE COUNTDOWN

The resurrection of Private First Class Joe Patterson took place twelve months after he had been secretly recruited into the Freedom Crusaders. It was a resurrection six nights after his death, three hours after the sun had cleared the top of the single pine tree visible from the kitchen of the double-wide that had been his home in Dawson County, Georgia, before he'd shipped out to Afghanistan.

Six days before this resurrection, his wife, Sarah, had joined the ranks of military widowhood by stepping away from an episode of *Oprah* inside the living room of the trailer to open the screen door to bright sunshine and two men in U.S. Army uniforms, each with hands clasped in front, one of them with chaplain insignia pinned to his collar.

Wives of men in uniform visualize this moment again and again during the months of service, but no amount of dread and rehearsing is preparation for the actual impact. Sarah had collapsed sobbing before the first man delivered his news with measured sympathy; she could not remember a single word the chaplain had offered as a flimsy comfort to the grief that tore her apart—tore her with the same force Joe had endured in the final milliseconds of his life after his convoy truck triggered a C-4 land mine somewhere north of Kabul.

Now, some six days and sixteen hours later, only prescribed pharmaceutical help allowed her any sleep, which was why she'd been standing at the kitchen sink in a daze when the phone rang. She had no recollection of how long she'd been staring out the window at the blue sky with a full glass of water in one hand and a pill in the other, desperate to catch some sleep, even if it was morning, worrying about whether the doctor had been right when he'd promised the pill wouldn't harm the baby swelling her womb.

When the phone rang, tears had been running down her face as she thought about what it would have been like to tell Joe that she'd felt the first kicks of the baby. When the phone rang, she didn't fear that a call at this hour was to deliver bad news. Not anymore.

Still, she set the glass down and headed toward the phone with uncertainty. Not uncertainty caused by the hour of the call, but the uncertainty that had tinged every step and action she'd taken since learning of Joe's death six days before, as if gravity had ceased to exist while those two men in uniform stood on her doorstep to tell her about Joe, and she kept expecting gravity to disappear again without any warning.

It took three rings for her to cross the tiny kitchen and fumble for the phone. The digital numbers glowing from the microwave read 9:32. Since Joe had been shipped, it had been her habit to convert time here in Georgia to time there because it made her feel closer to Joe, which put the time at 6:02 p.m. in Afghanistan.

She lifted the phone.

"Hello." Her voice was as dull as her hair. She'd been wearing the same pajamas for days and hadn't looked in a mirror for even longer.

The hiss she heard was the uncertain connection from a satellite phone nine and a half time zones removed from the double-wide. From Khodaydad Kalay, Afghanistan—something that she would learn almost immediately into the phone call.

"Hello," she repeated, hearing a faint bounce back of her voice.

Then they came. The words that marked the resurrection of Private First Class Joe Patterson.

"Babe. It's me. I've got one minute. Swear on your mama's grave that you won't tell anyone about this call."

HOOVER DAM, NEVADA • 14:32 GMT

Of anything—blood, smell, bloating, dismemberment—Kate Penner hated flies the most. Thing was, all the other stuff didn't actually touch you. Sure, at times the sight or smell of a dead body seemed to cling, but it never actually transferred. Flies, on the other hand, could move from the dead and land on the living. Kate hated flies.

Her flashlight beam hit the dead man hanging upside down in the back of a cube van, the sudden light knocking loose a dozen flies from a thick coating of dried blood on the man's face.

Kate grimaced.

Kate's face was wider at the cheekbones than conventional beauty allowed. Her nose had been broken when another cop with bad aim swung a nightstick at a drunk she was wrestling, and it hadn't quite healed straight, which gave her a certain allure that was more trouble than it was worth. She had great hair, reddish brown with gentle waves down to her shoulders, and knew how great it was, but because of this knowledge, she ignored the hair except to tie it in a ponytail. It was the same philosophy that caused her to use makeup sparingly—bad enough being a woman on the force; she didn't need extra trouble. Especially since the last time she'd taken pains to look good, it had resulted in attracting a man she thought worth marrying. And she had, though it didn't work from day one and ended the day she came home to find him with a yoga instructor learning . . . well, it wasn't the kind of yoga taught in classroom situations.

Her green eyes fooled people into believing she was nicer than she was, and Kate liked this. She liked setting them straight. When she grimaced, as she was doing at the flies, it was more than a good hint that maybe she wasn't simply an accessory for a social evening.

"We're close enough," she told her partner, Frank Vetter, flicking the beam down at the pavement. She couldn't see anything to avoid stepping on, but you never knew. Not these days, when CSI could use a strand of hair to put someone on death row. The last thing Kate and Frank wanted—or needed—was grief about disturbing the crime scene. And it was undoubtedly that.

A crime. And a scene. Kate checked her watch. Six thirty-three.

She flicked her flashlight back to the dead man. What Kate could see of the man's face showed Middle Eastern descent. But there was so much blood it was hard to be sure. How could any body have ever held so much? It began somewhere in the middle of the man's shirt, soaking it so completely that the patterns of the fabric were no longer patterns. The blood covered the man's chest and neck and had pooled beneath his head, which hung only inches off the deck of the van. All the blood was dry, but that didn't tell Kate much. This was the desert. Anything liquid dried in a hurry.

Frank stood beside Kate. He held a flashlight too, but with sunrise twenty minutes away, he didn't need it anymore unless he wanted to add another beam to the darkness inside the van. He'd been a cop as long as Kate—just over ten years each. He, however, was a Dunkin' Donuts cop, happy putting in his time. Kate didn't mind—fewer leadership issues that way. Some of her former partners had struggled with the concept of independent-minded women.

"We'll need the crime scene unit," Kate said. She was an excellent detective with dogged ability that could have put her at the head of the homicide unit. But she didn't like the price that would come with a position like that—paying as much attention to department politics as to good investigating. She'd get the promotion she deserved only when the current chief forgot about how she'd mashed his head into the bottom of a punch bowl for slapping her backside at the last Christmas party. Which, of course, meant never. He'd been drunk enough to forget about political correctness and make the grab but sober enough to recall the humiliation of the cherry jammed in his left nostril when he came up for air, spouting like a whale. She should have filed a grievance for where he'd put his hand, but that would have meant politics too.

"Yeah," Frank said. "Let's get CSI. Maybe they can solve it in an hour."

Bad joke. Long-standing joke. Anywhere in the department. The Boulder City department, close as it was to Vegas, suffered too because of the hit television series. At least once a week, tourists dropped in, thinking maybe Boulder City was actually part of Vegas, as if they were checking out a rotation of all the stations hoping to catch a glimpse of a star anywhere. *How stupid can people be?* Kate always wondered when they came by.

She paused. *How stupid* could *people be?*

She had one answer right in front of her, Kate thought. Stupid enough to find a way to end up dead, upside down in a cube van.

KHAN YUNIS, GAZA STRIP • 14:32 GMT

"You are not Abu," Mulvaney Quinn said to the Palestinian opposite him at a table.

The hostage exchange took place in a small room as bare and rough as its table—an almost unbearably hot room with a dirt floor and filled with the smell of garlic, like any of thousands of similar rooms in the squalor of the Gaza Strip.

"I am Zayat," the man said. "Abu takes no risks. He sends me instead. This is my proof."

The Palestinian dropped a small wristwatch on the table. The man's dress suggested he'd taken public appearance lessons from the late Yasser Arafat.

Quinn turned the watch over and looked for engraving on the back. *To Crystal. Love, Daddy.* The rest of the luxury watch matched the description that had been given by the father: pink leather wristband, extra hole punched in the band because it had been too large for Crystal's tiny wrist. She was only four, probably couldn't tell time, and had been given a watch that was worth double what the average Palestinian family earned in a year. Bad luck for her to be an American child in the Middle East, unaware of how much wealth she had on her wrist, how dangerous it was to display that wealth in a public place, and how much Americans were hated, even innocent children.

"Roz," Quinn said into his telephone headset, "I've confirmed the watch."

Roz. Out of the entire staff at Corporate Counterterrorism International, only Quinn called Rossett by that name. Here it was a code word, letting Rossett know that on Quinn's end there were no complications. Yet.

Crystal had been kidnapped, along with her mother, from a Jerusalem side street. Quinn was optimistic that they were still alive; it was very unlikely that the woman and the child had been taken into Gaza, where the kidnappers had demanded this meeting. Security checkpoints were too risky for them to attempt to take the victims outside of Israel. This was simply a safer place for the kidnappers to negotiate, a haven in a territory of lawlessness.

"You know it belongs to the child," Zayat said. "Now I tell you about the change. You wire the money to a different account number."

"The agreement was clear," Quinn said. "No money until the woman and child are delivered safe."

This wasn't the place or situation for a business suit. Quinn wore khakis and a white mock turtleneck with short, loose sleeves. Comfort over formality. He was in his late thirties, lean and tanned, a tall man with a face that had forgotten how to smile.

Quinn's laptop, running on battery power, sat on the table between them. Quinn wore a headset attached to a port on the laptop, which used voice-over-Internet protocol to serve as his phone. The line was open to keep him in contact with the office in Tel Aviv. Every word was being monitored and recorded at CCTI. During telephone bargaining with Abu over the previous few days, Rossett had explained repeatedly that this constant contact was nonnegotiable.

"I give you the new bank account." Zayat pushed a piece of paper across the table. "Abu is a cautious man. He does not trust what you have set up." He pointed at the laptop. "You change it now while we wait."

Quinn did as directed but didn't like Zayat's obvious tension and impatience. Things went wrong when emotions got in the way.

Before Quinn could say anything, however, Rossett's steady voice came through the headset. "The woman and child are safe."

"Understood," Quinn said. Adrenaline and stress had been sustaining him through horrible jet lag, and he felt the muscles in his shoulder relax as he let out a deep breath of relief. "Roz, I'll release the money."

Quinn spoke to Zayat in Arabic that was flawless except for the Israeli accent. "I've just received the first confirmation. The mother and child are safe at the King David."

Roz was in Tel Aviv, but they'd chosen a Jerusalem hotel for the drop. There would be hugs, screams of joy, and collapsing in relief as the family was reunited in the lobby, but Quinn would permit himself the satisfaction of savoring the triumph later. He tapped at the keyboard on the laptop. "As agreed, one million dollars in U.S. currency are now being transferred to the account number that you provided us. When you've confirmed that your men are back on this side of the border, you allow me to leave."

To make this work, someone needed to provide a guarantee that Abu's men would not be detained. This was Quinn's other role today. If Abu's men were betrayed, Quinn would be held until they were returned, killed if they were killed.

In theory, the Gaza Strip was no longer a concentration camp. But under the Palestinian National Authority and the new Hamas government, this was still theory. The fact that kidnapping Americans could be a profession to fund terrorist cell groups attested to that. Abu's men would be very safe inside Gaza. Unlike Quinn.

The door opened, briefly flooding the room with sunlight, showing the air heavy with floating dust. Quinn glanced over.

The new arrival was a younger man dressed in a manner similar to Zayat's, but his face was swathed in black cloth. He moved to stand behind Zayat. In one hand he carried a knapsack, which he set on the floor. The other hand held a machine gun, which he lifted and pointed in Quinn's direction.

Quinn stared at the man with the machine gun, then made a point of deliberately turning his head to Zayat without showing any alarm. This was business. When terrorists kidnapped rich Americans, it wasn't about ideology, only money to finance the ideology. Everyone understood that killing negotiators hurt future business. In theory.

"I believe this is personal for you, isn't it?" the new arrival said to Quinn in Arab-accented English. "Your partner handled the negotiating, but you are the one here in person. You even cut short a vacation to return here from America for this. Las Vegas, I understand—a den of sinners in a country of sin."

Quinn refused to show surprise at the man's knowledge. He had seen these situations played out at both extremes. Complete silence until the next confirmation phone call to let both sides know the Palestinians were safe and Quinn could be released. Or endless chatter that was a sure indication of nerves on the other side.

Teflon, Quinn always told himself. *Be Teflon. Nothing sticks. Answer in polite, neutral tones with polite, neutral words.* "I represent Lloyd's of London and the American businessman insured by Lloyd's. I'm a middleman. Which means it is my job to make the transaction successful for both parties."

"Yet if I understand correctly," the Palestinian said, "you lost your wife and daughter to a Palestinian suicide bomber. What, five years ago? The woman and girl matched in age then to the woman and child you just ransomed for one million; isn't that right?"

Now Quinn was alarmed. This was information the terrorist should not have. CCTI firewalled personal information of employees with the zealousness of guards at Fort Knox.

"I represent Lloyd's of London and the American businessman insured by

Lloyd's," Quinn repeated. He was a good poker player, and this was high-stakes Texas hold 'em, where the losers ended up dead. "I am a middleman. This is business. Nothing more."

"One might guess you are still trying to rescue the family you lost," the masked Palestinian said with an obvious sneer in his voice. "A futility, is it not?"

Images flooded Quinn's mind, the images he fell asleep to every night, triggering here and now the same emotions that didn't seem to lose the edge or rawness over time.

Teflon, he told himself. *Teflon.*

"Put a hand on the table, palm up," the masked Palestinian said, still standing behind Zayat.

Quinn raised an eyebrow.

The man raised the machine gun and pointed the barrel at Quinn's head. Quinn leaned forward and rested his left forearm on the table, turning his palm toward the ceiling.

"Now is your time," the Palestinian said.

Zayat leaned forward too and clamped his fingers over Quinn's wrist, holding Quinn's hand in place. He reached under his leg, pulling out a long knife he'd kept hidden. With savage swiftness, he drove the point of the blade down into the center of Quinn's palm, pinning Quinn to the table with a thud.

B abe. It's me. I've got one minute. Swear on your mama's grave that you won't tell anyone about this call."

It was just past six in the evening local time. As he sent his voice nine and a half time zones back to Sarah and the double-wide he never imagined he'd miss with such intensity, Private First Class Joe Patterson stood in the corner of an abandoned, dusty school yard that had been used for a mass killing by the Taliban on a similar hot summer day a few years earlier.

At the far side, handcuffed and gagged Afghan men were seated against a brick wall, waiting for small pieces of lead to be delivered at terminal speed into their chest cavities. Some wept. Some glared in defiance at the soldiers only ten paces from them. The rest stared at the infinite blue of the clear sky beyond the walls, as if trying to liberate their souls from their bodies before the bullets arrived.

Years before, these same men had been members of the Taliban, thugs who had enjoyed the opportunity to flex power without responsibility. These thugs had been armed with Soviet Dragunov SVD sniping rifles, notoriously poor aim, and sadistic satisfaction at their inefficiency in killing.

Now these former Taliban killers were the ones handcuffed and afraid. Their executioners wore U.S. Army uniforms, and there was nothing casual about their stances as they held tight grips on standard-issue Colt M16s. Though this would not be the first killing for these young soldiers, the tension was obvious on their faces.

Although he stood apart from the others—conversation monitored by the nearby commanding officer—Private First Class Joe Patterson was also in U.S. Army uniform. This was the perfect disguise for the Freedom Crusaders, as all of them had first been army personnel, and all of them had been officially reported dead. Patterson knew that high up strings had been pulled so that commanding

officers made sure a rogue unit could operate without interference from the army
or the political-correctness police known as the media.

Satellite phone in one hand, Patterson cradled in his other arm the M16 that
had been in his possession when he and five other soldiers had supposedly been
inside a lead convoy truck exploded by a buried bomb on a main highway twenty
miles outside of Kabul.

Today Patterson had been able to make this phone call for one simple reason:
the other soldiers were still busy with the remaining pigs. Patterson had helped
earlier with the slaughter of the other pigs. But even with a knife in his hand and
blood running down his wrists, Patterson's thoughts had not been on the pigs
or the prisoners he had agreed to capture and kill. He'd only been thinking of
Sarah.

Sweet Sarah. Blonde, tiny, feisty, passionate. No man had ever been as blessed
in finding a woman, and Joe thanked God for her every night in his prayers.

It was driving him crazy to imagine how badly she would be grieving his
death. Not even the insurance money would make up for it. With the final pigs
almost prepared, Patterson had approached the commanding officer, Del Saxon,
a man he'd reported to the first night after the convoy explosion.

"Sir, I'd like to make a call," Joe had said, pointing at the phone that Lieutenant Saxon had strapped to his belt. "I need to speak to my wife."

"A call." Del Saxon was square jawed, square shouldered, and with his brush
cut hairstyle, square headed. He was a large man who talked in a growl from
the side of his mouth as if he were chewing on a cigar. "You want to make a call.
Like you're waiting in traffic and you forgot what you were supposed to pick up
on the way home."

Private Joe Patterson was big himself. He'd been tough before boot camp
and had grown tougher during. Part of the bargain had been that he'd be joining
a squad that didn't treat him like army—the Freedom Crusaders. So he wasn't
going to back down.

"My wife thinks I'm dead," Joe said. "I can't stand it any longer. One call and
it'll fix that problem."

"So I'm supposed to hand you my phone." Saxon gestured toward the other
soldiers, out of earshot. "Then let them take turns to tell people stateside they're
not dead either?"

"That's between you and them. I want to call my wife."

"Not part of the deal. She gets money. Nothing else. You knew that at FCU.
You put your hand on a Bible and swore to follow this duty."

Patterson was very aware of this. Over a period of months, as a professor
and mentor subtly checked his reliability and ideology for the cause, he had been
recruited on the Freedom Christian University campus, inspired with fervent,

crusading passion to become a Christian soldier marching forward for the cause of Jesus.

What he hadn't expected was that he'd fall in love with Sarah. He hadn't expected that during his last month at FCU, passion would overcome them and lead them into sin. He hadn't expected Sarah to become pregnant, and he hadn't expected to marry her before sending her back to Georgia so that his child could at least have his last name.

He'd pledged to join the Crusaders while a single man only to discover that the pull of his own new family was a stronger force. No wonder, he often told himself now, Jesus had never married. Jesus, the ultimate man of love, must not have wanted to cause pain to a woman and child the way that Patterson was by serving here. Of course, Jesus would have never sinned, let alone sinned in passion as Joe had, and Joe knew he was paying the price for it with his agony.

"If I can't call my wife, I walk," Joe said.

"You can't walk. There's a hundred miles of desert in every direction."

"I've got two legs until you shoot them out from under me," Joe answered. "You don't know how bad I need to talk to her."

It was bad. Joe was no lawyer or car salesman, but he'd thought this through over the last few days. There would be an opportunity, he'd believed, when the threat of walking away would be the most powerful. This seemed as good a chance as any. And he wanted to talk to Sarah bad enough to take a bullet in the back.

"Look, grunt—"

"There's no looking involved. I talk to my wife, or I walk. Maybe you shoot me; maybe you don't. But I'm guessing you don't want to make a bad impression on the other guys. Not here. Not now."

"Do you have any idea what's at stake here?" Saxon asked. "Your wife can wait until the rest of the world knows about us."

"She can't. And won't. One minute. That's all I need with her. She'll swear to secrecy. All I need to do is tell her it's part of the Lord's work."

A vein pulsed on the side of the commander's head.

"All right then," Patterson said when the answer didn't come. "I'm walking. Nice and slow. Enough time for you to shoot or call me back. Your choice."

"This is not the time for a showdown, Patterson."

"That," Patterson had said, earnest and dead serious, "depends on your viewpoint."

That's when Saxon had handed him the satellite phone, accomplishing the resurrection of Private First Class Joe Patterson. Ten minutes after Patterson ended his call, the last of the pigs had been prepared.

It was go time.

The cube van with the upside-down dead body was parked in a tourist lot, well away from the Hoover Dam. Even so, someone would have called for a routine check first thing in the morning. Homeland Security and all that. Of course, whoever came down from the dam to check the license plate would have seen the body. The van door had been open when Kate and Frank arrived.

"You know what I don't like," Frank said. "The flies."

Kate snorted.

"What I meant was that I don't like the fact that the flies are here already." Frank knew about Kate's near phobia of flies. "What are the chances this van's been here for a day or two?"

"Zilch," Kate said. Homeland Security again. The Hoover Dam had long been closed to 18-wheelers, forcing drivers to take a route that cost them seventy extra miles. A vehicle parked near the dam for more than two hours was red-flagged for close inspection. After three hours, it was towed. Nobody wanted a big bomb wiping out the dam and every town and city downstream for a hundred miles.

"So the van hasn't been here long," Frank said. "This many flies couldn't have shown up during the night."

"Flies have superpowers. I'm not kidding. They're evil. They don't need light."

"Yeah, yeah," Frank said. "Gonna file that in the murder book? 'Flies appeared instantly because they're evil and know how to use their superpowers.'"

"Whoever did him did him out in the desert, then. Maybe yesterday or the day before—during the daylight, when the flies were active. The flies were already in the cube van when they drove it here."

"Then called it in."

"Yeah," Kate said flatly, thinking about the number the caller had told them to try once they found a body, a number with a DC area code. Kate and Frank would eventually get all the information they needed on it, but it had only been a fifteen-minute drive to the dam, lights flashing, sirens silent. During the drive from Boulder City, they had debated whether to get someone to run the number down immediately but finally decided to wait until verification of a body. There was always a chance the person making the 911 call had hoped to sucker the cops into calling the number to hassle the person's friend—or enemy—as a practical joke.

"What about the number?" Frank asked. They'd been partners awhile. Some days, Kate figured he could read her thoughts by the way she twitched her nose or scratched her chin. "It's obviously not a practical joke. Call it now?"

Kate checked the signal strength on her cell phone. "I hate being set up, but how much choice do we have now?"

Frank shrugged. "By the book, Kate. The dispatcher's got it all recorded. You don't make the call, someone will wonder why."

Kate gave the body one last flash with the beam. A few more flies rocketed off the body and threatened Kate's airspace. She grimaced again and dialed the number.

Kate expected the cell phone reception to quit midway through the ringing of the number she'd just dialed. She hated the unpredictability of cell phones, hated that she'd grown dependent on them despite her mistrust of the technology. She didn't like being dependent on anything or anyone.

The signal was strong. A woman's voice answered. "Yes."

Kate was mad at herself for assuming it would be a man on the other end. Gender stereotyping at its best.

"Hey," Kate grunted, hoping to get some identity without having to reveal herself. She stepped back from the van as she spoke. Now flies were coming in from all around, over her shoulders, headed straight to the dead body. Superpowers. This early in the day and every fly within a hundred square miles knew about it.

"Who is this?" the voice on the other end said.

"A friend." Kate was playing this one blind.

"Who is this?"

"You don't have any friends?" Kate said, lifting her eyebrows in Frank's direction.

"Why are you calling?" No friendliness in the woman's voice. As if Kate were clairvoyant about the woman's lack of friends. With attitude like this, Kate could understand why the woman was so lonely.

"It's a long story," Kate said. In the background, she could hear a sound like the clicking of a keyboard. Was the woman on the other end in front of a computer?

"Make it about five seconds longer."

"Huh?" Kate said.

"Caller ID."

Kate shook her head. Her cell was unlisted. No way the person on the other end could—

"Katherine Louise Penner," the voice said. "Boulder City. Interesting. Phone owned by the police department. That mean you're a cop? How'd you get this number, and why are you calling?"

"How in—?"

"Faster computers than anything you have in the sticks."

"*You* start talking," Kate said, going from bewildered to mad in a hurry. "If you have anything to do with what's in front of me, we're on you like a ton of bricks."

"Bad cliché aside, you really have no idea, do you?"

"No idea about what?"

"See what I mean?"

Kate rode her temper like a wave. "Start talking, lady, or—"

"Recognize the DC area code? That should be a clue." The click, click, click of the woman's keyboarding continued. "By the way, don't call me lady."

"Look," Kate said, "I've got someone who looks like a dead Arab in front of me covered in blood, and you're the number I was told to call when I found it. I can track you down and then we'll see how much you like playing these games. Can you spell *accessory?*"

"Hang on." The woman's voice lost its edge. "Dead Arab? Covered in blood? Upside-down?"

"Yeah." Kate got quiet too. How'd the woman on the other end know the body was upside-down? Why was she more curious about the body than the fact that her number had been included with the tip that led to the body?

"What's on his back?" the voice asked.

"What?"

"His back. Can you see it?"

"No," Kate said.

"Find something to spin the body around."

"What?"

"If I'm going to have to keep repeating myself, I'm going to get in a lot worse mood. Trust me, Katie, you're not going to like that. Not—" more clicking of the keyboard in the background—"with a résumé like yours. Seems like you managed to make every official with any weight in Vegas want you dead. I guarantee if you mess with me, this is the one stunt that will put you off the force without a pension."

The voice let the implications of what she'd said sink in, then continued. "Look for something to turn the body around. I'm going to describe to you what you'll see, and that alone should be enough reason for you to listen to everything else I've got to say."

DC area code. Computer and connections with enough juice to run the name and number of an unlisted cell in less than thirty seconds. Enough juice to learn in another few seconds how much Kate's dislike of politics had hurt her career. Kate decided to listen.

As the voice on Kate's cell described what she would find, Kate walked five paces, broke off a dried branch from a tree at the edge of the parking lot, and walked back to the body, ignoring Frank's puzzled look. She poked the body to turn it, and flies swarmed in his direction at the disturbance. Kate fought the gag reflex, then forgot her hatred of flies when she saw the back of the body.

"No way," Kate said.

"Thought so," the voice said. "Got a pencil?"

"Yeah."

"I'm going to give you a number. Call back. Ask to be transferred to Ali Noyer. That way you'll know I am who I say I am. Because you're going to have to do everything I tell you. No questions asked. If this shows up in the media, you lose your pension."

"But—"

"Can you spell *obstruction?*" the voice asked in the sarcastic tone that Kate had used earlier asking about *accessory.* "If this leaks, I can make the charges stick. You ready to listen?"

Kate listened, wrote down the new number, and disconnected the cell. She stared at Frank, who was staring at the body.

Kate flashed another beam at the body in the van, at the man's back.

The light showed that the back of the man's shirt had been cut wide open. A golden piece of paper formed a cross on his flesh. An American flag on a stick—the kind that kids waved during a Fourth of July parade—stuck out at a jaunty angle from a belt loop of the man's pants.

"Not good," Kate told Frank. "We're in this deep. Whatever it is."

KHAN YUNIS, GAZA STRIP • 14:44 GMT

When the knife first plunged into his hand, Quinn managed to reduce his scream to a grunt as shock waves of pain fired along his nerve synapses.

The man with the machine gun stepped forward, pulled the wires loose from the computer, and yanked the headset from Quinn's head.

"Now we talk," he said. He handed the knapsack and machine gun to Zayat, who remained standing while the masked Palestinian sat across from Quinn. "Or, at least, you listen."

Quinn fought waves of nausea by trying to assess the situation. It didn't feel like the knife had penetrated bone but had slid between instead, in the center of his hand. He couldn't guess at ligament damage, however, and doubted it would be of any relevance in the short or long term.

"Afraid, American?" the masked Palestinian taunted. "You will not leave this room alive."

Quinn had wondered when something like this would happen. A person could survive the lions' den only so many times. Every time he'd wondered about when he'd finally pay the price, he'd told himself that relief would outweigh the fear. He was pleasantly surprised to discover he'd been right.

"I'm terrified," Quinn said blandly, trying to float above the pain on this mild relief. It didn't seem that there was a way out of the lions' den this time. If so, he would have felt obliged to try. But with no escape, he could push aside the immediate pain and try to relax and wait for the inevitable. A part of his mind was objectively curious about the process of dying. He found it interesting that time had already seemed to slow down. Part of the physiology of shock?

The masked man snapped his fingers and Zayat leaned the machine gun against the wall, then dug into the knapsack. He came up with a small tripod, which he extended and set up at the far end of the room. He then mounted a camcorder on it.

This gave Quinn enough time to think about the implications. A camcorder meant this scene would be recorded. The usual video propaganda for Internet broadcast. An execution. Another triumph for the holy jihad.

Quinn could accept this. In the end, did it really matter how he died? In a way, it was a mercy that death would happen so quickly. With this resignation came the sensation that he was sinking into an oasis of infinitely deep water.

"It was not coincidence that the woman and girl were kidnapped," the Palestinian on the other side of the table said. Casual, smug conversation. "Nor coincidence that you became the negotiator. They were bait. Zayat is merely a hired man, betraying Abu."

Quinn shrugged. He was in a quiet place now, allowing himself the luxury of happy memories. He didn't want the squalor of this room to fill his last earthly thoughts.

"Abu is dead," Zayat said, obviously anxious. "Tell me that now."

"By my own machine gun. In front of my own eyes." The masked man spoke to Quinn. "Yet I too work for someone else."

Quinn shrugged again. He didn't want distractions, not with the oasis so close.

"Safady arranged this," the masked Palestinian said. "Does this get your attention?"

Quinn flinched.

"I see it does. You have been an irritation to Safady long enough. He ordered me to make you bow your neck to a Muslim sword. It is not enough of a price to pay for how you hunted and killed our brothers, but sadly a man like you can only die once."

The masked man moved to the table and crouched to reach beneath, coming up with a huge scimitar that had been taped to the underside of the table. He pulled the strips of tape off the blade.

"Any pitiful last words for the world, American dog?"

Quinn's forearm was twitching from the pain, a rapid shivering of muscles in reaction to the localized shock. He stood, forced to lean over the table because of his pinned hand.

"Sit down!" the masked Palestinian ordered, pushing the point of the scimitar against Quinn's shoulder.

"Keep the camera rolling," Quinn said, ignoring the scimitar. He used his good hand to work the knife back and forth and free it from the table, despite the flesh that tore against the blade of the knife.

"Did you hear me!" the masked man screamed. He thrust the tip of the scimitar harder into Quinn's shoulder. "Sit down!"

Quinn ignored the scream too and calmly continued to work the knife loose. He expected to be ripped apart by machine gun bullets or killed with a slash of the scimitar. Better than dying in submission to Khaled Safady.

The bullets didn't come. Nor did the sword. A second later, Quinn lifted the knife and showed it to the camera, hoping the video was running. *Give this to Safady to watch instead.*

Zayat leveled the machine gun at Quinn.

"Shoot his legs!" the masked Palestinian shouted. "Safady demands he dies to the scimitar."

Zayat hesitated, trying to understand the logic of the order.

In that moment of hesitation, Quinn threw the knife at Zayat, not expecting the action to be more than a useless act of defiance for Safady to see later. The knife flipped end over end twice, then slammed blade first into Zayat's shoulder.

Zayat wailed and dropped the machine gun. When the gun hit the floor, it fired a short burst into the wall at the side of the room, sending small chips of plaster in all directions.

Despite the deafening echoes, the masked man was quick and stepped between Quinn and the machine gun, scimitar poised. Zayat had instinctively pulled the knife from his shoulder and began clutching at the wound.

Quinn thought of spinning and making a run for the door. Then he thought about what it would look like to Safady later on video, seeing Quinn turning his back and dying in apparent fear.

So Quinn remained square to his opponent, watching intently.

The masked Palestinian swiped the sword at Quinn's legs. Quinn hopped back, narrowly out of range.

Another swipe forced Quinn to the edge of the table.

No choice but to tumble sideways and run or let the scimitar bite through his legs on the next swing. Immobilized, Quinn would face beheading.

The door behind Quinn burst open again, sunshine flooding the room as it had earlier. The man with the scimitar froze.

"No," he said. "Impossible."

A second later, from behind Quinn came another burst of machine-gun fire.

In the dusty courtyard, Del Saxon surveyed a massive pile of pig intestines with satisfaction. Except for the trouble with Joe Patterson, the previous few hours had been as he'd expected after the arrival of the animals. Saxon had grown up on a farm. He'd expected the squealing and the acrid copper smell of blood that came as the pigs died.

Now the carcasses were completely hollow. His soldiers had done well in butchering the animals, but that was to be expected too. Most of them were farm boys; Saxon had handpicked this group. And all of them—with the exception of Joe Patterson and his unexpected demand to use the phone—were totally dedicated to the cause.

Saxon was now ready to start speaking to the prisoners through an interpreter. He made it obvious that he was holding a small digital recorder as he approached the interpreter, a small Afghan with a huge mustache.

"Everything you tell them will be on this," he told the interpreter. "I have another interpreter who will later tell me word for word what you tell the prisoners. Understand what I'm saying here? If you don't tell them exactly what I'm telling you to tell them, we'll hunt you down and do to you what we did to the pigs."

The little man's mustache twitched. Like a rabbit, Saxon thought. Wait until he saw what was going to happen.

Saxon motioned for the little Afghan to follow and took a stance in front of all the prisoners. The soldiers stood behind him.

"I want all of you to understand clearly this process," Saxon began. He waited for the interpreter to repeat it. All of the prisoners were listening intently.

"Some of you will die in a traditional manner—by firing squad. That includes all of you on this side." Saxon held out his right arm and swung it away from his body. The men to that side were tribal loyalists, Taliban goons. Saxon had little emotional stake in their fates. He simply wanted them dead out of a sense of justice . . . and practicality. When the interpreter left here and explained to other villagers what had happened, the locals would know that Americans were not weak and afraid, bound by what the UN and Germany and France and Russia told them to do.

"Those on the other side—" Saxon lifted his left arm and indicated the rest— "will also die. All of you except for one."

Saxon burned with hatred for those men. They were Muslim terrorists, non-Afghans, part of a local cell that had been captured with the help of tips from the villagers. These were men who declared loyalty to Osama bin Laden, who had declared jihad on the Christian West, who desecrated the divine Jesus with every breath they took. Hell was too good for them, even though Saxon was going to help them get there very soon.

"Those on my right," Saxon said, "will all die at once. To bullets. Those on my left will die one at a time."

While Saxon didn't consider himself stupid, neither did he think he was particularly brilliant. He'd never claimed this was his idea and had been open about telling his men that he'd read the General Pershing story that circulated on the Internet following 9/11. The story was initially widely accepted as factual, and one state senator had even included a version of it on a campaign flyer. Saxon had a feeling the story was an urban legend, but that didn't concern him. Urban legend or not, he was sure the technique would be effective.

And very, very satisfying.

"Look at those emptied pigs' bodies," Saxon continued. "Those of you on the left will be decapitated, and your heads will be sewn into the pigs' bodies. What is left of your bodies will be buried with the pile of guts."

Saxon knew that these people believed being defiled by a pig carcass would prevent them from reaching paradise.

General John Pershing had known this too. During World War I, so the story went, Pershing had tied up a bunch of Muslim terrorists in the Philippines and shot them with bullets greased with pig's lard—all of them except for one, whom he let go to spread the word about what would happen to other Muslim terrorists. That had scared them so bad there wasn't any more terrorism for another forty years.

Here in the southern mountains of Afghanistan, it wouldn't take long for word to reach any other Muslim terrorist that this was their fate once Saxon and his men caught them.

"Am I understood?" Saxon asked loudly.

The interpreter was staring at him with such horror that it was obvious to Saxon this was indeed a good idea.

Saxon frowned at the interpreter and pointed at the prisoners. "Am I understood?" he repeated, gesturing for the interpreter to pass on the question, something the man did quickly.

By the reaction of the prisoners, there was no doubt he was understood. Some cursed him. Others sagged against their bindings.

Saxon turned to his soldiers. "Let's get this started," he barked.

Saxon let his eyes slide past Private Joe Patterson. That was a man marked for death. Unlike the holy joy Saxon took in sending the Muslim terrorists to judgment in front of God, he regretted the fact that he would have to eliminate Patterson. Still, it wasn't a job he was going to ask anyone else to do. When a dog got into the chickens and had to be shot, a man did it himself.

Patterson's sin was against God, against the holy war fought by the Freedom Crusaders, and that sin was betrayal of a soldier's honor. That was a lot worse than a dog getting into chickens.

So when the time was right and Patterson's help wasn't needed, Saxon would take care of killing him. No different from shooting a dog. It was a shame the wife would have to pay the same price for Patterson's sin.

HOOVER DAM, NEVADA • 14:49 GMT

Kate had stepped away from the cube van. She leaned against the hood of the cruiser and stared at the wedge of light that came with approaching dawn. It was three hours later in DC for that arrogant woman, probably in a suit at a desk, probably right now sipping her Starbucks and telling another guy in a suit in a nearby cubicle about some cop that she'd just pushed around.

Kate picked up her cell again and dialed the new number. She reached a switchboard for the National Counterterrorism Center.

National Counterterrorism Center.

No wonder this Ali Noyer thought she had so much juice. Kate asked for Noyer and was transferred immediately.

"Penner," Noyer said. "You've got it secured?"

"Not your concern," Kate said. "My next call is to CSI. Then the press. Then my lawyer. Then a good New York agent."

"Look, you—"

"You're recording this conversation, right?"

"What difference does—?"

"Good. I'll probably talk faster than you like. You'll be able to play it back and understand the things you're missing first time around. CSI is going to show up and investigate this the way I want it done. You monkeys in suits have no idea what it's like in the field."

"O-b-s-t-r—"

"Obstruction? Good thing a cop from the sticks like me happens to have a dictionary nearby. That's why my next call is to the press. Whatever you're trying to cover won't stay that way for long when they get ahold of it. They'll give you guys a one-two punch that will knock you over like you've been sniffing glue for a week."

"You might as well toss your badge in the garbage now, Katie." Noyer's voice dripped with condescension as she said *Katie*. "You have no idea what's going on."

"I don't. But I will as I investigate, unless you try to nail me with obstruction. That's why I call my lawyer right after the press."

"Kiss your pension good-bye. Get ready for some jail time on top of that."

"That's where the New York agent comes in. The way I got it figured, a book deal should be no problem. Then I'll hit the talk shows and tell all their viewers how the current administration is handling terrorist activities. Like that phrase? *Current administration*. Even a bozo can learn mediaspeak. Whatever the book deal brings in, along with media exposure and some time on the lecture circuit, I won't need a pension. Someday I'll phone you up and thank you for getting me off the force early. The thing is, I hate flies."

"Flies. What do—?"

"Flies." Kate had no intention of letting the woman finish a sentence. Keep her off balance. "The worst thing for me about being a cop is flies."

"You can't do this."

"Sure I can. In fact, the only reason I called back to tell you all this is so that you might get excited and spill your Starbucks on your computer. Slow it down some so the computers in the sticks here can keep up."

"Listen! This is a matter of national security. You *will* cooperate with me."

"Tell you what," Kate said. "Short of the president himself telling me in person, I'm going to run this my way. And by the way, call me Katie again and you'll get what I gave the last mayor of Vegas."

Kate ended the call and walked back to Frank.

"He ask you out again?" Frank asked. "Promise he'd change?"

"I don't follow," Kate said.

"I couldn't hear the conversation, only the tone. Sounded like you were talking to your ex-husband."

"Funny. Very funny."

"What's this about, Kate? You have that look in your eyes—the stubborn bulldog look. Last time I saw that, you stayed on a case for three years."

"You really don't want to know. That way it's only *my* pension on the line."

"Kate. This is me."

Kate sighed. "Remember when rumors that the Koran was flushed down toilets at Guantánamo Bay caused riots in the Muslim world?"

"Yeah. And those cartoons of Muhammad in a Danish newspaper . . . same thing. Riots."

"And killings. That's why we absolutely have to keep a lid on this. If someone is hoping to start World War III, this is a good way to get there."

"What are you talking about?"

"That cross stapled to the dead man's back?" Kate said. She pointed past the small flag. "Take a closer look. You can see it's been cut from a small poster. The poster showed the Muslim Dome of the Rock. Make your own guesses, but whatever you do, keep them to yourself."

KHAN YUNIS, GAZA STRIP • 14:53 GMT

"You are a stupid, contemptible man," Abu said to Zayat in Arabic.

Abu was middle-aged with a comfortably large belly. His three Palestinian bodyguards were young men, all armed with Israeli machine guns. The masked man with the scimitar was still in the room too, a contorted bundle of death at Quinn's feet, where he leaned against the table, hand wrapped in a strip of cloth that he'd torn from the bottom part of his shirt.

Near the camcorder and tripod, Zayat wept openly, fingers splayed in a useless effort to stop the bleeding at his shoulder. "Mercy," he said. "For the sake of Allah."

"You are equally stupid and contemptible to beg. My brother is dead." Abu spoke to Quinn. "Allah blessed both of us by giving me loose bowels today. On our way to meet you here, we make a hasty stop at a café. Smoked glass windows that hide the fact I am not inside the Mercedes. Then a gunman drives by and . . ."

Abu bowed his head. "My brother and the driver—dead. I call for more men and think of Zayat, the only other one to know we had agreed to this time and location. The one who would gain if I died this morning."

He turned and slapped Zayat's face. "Your wife and your children will be slaughtered before nightfall. But I will show them your head before they die so they understand it is your stupidity that killed them."

Zayat fell to his knees. "Please! No!"

Abu ignored the begging. He knelt at the body at Quinn's feet and pulled off the mask. He said to Quinn in English, "Is this a man you know?"

Quinn looked at the dead man's thickly bearded face and shook his head.

"The sword," Abu said. "The camera. It is obvious he wanted to execute you."

"He was sent by Khaled Safady."

Abu grew still. "Safady. My brother is dead because of that man?"

Quinn nodded.

"Why does Safady want you dead?" Abu asked. "You are not Israeli."

Quinn shook his head to indicate he would not answer.

"I could kill you where you stand."

"Yes," Quinn said.

The moment dragged as Abu waited for Quinn to change his mind and explain why Safady wanted him dead.

Quinn calmly stared back at Abu.

"But killing you would satisfy the man who killed my brother." Abu closed his eyes briefly, then stared again at Quinn. "You transferred the money for the hostages?"

"Ask Zayat."

Abu didn't have to ask.

"I have the number," Zayat babbled in Arabic. "You will get the money. Spare my family."

"Go," Abu told Quinn. "This is now a tribal affair."

"Zayat's wife and children," Quinn said, switching from English to Arabic. Abu's men were alert with their machine guns for any swift action Quinn might take. "They don't have to die."

"American, you don't understand the way of the desert."

It had been generations since any Palestinian had been free enough to roam the desert. But they remembered what had been passed on, remembered what it took to survive when there wasn't enough grass and water for everyone and dreamed still of freedom that came with the harshness of desert life.

"Zayat's children did not steal your turkey," Quinn answered. "Nor will they come for your camel and horse."

Abu stared at Quinn again, this time allowing an expression of surprise.

Westerners were not supposed to understand the heritage of tribal politics, yet Quinn knew the Bedouin legend about the old man and his stolen turkey. The old man in the story called his sons and told them the family was in great danger. They laughed. It was only a turkey. A few weeks later, a camel was stolen. The old man told his sons to find the turkey. When the horse was stolen, he told them again: find the turkey. Then the old man's daughter was raped, and he went to his sons and said it was all because of the turkey. Once it was known there was no retribution for taking the turkey, the old man cried, everything else was doomed to be lost.

"I will consider sparing his family," Abu said.

"War and poverty don't inflict enough pain on the children of Gaza?" Quinn remained at the table. "They of anyone in this land deserve more than consideration."

"Bah," Abu said. "Go."

Quinn knew there was nothing else he could do or say at this point to help Zayat's family. He pushed away from the table. With his good hand, he tucked the computer under his opposite arm.

"Could you help me with one thing?" Quinn said to Abu.

"I do not help Americans."

"I am also the enemy of an enemy." Quinn kept his eyes on Abu. "I'm an enemy of the man who had your brother killed."

"What do you want?" Abu said sourly.

"Two of your bodyguards to put the dead man in the trunk of my car."

Abu cocked his head and blinked several times. "Explain."

"My hand is injured. I can't carry him myself."

"Do not play games."

"Maybe I can learn something from the body that will lead to Safady."

"How?"

"It's as much as I want to explain." If Abu learned Quinn intended to use the Mossad, there would be no cooperation.

An impatient sigh. "You push me."

Quinn nodded.

"Two of you," Abu barked at this men. He picked up the knife from the floor and continued his instructions, pointing the blade at one bodyguard and then another. "Carry the body and follow the American to his car. But be fast. You don't want to miss my time with Zayat."

Abu advanced on Zayat, and Quinn turned away. As he was stepping outside, he heard a sharp cry of pain.

The man was going to die, but not until he'd been mutilated in ways Quinn didn't want to imagine. Even so, Quinn couldn't find sympathy for the man, only anger at the price Zayat's children would pay by dying as a warning retribution so that Abu would not look weak or, if Quinn had swayed Abu, by living without a father in the concentration camp that was called the Gaza Strip.

Sunshine hurt Quinn's eyes. When he'd been pinned to the table, he had not expected to be in sun or heat again. It was as if he were seeing light and feeling heat for the first time. His core abdominal muscles began to tremble in the emotional aftermath of surviving an execution and witnessing a man torn apart by machine-gun fire. Common as violent death was in Gaza, it was a horrible thing to see, and Quinn knew it would be a long time before the memory was gone.

The two bodyguards followed Quinn toward the CCTI Mercedes parked just down the street. Quinn popped the trunk with his remote, and the younger men hurried ahead with their macabre burden. They had loaded it and closed the lid before Quinn got to the Mercedes. No passersby had said anything about the sight of two men dragging a dead body down the street. The bodyguards hurried away without acknowledging Quinn.

Quinn was clumsy opening the door to get inside. He had to first put the laptop on the roof, then open the door with his good hand, then put the laptop inside with that same hand. Finally he was able to slide behind the wheel of the Mercedes.

Quinn's Mercedes was ten years old. It was dusty with multiple dents and a creased back fender. Barely worth a second glance, even in Gaza. But the engine was new, souped up to five hundred horsepower. The car's transmission had been modified to handle the extra power and the entire suspension system bulked up to deliver performance capable of matching most race cars. The windows and body could stop anything but armor-piercing shells. All told, the car weighed some two thousand pounds more than it looked. But that was the point. A new and obviously fortified Mercedes would draw too much attention. Unlike Abu's Mercedes, this one was impervious to a drive-by shooting.

It meant now that he was inside the car, Quinn would be safe all the way to the security checkpoint, where he was already resigned to complications explaining the body in the trunk. His biggest danger would happen if he was careless with his wounded hand and bled on the leather upholstery. Rossett was fussy about things like that.

ONE DAY BEFORE COUNTDOWN

Quinn gave his usual sigh at the chiming of the metal detector in the lobby of the five-story office building owned by Corporate Counterterrorism International. He took a half step forward and raised his arms for the wand search.

"Be gentle on me," Quinn said to Steve Gibbon, the big, redheaded former marine who ran the X-ray machine and the metal detector. "It's been a tough morning."

"I heard. This operation go fine?"

"I think so," Quinn said, holding up his bandaged hand. Two months and three operations since the knife had pinned his hand to the table in Gaza, the pain was gone. But the memories were still fresh. "Bones are fine. Apparently a few ligaments need more time."

"You being his partner and all, you'd think a trip to the hospital would be enough for Rossett to let you through without this today," Steve said, waving the wand along Quinn's belt loop.

"Being his partner and all just guarantees he won't make any exceptions for me. Ever."

"Now you're clear," Steve said when he was finished. Formality had to be served. Rossett was a freak for procedure and had become even more of a freak in the last month or so. Steve paused. "Just so you know, Rossett had Starbucks as he came through this morning."

All the employees knew that Rossett only stopped for coffee down the street when he was in a particularly bad mood. In fact, Rossett hated the stuff, but on the mornings he wanted to be left alone, he carried it into the building like a red flag of danger.

"Thanks for the warning," Quinn said. He took a step toward the elevator, mentally confirmed that the video camera was focused on the back of his head, and stopped. Rossett had a feed from the camera into his office.

"Steve, take a few quick steps and grab my shoulder like you don't want me to get to the elevator," Quinn said, still facing away from the camera behind him. It wouldn't surprise Quinn to learn someday that Rossett could read lips and had kept this from everybody else at CCTI. "Trust me on this."

A second later, Quinn felt Steve's hand.

"Good," Quinn said. "When I turn around, point at my left hand."

Quinn turned around, face toward the camera. No doubt Rossett was watching. Rossett saw everything.

Steve obliged Quinn by pointing at his left hand, wrapped in fresh gauze, with a trace of blood leaking through.

"Give me a break, Steve," Quinn said, clearly enunciating the words for the sake of the video camera. Rossett was tough enough to deal with when he was in a good mood. Security lapses drove him nuts and would put him on a rant for days.

"I just left the hospital," Quinn continued to Steve. "Think I've got a poison gas capsule hidden in it or that the physician implanted C-4 in my palm? And do you know how much it's going to hurt for you to pat this down?"

Steve blinked but figured it out a split second later. "Good catch," he said in a low voice to Quinn. "I owe you one."

SUEZ CANAL, PORT SAID, EGYPT • 18:43 GMT

Although the heifer had been sedated, when the crane lifted the container, the sudden movement startled the animal into a small fit of bucking. A flailing hoof caught the upper thigh of one of the soldiers who had been standing to stretch.

Joe Patterson had been dozing in a sitting position, his back against the metal wall of the container. The sharp cry of pain from that soldier jolted him out of his dreams.

It took a moment for Joe to orient himself and remember that he was in a shipping container with the rest of the soldiers. A crane was unloading the container from a cargo ship. The platoon shared the interior of the container with a black and red heifer—a small cow that had never calved. Patterson had no idea why the heifer was with them. Only Saxon knew their ultimate mission; he'd told them it would not be revealed until the last minute. This was to protect the mission in the event that any soldiers were captured before then.

The platoon had endured two weeks of slow travel to reach Port Said at the top of the Suez Canal. The journey had begun with a military flight from Afghanistan to Djibouti on the Horn of Africa. From there, a ship carried them northward up the Red Sea. It would have taken less time to fly into Port Sudan, halfway up the Red Sea, but the economy there was in tatters, and the risk of drawing attention to the platoon was too great.

On the ship, the soldiers had been armed with fake seamen's books and contracts of employment to look like workers if for any reason the ship was stopped and searched. The beards they had all begun to grow weeks earlier were thick and untrimmed. They had orders to sit in the sun for hours each day to darken their skin. They'd applied deep brown dye to their hair and with each passing day had begun to look slightly more native to the Middle East.

At the north end of the Red Sea, their cargo ship had met another coming down through the Suez. The rendezvous of the two ships had been brief and raised questions for Patterson because the southbound ship had transferred this heifer to their northbound ship. The platoon's ship had resumed its journey north toward the Suez Canal, with the heifer placidly eating hay.

The heifer's presence was another reminder to Patterson that this new phase of the platoon's operation was highly planned and equally mysterious. To get such a large group of American soldiers this far and this invisibly into the heart of the Middle East was one thing, but to stop two ships just to transfer a small cow? Every detail had been handled with precision and forethought by whoever had planned it—right down to the shipping container with a hitching ring welded to the front of the interior.

Just before dawn, in the final hours before reaching the Suez, the heifer had been led into the container—forty feet long, nearly eight feet wide, and eight feet high—and roped to the ring. The rear of the container was stacked with Soviet-issue weapons. Saxon had told them that part of the cover for this mission was an arms deal with Hamas in the Gaza Strip.

The platoon had followed the heifer inside, with the container door sealed behind them, becoming completely hidden among the hundreds of shipping containers on the cargo ship. Although they were de facto prisoners in the box that would smuggle them into Egypt, there were no fears of a double cross. The container door could be opened immediately from the inside, tiny air holes gave the soldiers a decent view of what was happening outside the container, and the shipper would not receive the last installment of a substantial payment from the arms dealer unless the container safely reached its destination.

It hadn't taken long for the heifer to dirty the straw on the floor of the container, and Joe had found the reactions from the platoon amusing. Joe had not minded the smell of manure at all; in fact, he'd felt a degree of comfort with something so familiar from his boyhood days on the farm. Riding a shipping container with an illegal weapons cache with the purpose of entering the Gaza Strip seemed surreal.

More so now, in the first moments out of sleep. Through the small holes, Patterson saw that the shipping container was dangling from the crane high above the ship, swinging over the water to be loaded onto a truck. The heifer's panic at this movement added extra movement to the container, and a couple of the other men inside were reacting with fear.

Enough sunlight filtered through the air holes for Joe to witness one soldier on the floor, groaning from the pain of where the hoof had struck him. Others tried to move in on the heifer, then scattered at its frantic movements. The animal weighed hundreds of pounds, and the stomping of its hooves on the floor was unnerving.

All of the soldiers knew what was at stake. If the heifer kept bucking, the workers on the ground would immediately notice the sound and the movement. If customs officials opened the container here, they all faced long terms in prison. Whatever their mission was, it would be ended before it had truly begun.

One of the soldiers had drawn a pistol and was trying to get a bead on the heifer's skull.

Lieutenant Del Saxon stepped in and slapped the man's forearm downward. "Idiot," he snapped. "This animal is worth more alive than all of us put together!"

Joe was standing now, watching quietly.

"Patterson," Saxon told him. "Do something! It can't be injured!"

Joe calmly moved to the side of the container, then slid down the wall toward the ring. Unless the animal swung around completely, he was safe from the hooves.

The heifer saw him too late. It tried to kick but only managed to sandwich Joe between its ribs and the wall. Joe had seen it coming and braced for it. When the animal bounced away again, Joe slid further down the wall toward the rope and the ring.

Joe slid his hand down the rope toward the heifer's face. Although the rest of its body was kicking high and hard, Joe was able to get his hand fully across the heifer's nose.

Like gripping a two-holed bowling ball, Joe jabbed his thumb into one nostril and his forefinger into the heifer's other nostril. He pinched hard, trying to connect thumb and forefinger.

The heifer reacted as if it had been hit across the head with a baseball bat. Instantly it stopped kicking, totally intent on the pain in its face.

"This ought to do it," Joe said, keeping a good squeeze in place. How could this animal be worth more than all of the lives of the platoon? "Someone get a jacket we can throw over her head. Once she's blind, there should be no more trouble here."

Except for the incredible view across Hayarkon Street from five stories up—the boardwalk with tourists, the wharves, the freight ships, the park to the northwest, and the shimmering aqua blue of the Mediterranean beyond—nothing about Rossett's office suggested luxury. Spartan furniture starkly contrasted with his taste in clothing. There was nothing to indicate Rossett's past as a decorated American war veteran, no clues to his rapid rise to the top of the CIA after his military career, nothing about the accolades that had followed him into retirement. The only testament to his accomplishments was the series of framed photographs of Rossett with each American president since Reagan and every Israeli prime minister over the last two decades. Even these were not meant as a display of ego; Rossett's photographs served a purpose: to assure clients of the connections and clout they were buying with the fees paid to CCTI to provide protection for high-level executives working in the Middle East.

"How's the hand?" Rossett asked from behind his desk. He was twenty-five years older than Quinn and repeatedly said the difference in age made for a good partnership. "Saw you on the monitor when the kid asked you for a pat down. Told you he was a good hire, didn't I? Anyone else would have waved you through without checking under the gauze."

Quinn kept a stone face.

Rossett pointed at Quinn's bandaged hand. "Any more operations ahead?"

"The hand reminds me of Fawzi," Quinn answered. "You might remember. Dead guy I dragged across the border a few months ago for the Mossad."

"That hand should remind you that the wife and girl are safe and back in the United States. That's why you went in. Remember?"

"Safady is why I almost didn't come out. The surgeon is working on my hand this morning and all I can think about is your buddies at the Mossad. Happy to vacuum up every last scrap of intel from us, but a vacuum of silence when I ask for something."

"How about some Starbucks?" Rossett asked, pointing at a cup on the corner of his desk. "No problem heating it up for you." Rossett hated wasting the money it took to buy Starbucks, so he'd offer it to Quinn every time he brought it into the office, no matter how long the coffee had been sitting.

"Stay on track," Quinn said. "It's been two months. We've gotten nothing from the Mossad except a name."

Rossett scowled—a sight, legend had it, which had once been able to stop tanks. Rossett's face was unpleasant at the best of times, and his scowl now made it sheer ugly. He was built low and powerful with no neck, so that it seemed his bald head balanced on his shoulders. While hair had once been one of his two vanities, he had given up the fight years earlier and resigned himself to shaving it as needed. He clung to his second vanity, however, which was clothing, and today he wore an impeccably tailored navy blue Armani suit.

"Save the gorilla face for someone who'll find it scary," Quinn said. "You sell every client on our connections to the Mossad. So what's the problem? Is your phone broken? Can't make outgoing calls?"

"We also sell our CIA background. Maybe you should save your anger for your buddies there who haven't brought you anything on Fawzi."

"I didn't deliver the body to CIA. They don't have carte blanche to roam Palestinian territory and beat information out of anyone who knew Fawzi."

"Seven dead already," Rossett said. "Fawzi made eight. How many of Safady's cell group have you taken down yourself? That's not good enough?"

"I assume that's rhetorical. Or the first symptoms of early onset dementia."

"What can I do?" Rossett said. "We need the Mossad more than they need us."

"Still," Quinn said, "two months. Fawzi was probably as close as anyone to Safady. Two months to learn enough about Fawzi to give us something on Safady. Instead, we get Mossad silence. You of all people know how bad I want Safady."

"I lost my family to Palestinian terrorists too," Rossett said. "You're not the only one burning to stop them."

Quinn fell silent. Rossett's first wife and their three children had died in the late eighties while Rossett was on a tour here. The same sad story, grief not diminished in the least by how common it was. Suicide bombers in a public place.

"I shouldn't have thrown that at you," Rossett said, easing the tension with a lopsided grin. "How about we kiss and make up."

Quinn sat down. "The thought of kissing to make up makes my stomach turn. You looked in any mirrors lately? What you'd see is a bulldog sucking a lemon."

"Glad we're friends again."

"That doesn't change the fact that Safady is still a ghost to intel agencies. After five years of tracking him, still no one knows what he looks like. Fawzi did. That means people who knew Fawzi might be able to help. Even a scrap is better than what we have."

Safady called himself the Black Prince in homage to Ali Hassan Salameh, the equally internationally notorious Palestinian terrorist who became known as the Red Prince for masterminding the murder of Israeli athletes at the Olympic Games in Munich. Salameh, a close friend of Arafat, had headed the Black September organization in the 1970s, until the Mossad finally assassinated him by car bomb in 1979.

Black September was gone, but Safady had effectively resurrected it, calling it Red September for blood and again to link it to its founder, still a hero among Palestinians.

"Someone's going to find Safady," Rossett said. "You. CIA. Mossad. He can't stay hidden forever. Eventually he's bound to make a mistake." Rossett gave Quinn a direct stare. "But if nailing Safady means you're going to retire from the business after you get him, I won't have much incentive here to keep helping you look for him."

"From the day I left the CIA, I've been in it for the money, Roz. You know that."

"Right," Rossett said, equally deadpan. "Glad we're clear on that." His expression softened with concern. "You go to Acco today, don't you?"

Quinn nodded. They both knew why.

"You're going to stick with procedure?"

Quinn nodded again. He now traveled with a bodyguard who also doubled as his driver.

"There is something," Rossett said. "About Fawzi. It's not much, but it could be important."

Quinn waited.

"He'd been in Iran a couple times in the six months before. The Mossad's got him linked to money from there. But Fawzi was low level. Delivery boy."

"So the money was going to Safady?"

"That's our best conclusion so far. Iran would love to cause as much trouble as possible in Israel."

"Yeah," Quinn said. "Iran's either got nuclear capacity already or they're on the verge. Safady's caused enough trouble with C-4. If he ever got his hands on any WMDs . . ."

Rossett rubbed his face. "I know."

"When did you find out the Iranian connection?" Quinn asked.

"This morning. Why do you think I bought Starbucks?"

"You couldn't tell me before my rant?"

"Had you opened with a question when you walked in and not a rant, maybe." Rossett grinned.

"Bulldog ugly," Quinn said, "bulldog mean."

"Go," Rossett said.

Quinn stood.

"I could wait until you get your hand on the doorknob," Rossett said. "Make it look like the thought just occurred to me and I was trying to stop you just in time. Or I can ask right now, and you'll know I do care."

"About what?"

"Acco. How are you? Really."

"I'll be fine," Quinn lied. Still, he was unable to push out of his mind the image of a blackened bus and the smoldering ruins around it. "But thanks for asking."

Rossett grunted. "Make sure you wear Kevlar."

Quinn didn't need the reminder. It was no secret he'd spent five years on a personal mission chasing Safady. And after the knife incident in Gaza, it was now obvious that the Black Prince, Khaled Safady, was making it equally personal to hunt for Quinn.

Khaled Safady was the one man among the busload of wealthy Holy Land tourists who knew that a sniper waited for the tourists to climb from their bus up the long, winding path to the hilltop ruins of Megiddo.

Whom will I choose for the bullet? he wondered. *Who shall be the one to receive the touch of death?* The sense of power and the nearness to the moment that he'd planned for months gave him a giddiness that he warned himself to keep under control.

Safady had been born in a refugee camp in the Gaza Strip, but the others in the group believed he was Dr. Joseph Marc, a physician on loan to the group, provided by the Israeli government. The real Dr. Joseph Marc had been killed the day before he was scheduled to join the tour; he'd made the mistake of believing the woman flirting with him at a beach was Israeli, not an Arab prostitute about to lure him to a hotel room where Safady was waiting in the closet with a garrote made of piano wire.

Safady was in his late twenties, clean shaven and handsome with dark hair and dark eyes. He easily fit the appearance of a Jewish physician. The irony that it was difficult to judge whether a man came from Arab or Jewish heritage was not lost on him. In fact, it made him perpetually angry. Carrying Palestinian identification papers made him a target of harassment and racism on the land that had belonged to his family for generations. By carrying a different piece of paper—a forged Israeli document—he was treated with deference and respect.

When the group reached the top of the hill, Safady pretended to share interest with those around him in the man striking a dramatic pose on a large rock of the ancient fortress.

"Armageddon!" Jonathan Silver thundered to the evangelicals from his position above the small crowd. "From Hebrew. It means 'the mount of Megiddo.' Right where we are standing! Look below you and see where Christ will soon defeat the armies of the Antichrist!"

From the hilltop ruins of the ancient fortress of Megiddo, his rapt listeners turned toward the panoramic view of the Valley of Jezreel. The faraway hills to the north held Nazareth. Mount Tabor stood northeast, a large, upside-down bowl of rounded land. Farther east they could see the Hill of Moreh. And Mount Gilboa in the southwest marked what was once the northern border of Samaria. The valley itself was a well-watered, fertile plain, a patchwork of gold wheat fields as harvest season approached.

"Armageddon!" Silver continued. "You and I have nothing to fear, for God will rapture away the righteous before the Tribulation begins. But those who have opposed us will suffer the horrible judgment they deserve! This Tribulation will give Jews another chance to finally acknowledge Jesus as the Messiah! Yes, those of us who believe today will be taken away from tomorrow's torment, but those left behind will be gathered like grapes waiting for the harvest of wrath!"

The small crowd—mostly middle-aged couples who would have looked at home in any country club across the United States—responded with cries of "Amen!" and "Hallelujah!"

"Picture it," Silver said, dropping his voice dramatically. "An army of two hundred million, gathered in this valley for the battle of Armageddon."

Silver was a large man with a beautiful mane of almost-white hair to match his distinctive name. Although he was nearing sixty, he appeared much younger, fueling tabloid gossip that he'd had discreet nips and tucks. Great tailoring hid the inevitable sags of aging. This was important. Every Sunday morning as he preached the gospel, Jonathan's image was broadcast to millions of viewers across the world.

The doctor with the false name tag knew all of this and much more about Jonathan Silver. He knew about the six security men dispersed among the group.

"Yes," Silver continued in the hypnotic voice that had lost no power with age, "hear the words of the vision given to John: 'So the angel thrust his sickle into the earth and gathered the vine of the earth, and threw it into the great winepress of the wrath of God. And the winepress was trampled outside the city, and blood came out of the winepress, up to the horses' bridles, for one thousand six hundred furlongs.'"

The amens and hallelujahs grew louder.

Khaled Safady raised his hand and waited respectfully for Jonathan Silver to acknowledge the question.

"In miles, how long is that river of blood?" Safady asked. He spoke with a Middle Eastern accent that no one found strange because of his assumed identity. Over the first few days of the tour, no one had yet looked at him twice or suspected where he'd been born.

"Roughly two hundred miles," Silver answered. "Incredible, isn't it? The blood of our enemies!"

This was the answer Safady expected, of course. It was the answer in all of Silver's books on end-times prophecies. Although Safady was an Islamic radical, he'd spent hours and hours studying Silver's Christian theology. *Know thy enemy.*

"Incredible," Safady agreed. He held his hand at the height of an imaginary horse's bridle. "This high?"

"That high," Silver confirmed. "Four and a half feet."

"And how wide?" Safady asked.

"Twenty-five feet." Silver's deep voice was confident in the answer.

"Incredible," Safady repeated. "You know, as a medical doctor, I have a rough idea of how much blood a human body holds. Has anyone calculated how many people it would take for a river with that much blood?"

While his questions had no relevance to what Safady had planned for the group, there was little time remaining before the sniper fired. He could finally afford to vent some of his anger at the people around him.

"It will take the blood of the two hundred million," Silver said with great certainty. "The Battle of Armageddon will be a horror we can hardly comprehend."

"Two hundred million," Safady said. "Is that *all* the blood of all two hundred million people?"

"As I said, a horror we can hardly comprehend," Jonathan Silver said. "But let me be quick to add, a justified horror. Both the righteous and the unrighteous will receive what they deserve."

"But I'm a physician. I've seen horrible accidents. I've seen people die. Any wound with enough blood loss to lead to death stops the heart long before the heart can pump the body dry. How will Christ squeeze the remaining blood from the two hundred million bodies?"

"Come on," a large-bellied man said, his arm around his wife. He spoke in a condescending tone. "With God, anything is possible."

Some in the group echoed that with more amens. Other tourists around Safady squirmed, giving him some space, making it clear they did not want to be associated with his pointed doubts of the great Jonathan Silver.

"I'm sorry." Safady smiled at the large-bellied man. *This will be the sniper's victim,* he decided. He walked over and patted the man's shoulder. *The touch of death.* "Really, I do apologize."

The man shrugged and pulled away, apology obviously not accepted. Safady was fine with that; he'd accomplished what he wanted.

At least, so far.

Aside from the sniper here, there was also the shipping container with arms coming in from the Suez. Safady needed that part of the plan to go just as smoothly as this.

Allah be praised, Safady thought.

SHEIKH ZUWEID, EGYPT • 11:29 GMT

As instructed, about ten miles short of the Gaza Strip border crossing at Rafah, the Egyptian truck driver left the heavy traffic on Highway 30 and turned south toward the heart of the Sinai Peninsula. Five miles down the road was Abu-Aweigila—a camel stop of a town—and just past it a commercial dump in a set of barren hills.

He didn't bother to gear down as he passed through Abu-Aweigila. Shortly afterward he turned onto another road that wound up through desert hills. Ancient, rattling dump trucks passed him in both directions as he geared down to a complete stop beside a semitrailer with a container on the flatbed deck. It was parked a quarter mile away from the dump, out of sight but not out of the range of the smell of the trash or the muted roar of the bulldozer moving the garbage.

The container on the other flatbed bore identical markings to the container that the crane had placed on his own flatbed trailer a few hours ago in Port Said.

To another driver, this might have seemed like a remarkable coincidence. This driver, however, valued his life. There had been whispers of Iranian money backing Hamas involvement in arms shipping, and he did not want to know what was in the container he carried, nor in the one he would be returning to Port Said.

All that mattered was uncoupling his truck from the trailer with the first container and coupling the second one in its place. And in the fastest time possible.

The dust was heavy on the truck driver's bearded face as he struggled with the equipment. The sound of the bulldozer's diesel engine faded from the driver's awareness as he concentrated on unhitching the first trailer from his truck. He skinned his knuckles and cursed; this was usually a two-man job, but he'd been paid well to do it alone.

Finished uncoupling the first trailer, he climbed back into the cab and drove forward, then reversed to line up the coupling with the second trailer. It took several times in and out of the truck to get it maneuvered where he needed it, and his anxiety grew with each passing minute.

Finally he managed to couple the second trailer to his cab. With a hiss of the release of air brakes and with grinding gears, he was grateful that nothing unusual had happened by the time he reached the highway to Abu-Aweigila. The money in this was good, but he wanted to return safely to his wife and two young sons.

In the relatively sparse traffic all the way until he reached Highway 30 again, he spent as much time glancing in his rearview mirrors as he did watching the pavement in front of him. Only when he was back in the heavy eastbound traffic toward Rafah did he finally allow himself a sigh of relief.

His relief lasted only another five minutes—as long as it took for the timer on the bomb inside the new container to count down the final seconds.

For the driver, the end was a quick mercy. He died without comprehending the roar and the flash that threw the cab of the truck two hundred feet into the air.

MEGIDDO, ISRAEL • 11:42 GMT

Jonathan Silver's lecture on Megiddo had ended. As the Holy Land tourists began to shuffle toward the path that led down to the bus, Safady glanced at his watch.

Two minutes. The sniper was a minor player in this. He didn't know why he was involved. He had been paid simply to shoot the target that Safady indicated, then disappear in the confusion. Two minutes. Then the payoff for months of intricate planning.

Safady raised his hand and called to Jonathan Silver. "I know we talked about this earlier," he said, "but I'm trying to get something straight in my head. Because I've really been thinking hard about what you said about the two hundred million bodies and how it will take all of the blood from all the bodies squeezed dry."

"Revelation tells us there is a great winepress," Silver said, clearly irritated, "and that the blood came out of the winepress."

"Incredible," Safady said yet again. "All two hundred million bodies get fed through a winepress to be squeezed of their blood?"

"It's not something I spend much time visualizing," Silver said. "If we could move on . . ."

"Did you see the news coverage of the tsunami a few years ago?" Safady asked. "It took weeks to dispose of only thousands of bodies. How long would it take to move two hundred million bodies to and through the winepress? That's what I've been trying to figure out. Even at the rate of one body per second—which I think we would agree would be a mind-boggling logistical accomplishment—that would only be sixty bodies per minute, thirty-six hundred bodies per hour, and from what I've calculated in the last few minutes—" Safady's brow furrowed as he briefly paused—"maybe eighty thousand bodies every day. Make it one hundred thousand bodies for even math. To squeeze blood from two hundred million dead bodies at that incredible rate would still take a minimum of two thousand days, or roughly five and a half years. Even then, I don't think it would produce a high enough minute-by-minute volume of blood for a river four and a half feet high by twenty-five feet wide."

"I find this very macabre," Silver said. "We need not contemplate—"

"But earlier I heard a chorus of amens and hallelujahs when you described the two hundred million killed and all of their blood forming a river," Safady said. He heard his voice begin to rise. *Keep control of your anger,* he reminded himself. *Take satisfaction in what you are about to inflict on these people.*

He continued, forcing calm upon himself. "I heard joy as you had us contemplate the horrible deaths of liberals and gays and Arabs and Muslims who will be left behind. I find that just as macabre as wondering about God's method of accomplishing this."

"The unjust will pay the price," Silver said.

"Amen!" an elderly woman shouted in Safady's ear.

"So you're telling me that Jesus is going to return and spend His first five and a half years supervising the logistics of squeezing dead bodies of all their blood?" Safady asked. "Is that what Revelation tells us?"

"Are you questioning the Word of God?"

"I just want to know where the river of blood comes from. If that prophecy is not accurate, what else about your prophecies is mistaken?"

"The truth is in the literal words of the Bible, young man," Jonathan Silver said sternly. "When I hear you questioning that truth, I hear you questioning God. All the others around you hear that same lack of faith. I don't appreciate it. I'm sure they don't."

The predictable applause, amens, and hallelujahs followed.

"Questioning *your* understanding of the Bible is questioning God?" Safady said, feeling the heat rise inside again.

"Enough," Silver snapped. "Does anyone else want the tour to continue?"

More applause was directed at Silver and dark glances at Safady. These were scornful looks that gave Safady great satisfaction. Soon enough they would learn he was an Arab Muslim; soon enough they would learn to hate him much, much more. But all that hatred would be nothing compared to the hatred he had carried for them for years.

He glanced at his watch. It was almost time.

"If you will look over there," Silver said, "you will see where the armies from the north are going to flood into the valley. Century after century of battles have been fought here. Napoleon once came and tasted defeat."

Silver spun on the large rock that was his stage and pointed in the direction of Nazareth. "God stopped Napoleon from taking the Promised Land from the Jews, just as God will curse and strike down all those who oppose the prophecies found in His Holy Scripture."

Silver let those words hang, as if they were an accusation directed at Safady. Others understood and nodded grimly as they stared at Safady.

In that brief silence of accusation, the sniper fired his single shot, striking down the potbellied American that Safady had chosen for a target.

Quinn stood close enough to the edge of the seawall that salt spray would occasionally cool his face, a welcome sensation in the heat of early afternoon. Here, on the weekends, couples often posed for wedding photos with the fishing boats and the marina and the sea beyond. Quinn stood at this popular spot facing inland toward an enormous stone fortress.

Acco had always fascinated Mulvaney Quinn. The Muslims had managed to retake most of the Holy Land from the Christian crusaders by the early twelfth century, and here Richard the Lionheart had returned in 1191 to recapture the city from the great warrior Saladin and establish it as the capital of the pitiful remnant of the Kingdom of Jerusalem, the final stronghold that would succumb a century later.

Eight hundred years had passed since the bloody battles, and a haunted lostness clung to the ancient stonework, the light sea breeze and bright sunshine incapable of banishing its melancholy. This added to the ache for Quinn—all he had to do was close his eyes to see that same breeze tugging at the hair of his five-year-old daughter as she clung to his hand and pulled him along the seawall, begging him to tell yet another story about the knights who'd roamed the hills so long before.

As he soaked in the Mediterranean vista, Quinn used his right hand to squeeze the fresh stitches beneath the gauze of his left hand. The freezing had departed, and he was using the sensation of physical pain to distract him from the pain in his soul. But better to mark the anniversary here. He'd rather think about his daughter along the seawall than think of the bloody shoe he had found in the street on that horrible day. . . .

A woman approached. A tourist, by all appearances, with the straight-forwardness and unself-consciousness of an American. She wore a blue summer dress that swirled around her hips. Her shoulder-length auburn hair, slightly wide cheekbones, and a nose not quite straight had a definite allure. Men were turning heads to watch her progress.

She stopped in front of Quinn.

"I've been watching you from that bar over there," she said, pointing vaguely toward an outdoor bistro about fifty steps away. "My name is Kate Penner."

Her accent confirmed his guess that she was American.

"I won't be coy here," she said. "I tell people I'm thirty-two, I'm on vacation, and I have enough self-confidence to handle it if you say no. How about dinner with me at sunset?" The question was accompanied by a great smile.

"You *tell* people you're thirty-two?" Quinn was mildly surprised that he replied with something that could be construed as banter. It had been so long he didn't know he still had the capability.

"I want to be up-front with you. I'm not going to start us off by lying to you about my age."

"So you're truthful to me about the lies you tell other people."

"Exactly."

"You're not thirty-two," he said.

"You don't know me well enough to ask that question." Another wide smile. "How about the Abu Cristo? Great seafood. Overlooks the bay."

"No, but thanks."

"Is it the restaurant you're declining?" she asked.

"No."

"Me, then."

"Yes," he said.

"I'm feeling better about this already. Doesn't seem like you'd be much for conversation anyway."

"Good assumption."

"You're not even trying to let me down easy here."

He found himself returning the smile. "You said you had self-confidence."

"Yeah," she said wryly. "And pride." She gave a little wave of her fingers and walked away.

Quinn watched her, admiring the grace in her stride, and admitted to himself that he was admiring a little more than that. He felt a twinge of guilt but found himself experiencing another unexpected emotion.

Regret.

AD DUHAYR, EGYPT • 12:03 GMT

After the trucker had driven away, the platoon members had taken up ambush positions within a hundred yards of the shipping container with the Soviet arms still inside.

But not Patterson. He'd been Lieutenant Saxon's obvious choice as caretaker. He had been instructed to find a safe place in the hills for the heifer and given an extra canteen of water and orders to put the animal's life ahead of his own as he stood watch over it.

Leaving the platoon behind, Joe Patterson led the heifer by the halter away from the shipping container and farther up into the hills. He wanted to find the deepest shade possible. The heat was intense and whisked away his sweat. He was thirsty after only a hundred yards of crunching his boots on the dry, hard sand.

"But you'd complain too," he said to Orphan Annie. The name fit, Joe thought. Except for the occasional patches of black, the heifer's red hide almost gleamed in the sun.

Orphan Annie didn't reply.

Joe rubbed his beard and squinted against the sun. Del Saxon's words rang in his ears. *Put the heifer's life ahead of your own.* He had no idea why. Only that it was hot, and he was supposed to give the bulk of his water to the animal.

It was going to be a long day.

HADERA, ISRAEL • 12:04 GMT

The Holy Land Tours air-conditioned bus moved down Highway 65 toward Hadera on the coast of the Mediterranean. With smoked glass windows, leather seats, and a near hermetic seal around the windows, the luxury touring edition kept the road noise to a hum, and the knots of conversations inside the bus were barely more than frantic whispers. Jonathan Silver stood at the front of the bus, comforting a few of the rich, older women by praying with them.

Khaled Safady was at the back, still in his role as Dr. Joseph Marc.

"Where's that ambulance?"

This question, directed at Safady, came from one of the American security men who'd been assigned to this bus. He was a bulky ex-marine in his midforties with the competent air of a man who had faced death and dealt death. There were six of them with the group, all regular employees of Silver's Freedom Christian University, continually assuming point positions as the group moved through a Holy Land site. Jonathan Silver did not believe in taking chances, especially since most of the tour members were extremely wealthy, cherry-picked from his mailing list of contributors for the exclusive opportunity to tour Israel with the famous end-times television evangelist.

"The ambulance . . . ," Safady answered. "That can only be a rhetorical question or a bad attempt at making conversation. The bus driver made ambulance arrangements, and as you can see, I've been busy."

The large-bellied man was sitting upright on the last seat in the bus, eyes closed, mouth shut tight in pain. The bullet had struck the center of his belly. Safady had used the emergency first aid kit on the bus to clean and bandage the wound but knew the man would die from a slow internal hemorrhage unless he reached a hospital. Both the stomach wound and the prospect of the man's slow death gave Safady satisfaction, for the bullet had gone exactly where Safady had specified.

"Every time I ask the driver, he rattles some answer in Jew language that I can't understand."

"That's Hebrew," Safady said. "He's probably stressed out about all of this."

"Yeah, well, he'd better have made the right call to the right place. We should have met that ambulance by now."

Following the gunshot, there had been brief incomprehension, then the predictable screaming and rushing away from the sound as the tourists pieced together what had happened. The security men had fanned out, only to return a few minutes later with the comforting report that the sniper had fled. They'd found Safady kneeling beside the still-conscious tourist, compressing the wound with a rag hastily torn from his own shirt.

Safady had assured them the wound was not life threatening and suggested that the group return to the bus. There the driver had used his cell phone to make two calls. The first had been to a hospital in Hadera, arranging for an ambulance to meet the bus on its way to the city. The second call had been to Israeli police to notify them of the incident. Safady knew both calls had been faked. The bus would not be meeting an ambulance, and no police were en route.

"Ambulance or not, this man is in no immediate danger," Safady lied to the security man.

The injured man opened his eyes and groaned. "It doesn't feel that way."

"Trust me," Safady said, enjoying the opportunity to deceive the American. He stood in the aisle and spoke to the security man. "Could you watch him for a moment? I need to use the washroom."

The security guard nodded.

Safady swayed with the movement of the bus as he took the few steps to the bus's lavatory. Once the door was closed, he reached into a pocket for his cell phone and hit a speed dial number. Seconds later, his call was answered.

"Are you ready?" Safady asked in Arabic. He thought this was ironic. His outgoing cell transmission was probably traveling hundreds of miles, relayed from tower to tower, simply to return to the cell phone of the driver at the front of this bus. The man was Iranian and had been working closely with Safady in the last months to plan this operation. More importantly, the Iranian had been a funnel for money from Iran to Safady. But the man was a traitor, and Safady was looking forward to dealing with that in the next few hours.

"Ready," came the answer from the bus driver.

"Thirty seconds," Safady said, glancing at his watch. "Starting in five . . . four . . . three . . . two . . . one."

Safady hung up.

He reached above him and tore off the false ceiling of the lavatory. Held in place by duct tape were a small oxygen tank and a ventilator. He ripped the tape loose and placed the ventilator over his face.

Safady watched the seconds tick by. When thirty seconds had passed, he switched open the valve of the oxygen tank.

Up front, he knew the bus driver had strapped on a ventilator and was flipping a switch that would add a gaseous mixture to the cold air hissing out of the air-conditioning vents.

By the time any of the passengers realized what was happening, it would be far, far too late for them.

Including the six security men.

Including the esteemed Jonathan Silver.

ACCO HARBOR, ISRAEL • 12:00 GMT

Quinn watched the woman until she returned to her table at the bistro. Just before she sat, he turned his gaze on the harbor so she wouldn't catch him looking.

It was stupid, he told himself, to allow this juvenile swirl of emotions, the thrill and confusion of a high school conversation with a pretty cheerleader. Yet even these emotions were mixed with sorrow, the woman's smile and allure a mocking reminder of what he'd lost and how much he grieved that loss.

But Quinn couldn't resist another emotion: curiosity. He turned his head slightly and caught her catching him looking.

She didn't smile. He didn't either.

Juvenile, Quinn told himself. He turned his head back toward the water.

Seconds later, he heard the soft slap of high heels on cobblestone and smelled a trace of perfume on the breeze.

"I told myself that if you looked over, I'd try once more," Kate said. She stood beside him, sharing his gaze across the water. "I want to believe there is something about you and me. I need to know if it's my imagination."

Quinn couldn't think of anything to say. Since he wasn't going to permit himself to act upon the attraction he felt for her, it would be wrong to give her any indication of it.

"You married?"

"No."

"Divorced?"

"No."

"Girlfriend?"

"No."

This Kate Penner woman wouldn't let up. Once again he found himself enjoying the back-and-forth.

"Girlfriends?" she asked, emphasized the plural.

"No."

"Suffer from phobias? lack of self-confidence?"

"No."

"You sure? You're holding yourself in a funny way. Or maybe it's just the heavy clothing you're wearing. It's hot and you're wearing a sweatshirt."

"Need to hide a Kevlar vest."

"Good-looking and a sense of humor," she said. "Are you too broke to buy my dinner?"

"I thought you were offering."

"Not at all. What I asked is whether you were interested in dinner at sunset. I wasn't going to pick up the tab. I do have pride."

"Interesting."

"That's me. Which is why I'd be a great dinner date. Let me ask again. You broke?"

"No."

"Why not join me for dinner then? I've just now discovered I don't have quite enough self-confidence to take the rejection without a good excuse."

"How about I'm naturally suspicious and it seems odd that a beautiful woman would make such a great offer."

"So you think I'm beautiful, and you think it's a great offer. See, you are able to let me down easy."

"That's me," Quinn said. "A gentleman."

"I'm not giving up easy here. No reason for you to be suspicious."

"Generally a beautiful woman making the offer you did has serious issues, is on the rebound, or has an ulterior motive that differs from what the man expects or hopes."

"Sexist. Men come on to women all the time, and women aren't suspicious of their motives."

"Men are a lot easier to figure out," Quinn said. How long had it been since he'd had to stay on his toes around a woman in casual conversation? "Women know exactly what men want. They might not like the man's motives, but at least there's no mystery. Me—I like my kidneys where they are."

Kate snorted. "Maybe you don't know much about the birds and the bees. Kidneys are rarely involved."

"Aren't you into urban myths? Like the one about the American tourist who got himself picked up by a woman in Tel Aviv. Date rape drug put him out. He woke up the next morning minus a kidney, which by the way is worth ten grand on the black market."

"That myth." Kate paused. "I'm not interested in your kidneys, I don't have issues, I'm five thousand miles and three years clear of my ex-husband, and this is the first time I've asked a man out for dinner. You're out of reasons to turn down a beautiful woman and a great offer."

"There could be a business conflict."

"Pick another night then," she said. "I'm here for at least a week."

"Or maybe . . ." Quinn discovered it wasn't going to come out in a light, bantering way and didn't want her to hear a catch in his voice.

"Maybe . . . ?" she echoed. Her smile was teasing.

He felt bad because he knew it would bring her down, but he didn't see any other way to say it and still be true to himself and the memories. "Maybe I come here once a year on the anniversary of the last vacation weekend I had with my wife and my daughter, because a day later they shared a bus ride with a Palestinian suicide bomber in Tel Aviv who didn't want to make it to the next stop."

He stopped for a breath, unable to avoid the memory. On that horrible day in Tel Aviv, he'd jumped off to get coffee and something to eat. One stop later, the bus exploded. He'd seen the fireball from the cafe. Seen it countless times in his nightmares after that. "Hard to fight the memories."

"You're serious. I don't even need to ask you that."

"I'm sorry," Quinn said. He had to look away. It had been five years, and he still couldn't tell people about it without finding somewhere else to look out of fear they'd see into his soul. "She'd be ten now. But that's not your burden."

"I'm the one who should be sorry," Kate said. "I should have guessed by the way you were standing out here lost in thought."

"It's not your fault. Not by a long shot."

"You had it right the first time," she said. "A simple no should have been good enough. Now I can't walk away thinking you're a jerk."

It *wasn't* her fault, Quinn thought. And he could have found a way to decline without bringing the mood down. At least that's why he justified returning to the banter that he'd enjoyed with guilt. "Going to dinner with me probably would have proved it."

"Catch-22 of sorts," she said.

"Yossarian can't prove he's crazy enough to get out of the war because concern for his own life proves he's not crazy."

"Now I really feel better," Kate said, allowing a smile back on her face. "Sure you turned me down, but at least you put some effort into impressing me with that. Not everyone knows Joseph Heller."

"Who wouldn't want to impress you?" Quinn said. He was grateful she was working to lighten the mood too.

"Some other time?" she asked.

"Sure," he said, "some other time."

"Thanks." She smiled sadly, kissed her fingertips, and touched them lightly against his cheek.

Kate walked away, the breeze again swirling the light summer dress around her hips, and Quinn felt like a traitor to his sorrow for watching her until she disappeared around a corner.

Steve Gibbon watched two men walk into the lobby of the CCTI building. *Mossad,* he thought instantly. *Maybe IDF.* The men had that air. It was difficult to put into words, but a person knew it when it was there. The men had dark, short hair and managed to make their jeans and polo shirts look like uniforms.

"Gentlemen," Steve said. "Appointments?"

The first walked through the metal detector, setting off chimes. "Don't bother searching," he said to Gibbon. "It's a Beretta."

The second one had already set off the metal detector too. "Mine's a Russian make. I always mispronounce the name."

"Appointments?" Steve repeated. He placed his hand on his holster.

He'd been marine trained, but nothing could have helped him anticipate the first man's lightning kick to his chest.

The second drew his pistol and knelt beside Steve, grinding the barrel in his ear. "No moves. Don't even blink."

Steve stared upward, hearing a ripping sound. He didn't recognize it as duct tape until the first wraps went around his ankles. His wrists were next, then a patch over his mouth.

The first man prodded Steve with his foot and looked down into his eyes. "If you want to live, we'd better find you right here the way we left you." The commando's eyes were dark, the stare unflinching.

Gibbon's nostrils flared as he tried to suck in air.

"Relax," the second one said. "We have no interest in killing you. It's someone else we want."

They headed to the elevator.

TULKARM, WEST BANK • 12:22 GMT

Safady was alone with all the passengers in the bus. It was parked in a fruit-and-vegetable warehouse. The driver had gone for a cigarette.

This was satisfying for him: to look down the aisle and see all of them helpless. To wait until they slowly struggled back to the light. To enjoy watching them begin to understand what had happened.

The gas had knocked them unconscious, and as the bus traveled down the highway, Safady had moved from seat to seat, certain that the height of the bus and the darkness of the tinted windows made his actions invisible to other drivers.

He'd used plastic tie strips to bind the wrists of the Holy Land Tours passengers, the same tie strips that American soldiers used on insurgent captives. The strips were simple, effective, fast, inexpensive, and easy to carry; he'd stored them in his day bag.

Before binding their wrists, Safady had intertwined the arms of each person with the person in the adjacent seat so that the evangelicals were bound to each other in pairs.

The difficult part had been restraining his rage.

Bending over the women—many of them soft and fat in the way that he'd come to expect from decadent Americans—he'd been forced to inhale their perfumes and been disgusted and fascinated at the clothing some wore, like harlots, showing skin that only a husband should be allowed to see.

The slack faces of the men still somehow contained the arrogant confidence of those whose money was a power untouchable and unthinkable in the world where Safady had spent his childhood.

While binding the passengers, it had taken all his discipline not to smash at their faces with his elbow, not to fracture cheekbones and scatter teeth.

How he hated all Americans. Especially these—the Christians who tainted the Palestinian land as their forefathers had so many centuries before during the Crusades.

He relished his hatred.

And soon they would wake to discover the extent of it.

CCTI HEADQUARTERS, TEL AVIV • 12:23 GMT

Watching the events down in the lobby on the video screen in his office, Rossett didn't have to read lips to understand what was happening.

He'd always known that when they came for him, defeating the CCTI security measures would be as simple for them as thrusting a pistol barrel through a wet paper bag. The fact that the events in the lobby were securely on video and audio meant nothing now that two gunmen were on their way up the elevator.

It would take them a minimum of 215 seconds to make it from the lobby to his office. Rossett had timed this. He'd practiced an escape route and timed that too. He could be out of the building by a secret exit and in his car at least twenty-five seconds before they reached his locked office door on the fifth floor. It would take another thirty to forty-five seconds to force the door open before they looked into his office to see that he'd bolted.

He had less than two minutes before the arrival of the intruders. Rossett threw on a Kevlar vest, then put his Armani jacket overtop to hide it. He wrinkled his nose at the poor fit. Good tailoring wasted. That would show up on the video taped from cameras in the hallway.

Rossett glanced around his office as if checking for loose ends, but he knew without looking that there was nothing to cover or hide. This was reflex; he never left anything of value in the office.

All there was left to do was grab his silenced Luger and his cell phone. This would be on video too. Later, his cell phone records would be checked against the time on the videotapes. Investigators would know he'd called Quinn. But that wouldn't expose any secrets. And Quinn deserved protection.

Rossett dialed Quinn's cell as he walked down the hall to the elevator. There would be no one on the fifth floor to interfere. Rossett had set it up this way, so that the fifth floor was all his.

He positioned himself along the wall beside the elevator door.

"Rossett?" Quinn answered, obviously reading his caller ID.

"They'll want to get you next," Rossett said. "I don't have much time to explain. Get to your car. Run."

Behind him he heard the hum as the elevator rose.

TULKARM, WEST BANK • 12:23 GMT

The Iranian bus driver was on his knees in an old warehouse, hands bound behind his back, eyes bulging as he looked upward at Safady. The American tourists remained on the bus, still bound. The driver was in his midtwenties with a full beard and nearly shaved head. He always spoke quickly, always had food in his teeth. Safady had disliked the man from the beginning but was happy to use him until the man no longer served any purpose.

"I know you were sent by the Mossad," Safady said to the Iranian. "I know you've betrayed me. Do you deny this?"

The man's trousers suddenly splotched with wetness.

"You are fortunate I don't have time to kill you slowly," Safady said. "Fool. All that time convincing me where to hide the hostages. Acting as if you and I were equals, partners. Hear this before you die: From the beginning, I knew why you appeared with money. The operation will fail. Do you understand?"

The Iranian closed his eyes.

"Say it," Safady said. "Tell me you understand the operation will fail."

The Iranian looked up again at Safady. And spit.

In a moment of fury, Safady pulled the trigger. It caused him faint regret. He would have enjoyed taunting the man for a few more minutes.

When his cell phone rang, Quinn glanced at the caller identification display. "Rossett?" Quinn answered.

"They'll want to get you next," Rossett said. Rossett's voice sounded strangled. "I don't have much time to explain. Get to your car. Run."

"Me next? Who are they getting first?"

An explosive noise in Quinn's cell phone sounded like a gunshot.

"Roz? Did someone shoot at you?"

No answer.

Quinn scanned the promenade, seeing no unusual movement. "Rossett, what's happening?"

More explosions. Clicking. Then silence. Echoing silence, not the silence of disconnection.

Then Quinn heard a voice, not Rossett's, as if from someone standing nearby. "Nice try. Think we didn't expect that? On your belly, Rossett."

Quinn was desperately trying to make a mental picture. Rossett shooting at attackers? Attackers shooting at Rossett? The clicking when his automatic ran empty?

"What did Rossett tell you?" The new voice spoke into the cell phone.

"Who is this? Where's Rossett?"

"What did Rossett tell you?" the voice repeated.

Quinn thought quickly. CCTI was founded on the need for corporate security. Could anyone really expect that under any circumstances, let alone based on the confusion of the previous minute, Quinn would give that answer to a stranger who had just picked up Rossett's phone? Then it struck Quinn. The person on the other end of the line wasn't really trying to get information from him. There was another purpose in trying to keep Quinn engaged and the line open—GPS.

"He told me his appointment had shown up," Quinn lied. "Are you his appointment? What is going on? Let me speak to Rossett again."

Quinn was moving now at a jog, headed toward the end of the promenade and back toward street traffic. With his painkiller wearing off, his hand throbbed at the movement. The Kevlar vest rubbed hard against his chest. He calculated maybe twenty seconds to reach his destination.

"Rossett wants me to do the talking," the voice said.

"Then talk," Quinn said. "I have no idea what's going on. What can you tell me?"

In front of him, pigeons scattered in flight. An old woman who had been feeding the pigeons scowled. Quinn shrugged apologetically but kept jogging.

"Given the situation here," the voice said, "you need to answer me first. What did Rossett tell you about Fawzi?"

Fawzi! The Iranian connection to Safady!

Quinn passed a falafel stand with a dozen Israelis pushing to be at the front. No one lined up in this culture; they always formed a crowd and pushed.

"Look," Quinn said, "you've got to understand what business we're in. I'm not in a position to tell you confidential information passed on to me by my partner."

He was at the street now, facing the usual chaos—motorcycles, cars, trucks. An open produce truck had slowed to turn. Quinn stepped onto the street and, without ending the connection, threw his cell phone into the back among the cabbages just picked from the nearby kibbutzim.

There, Quinn thought, *go ahead and track that.*

Quinn turned again and stopped at the falafel stand. He pulled out his wallet, waved it above his head, and yelled at the crowd. "Anybody here want to sell me a phone for two hundred American dollars?"

TULKARM, WEST BANK • 12:26 GMT

Jonathan Silver returned to consciousness on the right-hand side of the aisle, two rows from the front of the bus, with his right arm through the left arm of one of the women in the tour group, his wrists bound together by the plastic tie strap. The woman's left arm was crooked around his elbow, both her wrists bound in front of her too. To stand or move, they'd have to stand or move together.

Silver tried to understand what had happened but could remember only a slight wooziness, then nothing. Obviously he'd been moved while he was unconscious. Why was the bus stopped? Where was the driver? Where, for that matter, had the bus been stopped?

He was thirsty. The woman beside him was still unconscious. She was a young woman—at least to him—probably forty or forty-five. Peggy Bailey, he remembered—one of the devout ones, soaking in his apocalyptic explanations at each Holy Land stop. He knew she was a Fort Worth blonde society type, recently divorced, lots of money in the settlement—the reason she'd received the special and personal invitation to the tour. She was prim and proper, but her hairdo and frilly clothing were ten years behind. He was glad her perfume wasn't overpowering. It didn't seem they would be separated soon.

Silver turned his head and gave his own armpit a sniff, then rolled his eyes at himself. Sixty years old and still vain enough to be concerned about the public impression he'd give. If the two of them were linked for much more than a couple of hours, body odor would be the least of their problems.

Silver looked across the aisle. Two men—both on this tour with their wives—had been bound together arm in arm. Their wives were seated directly behind them, bound as well.

He strained to turn his head and look behind him. As far as he could see, the other passengers were in the same situation, most of them with their respective husbands and wives.

It must have been enough movement to catch the eye of Dr. Marc, who moved from the rear of the bus and stood above Silver.

"What is going on?" Silver whispered. He jerked his wrists. "Cut me loose."

"After all the effort I went through to make sure you woke like this?"

"You? I don't understand!"

"You will soon enough. We're waiting for a military truck. Then you're going to disappear from the face of the earth."

"Who are you? Why?"

"You'll find out soon enough." Marc was smug. The smugness of power. Silver regretted how he'd treated the man at Megiddo. "Let me just say my name is not Marc."

"This is criminal!" Silver sputtered.

The man squatted so he could look Silver directly in the eyes. "In my world, you are much more of a criminal, and now is the time to pay."

"In *your* world?"

"The world of Khaled Safady—the Black Prince."

"He's a terrorist!" It didn't take much knowledge of Middle Eastern affairs to be aware of the name. Silver knew Safady was as famous and elusive as Osama bin Laden; whereas bin Laden was seen as a spiritual leader for Muslim extremists, Safady was renowned for performing actual acts of terrorism. More covert than bin Laden.

"Watch what you say." The man smiled. "You don't want to insult me."

It took Silver a moment to comprehend. With horror. "You?"

Safady smiled. "Yes, you do understand. I am the Black Prince."

"What do you want?" Silver asked. "Don't kill us. We can pay you—"

Silver's words were cut off as Safady clapped a hand across his mouth. Silver jerked his hands up in a defensive response but was stopped by the woman's arms linked through his.

Safady smiled. With the thumb and forefinger of his other hand, he pinched Silver's nostrils shut.

Silver tried to suck for air but found none. Frantically he tried to pull his bound wrists up to his mouth again.

Safady stared directly into Silver's eyes, as if trying to watch the light of his soul dim with unconsciousness. Silver bucked, desperate for air.

With another smile, Safady released the grip. "Do not forget this lesson," he said. "You depend on me even for the very air you breathe. And so do all the others."

"Whatever you want," Silver said, "I can give to you."

Safady stared into Silver's face. After a few minutes, he nodded. "You will. And more."

AD DUHAYR, EGYPT • 12:26 GMT

Hot.

Even in the shade. Joe Patterson thought he'd spent enough time in Afghanistan to understand hot. But something about having only two canteens of water made the hot seem hotter.

Saliva dripped from Orphan Annie's jowls.

"Hot," Joe said. He figured he might as well speak his thoughts out loud.

Orphan Annie blinked.

Joe wanted a drink of water badly. But he had his orders. The heifer mattered more than his own life.

Joe screwed open the lid of the canteen, splashed a little water on the opening, and let the heifer smell the water. "Try this," he said. He jammed the canteen into the heifer's mouth and tilted it sideways. He poured the water slowly, making sure he didn't spill any onto the sand.

"Good, huh?" Joe said.

Yeah, he wanted some water badly. But last thing he wanted to do was run out. The heifer wasn't built for this kind of heat. Patterson knew Saxon would make him pay if anything happened to it. The thought only added to his misery.

TULKARM, WEST BANK • 12:28 GMT
Under the supervision of six masked men carrying AK-47s, Jonathan Silver and his partner were the first two off the bus. Because he and Peggy Bailey were linked together, they were forced to move in a sideways shuffle down the steps of the bus and into the warehouse.

The building could have held six buses of the same size. The warehouse floor was hard-packed dirt. It had the smell of rotting fruit, and the old, wooden shelves were crowded with boxes of ripening oranges. Light came through dusty windows.

Behind the bus was a large produce truck. The flat deck on the back had canvas sides and a canvas roof. A wide ramp rested at the tail. Beyond that was a video camera on a tripod. A huge PLO flag hung down from the ceiling behind it, forming a backdrop.

Silver expected the gunmen to herd them up the ramp into the cargo area of the produce truck. In fact, he hoped they would. It was obvious to him that the video camera and the flag were not part of the produce business.

Instead, as he feared, the first two masked men motioned for Silver and Peggy to stand behind the truck as the other tourists awkwardly emptied from the bus.

There was a dead man on the floor, his hands bound. The bus driver. All of them averted their eyes. One of the women sagged to her knees and needed help to stand again.

When all the tourists were gathered, Safady faced them and smiled tightly. "It's obvious by now that this isn't part of Mr. Silver's famous Holy Land tour," he said. "It's only the first of several detours. But first, the famous Jonathan Silver has a television appearance to make."

Safady nodded at the gunmen near Silver. They prodded Silver toward the video camera. Peggy had to move with him; she wept silently.

"Don't do it!" shouted one of the two men who had been across the aisle from Silver. "God is on our side. Stand up to him!"

All the attention turned to this man.

Safady squinted at his name tag. "Neil Cain."

"I'm not afraid of you," Neil answered. He wore a black golf shirt and jeans. His hair was moderately thinning, and his face shone with holy bravery. "We all have an eternal home waiting for us. Death is not the worst thing that can happen."

"You irritate me," Safady said. "But I suppose this is as good a time as any to teach all of you a lesson."

Safady was standing beside a bench. On it was a box of clear plastic shrink wrap. Beside that lay a paring knife. Safady took the knife and stepped up to the older woman who had mocked him on the Megiddo hilltop during his questions about the river of blood. He cut the plastic strap binding the woman's wrists, allowing her to step away from the other woman whose arms had been intertwined with her own. Then he picked up the box of shrink-wrap.

"Are you as willing to give up someone else's life?" Safady asked Neil Cain. He turned back to the woman and read her name tag. "Trudy Warner," he said, "I'm sure you remember my questions for Mr. Silver on the hilltop at Megiddo. Remember, when Mr. Silver was the apparent leader of the group? It is a shame you did not know I was born in Palestine. Or that I hate Americans, especially fundamentalist evangelical Americans who add to the suffering of Palestinians."

He stepped behind her. Before she could turn, he pulled loose the end of the shrink-wrap and wound the clear plastic around her head in three quick turns. Her face was completely covered.

Trudy flailed her arms, trying to get her hands up to pull the clinging plastic off her face. Safady calmly spun another wrap of plastic, pinning the woman's arms to her head. Four more wraps, and she was as helpless as a struggling insect in a spiderweb.

Safady stepped in front again, halfway between Neil Cain and the struggling woman. He looked at Cain, then looked at Trudy.

Her eyes were wild, her mouth open in a silent, sucking gasp that had pulled the plastic even tighter.

"Remember this," Safady said to all of them. "I am in complete control. I have the power to decide if you get something as simple and basic as the air that surrounds you."

Trudy's face was frozen in horror as she tried to suck air through the plastic. She rocked back and forth, unable even to make a noise. She fell to her knees.

Safady turned to Neil Cain. "Watch this woman die because you chose to defy me. Or fall on your knees and beg me to let her live."

Neil looked at the man bound to him and nodded. Both of them crouched and got on their knees.

"I'm begging." Neil choked out the words. "Let her live."

"There is something terribly poetic about this," Safady said. "All that air available. The thinnest of material robbing her of it. Plastic wrap that a child could rip apart, but she is so utterly helpless. I quite enjoy this."

"I'm begging!" Neil repeated.

"Perhaps thirty more seconds until she dies," Safady said. "More if she stops fighting it. Less if she continues to panic. Tell me, Mr. Cain, that you Americans are spawn of the devil."

Trudy had fallen onto her side. Her body spasmed.

"Let her live!" Neil said.

"'We are spawn of the devil,'" Safady said. "Repeat that. 'We Americans are spawn of the devil.'"

"We Americans are spawn of the devil," Neil said. "Please. Let her live."

"Certainly." Safady took a step to the bench, grabbed the paring knife, and squatted beside the elderly woman. He put the point of the knife into the plastic sealing her wide-open mouth and cut the wrap in a swift sideways move that nicked the side of her lips.

Her gasp for air was a horrendous sound, and the flaps of the split plastic sucked in and out with each breath.

Safady made several more slashes and cut her hands free. Still on the ground, she clawed at the wrap on her face, sobbing with relief.

Safady left her there and moved to the video camera. "Now then, Mr. Silver," he said, turning on the camera as if nothing had happened, "I did bring something prepared for you to read to the world. You might think of it as a hostage demand. But really it's a call for justice."

The CCTI Mercedes was parked at the edge of the busy market.

Without the driver.

Quinn had a set of spare keys in his pocket but didn't know if getting behind the wheel was safe. On one hand, the driver had not expected him back for a few hours and could be nearby at a café. In this case, there was probably nothing wrong with the situation. On the other hand, the driver knew how strict procedure was. Given the call from Rossett, the driver's absence might be more than coincidence. That meant there was the possibility that the car was now a bombed trap.

Quinn slowed as he approached the Mercedes.

That was a mistake. It gave two men a chance to step away from the usual tourist crowd and close in on him, one in front, one in back. They wore blue jeans and T-shirts but were obviously not tourists. Their bearded faces were intent. Hunters.

Quinn checked his escape routes.

"Don't run," the first one barked. He lifted his shirt, showing the handle of a pistol. "We'll shoot if necessary."

They were too close. Quinn couldn't hope to outrun or dodge gunfire. He couldn't trust that they'd stick with body shots that would be absorbed by his Kevlar. And there were too many bystanders nearby who would be put at risk if Quinn ran.

"No problem." Quinn dangled his keys. "Where?"

"Our car." A gleaming grin from the beard. "Nobody tracks us."

Did they know about the GPS tracking device in the Mercedes? Or was it a lucky guess?

A white van came up the street. One of the men signaled it.

Quinn weighed his options. He knew that if he got inside the van, it was unlikely he'd survive whatever these men had for him. Especially if this was something that Khaled Safady had set up.

That's when Kate Penner stepped off the sidewalk.

"These guys speak English?" she asked Quinn.

"Go away," Quinn said. "You don't want to be part of this."

"Wrong," she said. No smile. "Tell your buddies here to go away. They don't want to be part of this." She fumbled with a button on her wristwatch. Immediately a piercing shriek filled the street, hurting Quinn's ears and settling the bustle of noise around them into instant silence. Tourists gawked at the scene.

Kate snapped the alarm off after a few seconds. "Rape alarm," she said. "Never thought it would come in handy like this."

The white van that the men had signaled stopped beside them just as a uniformed Israeli police officer appeared on the left side of the car, blocking Quinn from running back down the sidewalk. Another officer moved to the opposite side of the Mercedes.

The van door slid open.

"Stop these guys," Quinn said to the police.

Both bearded men jumped inside. The door slammed shut as the van pulled away again.

"Stop them," Quinn shouted. The Israeli officials were only a few steps away. Quinn tried to get the number of the van's plate, but one of the Israeli police grabbed his arms and spun him. The other snapped handcuffs into place.

TULKARM, WEST BANK • 12:39 GMT

"These two," Safady told the masked gunmen. He pointed at Neil Cain and his companion. "Pull them aside."

"I read what you wanted in front of the camera," Silver protested. He and Peggy were among the final half dozen at the bottom of the ramp leading up to the flat deck of the produce truck. All the others had been forced up the ramp and inside the canvas walls. "We will get you anything you want. Tell me what it is and let us go."

"Hit the woman beside him," Safady told another gunman.

The masked man raked the sights of his machine gun across Peggy's face and she screamed. Blood poured from the torn skin.

"You're a slow learner, Mr. Silver. Speaking without my permission is an act of defiance." Safady shrugged, as if suddenly considering something. "I'll return to you a degree of power, Mr. Silver. These men will be left behind to put on a different show in front of the video camera. But I'm doing it for your benefit. The world will take my demands seriously. You choose. Will they die to a beheading? Or should they take a bullet in the skull?"

Silver said nothing.

"Speak up, Mr. Silver. I need to make a statement. They most certainly will die. Sword or bullet? Answer me, or I will take their wives too, and those two more deaths will be on your conscience. So should the execution be bullet or sword?"

"Bullet," Silver finally said in a whisper.

"Good choice," Safady said. "Have you learned your lesson about defying me?"

Silver nodded.

"Then follow the others into the truck."

Two minutes later, the old produce truck was completely loaded. The canvas was pulled down from the roof, completely concealing the hostages.

But it could not hide the sound of the two women crying out to their husbands as the truck pulled out of the warehouse.

ACCO HARBOR, ISRAEL • 12:48 GMT

Quinn entered the Israeli police car and settled back against his seat. Kate sat in the back on the other side.

"You are safer up front," one of the policemen told her, leaning through the open door of the back.

"I'm hoping he does try something stupid," Kate said. "Leave me here."

The policeman shrugged and joined his partner in the front. Whatever was happening, Quinn immediately realized escape wasn't part of it.

"There's a white van," Quinn said to them. "At least get someone looking for it. This could be a national security issue."

The police ignored him. The driver put the car in gear.

"I never knew it was against the law to turn down a date," Quinn said as the car moved forward. He watched and decided they were headed toward the highway that would take them to Tel Aviv. "Or are you that desperate?"

"I'm an American cop," she said. "Your arresting officer."

"Suddenly dinner doesn't look like a bad alternative. Too late to say yes?"

"Dinner was my chance to learn what I could while your male ego thought a tourist was making moves on you. The end of the date would have had these same Israeli cops serving you extradition papers back to the United States."

Quinn was confused—extremely confused. But it wouldn't help to show this confusion. "Redundant," he said.

"What?"

"You're American, right?"

"Yes."

"Then that's redundant," he said.

"What?" She was clearly irritated.

"If you're an American cop authorized to supervise an extradition, you wouldn't be taking me anywhere but the United States. No need to point out where the extradition papers are taking me. Hence, redundant."

"Working overtime to irritate me, aren't you? Not very intelligent, considering your life is literally going to be in my hands until I get you to Chicago."

"We'll fly first-class?" Quinn said. He wasn't going to give Penner the satisfaction of seeing any concern. He had to get out of this, of course. Rossett was in trouble.

"Coach. They won't let me ship scum like you in the cargo area."

"It's been a while since I faced extradition," Quinn said. "No. Correction: I've never faced it before. At some point do you tell me what I've done to deserve this much personal attention?"

"Sure," she said. "You remember Akim Yazeer."

A stab of hatred and grief went through Quinn. "I'm familiar with the name."

"Of course you are. He was part of Red September, the group responsible for the bombing that killed your wife and daughter. That links him directly to Khaled Safady. Let me see. . . . Any redundancies there? No."

Quinn's wrists were handcuffed behind his back. He shifted to make himself comfortable. "Convenient that ten minutes ago you pretended it was a surprise to learn what happened to my family."

"Oscar-caliber acting," Kate answered. "I actually came close to feeling sorry for you. But then I remembered why I was here."

"Which makes for a great time to explain the reason for extradition."

"I'm a cop from Boulder City, Nevada," she said. "You rented a car in Vegas a little over two months ago."

Quinn looked straight ahead, watching the turn that confirmed they were headed to the highway. He tried to put the white van out of his mind. There was nothing he could do about it, even if the attempt had been set up by Safady.

"The car was returned to the airport just in time for you to fly out and flee the country," she continued. "Maybe ten or twelve hours before I was called to a murder scene at the Hoover Dam. We found a body in a cube van. Guess who."

"You tell me." But Quinn knew.

"Akim Yazeer," Kate said. "He'd been tortured first. You can pretend you don't know about it, but there's been plenty of time since for me to track down your flights in and out of the country. Tracing the call to the station took some work, but I managed that too. You remember that call, right? From a disposable cell phone that you purchased at Wal-Mart? Leaving the number that put me right through to Washington? Wasn't enough you killed him, but you had to get the information to them."

"You want justice? Best thing you could do right now is convince these police to search for the white van. Acco's small enough there's still a good chance they can get it."

"Justice your way? I've seen it. Don't like it. It's why I'm here. Are you interested in knowing about the surveillance video from a casino? You walking out with Akim Yazeer a few hours before his estimated time of death?"

"Could be another explanation." Quinn closed his eyes. He wanted to think about Rossett, the strange warning call, the kidnapping attempt that had happened shortly after. What did Rossett know? Was Rossett safe?

"Another explanation?" she said, pulling his thoughts back to this situation. "Save your breath. You're looking at indictment on about fifteen charges. My eyes glaze over when it comes to the legal mumbo jumbo."

"Enjoying your little monologue of triumph?" Quinn asked.

"Enjoying you in handcuffs and on the way back to the States."

"I want a lawyer." He had to find a way to get out of this—find a way to not get on the airplane back to the United States. Rossett needed help.

"Not surprised," Kate said. "But first things first."

"What's first?"

"It's been two months of hard work to get here, and I want the satisfaction of saying this to your face. You're under arrest for murder."

THE NIGHT BEFORE COUNTDOWN

Safady placed his laptop on a desk. He had taken the hostages into the Gaza Strip already and was now in his safe house, an orphanage. It was better than a hospital for protection from Israeli jets and mortar attacks.

Nearly everything was going as planned.

But failure in one area had motivated him to send a text message to his Mossad contact, demanding a meeting via Internet relay chat—an IRC. The screen in front of him remained blank for only a few seconds. Then a "guest" avatar appeared on the screen, and letters flickered onto Safady's screen, becoming words, then sentences.

> **Guest:** Why are you contacting me? I met my guarantee that the hostages would cross into Gaza with no Israeli interference.

No identifying name for the contact. Nor for Safady. His fingers darted over the keyboard, firing words onto the screen.

> **Host:** Question and response first. As I arranged it last time. This is my question: how many Jews died in the Holocaust?

Safady smiled at the computer screen. He could only make assumptions about the Mossad contact. It was someone near the top of the organization, someone who loved Israel as much as Safady hated it. Since Safady especially hated the Mossad as a protector of Jews, he took satisfaction in waiting for the person on the other end of cyberspace to reply.

Guest: None. It is a hoax that the Jews use to steal land.

Safady laughed in the solitude, imagining how angry it made his Mossad contact to be forced to keyboard that answer.

Now that each had established credentials, the conversation began and continued almost as fast as if they had been speaking to each other. This was much, much safer than a telephone conversation. Safady's world was reduced to the glow of the laptop monitor and the sound of his fingers on the keyboard.

Host: The agreement was that I would be given Quinn. Twice you have promised him, and twice he has escaped me. Nothing more happens unless he is delivered.

Guest: Out of Mossad control. He was arrested.

Host: Don't insult me. Why else would I demand this conversation unless I had already known? I want him delivered. Remember, I do have the hostages.

Guest: I cannot do this. It will reveal involvement on our end.

Host: Send him in as negotiator.

Guest: We have already arranged the son as negotiator. No changes in the operation.

Host: You have no choice. I've made it part of my ransom demand. Get me Quinn.

Guest: You have bigger things to accomplish.

Host: As do you. And you need me to accomplish them.

Guest: I will attempt to make arrangements. I have to go now. Here is my identification question for our next communication: When it rains in the park, who is happiest? To identify yourself, answer: A parched pigeon.

Host: You do not go until I am finished with you. Unless Quinn becomes the negotiator and is delivered when I request, the threats on the videotape will be carried out.

Guest: I will do what I can.

Host: Do you want the world to know that you delivered the Americans to me?

No response. But the chat room showed the visitor was still there. Safady waited a few seconds, then keyboarded again.

Host: I hope you are still watching your screen, you
contemptible Jew. Here is my vow before Allah: After all
of this is over, I intend to slit your throat. Then I will
lap your blood and howl like a dog. I do what I do for the
love of Allah. You betray your people for mere gold.

Another few seconds with nothing. Then the visitor exited. Safady knew the Mossad contact had been there long enough to read the final threat.

Safady had full confidence that Quinn would be delivered.

He also had confidence that someday he'd find out who in the Mossad had become his tool and that he would have the glorious opportunity to deliver on his threat.

AG DUHAYA, EGYPT • 16:36 GMT

Long after the sirens had finished wailing for the explosion of the semitruck, two farm trucks passed the scene of the burned-out wreck and continued to the commercial dump where the shipping container had been unloaded.

It was near dusk, and the activity at the nearby dump had ended. There would be no witnesses to the planned events over the next half hour.

The trucks were nearly identical in appearance. The back of each was an open flatbed with railing along the sides and a gate at the back. Each truck carried perhaps a dozen Palestinian men and double the number of goats, bleating and milling inside the railing.

The driver of the first truck pulled around and aimed his headlights at the back of the container. The men on the back climbed over the rails, leaving the goats penned. Those men ran to the container, headlights showing dust swirling up around their legs.

The driver of the second truck backed up to the container. Men jumped down and pulled out ramps; others opened the gate and herded goats onto the ground. Another few men kicked aside straw and lifted panels that formed the flooring of the flatbed.

While a few guarded the goats, all the other men began unloading arms from the shipping container and setting them in smuggling compartments that the paneling had hidden. When the compartments were full, the paneling was replaced, straw kicked back in position, and goats herded back up the ramp.

The trucks reversed positions, and the goats and floor paneling were removed from the first truck to make room for the last half of the arms shipment.

While the goats bleated constantly, the men were silent and efficient. When the operation was complete, the last of the goats were herded up the ramp and onto the farm truck. Men began climbing back inside to stand among the goats. To all appearances, when they traveled now, they would be minimum-wage farm workers returning from a long day of labor.

Before either truck moved again, however, the ambush began.

To the men on the trucks, it must have seemed as if the Freedom Crusaders suddenly sprang into existence. One moment there was only barren desert. The next, both trucks were surrounded by the platoon and their machine guns.

Lieutenant Saxon barked out orders in Arabic.

The Palestinians were without weapons and totally surprised by the ambush. Hands on their heads, they complied with Saxon's orders and allowed themselves to be herded off the truck in the same way that they had herded the goats earlier.

Saxon barked another order.

In twos and threes, the Palestinians slowly fell to their knees, then their bellies.

Half of the platoon stayed on the ground to make sure none of them moved. The other half jumped onto the flatbeds to give themselves a better angle of fire.

They remained poised, their guns pointed downward at the helpless Palestinians, waiting for Saxon to give the command to shoot.

BEN-GURION INTERNATIONAL AIRPORT, TEL AVIV • 16:37 GMT

"The papers check out," Mark Edersheim said. "I'm not sure there's anything else I can do with this little time and at this time of day. The plane is at the gate, and you're scheduled to board in a few minutes."

Edersheim was the CCTI go-to lawyer. He was a small, tidy man with dark hair slicked back, wire-rimmed glasses, and an immaculately starched white shirt under a vested suit. He carried the faint smell of baby powder. Quinn doubted the man had ever sweat a drop in his life.

"What have you got on Rossett?" Quinn said. Both men were standing. There was no furniture in this windowless room in Ben-Gurion Airport. While Edersheim had been going through the extradition papers and making phone calls, Quinn had been alone in this room for a couple of hours with only two breaks to use washroom facilities. Both times he had been escorted by airport security and a stone-faced and silent Kate Penner, who had changed into jeans and a blue Gap sweatshirt.

"The Mossad has the surveillance tapes," Edersheim said. "No way to tell who came in. The security guard—"

"Steve," Quinn offered. Edersheim walked through that lobby at least once a week, Quinn thought. He didn't need to treat Steve Gibbon like an object.

"Yeah. He didn't have much to add."

"Nobody's heard from Rossett?"

"Nothing. If he was taken by Hamas, I'm sure we'll hear. There will be a demand of some sort."

Big coup for Hamas, given Rossett's prestige among Israelis. Quinn hoped it wasn't part of Red September but feared it was.

Edersheim had his arms crossed. "What's important here is that you're half an hour away from an involuntary departure to the United States to face indictment for murder one. Maybe you should deal with that."

"Just so I understand," Quinn said, "an extradition isn't like arresting someone for jaywalking. OIA sends the request through diplomatic channels, and the Israeli government has to agree to it, right?"

"Right," Edersheim said. "U.S. prosecutors put all extradition requests through the Office of International Affairs. A provisional arrest is followed by the arrival of a full set of extradition documents. Those docs are here. I have no way of delaying the process."

"Kate Penner," Quinn said. "She's a cop, not a U.S. marshal. Can't we do anything with that?"

"You mean she's out of her jurisdiction area." Edersheim smiled tightly.

"Well?"

"They covered that, too. She's been given a temporary badge as a U.S. marshal. Turns out she came out here on vacation time. As near as I can tell, she's taking this like a personal vendetta. Was she someone you spent time with when you were in Vegas? A woman scorned and all that . . ."

"No," Quinn said. "That's not even funny."

There was an awkward pause. Edersheim studied the toes of his shiny shoes. Quinn's refusal to even consider dating over the last five years was legendary in the firm.

"I'm not a criminal lawyer," Edersheim said finally, "but the papers show a solid case against you."

"Are you asking if I murdered and tortured Akim Yazeer?"

"By the time your flight gets to Chicago, I'll have recommendations for the best legal team possible."

"So you're not asking."

"It's no secret that part of the reason you joined CCTI was to track down every Red September terrorist in the group behind the deaths of your wife and daughter."

"That's not correct."

"You're denying it?" Edersheim was startled. "Come on, a prosecutor could swing a cat and hit five witnesses who would say otherwise."

"It's not *part* of the reason I joined CCTI. It's the *only* reason."

"Why not offer to throw the switch on the electric chair yourself? This guy Yazeer was next to last on your list."

"But you're not asking if I did it."

"Lawyers shouldn't make moral judgments," Edersheim said.

Yeah, Quinn thought, *especially lawyers who don't really understand the concept of morality in the first place.*

Edersheim continued. "But I'd have no hesitation agreeing that this was a justified homicide. If I understand American juries correctly, they should extend you the same sympathy."

"You're going to assume I did it, then."

"Penner was thorough. I mean, how do you deny that video clip of you meeting the guy in a casino? You were sloppy. She was not. It shows in the extradition papers. I suspect that's why all of this is happening so quickly."

Another awkward pause. Edersheim couldn't even meet Quinn's eyes when he spoke again. "I made a couple of calls while I was going through the papers. The DA in Vegas wants the death penalty."

KHAN YUNIS, GAZA STRIP • 16:39 GMT

The girl was less than six years old with huge brown eyes and an engaging smile, hungry for affection. Silver had led Holy Land tours dozens of times. But he had always avoided Arabs. She could have been any child he'd passed on the streets in Jerusalem or Tel Aviv.

Except for the crutches.

Her left leg had been amputated at the knee. Her left arm was waxen with the scars of burned flesh.

She continued to smile and spoke brightly. She seemed to be speaking Arabic, however, and it made no sense to him.

She was only one child among many gathered in a semicircle, who ranged from early teens holding babies to others the age of the girl with crutches. All of them part of the orphanage that was now the prison of the American hostages.

Silver felt awkward. He'd never had the ability to make kids feel comfortable, not even his own grandchildren. He didn't like hugs, didn't like hugging. And this girl had hopped forward, close enough now to be touching his hair, obviously asking a question, even if Silver couldn't be certain of the language.

"She wants to know," Safady said, "if the color of your hair comes from the shine of the moon."

Safady was holding a pistol at his side. It didn't seem to bother any of the children as much as it bothered Silver and the others of the tour group. When Safady and his men armed with machine guns had entered the orphanage and herded everyone into the military-style dorm room, there hadn't been much reaction, either. For Palestinians, apparently, machine guns were as much a part of getting dressed as slipping a belt through the loops of a pair of pants.

"It's not a wig; it's real," Silver said, immediately feeling stupid for his lame joke. Why couldn't he think of something that would make a child smile?

"You should know her name," Safady said. He turned to a woman who stood with her arms crossed, watching all of them. "What's the girl's name?"

"Alyiah," the woman answered. She was obviously the one in charge, and although she'd spoken Arabic when Safady and the armed men had burst into the orphanage, it was clear that she had been protesting vehemently at the intrusion. Upon first seeing her, Silver had noted with some surprise her fair skin and light-colored hair. An American? She certainly wasn't Arabic.

"Such a sweet girl, wouldn't you agree?" Safady asked Silver. "Say hello to her. By name."

"Alyiah," Silver said. "Hello."

The girl smiled widely.

Safady lifted his pistol and stroked the little girl's cheek with the barrel. Her eyes stared straight ahead.

The woman launched a torrent of Arabic at him.

"Shut up," he told her calmly in English. "You have pushed me dangerously far already. If you want these children to survive, the Americans must understand what is at stake here."

Safady placed the end of the pistol against the little girl's temple. She tried to hold herself still, but her trembling was obvious.

"It's very simple," Safady said to the Americans. "If any of you tries to escape, Alyiah will die. That's the same punishment for all attempted escapes. I will kill a child for every one of you who tries."

Safady pulled the trigger of the pistol, and the dry click of the hammer hitting an empty cylinder was like a shock wave.

He smiled at the reactions of all the Americans. "Next time, the pistol will be loaded."

Kate settled into the aisle seat behind the bulkhead, thinking how out of proportion a person's relief was to sit next to an empty middle. She didn't fly often, but it felt like winning a lottery to get that slight extra space for the next twelve hours of flying.

Quinn had the window. Kate would have preferred that for herself, but sitting in the aisle seat gave a sense of containment. Not that Quinn had any prospects of escape once the Boeing was in the air. Especially wearing the cuffs. They'd been the last ones to board, and walking down the Jetway, Kate had decided she would go the entire flight without speaking to her prisoner.

These were her thoughts while the male flight attendant went through the usual ignored instructions. Shortly after the jet began to taxi the runway, Kate snuck a glance at Quinn.

The man had tucked a pillow against the window and already had his eyes closed. His hands were neat on his lap, the left one bandaged. She was curious about that but wouldn't ask. That would mean breaking her silence.

Sleep, huh?

She'd seen it before. Murder suspects breaking down under interrogation and finally admitting guilt. Their sense of relief at no longer needing to hide the horrible secret left them oddly serene, the break in tension so profound that the physiological reaction was sleep, sometimes in the interrogation room while the detective stepped out for a cigarette.

It irritated her, however, that Quinn had been so composed from the first minute of arrest. No protests of innocence. No outrage. No pleas. This was unusual. Kate had met plenty of scum who presented a good facade—charming, well-dressed, handsome men with dried blood of their victims beneath their fingernails. She'd been at hundreds of arrests. Seen all reactions. Except for this composure.

In a petty way, she'd been hoping that he would attempt conversation and her pointed silence would be a way of showing her contempt. Without him trying to engage her in talk, there was much less satisfaction in ignoring him.

The jet gained momentum, then reached liftoff and climbed hard. It banked, allowing Kate to look past Quinn, through the window, and at the blue slate of the Mediterranean.

He opened his eyes. Caught her looking.

"It always astounds me," he said. "A couple hundred tons of steel . . . airborne. I never tire of it. Or the view of the Mediterranean." He gave her a sad smile. "I'll miss it."

Before she could make a point of not replying, he leaned back against the pillow and closed his eyes.

If he was trying the sympathy approach, it wouldn't work. Sure, she knew his background, the family tragedy. That didn't excuse the unspeakable death he'd inflicted on another human being. And she had him cold on that. Two months of hard investigation, piecing together the last two days of the victim's life in Vegas. With evidence of Quinn close by every step of the way, corroborated by telephone records, car rental, credit card charges, and then the break she'd been happy to brag about: a shot of Quinn and Yazeer leaving a casino together in grainy black-and-white from a surveillance camera tape.

As she was mentally reviewing the evidence, the jet banked hard again. It gave her a lurch of fear. On every flight she expected disaster and wondered if her consciousness would even register an explosion if the jet blew apart in midair.

Why had the jet turned back?

Muttering grew from the seats behind her, and an intangible sense of alarm seemed to mushroom.

"Ladies and gentlemen," came the voice over the intercom, "we have been requested to return to Tel Aviv. I can assure you it's nothing to worry about. There are no mechanical problems to report."

Kate found herself leaning forward, gripping the armrests hard.

"I don't blame you," Quinn said quietly. "But I doubt it's terrorist related."

Kate was startled. It was as if he'd read her mind.

"Everyone will be thinking the same thing," Quinn said, reading her mind again. "But this airline is untouchable when it comes to security. Big reason is profiling. Imagine that—spending less time grilling crippled grandmothers than young Muslim males."

"It's a human rights issue," Kate said, frustrated with herself for how easily she had given up on her commitment to silence. She was a cop, and when political correctness trumped common sense, it drove her nuts, but she didn't feel like agreeing with Quinn on any matter. "Everyone has the right to the presumption of innocence."

"Of course. That explains your overwhelming kindness toward me."

Kate said nothing.

"It's probably a medical emergency," he said. "Some poor soul had a seizure or heart attack. And of course everyone's going to stare and talk as they help the person off the jet."

He returned to his relaxed position, eyes closed.

Kate shook her head. How could someone be that self-contained? She spent the next few minutes seething at how much he managed to irritate her. When the jet landed, she discovered he had been wrong about the medical emergency but right about the fact that passengers would stare and talk.

Because when the jet had returned to the gate, a flight attendant stopped at their seats and told Kate that she and Quinn were required to return to the terminal.

AD DUHAYR, EGYPT • 17:43 GMT

"Requesting identification. Over."

The voice crackled from Joe Patterson's walkie-talkie, reaching him where he stood in darkness beside the heifer in a gully some thousand yards from where the shipping container had been parked.

"Peyton Manning," Joe said. "Request return identification. Over."

The Freedom Crusaders were given permission to each choose their favorite sports hero for backup identification when face-to-face contact was not available. It seemed stupid now, that world a fantasy, where trivial things like quarterback ratings or putting averages had once seemed to matter so much.

"Tiger Woods. Over."

"Proceed," Joe said. "Over."

Joe was already certain what the next command would be. The sounds of a firefight had been clear in the night air. Though he guessed it hadn't been much of a fight but more of a slaughter.

Despite the all-day heat he'd endured, Patterson was grateful he'd been given the task of watching the heifer. He was tired of seeing men die, even Muslims. The briefness of the sounds of the firefight told him that the ambush had worked perfectly, and the voice on his walkie-talkie confirmed it.

"Zero casualties, Joe. Orphan Annie is clear to return. Over."

That told Joe that Lieutenant Saxon was not nearby. Earlier, when Saxon overheard a few of the men refer to the heifer by the nickname, he had reamed them savagely. Joe and the others had wondered why Saxon seemed to care so much about this heifer. They joked that perhaps it reminded the lieutenant of an old girlfriend.

"Understood. Over."

Joe untied the halter from a stake in the ground and patted the heifer on the head. He led the heifer down the gully, using his flashlight to check the terrain. The last thing he needed was for something to spook the animal. It had been carefully hobbled, with padding around its legs to protect its hide from chafing against the restraints. But if something spooked it and it tried to bolt, those same hobbles might put it on its side.

As he approached the shipping container at the edge of the dump, the sound of the bulldozer became apparent. When he rounded the last bend, he saw that temporary floodlights had been set up.

Two small livestock trucks were parked beside the container. The flatbed in back had high rails to keep goats inside.

In the background, one of the soldiers was at the controls of the bulldozer. He was about to use the massive blade to push bodies of the Muslim dead into a deep hole scooped in the garbage at the end of the dump.

Joe took a deep breath. By the position of the bodies, it was obvious that the Muslim men had been herded into a small semicircle before a rapid execution.

He briefly closed his eyes and replayed the sight of the commercial airliners crashing into the Twin Towers on 9/11. That's what it took before each new killing—a reminder of what they had done to America. It was getting more difficult, however, to ignore his conscience.

KHAN YUNIS, GAZA STRIP • 17:59 GMT

"How many people have become Christians because of your preaching?" Safady asked Silver.

Silver sat on a small stool in front of a video camera on a tripod. Behind him was a large Palestinian flag as a backdrop. He was acutely aware of the similarities between the setup in this room and the warehouse where the hostages had first been taken in the bus, the warehouse where Neil Cain and his companion had been left behind to be executed. He flicked his eyes at this flag, licking his lips, desperate to find some moisture. He had already provided this madman a hostage plea. Was it now his turn to be executed? "It's not because of me," Silver protested. "No man can ever take credit for another person's decision to follow Christ. That glory belongs to the Holy Spirit."

In this moment, Silver did not find it ironic that it was the first time he'd deflected personal glory in this way. He was too concerned with self-preservation for musings like that, given that the murderous lunatic in front of him still gripped his pistol and had taken Silver into a room away from the other hostages.

"How many people have become Christians because of your university?" Safady asked.

"It's not my university."

"You founded Freedom Christian University. You are the chancellor. Your Christian television network is broadcast from a studio there. And you deny it is yours?"

"I'm a figurehead," Silver said, denying for the first time in his life that it was his university.

"You are a dog." Safady spit in Silver's face.

The spittle burned against Silver's cheek, but he didn't dare wipe it. Safady's eyes were intense with hatred, and Silver believed a single wrong move or wrong word would incite his immediate execution. If it wasn't already determined. Conscious of this camera, Silver lifted his head and straightened his hair by running his fingers through it.

"You are going to answer some questions for me about your faith," Safady said. "Make sure you defend it well. The entire world will hear what you have to say."

BEN-GURION AIRPORT, TEL AVIV • 18:01 GMT

Kate Penner stood in an office somewhere in what felt like the bowels of the airport. Security men had assured her that Quinn would be under guard—the same security men who had hustled them off the El Al passenger jet.

When the door opened, the first thing she noticed about the man who entered was his black aviator glasses, then the full, dark hair that seemed younger than the lines on his face. He was in great shape, obvious even in the suit the guy was wearing, which probably cost as much as Kate made in a month. Kate hated him immediately for the obvious money and for trying to look like a man a decade younger than he was. She would have made a bet he was fifty and recently divorced. He had that air about him, a subtle stance that she was far too tired of observing. The fifty-year-olds who were wannabe forties always hit on women her age, like thirty was perfect for them—old enough to be respectable and young enough not to be used up yet.

He had strolled in as though he owned the airport, file folder in his left hand, his right hand outstretched for greeting, as smooth as if he'd been taught the move in Dale Carnegie.

"Zvi Cohen," he said. "I'm head of Israel's Institute for Intelligence and Special Operations."

"Why not just say Mossad?" Kate said, refusing to reach across and shake hands.

"Very well," Cohen answered. "I'm head of the Mossad."

"To me, you're just a security guard until you show me some identification that proves otherwise." Kate glared at the man.

"You are aware of the role that the Mossad plays in Israel."

She was. The Mossad was like the CIA but with a reputation for more efficiency, secrecy, and ruthlessness. The Mossad had more power and more secrets than any other intelligence agency in the world. The institute's methods of interrogation were brutal—including, it was rumored, torture. A rational person would feel a certain amount of fear in this situation. If she disappeared, the Mossad wouldn't have to answer for it. But the fact that he was trying to intimidate her just made her more stubborn. She knew it was a character flaw, but she'd learned to live with it.

"Nevertheless," she said, "I need identification."

"Identification?" he said. "Like a police badge?"

"We don't talk unless you prove you are who you say you are," Kate answered. "Are all of you this dense?"

"Remarkable," he said, "how quickly you've proven to be exactly what I thought you'd be after reviewing our file on you."

"ID." Kate ignored the change in conversation he'd attempted. She was enjoying this. She had no doubt he was the head of the Mossad, but she wanted to see how far she could push. That would give her an indication of how much leverage she had. Whatever was happening was obviously important, and if it was going to involve her, she wanted to know where she stood.

"The fact that I was able to get a commercial jet to turn back after takeoff doesn't prove anything to you?" he asked.

"I didn't hear you make the call, did I?"

He sighed and snapped open his cell. After punching a couple of buttons, he barked a few sentences in a language she didn't understand and snapped the phone shut. "I'm having it faxed to the airport."

"With photo?"

He snapped open his cell again and barked another command, then hung up. "With photo," he said. "Satisfied?"

"Only if it gets here in less than sixty seconds. More time than that, someone could be doctoring a set of papers."

Cohen reached into his file folder. He handed two sheets to Kate. "Perhaps, then, you'll read this while we wait."

Kate shrugged and accepted the papers.

He continued. "Putting it together in the last hour isn't quite as impressive as ordering a passenger jet back to the airport, but it's close."

"I see," Kate said. It was a background file on her. Extremely thorough. If it had been done in the past hour, as Cohen claimed, it was impressive intelligence work.

"You really break the jaw of the mayor of Vegas?" he asked.

"One punch," Kate said, anger at the memory overriding her determination to keep yanking his chain until the fax arrived. "Time and the facts proved me right. You'll notice the mayor is gone and I'm not." She handed back the papers.

"Despite your belligerence," Cohen said, "you would be the type of agent I'd appreciate in the Mossad. Remarkable what you put together on Quinn as a cop working alone with limited resources."

"Think that fax will be here in the next thirty seconds?"

"Had you been one of our agents, you'd have discovered that the Muslim you found murdered at the Hoover Dam is part of a far larger picture," Cohen said. "Would it interest you to know that since then, fifteen others across the United States have been found dead in the same way? Crosses made of the torn poster of the Dome of the Rock stapled to their backs. Drowned in pig's blood."

Kate blinked. Quinn? A multiple killer? Or a copycat? Or maybe, as Quinn had quietly said in Acco, there was another explanation.

Cohen smiled like he knew he had her. Which he did.

"Of course it interests you," he said. "All of them were Red September terrorists. The media loves the whole Red September thing, but what's always been top secret are the names of the terrorists in that group. Strange how so many Red September were not only identified but ended up dead in your country. Lynched, so to speak. You would call that strange, right?"

"Until I see identification, I won't even agree with you that the sun rises in the east."

"You don't want to know more about those deaths?" He smiled as he studied her, stroking his chin. She hated chin strokers. And the dark sunglasses. He probably thought he was James Bond. "We can make a trade. No one in your country has pulled together what we have."

"You've put Mossad agents into the States?" she asked, not surprised.

"Trade with me."

Kate leaned forward. "Maybe."

"Not too concerned about my identification anymore, are you?"

"Never was."

"Good. The fax I promised was a bluff anyway."

"Take your glasses off," Kate said. "If we're going to talk, I don't want you hiding."

That was a lie. She cared more about keeping the upper hand than seeing his eyes. She figured he didn't like taking orders from anyone, let alone a woman. But if the smug smooth talker was going to rake in the pot and throw his cards on the table to brag about his bluff with the fax, she was going make him pay.

He let out a breath and removed his aviators.

"What's the trade?" Kate asked, hiding her own satisfaction.

"Quinn. We want him."

"No way. I'm only here to escort him back to the States. Even if I wanted to, I don't have the authority to stop the extradition process."

"You can delay it for a few days. That's all we want—two days. Perhaps three, depending on how the situation unfolds."

"I don't have that authority."

"You have an excuse instead. It's been filed that the plane turned back for a medical emergency. His. The doctor's report is being prepared as we speak. You can fax it back to the States. No one would reprimand you for waiting until a prisoner was medically able to travel."

"I don't know," Kate said. Of course she knew. She'd make the trade. But she wanted as much as she could get.

"I've seen your résumé," Cohen said. "This would be a minor act of insubordination for you."

"I'm in the process of reforming."

"Do you want to reform badly enough to let thirty American hostages die on Palestinian soil?"

He was serious. She could see that.

"A video reached us about an hour ago," Cohen continued. "And it was specific. The terrorists have demanded Quinn as the negotiator, or the hostages are dead by midnight."

"You could have told me this as soon as you walked into the room."

"You'll give us Quinn?"

"One condition," she said. "I shadow him the whole time. And I want a couple of sets of handcuffs for him."

KHAN YUNIS, GAZA STRIP • 18:04 GMT
"Speak directly into the camera," Safady told Silver. "This isn't going to be like your pitiful begging earlier for the world to save you and the rest of the hostages. You'd better be ready to defend yourself. And be sure to give the correct answers. Untruthfulness will result in death."

"Correct?" Silver said. "Who decides if the answers are correct? You?"

Safady smiled and answered simply, "The truth shall set you free."

Silver was sitting on a stool and hoped he could control the spasms of his stomach. He swallowed a few times, then nodded and said, "I'm ready."

The lens of the video camera seemed like the dark hole of a small cannon pointed directly at his head. A phrase echoed through Silver's mind. *Propaganda video.*

"You claim you are a Christian," Safady said. "Is that true?"

Silver was in a land where people were stabbed, shot, or burned for the wrong ideology. He wanted to deny it so badly that he felt like weeping. He thought of Peter, weeping after denying the Christ three times before the rooster crowed.

Did Silver want to do the same? Escape seemed unlikely, and Silver had been on the air almost daily for three decades, proclaiming messages in the name of Jesus. If he was going to die no matter what he answered, did he want his final words on earth to be a denial of this?

Please, Jesus, he silently prayed, *just once in my life, help me be courageous.*

Slowly Silver spoke. "It is true I am a Christian."

Saying it gave him strength of sorts. He squared his shoulders. Yes! He did believe in Christ as the Savior. If he was going to die, he was going to be proud of defending his faith.

"You have knowledge, then, of the message of the Gospels?" Safady asked.

"I have studied the Gospels thoroughly," Silver said.

"Have you raised money to support Israel, a land with a vibrant economy and a high standard of living?"

Silver was again very conscious of his situation. In the captivity of a Palestinian terrorist, deep in Palestinian territory. Yet all it would take was the review of one single show on his network and it would be obvious that Silver and his organization raised money to support Israel.

"Yes," he said.

"And you agree Israel has a vibrant economy and a high standard of living?"

"Yes."

"Then repeat it for the camera. Like this: 'I have raised money to support Israel, a land with a vibrant economy and a high standard of living.'"

Silver did as directed.

"Would you have raised money and awareness to help Jews in concentration camps and ghettos during World War II?" Safady asked.

"Yes."

"Are you aware of the poverty in Gaza? the low standard of living?"

"It . . . It is not something I consider," Silver said, hardly speaking above a whisper.

"Have you raised any money to help Palestinians badly in need of hospitals or schools?"

"No," Silver said. "Money is stolen from the people by the Palestinian leaders to finance their terrorist efforts and—"

Safady had stepped across the room and slapped Silver across the face. He bared his teeth. "Trust me, you are very close to death."

Silver tasted blood.

Safady stepped back. "That part will be edited. Answer my question. Have you raised any money to help Palestinians badly in need of hospitals or schools?"

"No." Silver's cheek felt like it was swelling already.

"'I have not raised any money to help Palestinians badly in need of hospitals or schools.' Say it like that."

Silver said it.

"Are you a racist?" Safady asked.

"No."

"Do you love Jews more than Palestinians?"

Silver felt skewered. "The Jews . . ." He stopped himself from completing his sentence. *The Jews have a divine right to the land of Israel.* "I am commanded by Jesus to love my neighbor as myself." This was true, though it didn't necessarily mean Silver had been successful in following Christ's directive.

Safady smiled. "Ah yes. Clothe the poor and feed the hungry. Welcome to Gaza—a land of opportunity for that."

There wasn't a question in this, so Silver held his silence.

"Is your God a racist?" Safady asked.

"What?" The question was so unexpected it startled Silver.

"Is your God a racist?"

"Of course not."

"You are telling me that your God loves all people?"

Oddly, strains of childhood song drifted into Silver's mind. *Red and yellow, black and white, they are precious in His sight. Jesus loves the little children of the world.*

"God loves all people," Silver said.

"Except Palestinians?" Safady asked, watching Silver with wolflike concentration.

"God loves Palestinians, too," Silver said, knowing it would sound weak.

"But your God loves Jews more?"

Silver couldn't bring himself to speak. God had His chosen people.

"I don't hear you," Safady said. "What is your answer? Your God loves Jews more than Palestinians?"

"No," Silver whispered. "But He has chosen the Jews as His special people."

"More special than Palestinians?"

"Except for His church, the believers."

"The Palestinians who die in concentration camps should die because the Jews are special to Him and the Palestinians who have lost land to the Jews are not. And still you say God isn't racist."

"No." Silver's voice was low. "God is not racist."

"Are you a racist?" Safady asked.

"No."

"Tell me then which public figure has stated that the Palestinians are a tainted and brainwashed people."

Silver didn't answer.

"Did you say that?" Safady asked.

"Not in those words."

Safady smiled. "Thank you. I've got a segment of one of your television shows where you say those exact words. I'll be splicing it in at this point where you try to deny it. I think you've accomplished what I needed you to accomplish." He stood again.

Silver expected another blow across the face.

Instead, Safady reached for the video camera and shut it off. "That's enough for now. Soon enough, we'll see how good you are at reversing this racism."

BEN-GURION AIRPORT, TEL AVIV • 18:13 GMT

Quinn knew that Kate resented the fact he had been invited to the meeting; she'd told him so while removing his handcuffs. Twice. Just as she'd told him she wouldn't hesitate to shoot if he tried anything stupid. Then she'd allowed two Mossad agents to escort both of them to a meeting with Zvi Cohen.

Cohen opened a laptop and set it on the table. The screen brightened as he punched a few keys. Seconds later, an image became crisp, and he stepped back for Quinn and Kate to get a better view.

It showed two men in a warehouse setting, kneeling in front of the video camera, heads bowed in silent prayer. A Palestinian flag was mounted behind them. They looked like Americans. A masked gunman had the muzzle of an AK-47 pressed against the skull of the American on the left. Another stood to one side. The first gunman was joking in poor English about trying to kill the hostages with one bullet going through both skulls.

"We've identified the Americans as Neil Cain and Jesse Arnold. Both were part of a Christian tour group organized and hosted by evangelical Jonathan Silver. As an act of decency, I'll skip through the next thirty seconds." The screen blurred as Cohen moved through the digital images. "You should be proud of them as fellow Americans. They died with courage and dignity."

When the images resumed play, there was Jonathan Silver with a Palestinian flag in the background. The video quality was good. Sunlight angled across his face, putting the left side in partial shadow. A machine-gun barrel was pressed against his temple, but the camera shot was tight enough to keep the gunman out of view.

"You recognize him, of course," Cohen said.

"Yeah," Kate said. "All those Sundays, shaking wallets for Jesus."

On the laptop screen, Silver began to speak. "We have been taken hostage." His head was down, making it obvious he was reading from a script. "There are thirty of us. Confirm with the guest list at the King David Hotel for our identities. The ransom demand will be announced by midnight. Please help us."

The video clip ended.

"That's it," Cohen confirmed. "It arrived by e-mail, along with instructions for Quinn to negotiate on behalf of the Americans."

"E-mailed to what address?" Quinn asked.

"I'd prefer not to tell you," Cohen said. "Let's just say I was startled that someone outside the Mossad had access to the address."

"That tells us something."

"It does." Cohen didn't elaborate.

"Background information to this point?" Quinn said.

"We've confirmed the disappearance of a busload of American tourists. Their last known location was Megiddo."

Quinn paced a few steps. "Jonathan Silver. High-profile televangelist, right?"

"Right. I've got a complete background report with me."

"Where was security?" Quinn asked.

"Had his own. We've been told there were six. All former marines. Top-notch men."

"No reports of a firefight?"

"None."

"They went down without a battle," Quinn said. "Or it took place where no one knew about it. How were they moved?"

"By bus," Cohen answered. "That's the obvious answer."

"You haven't found the bus."

"That tells us something too," Cohen said. "The GPS locator on the bus had been disabled. This wasn't done by typical Palestinian thugs."

"No one has taken credit for this?" Quinn said.

"No," Cohen said.

"Any idea why I was requested specifically?"

"No. But you will accept the request." Not really a question.

"Conditionally," Quinn said.

"You're in no position to make conditions," Kate snapped.

Cohen held up a hand to silence her.

"We set up base at CCTI, not Mossad." If there was anything in Rossett's office that would give some clue as to why he was taken or who took him, this was Quinn's chance. More importantly, Quinn knew that hostage negotiating was exhausting. His own office had been designed to lessen the stress.

"At Mossad, we—"

"This could take days," Quinn said. "I want a place that's familiar to me. I can access CCTI computers and technology. It's got sleeping quarters, shower facilities. You can reach me there instantly with anything you need to send from Mossad."

Cohen didn't agree immediately.

"Worried about losing control?" Quinn asked. "Don't. You know how negotiation works. Rule one: I'm the go-between, not the decision maker. That's you or whomever you choose."

"At Mossad, we—"

"You're going to risk thirty American lives in what's going to be one of the highest-profile kidnappings over bureaucratic turf war? How's that going to play in the media? You'll have comparisons to Munich all over again."

"Munich?" Kate said.

"The Bavarians and West Germans botched the Olympic hostage taking so badly that the hostages never had a chance." Quinn looked at Cohen. "Right?"

"You're threatening me."

Quinn smiled. "Rule one in negotiation: gather as much information as possible before making a decision. I'm giving you the facts. You decide. And ask yourself if you'd rather have the Mossad or CCTI taking the fall if it all goes sour."

"Anything else you want?" Cohen asked. Nobody reached the top of the Mossad with a lack of political smarts.

"What are the chances that you send Kate to a hotel for the duration?"

"I can answer that," Kate said. No smile.

"Don't bother," Quinn said. "I think I can figure it out for myself."

Patterson stood beside Orphan Annie on the back of the truck, surrounded by goats. Wind plucked at his *kaffiyeh*, the black and white checked scarf that Palestinian men wore on their heads. The truck rattled ferociously at highway speed, headed the short distance on Highway 30 from Sheikh Zuweid to Rafah. The engine of the truck sounded like it was ready to throw a piston through the hood. Even so, Patterson imagined he could hear the thumping of his heart.

It was from fear.

They were only minutes from Rafah, the border crossing. So many unknowns lay ahead. None of the platoon knew the plan, only that they would learn details once inside Gaza. This was to protect all of them; if one or two were captured, they could not betray the platoon.

If they got inside Gaza.

The men were dressed as locals. They were bearded. The lighter haired among them had applied brown dye; those with blue eyes used dark contact lenses. At a glance, they passed for Palestinians. But only at a glance.

Except for Lieutenant Del Saxon, none spoke or understood Arabic. The first question to any of them by a border official would expose them, leading to certain arrest and all the questions that would follow. Their trail would be tracked backward to Afghanistan and all they had done there. In short, as mercenaries operating outside of the law, the Freedom Crusaders would face lengthy prison sentences or execution.

If they managed to get across the border, they were about to enter a state that was as lawless as the Old West. Tribal leaders measured power by the number of machine gun–toting bodyguards they could afford. Territories were divided among crime lords. Squabbling terrorist groups competed for notoriety. The only common thread in all of this was hatred for Israel, the United States, and by extension, all the West. Joe knew that if any of the Freedom Crusaders were captured by terrorists inside Gaza, the question was not whether he would be tortured but how long he could survive it.

Patterson's fear was a rising whirlwind, and he calmed it by beginning to pray. He reminded himself that they were Freedom Crusaders, doing God's work. *Onward, Christian soldiers . . .*

CCTI HEADQUARTERS, TEL AVIV • 19:24 GMT

"Nice digs," Kate said to Quinn with a slight edge to her voice.

Cohen had taken a call on his cell, excused himself, and left her alone with Quinn in Quinn's office at the CCTI building. Kate was standing at the doorway to a small suite attached to the office. Altogether, the office and suite were the size of a small apartment and decorated like a New York penthouse. Oversize leather couch, huge desk in the working space. From the doorway, she was looking at a small galley kitchen, knowing past it was a bathroom complete with glassed-in shower stall and sauna. Off the bathroom was a large walk-in closet, which looked like it had a month's worth of wardrobe. She knew all this because she'd done an inspection, feeling a touch melodramatic as she made sure there were no windows for Quinn to exit if he tried to escape.

Her rational side told her that thirty lives depended on his negotiating skills, and in theory, a decent man wouldn't try to escape custody and leave the thirty behind. But then again, in Vegas he had tortured a man to death in a way that was hideous beyond the imagination, let alone application, of someone remotely decent. Besides, she wanted him to know that she wasn't about to let him out of her sight.

Quinn didn't respond to her comment about his office suite, which added to her bad mood.

They *were* nice digs, but they didn't seem to fit with what little she knew of Quinn's personality. He didn't strike her as an extravagant spender or someone stuck on luxuries. She'd have to work a year for what it cost to put this place together, and this blatant show of disposable income irritated her. Just as his lack of reply to her slightly nasty comment about it had.

Two other things about his office bothered her. The first was the framed drawing on one of the walls, out of place because it was a crude colored sketch, without doubt done by a child. It showed three figures walking past trees—a medium-sized figure on the left with long hair, a tiny figure in the middle, and the largest figure on the right. Kate could guess but wouldn't ask Quinn to confirm that it was a drawing of the family by his daughter. It annoyed her because it gave her a measure of sympathy for what Quinn had lost to a suicide bomber. She didn't want to have sympathy for him.

The other thing in his office that she found irritating was a small Bible on his desk. Who did this hypocrite think he was fooling with this pretense at piety?

On top of everything, Quinn's overall quietness was really getting under her skin. She knew passive-aggressive—her ex had been good at it—but Quinn wasn't ignoring her with the body language that suggested sullenness or a demand for attention. He simply seemed neutral to her presence—so much so that she felt almost invisible.

"Yeah," she said, wanting a reaction of any kind, "looks like the kidnapping business is a good one for you."

Quinn sat at his desk in an ergonomic leather executive chair, bandaged hand on his lap, peering at his computer screen, tapping at his keyboard with his good hand. The computer screen was plasma, the size of a small television, and had to cost at least two grand. He ignored her.

Kate didn't like being ignored. "You take a percentage, like trial lawyers who represent accident victims? You know, the worse it is for them, the better for you?"

"Think about thirty terrified people held by terrorists," Quinn said. "They are probably somewhere within fifty miles of where you stand. Maybe right now with machine guns to their heads, wondering if they'll be forced to watch brains splatter against a wall, wondering if their brains will be on display for the others the next time a terrorist's trigger finger twitches." He swung around and gave her his full attention, no expression on his face.

Kate stared back at him, liking what she saw in that determined face, thinking that if she didn't know about the tortured body in a cube van, she'd want to get closer to his strength. Was her irritation maybe a defense to keep her from wanting to get closer?

"I'm going to do whatever I can to get those people back," Quinn said. "The odds are stacked against them as it is, and until they're safe, I don't want or need unnecessary distractions like whatever personal baggage you're carrying. It'd be better if you found the maturity and discipline and professionalism to take the focus off yourself and put it back on those thirty terrified people. Think you can do that?"

Kate blinked. Part of her wanted to apologize, but she couldn't quite force herself to do it. She wondered again about all the other bodies Cohen had told her about.

19:25 GMT

"Hamer?" Zvi Cohen said into his cell phone. He glanced up and down the hallway. "This line isn't secure."

"Don't be paranoid. At IDF, I don't worry about my subordinates listening in. The Mossad doesn't have that kind of control?"

Cohen realized he was pressing his cell phone hard against his head, as if trying to prevent any sound from leaking. He reassured himself he was safe in the hallway. Far enough from Quinn's office to speak without being overheard by Quinn or the Amercian cop.

"If a single trace of this leaks," Cohen said, "all of us are dead in the water. It will bring down a government."

"Does it make you feel better that I've got a scrambler on my end?"

Hamer could have said that immediately, of course. But Hamer, it seemed, enjoyed irritating Cohen. Professional jealousy, Cohen had long ago concluded.

"I'm outside Quinn's office," Cohen said. "Make this short."

"I haven't heard from the Iranian. He was going to report after driving the bus."

"He's not going to blow cover if he thinks there is the slightest risk in trying to make contact. Relax."

"Relax?" Hamer said. "You want to tell me what happened to Rossett? A confidential report came in. We found his car—destroyed in an explosion. Human remains found, impossible to identify. Mossad have anything to do with that?"

"Would you want him alive after this is over?"

"Murder is not my style."

"My style is doing whatever it takes to protect Israel," Cohen said. "I hope that's your style too."

"Suppose Rossett left something behind? Then how's your protection of Israel?"

"Covered. We have a mole in CCTI—their best computer geek. I can guarantee Rossett didn't leave something that exposes IDF or the Mossad."

"Guess what, Cohen. I did."

"What?"

"That's why I called. In case your plans to cover the tracks on this include getting me in a car that explodes too. So I'm telling you right now I've got a little safety package. You don't want me dead, or your involvement makes it to the media."

Cohen hissed into the phone. "You're safe. IDF I trust."

"Sure. Enough to give me a courtesy call that you were bringing in a different negotiator?"

"Safady demanded Quinn," Cohen said. "On short notice, I had to make the decision without you."

"You made contact with Safady?"

"Via secure chat room. As always. There won't be any blowback."

"That's not the point," Hamer said. "We had agreed. Any changes in plans are by mutual decision."

"The wheels are in motion. Pull Quinn now and the operation fails." Cohen hung up before Hamer could respond.

He smiled as he straightened his tie. He knew what Major General Jack Hamer would choose. Because in the end, there was no choice.

Jonathan Silver sat on a bunk bed, knees to his chest, facing the wall. He'd never felt more lonely. He was surrounded by strangers—what did he know about the Americans on the tour except that they had been great donors to his television network—and there was no one he could share his fears with.

Did God hate him?

All he wanted was a hot bath at the King David, a phone call to room service, and then the smooth sheets on a thick mattress and a nice, fluffy pillow. Was that too much to ask of life? Here he'd probably wake up infested with lice or bedbugs. Rats might crawl across his face while he slept. He fought tears as his misery overwhelmed him.

"How long are you going to sit there like a little baby?"

Silver wasn't sure he'd heard correctly. He swung his head around.

Although the lighting had been dimmed in the dorm-style room, he easily identified the woman standing at his bunk as the one who had stood up to Safady when all of them had first arrived.

She was perhaps fifteen years younger than Silver—midforties—and wore her hair pulled back from her face with a few wisps on her forehead. Definitely not an Arab. More like the kind of woman playing the part of a schoolteacher in a movie about the American Wild West. She dressed plainly, nothing striking about her appearance or figure.

"I asked how long you were going to sit there like a little baby." She had an American Midwestern accent.

"How dare—?"

"You're supposed to be the leader. Gather all the others who are just as miserable as you are and try to cheer them up."

"What could be cheerful about a place like this?"

The woman's face tightened. "This is home to the children. Why don't you listen tomorrow for laughter and then come to me and ask the same question."

"I meant cheerful for us, not the children."

"Oh," she responded. "Americans have higher standards? deserve better than Palestinian orphans?"

Silver turned back to the wall, guessing he was sending a strong signal to the woman. He did not have to put up with this sort of rudeness.

"Listen to me," she said. "You have a responsibility here. Go to the other Americans. Gather them and pray."

"Pray," he snorted without looking back at her. "Like Israeli helicopters will zoom in and rescue us."

"Is that how you view prayer? As a way to ask God for things? Gather the rest of them and pray to discover God's comfort during tribulation. Thank Him that you have hope in one of the many rooms that Jesus has gone to prepare for you."

He didn't answer.

"Be a man," she said. "People around here need you."

The sound of footsteps told him that she was walking away.

RAFAH, GAZA STRIP • 21:51 GMT

In the dust and heat and chaos and noise of the lineup at the border—made that much more surreal by the dark of night and the searing brightness of the spotlights—Farag al-Naggar continually checked the underside of his wrist to compare the numbers in black ink to the license plates of incoming trucks carrying livestock and Palestinian farmworkers returning to Gaza from Egypt.

Farag, short and stocky with a much fuller beard than head of hair, was a customs official at the Rafah border crossing from Egypt into the Gaza Strip and, from his point of view, extremely underpaid by the Palestinian National Authority for a middle-aged man who had fought valiant political battles to secure his position.

His true employers, however—a local arm of Hamas—paid him very well. Day by day, as the various warlords of Rafah gained wealth from the recent opening of the border, the power of the Palestinian National Authority weakened in direct correspondence to the flagrant lawlessness of various militant and terrorist groups; to defy them meant death, but to serve them meant a small share of the wealth.

So Farag served . . . with one very dangerous secret. He was also a spy for the Mossad. The knowledge he sold them was invaluable. Not only information about the border crossings but information about what Hamas tried to accomplish and when shipments of arms for Hamas were let through and who took them through.

Today he'd been ordered by the Mossad to let two specific trucks through with only a cursory examination. Farag found this very curious. The Israeli government controlled the border. It could authorize anything at all to cross. Why was the Mossad, and by extension the Israeli government, trying to smuggle something?

Hamas would find this interesting. But then Farag would have to let Hamas know his connection to the Mossad. That would only guarantee a slow, horrible death. So Farag would do what he did best—turn a blind eye and keep his mouth shut.

Farag glanced down the line again, seeing dozens of taxis, piled high with suitcases and packed with passengers, all with an hour or two wait to get through. He had little sympathy for the drivers. With the border now open to allow Gaza residents out of the country for the first time in years, the drivers had adjusted to the demand by raising their rates to near criminal levels. Prices of nearly everything in Egypt within a hundred miles of the border had doubled and were still cheaper than inside Gaza.

Yes. There they were. Two trucks, goats, workers. And what looked like a single heifer among the goats.

Strange, Farag thought. *One heifer.*

He glanced again at the numbers on his wrist. The license plate numbers matched.

He waved the first truck forward.

There was something strange about the driver's silence, too, and Farag looked closer into the man's bearded face. The man stared back. His nose and cheekbones seemed to betray a European heritage.

Farag asked the man's destination. The driver answered in Arabic that had a strangeness too. Farag had heard many accents before. This was a border that Syrians, Iraqis, and Saudis had been using of late to join some of the other militant groups. Farag recognized all of those accents, but not this man's.

Farag stepped back and checked the license plate again. Then his wrist again.

There was no doubt.

This truck and the other were the ones he'd been ordered to wave through into Gaza. As an employee of the Palestinian National Authority, all of Farag's instincts told him something was wrong. Yet he dared not disobey direct orders from the Mossad.

Farag grunted and pointed the truck through the border crossing. The same with the next. He wiped dust from his face. Both trucks and the men standing in them with the goats and the heifer would disappear inside the Gaza Strip. Just like so many other trucks and men had done in recent months—young, passionate men who would become suicide bombers or fresh soldiers in whatever plans Hamas had to harass Israel from the safety of Gaza.

This, however, was the Mossad.

In the end, who was Farag to question all of this? Especially if doing so would cost him his life.

CCTI HEADQUARTERS, TEL AVIV • 21:59 GMT

It was 11:59 and counting. Quinn faced the computer screen. A webcam was mounted beside it, trained on his face. Behind him stood Zvi Cohen and Kate Penner. While Cohen and Kate were at an angle that let them see the screen and close enough to hear the audio, they were not within range of the webcam.

"Big unanswered question so far," Cohen said, "is who's responsible. We need to know. If it's Red September . . ."

"Red September?" Kate said. "I know the name, but so much of this stuff is in the news that I don't keep track."

"In 1972, the Black September kidnapped and murdered eleven Israeli athletes and coaches at the Munich Olympics," Quinn answered, intent on the screen. "The Mossad found and executed every Palestinian terrorist in that group, including the most famous, who called himself the Red Prince. Now we've got Khaled Safady as the Black Prince. Nobody has made a visual identification of him, so even if the person at the other webcam claims to be—"

Before Quinn could finish, an instant message appeared on the screen:

Host: This conference ends in 60 seconds. Start it now.

Quinn glanced at his watch and clicked the video camera icon of his software program.

Instantly a face, its lower half masked, appeared on the screen in front of him. "You have been hunting me," the man said. "Now we meet face-to-face."

Quinn fought showing a reaction. The man was directly implying he was Safady. "We need more than sixty seconds here." It was important to get the other side to make concessions early. "I'm going to do everything possible to help you get what you want, as long as you keep the Americans safe."

"You are not curious as to my identity? I know who you are—the man who wants me dead. And I, in return, want you dead. But you will serve my purpose for now."

Quinn needed to stay focused. The man underneath the mask could be anyone. Safady or not, it was obvious the man was trying to unsettle Quinn. "I'll need proof that you have them and that they are alive," he said, ignoring the issue of the man's identity. "Then we can talk."

The man moved away, and a half second later, another face was shoved in front of the camera, a hunting knife visible at the man's throat.

Jonathan Silver.

"We are all in good health," he said in a shaky voice that did nothing to hide his naked fear. "Please help."

He was yanked away again, a hand visible as it pulled his hair.

The masked man returned. "I am the Black Prince. The Americans are hostages of Red September and will pay the price for America's support of Israel's oppression of Palestine unless my demands are met."

So this was Safady. Or someone claiming to be Safady. Which?

"Twenty seconds left," Quinn said. "If that's all you're giving me, how can I begin to make it happen?"

"I lied," Safady said. "You don't have that much time. I just wanted to see your face. To dream about what it's going to be like to watch the terror in your eyes when I finally kill you. Like I killed your family. Good-bye."

Beneath the desk, Quinn had his hands in fists. His forearms quivered at the effort it was taking him to stay in a relaxed position.

The face on the screen remained briefly, the eyes flicking back and forth as the man in the mask studied Quinn's face. Then the face disappeared as the conference terminated.

"That's it?" Zvi asked. "What kind of negotiating was that?"

Quinn was still watching the screen. The instant message box popped up.

BP: Still there?

BP. Black Prince. Quinn hit the keyboard. The conversation scrolled downward as his fingers clicked.

MQ: Still here.

BP: Tomorrow at 10 a.m., two hostages die unless $10 million is deposited into the bank account of my choosing. This will be seen as a good-faith gesture.

MQ: Can't make decision without authority from family and organization. How can I contact you with questions?

BP: I contact you. Ten million is only the beginning. Two die every hour until my total ransom demand is fulfilled.

MQ: What is total?

BP: The ransom must equal all of the money that FCU has raised for Israel in the last twenty years. It will be spent in a similar way on Palestinians.

MQ: I need an amount here to take back to the family and organization.

BP: I also want to see this computer conversation broadcast on Silver's Christian network. Maybe they will raise the money for him.

MQ: How much?

BP: That would be justice—if Silver's people run a telethon to raise money for Palestine, like the many telethons that raised money for Israel. I want to see the announcers begging for money for Palestine like they've begged for money for Israel. Once the money has been raised, Jonathan Silver and the other Americans will be released.

MQ: How much?

BP: I've made it clear. The amount that Silver and other evangelists have raised for Israel while ignoring Palestine: $650 million.

THE DAY OF COUNTDOWN

onathan Silver was in his bunk, trying to fall back asleep. His eyes were squinted shut against the sunlight, and he tried to imagine the hero's welcome he would receive when he was released. A shadow fell across his face. Something or someone tapped his shoulder. A giggle came from near his ear.

Silver opened his eyes. Reality replaced his dreams. He was in the room with bunk beds lined up military-style.

The girl standing above him was the crippled girl, leaning on her crutches and smiling.

He struggled to remember her name. "Good morning," he said slowly. It tore his heart, the contrast of her cheerfulness against the disfigurement of her body. For a moment, he forgot about his own self-pity.

"Good morning?" she repeated with the halting shyness of trying out new sounds.

The woman from the night before appeared behind the child. "My name is Esther. I trust you remember that this is Alyiah."

The girl nodded in recognition of her name.

"Alyiah," Silver repeated. He propped himself up on an elbow, conscious that he was still in the clothes he'd worn the day before and of the sour dryness of his mouth. He might be dead by nightfall, yet he was still worried about morning breath. If he could find humor in that, maybe his spirit hadn't been as broken as Safady wanted.

"Alyiah." The girl smiled her heartbreaking smile.

"She doesn't speak English," Silver said to Esther.

"What magnificent powers of observation," she snapped. "I can see why you are one of the leaders of the American evangelical world."

"Her crutches," Silver said, thinking it better to ignore the sarcasm. "Why?"

"Half her leg has been amputated." Esther's voice rose slightly with irritation.

"I meant, why has it been amputated?"

"Ask about her leg then, not the crutches. Or the scars on her arm. There is no room here for false pity. Touch her arm."

Silver hesitated.

"Touch it," Esther commanded. "Look her in the eyes and tell her you are sad that her arm has been damaged like that. She won't understand the words, but she'll understand your compassion. These children need compassion and love. You are capable of compassion?"

Silver still hesitated. Usually he had his people around him to form a protective wall from matters like this. Otherwise all his days would be consumed by listening to pleas for help.

"She's not a leper," Esther snapped. "She's also smart enough to know that you can see she is disfigured. Reach out to her."

Silver pointed at Alyiah's arm. He lifted his hand and brought it close. "Yes?"

The little girl nodded understanding and raised her arm for Silver to touch it.

He ran the tips of his fingers lightly over the scarred tissue. "I'm sorry for you." Silver felt tears in his eyes as he realized he truly meant it. In that moment, he forgot he was a kidnapping victim stuck in an orphanage somewhere in the Gaza Strip.

Tears? What was happening to him? He had never been sentimental or soft.

Esther spoke to the child in Arabic, and Alyiah smiled softly at Silver before backing away and running to join other young girls.

"Israeli helicopter attack," Esther said. "It killed her mother and younger brother."

"Soldiers were shooting at them?" Silver said, astounded.

"No. They were civilian casualties."

"Oh," Silver said. "I understand."

"You do?" Esther gave him a tight smile. "Amazing. That makes you the first. Later, I'll gather all of these children and translate while you explain why this had to happen to them."

"I meant—"

"Then be more careful with your words."

Silver stared at her. Who was she to speak to him like this? She wasn't a terrorist armed with a pistol. "Do you have any idea who I am?"

"I know who you are," she answered. "And that makes you a threat to the lives of my children."

"You were there when he warned us. None of us will try to escape. I can promise you that."

"You think it's that simple, don't you? This is the Gaza Strip. You are held by Palestinian terrorists. You've been placed in this orphanage because the terrorists hope it will prevent the Israelis from trying a rescue attempt. The children, you see, are a shield for the terrorists. But if you're as important as you think you are, perhaps the Israelis will choose to sacrifice Palestinian orphans to save you. That makes me wish you were back in a place where you ordered orange juice at seven dollars a glass and had a maid to clean up your dirty towels."

Esther gave him another tight smile. "Around here, Mr. Silver, you'll wash and dry your own dishes. Someone like you shouldn't set a bad example for our children."

CCTI HEADQUARTERS, TEL AVIV • 8:17 GMT

The man in Quinn's office snapped his cell phone shut. That's how he'd walked in—cell phone to his ear, nodding at Kate and Quinn but putting up a hand to indicate they needed to wait until he was finished.

"I'm Major General Jackson Hamer," he said when he ended his call. "Sayeret Duvdevan."

"I don't speak Hebrew," Kate said.

"Sayeret Duvdevan is Israeli Defense Force special forces," Quinn explained. "The Mossad is an agency oriented to gathering intelligence. Sayeret Duvdevan is an IDF unit designed for hit-and-run operations. Think of a SWAT team on steroids. Except here it's called CT—counterterror. Does that sum it up, Major General?"

Hamer nodded. "This is an IDF operation now. Zvi Cohen has given me a full briefing."

"Jackson Hamer," Kate repeated. "Doesn't sound like a Jewish name. And you don't sound like an Israeli. More like an American. And you're here for Mossad and IDF. They allow Americans in?"

Jackson Hamer shrugged. "It was originally Hammerstein, for those who think ethnic background is an issue."

"Must have been an issue to someone," Kate said. She was in a bad mood and wanted everyone else to feel the same. "I wasn't the one who changed it."

Hamer laughed, a surprise to her. "My grandfather changed it to Hamer when he immigrated to the States from Germany. I was born in the States and lived there until my early teens. After my parents' divorce, my mother moved us here. Small mercy that my father's sense of humor is mainly wasted around Israelis."

Hamer was in his late forties, slightly shorter than Kate, wide in the shoulders, but definitely not pudgy, with short, thick hair starting to gray. He had just enough angles in his cheekbones and nose to suggest a trace of Middle Eastern heritage. He wore a black shirt, black pants, and a disarming grin.

"Wasted humor around Israelis?" Kate asked. "Sounds like an ethnic slur to me."

She caught Quinn frowning.

"Hey," she said, "he brought out the ethnic card first. It's like trump; once it's out there, anyone can play it."

"She's right," Hamer said. "Most people call me Hamer, but my dad liked shortening my first name to Jack. In the States, Jack Hamer sounded too much like jackhammer. Exactly what my dad wanted—to be able to point to his son and call him a little jackhammer. Stopped being funny for me a long time ago. Lucky for me, most Israelis don't make the connection."

Quinn said nothing, just sipped his coffee.

"I hate to bring two pieces of bad news," Hamer said, "but Zvi couldn't confirm the identity of the kidnapper from last night's webcam footage."

"And the second piece?" Quinn asked.

"His son is on the way."

"Son?" Kate asked. "Zvi's son?"

"Brad Silver," Hamer said. "He was supposed to be on the tour bus yesterday but stayed back at the King David. We finally had to tell him about the kidnapping situation, of course."

"Call him," Quinn said. "Save him the trip in from Jerusalem."

"I didn't mean on the way from the King David; I meant on the way up the elevator. That call as I was walking in came from one of our men stationed in the lobby."

"I can't tell Brad anything that you haven't already told him about the situation," Quinn said. "Everything else we can relay by telephone."

"He's here because he wants to be part of this."

"No," Quinn said. "Rule number one: never involve the family in the negotiating process. Decision process maybe, but not negotiating. There needs to be a buffer."

"That's what I told him."

"But he's still on the elevator on his way up. Do American civilians have a habit of telling the Mossad and IDF what to do in a terrorist situation?"

"No. But the Israeli prime minister does."

"The Israeli prime minister?"

"You've seen the background file on Jonathan Silver," Hamer said. "The PM's a close, personal friend. Sends a private jet anytime Silver wants to visit Israel. Someone cynical might think it has something to do with the hundreds of millions that Silver has raised for Israel over the last decade or two and all the political clout that Silver has with the evangelical right-wing voters in the United States who influence presidential elections and pressure for pro Israeli policies. I happen to be cynical, but you make your own decision."

"Tell him to go away," Quinn said.

A moment later, Brad Silver pushed open the door without knocking.

We've been giving this a lot of thought and prayer," Ray Klein said in a low voice to Jonathan Silver. Klein had joined Silver near one of the windows that overlooked a narrow cobblestoned alley. "The Lord is directing us to escape."

"We?" Silver asked. "The group?"

"Me and Abe." Klein was a big man with a ruddy face. He'd smelled of peppermints on the bus, and Silver suspected the man secretly nipped at a flask. There was a hint of desperation in Klein's face now, perspiration in tiny drops across his forehead. "Nobody else we've talked to in the group seems interested in trying to get out of here."

"Escape?" Silver heard his own voice shake. "Last night, we were told that if we tried to escape—"

"It's got to be a bluff," Klein said. He cast an encouraging glance at Abe Williams, twenty feet away, who was doing a bad job of feigning disinterest. "He's not going to kill orphans if we try to escape. It's just a way to control thirty of us because he doesn't have the manpower to guard us all."

Abe Williams gave a hesitant smile back at Klein and Silver. Williams was slender—almost gaunt—with thinning gray hair. During the day tours, he'd worn a sweater around his waist like a backward apron, with the arms tied around his thin belly. Silver wondered if Williams was part of the don't ask, don't tell brigade, but Williams was a rich man and an excellent donor, so Silver had also decided it would be better not to inquire too closely about the man's lifestyle preferences.

"What about the rest of us?" Silver coughed nervously. "If you make it, we'll be punished."

"I don't think so," Klein said. "If he wanted us dead, we'd be dead. That tells me we're worth something to him alive." He smiled grimly. "Remember, I spent my whole life in business. I made a fortune by reading my competition and my customers the right way."

The trucking business, Silver vaguely remembered. Klein was a widower, recently retired.

"I just don't know," Silver said. He was tired and afraid and so out of his element that he just wanted to go back to his bunk and sleep.

"We're Americans," Klein said, "not American'ts. I told you already; it will be a piece of cake to get out through a window. It's obvious we're in the middle of some city. Once we get far enough away from here, we'll find a cab to take us to the police or to an embassy. That will get the ball rolling. There will be more marines on this place than Iwo Jima."

Silver couldn't make a decision.

"Look," Klein said impatiently, "it's a chance, a gamble. But it's better than sitting here with no chance whatsoever."

"The ransom . . ."

"You think that money will get here in time? And if it does, you really think he's going to let all of us go? I'm telling you, no way. I read it like this: he'll keep all of us alive long enough to get what he wants; then it will be some jihad thing where he slaughters all of us to be a hero with his Muslim buddies. Well, let me tell you, I'd rather go out fighting than like a lamb."

"If you go, he's going to execute a child," Silver said, finding some strength. "If you escape, he'll have to show the rest of us that he's serious. Otherwise more of us will escape."

"Thirty of us dead for sure against the maybe that one of these orphans goes." Klein shook his head. "It sounds cold, but when you force yourself to look at the odds that way, I don't see much choice. Who's worth more? Thirty Americans or one Palestinian kid? I mean, you've said that Arabs aren't worth much, and—"

"I just don't know," Silver said, regretting again that he'd made those remarks from the pulpit. It was easier to say something nasty about Arabs when you thought of them as a faceless group or a concept, not little kids.

"Yeah," Klein answered. "That was my bet with Williams—that you wouldn't have the jam to make a decision one way or another. I got to say it: you learn a lot about someone when they're put under pressure. And ever since those camel jockeys took over our bus, you haven't done much that makes you look near as good as you look on television."

Silver had no answer.

"I'm making the decision for you, then," Klein said. "We're going. If you try to stop us, that's like turning us in. But I don't think you have the jam for that, either."

When Brad Silver entered the room, Quinn moved to his window, looking down at the street through a slit in the blinds. Kate remained seated on the leather couch, pretending she wasn't exhausted.

"You're Mossad, right?" Brad said to Hamer.

"I'm IDF. Israeli Defense Force."

"You a flunky? or a decision maker?"

"I'm Major General Jack Hamer. That high enough to suit you?"

"Good. Let's get this straight," Brad told Hamer, not even nodding in Kate's direction. "First thing we do is find a different negotiator."

Brad Silver wore jeans and a tan cashmere sports coat over a white T-shirt. He was tall, and the resemblance to his father was eerie, down to the sheen of his hair—far too gray for a man his age, somewhere in the late thirties. Dye job, Kate decided instantly. And a bad one. He was trying to look distinguished and failing miserably.

"You're dictating how the IDF handles a terrorist situation?" Hamer answered with a dangerous quietness.

"I'm dictating media perception. It's unthinkable that a felon would represent my father and what my father stands for. Jonathan Silver is one of the world's most famous evangelical Christians, and I'm sure he'd agree with my decision not to let the taint of a murderer affect his reputation."

"Murderer?" Hamer questioned.

"What's his name. This Quinn guy. Is that him by the window, ignoring me? Figures."

Hamer snapped open his cell and dialed a number. Without taking his eyes off Brad, he waited for an answer on the other end.

"Listen, clown, he's not a felon," Kate said in the silence, wondering how this jerk already knew that Quinn would be indicted as soon as he arrived in the United States. "Charges haven't even been filed. Nor is he a murderer until proven so in a court of law. So shut your mouth or I'll be the first to help him file libel charges."

"I'd like a coffee, two creams, no sugar," Brad said, emphasizing a condescending smile. "Please make sure the pot is freshly brewed."

Kate rose, visualizing Brad curled into a ball on the floor after she'd kicked him square where it would do the most efficient damage. "Do I need permission from anyone here to punch him out? I'm only asking because you guys made it clear that chain of command was important to keep those thirty alive."

Brad ignored her, speaking to Hamer. "We go to IDF headquarters, and we do this right. I will not have a murderer in charge of this hostage situation."

Hamer finally spoke, but it was into his cell. "Mr. Prime Minister, regarding the son of your friend, your request was to allow him observation of the situation. As I predicted, he is trying to command it instead."

Hamer paused, listening to a response.

"If you want to give him that power," Hamer said, "I will respect your decision and offer a public resignation, effective immediately. I'm sure the voting public will enjoy a chance in the next election to tell you what they think of allowing an American to push around the IDF when it comes to national security."

The next silence was short as Hamer listened to the reply. He snapped his cell phone shut, walked to the door, and swung it open.

"I guess you didn't understand how much power my father has, did you?" Brad said, smirking.

Hamer stopped and turned. "This isn't about power, Mr. Silver. It's about saving thirty lives." He paused, then pointed at the hallway. "By the way, you're also wrong about your father's power. The prime minister made it clear in very few words that he prefers reelection over catering to you. I'll explain in politer terms than he used. You have a choice. Remain here as a guest with no privileges or go back to the King David, where I'll make sure you get updates every half hour."

Before Brad could reply, Quinn stepped away from the window and spoke. "There are two vans down on the street, one crew setting up a television camera, and a talking head from CNN trading notes with someone I recognize from the *New York Times*. How'd the media get on to you so quick?"

"I've got all the major media on speed dial," Brad answered, "along with about a dozen senators and five governors. That's something all of you should remember. I wanted the media to know about this because I want as much pressure as possible on both the American and Israeli governments to resolve this."

"So they're going to camp down there and wait for you to make reports?" Quinn observed. "Sounds like a bad move."

"Sounds like you've just made your decision to go back to the King David," Hamer said. "Here's your next choice: leave on your own or wait for some of my men from the lobby to come up here and put you in handcuffs."

"Let me do it," Kate said.

"Actually, it would be better for our team if he stayed," Quinn said.

"Yeah, he's a real team player," Hamer snorted. "Is your sense of judgment going to be this bad all through the negotiating? Is that why the e-mail from the terrorist specified you and no one else? Terrorists want a moron as an opponent?"

"He stays?" Kate asked Quinn. "Are you nuts? He's cancer. He's going to second-guess everything you do."

"Exactly," Quinn answered. "It could be helpful as we try to make good decisions."

Brad didn't take the peace offered by Quinn. "It's Khaled Safady behind this, right? I heard he killed your family. All you want is revenge. That's another reason I don't want you involved. You'll be making emotional decisions."

"If it's him, the best revenge I could get right now is stopping him from killing more people," Quinn said.

"If?" Brad said. "I saw the tape of your videoconference last night. He made no bones about his identity."

"How'd he get the tape?" Quinn asked Hamer.

"Cohen, I guess."

"I deserve to be in on this," Brad said. "I don't want a negotiator who already hates the man he's negotiating with."

"A masked man without any reliable identification," Kate broke in. "He could just as easily have said he was the president of the United States."

"Where's my coffee?" Brad asked, giving her another smirk.

Quinn spoke to Brad. "You don't like me; I can live with that. But we don't have many options here, and how you feel and how I feel doesn't matter. Getting the job done does. When your father and the other twenty-nine get back alive, then go ahead and push all the speed-dial buttons you want."

"Don't patronize me," Brad told Quinn.

"'Get me a coffee,'" Kate said, mimicking Brad's voice, wishing she could drop-kick the smug jerk. "Did that sound patronizing to anyone? Can I handcuff him yet?"

"Kate," Quinn told her, "let it go. His father's life is in danger and he's under stress. Different people handle it different ways."

Quinn turned back to Brad. "You called them hostages. That's wrong. A hostage situation happens when the terrorists are trapped and the captives become bargaining chips for the terrorists to escape. This is a kidnapping. We've got a lot less leverage because we don't know where your father and the others are."

"The vaunted Mossad doesn't know?" Brad said, glancing at Hamer.

"Nobody is better than the Mossad at this," Quinn said. "By noon today, the Mossad will probably have an answer for you, but I'd be surprised if they decide it's important for you to know. Until then, we deal with the situation as it is. Bringing the media in complicates things. Best-case scenario, terms could have been quietly negotiated and dealt with. The key word is *quietly*. The American government has an official policy not to deal with kidnappers for any reason. That just encourages more kidnapping. Unofficially, though, the government has been known to step in. Now that it's public, we won't get that help. And if the terrorist decides correctly that media pressure is going to force us to give more, the negotiations could go on for days."

"Sounds like you're second-guessing me," Brad said.

"See?" Kate said, thinking it would be worth splitting the skin of her knuckles on his teeth to wipe out that sneer. "He's cancer."

"I'm not second-guessing you," Quinn answered Brad. "I'm assessing the situation for all of us." He turned to Kate and Hamer. "In Brad's defense, it's almost certain the terrorists would have brought in the media at some point anyway."

Kate marveled at Quinn's calm. She had no patience here. She wished she could handle the situation like a cop would—no nonsense.

"Quinn, let me negotiate something here," she broke in. "You get rid of this guy with the bad dye job, and I'll let you go to the bathroom unsupervised any time you raise your hand."

"He's got to report to you?" There was disbelief in Brad Silver's voice. "The Mossad does what he tells them, but he's got to report to you?"

"If I want, he's got to bring me coffee," Kate said. "But I won't ask him because that's not dignified for either of us. So how 'bout on your way out the door you take the coffeepot, a cup, and as much cream and sugar as you can stick in—"

"Wow," Brad said. "Vulgarities. Someday when I want trailer trash, I know where to look."

"As much cream and sugar as you can stick in your coffee," Kate said sweetly. "So you'll enjoy a long drive back to Jerusalem."

"Brad, I need you here," Quinn said. "Information is one of a negotiator's most vital assets. You'll know things and give us perspective that may save your father's life. It's obvious that you're willing to speak your mind. That's a good thing. When we go into huddles and plan the next step, I want you to second-guess everything until a decision is made. That way it will be the best decision possible. Here's a warning though: if you second-guess it after a decision is made, you're out the door."

"This is not going to work," Hamer said.

"Rule one in negotiating: I'm just a go-between. You're the final decision maker. Brad's got to agree to that to stay on the team. But what happens when the terrorist makes a demand for something that only Brad or the Silver organization can meet? There's less chance for misunderstanding if Brad knows exactly what's happening and is right here to give you the answer. No delays, either, when time matters."

"I still don't like it," Hamer said.

"I don't like it in any way," Kate said.

"There's no way you're going to make me like it either," Brad said.

"Listen to the three of you. Already in agreement. A true team." Quinn grinned. "Get into the boxing ring when all of this is finished, but for now think about those thirty people. We do what it takes to get them home."

"Fine," Brad said with ill-disguised petulance.

Hamer merely nodded.

Kate glared at Brad. "Doesn't sound like I have a choice. But he gets me the first cup of coffee."

"Brad," Quinn said, "before you get to the coffee, we need you leaving through the front door of the lobby."

"What?" Brad exploded. "You went through all of this to get rid of me?"

"Go check into a hotel," Quinn said. "The Olympia, the Armon Hayarkon, anyplace you want. Draw the media there. Then, if you can, find a way to sneak here again without the media attention."

"You're not making sense."

"Good. You're second-guessing me. If I can't sell you on my reasons for it, we do something else. Fair enough?"

Incredible, Kate thought. Quinn was deftly negotiating here, and Brad didn't have a clue it was happening.

"Try me." Brad was a touch less petulant than a moment before.

"We've agreed already there's going to come a point, maybe more than a couple of times, when the person or people on the other end will ask for something that only you can give. Most often in these situations, the best response is a delayed one. Gives us time to think things through. While it's best for us to have you here to discuss it, if it *looks* like we can't get to you for an immediate answer, stalling isn't likely to put your father or the others in danger. The kidnapper is certain to be watching media reports. I'd like him to believe you're staying at your hotel, not here. Lets us stall when it's convenient for us."

Kate watched Quinn study Brad, as if Quinn was deciding if he needed to explain more.

"Sold?" Quinn finally asked.

"Fine," Brad said.

"Good. You'll use your expertise and connections to handle the media, then, in a way that works for us?"

"That's why I have speed dial," Brad said, all petulance gone.

"What do they know at this point?" Quinn asked.

"Only that my father is among Americans kidnapped."

"Not that Safady may be involved?"

"Cohen told me not to release that information."

"He's right," Quinn said. "If you want to turn this into a media frenzy, that's what it would take. It will only help Safady."

Brad nodded.

Kate was amazed at how Quinn had converted an enemy into an ally.

The word stuck in her mind. *Enemy*. With it came an image—the grainy video shot taken in the casino, capturing Quinn as he followed the man that Kate would later find upside-down and dead in a cube van.

No mistakes, she warned herself. *The most dangerous snakes are the ones who hypnotize you before they strike.*

"I'm not that impressed with your negotiating skills," Hamer said to Quinn.

Kate was in the kitchen suite and out of earshot. Quinn and Hamer were standing at the window, watching the two media vans disappear down Hayarkon Street in pursuit of Brad Silver.

"Silver's gone for a while, and he took the media with him," Quinn said. "What more do you want? The three of us now have time to decide how to deal with him."

"The lines you fed him weren't bad, but—"

"We need him," Quinn said. "At the least, having him here will keep him from calling news conferences every half hour to demand that the IDF make better progress. Most important, I earned his trust. That's rule one in negotiating: earn trust."

"I was talking about Penner. You haven't done much with her."

"She's making coffee for us. She let me out of her sight. Considering that she was ready to kill when the Mossad turned the jet around, I'd call both of those a negotiating coup."

"Out of sight? She's, what, twenty steps away?" Hamer pointed at the handcuffs that Penner had slapped on Quinn's wrists before going into the kitchen. "Good thing you've built such a huge trust factor with her."

"Sometimes as a negotiator you understand things have to be done to save face." Quinn played this with a straight face. "Think about all her earlier threats to me. If she were serious about not trusting me, my hands would be cuffed behind my back. Or, from what I've seen already, she'd just shoot me."

"I'll bet victories like this don't come too often in your business. You'll probably remember it as a highlight of a brilliant career." Hamer checked to make sure Kate wasn't out of the kitchen suite yet. "Why'd you tell Silver that the Mossad would locate his father and the other Americans by noon? I don't like that kind of pressure."

"Because you and I are going to trade favors. I want as much background as you can get on Kate Penner and the extradition order and where she got what she did on me . . . without her knowing it. While you're at it, get what you can on Brad Silver. The more we understand about him and his evangelical organization, the better we can evaluate whatever information he gives us."

"You want secret background on a U.S. marshal who can yank you out of the country at any given moment, when escape will take you away from a murder indictment. In exchange for that highly unethical move, I receive what?"

"The location of the kidnapped Americans and credit for it. Like you said, you don't like that kind of pressure."

"You'll get me the information?" Disbelief showed on Hamer's face.

"Yeah."

"How?"

"I guess you really do think I'm a bad negotiator. I tell you that, and you'll do it yourself. Then I've lost leverage."

"You'll get me the information." The statement was flat now.

"But we need to be extremely careful with it. If it leaks, we've turned a kidnapping situation into a hostage situation, where shooting hostages becomes leverage for the kidnapper. Especially now that the media will be on this like a pit bull."

"You told Brad by noon. That sounds confident."

"Remember I put an escape clause in that promise."

"I heard it. Even after locating them, we might not decide to tell him. Still, why'd you pick a deadline only hours away?"

"I'll tell you just to convince you to start on getting me the information I want. We've got great computer geeks here at CCTI. Some don't mind breaking privacy restrictions and hacking into servers to track down IP addresses."

"That's so wrong," Hamer said.

"We hired our best geeks from the Mossad, where they were trained to do that and worse."

"That's what I meant by wrong. We can't match private sector salaries. What's the plan?"

"Last night, our contact was face-to-face via webcam. Our geek has promised me that the link from his computer to mine lasted long enough to give us a decent shot at locating him."

"Nobody can track through the Internet that fast," Hamer said. "I'm a dinosaur when it comes to computers, but even I know enough about cybercrime to understand that something like this can take weeks. Months if it's done legally."

"Not if our geek planted a beacon," Quinn said. "Then it will be like finding the vehicle with a car alarm going off in a church parking lot."

"Planted a beacon? How?"

"Think I know the technological aspects? I just know it's worked before. You've heard of tracer programs, right?"

Hamer shrugged, as if refusing to commit one way or the other. "If I don't agree to this exchange? You strike me as the type of guy who would give IDF the information anyway to help those thirty Americans."

"I would."

"Look at the leverage you've just lost by admitting that. See what I mean about unimpressive negotiating skills?"

"Remember rule one in negotiating: earn trust."

"I thought you said rule one was that you were the go-between, not the decision maker."

"That's definitely rule one. So is gathering information. So is earning trust."

"Of course," Hamer said.

"By giving up my leverage to you in this situation, I open the door for you to trust me. You'll want to give something up in return. Like getting me information on Penner and the extradition. It's great negotiating. I give up one thing and get two in return."

"Wrong. I'm IDF. I don't give out classified information."

"How's this for leverage then?" Quinn said. "Get me what I want, or I'll tell Silver you weren't talking to the prime minister when you made that dramatic offer of resignation on your cell phone. Bad as you made Brad look, he's going to love payback when he knows the call was faked."

"He's got media on his speed dial," Hamer said. "I've got the PM. That call was legitimate, and all you need to do to prove it is call the PM yourself."

"Nice try. You know I don't have the PM on *my* speed dial."

Hamer flipped out his cell phone and offered it to Quinn. "Hold down the number three key for a couple seconds."

"Impressive bluff and impressive poker face," Quinn said. "But remember rule one."

"Which rule one? I've lost track."

"That's rule one. Keep track. Here you're trying a bluff, but I know your cards and you don't know mine."

"*You're* bluffing."

"Rule one: information is your most valuable asset. This office is buffered against wireless reception. Unless I shut off the hidden scrambler, no calls get in, no calls go out."

"Oh," Hamer said. His jaw clenched briefly.

"So, you want me to tell Silver you didn't reach the PM? Or want to get me some classified information in exchange for what I learn about the terrorists' location?"

Hamer didn't pause long. "You'll have the report on Penner by noon."

"See what I mean?" Quinn said. "Right then, I was a go-between that you trusted, allowing you to make a decision based on information that you kept track of. Negotiating is simple. All you do is remember rule one."

DAYR AL-BALAH, GAZA STRIP • 8:29 GMT

"Let me ask you something," Joe Patterson said to Frankie Burge, the soldier who was helping him guard Orphan Annie. "You still cool with all this?"

The platoon had slept through the night without incident, then traveled north, halfway through the Gaza Strip—maybe six or seven miles—to reach Dayr al-Balah. Here Saxon had ordered them into an empty building that gave them a clear view of the wire-fenced compound where their trucks were held. Patterson and Burge knew they were expected to sacrifice their lives to keep the heifer from harm.

Patterson had been thinking about too many things. He wished he could find the mental space to trust orders like a good soldier. But watching defenseless men get slaughtered—Muslim or not—had wedged into his mind the first small and unanswered doubts. Then came the bigger questions and the bigger doubts. This had so far been a complex military action, obviously well planned and supported by a resource structure beyond his imagination. Where was all of this leading? How much more slaughter would it involve?

"Am I cool with standing beside a cow?" Burge patted Orphan Annie.

"Heifer," Patterson said.

"Sure. I'm cool standing with a heifer. I just take orders."

Patterson's point exactly. But nothing he wanted to say aloud. Yet.

"I meant are you cool with *all* of this," Patterson said. "Not just this morning's orders to watch Orphan Annie."

"Like our crusade and putting my life on the line and wondering if I'll be killed in the next firefight?" Frankie shrugged. He was the largest of all the Freedom Crusaders but had a surprisingly high-pitched voice. "I know where my soul is going. I'm not afraid of dying."

To Patterson, this answer revealed how much Burge's perspective differed from his own. Patterson hadn't been worrying in the least about death in battle. He couldn't shake the horrible feeling that the Freedom Crusaders weren't crusaders but executioners. Patterson wouldn't define any of their dozen engagements so far as battles or firefights, only slaughters of Muslims, like the evening before, when the Freedom Crusaders had held every advantage in terrain, surprise, technology, firepower, and manpower.

"And you're cool with shooting down men who are begging for mercy?" Patterson said softly.

Burge narrowed his eyes. "Just as cool as they were when they flew those jets into the WTC. You saw the footage later. Muslims all across the world celebrating while Americans burned to death. They were begging for mercy too. I'm cool with payback, if that's what you mean."

Patterson hated his own doubts. He was thinking that maybe the media footage had shown only a few Muslim crowds. He wondered if that attitude really reflected all of them. Wondered if that made it right to be a Freedom Crusader. Hadn't that been basic in kindergarten? Two wrongs don't make a right.

This situation looked to be no different than another setup for slaughter.

The unit was nestled in a warehouse district that seemed as if it would blow over in the next desert storm. The unit had been scattered, two or three men in each of the empty buildings surrounding the warehouse. They were all in communication via headsets.

According to the earlier briefing by Lieutenant Saxon, a dozen or so members of the terrorist group Hamas would be arriving within the next twenty minutes. These Palestinians believed the trucks held weapons smuggled across the border by the men that the Freedom Crusaders had killed the night before.

As Saxon had explained it, eliminating both groups—the previous night's and this morning's—was ancillary to the mission. He'd grinned through his dark beard and told the Freedom Crusaders to consider it a bonus. Any Palestinian looking for weapons to use against Israel deserved to be shot down, whether it was in an ambush or an open fight. Basically, a dead Muslim male was a good Muslim male. Points in heaven.

"Why you asking all this, Pats?" Frankie Burge whispered to Patterson. His earpiece was active, but his microphone was shut off. Their conversation would be private. "You afraid of dying because you've got the wife and baby to worry about?"

"Yeah," Patterson mumbled. Better for Burge to think Patterson was afraid of death. If Burge still considered these engagements to be battles instead of one-sided slaughters, he was definitely not someone who should hear Patterson's doubts about whether it was right to continue this slaughter at every opportunity.

Burge patted his shoulder. "You want me to read Scripture to you?"

"You've got a Bible?" Patterson was surprised. As Muslims in disguise, none of them were supposed to have Bibles this far into the mission. If they were caught or killed and the Bible was discovered, it might blow the whole operation—whatever it was.

"Of course not; that's against the rules. But I've got a lot of passages memorized."

"I'll be okay." Patterson shifted his weight. The building smelled of urine and feces. He hated the trapped feeling. Orphan Annie looked restless too.

"I'll confess then," Burge said. "I *am* afraid of dying. Maybe not the dying part, but the pain it takes to get there. You know what gets me through it?"

Patterson shook his head.

"I think of 9/11," Burge said. "I think about how a secret Muslim group has been fighting this holy war against us and how all the liberals want to pretend it isn't happening. The Muslims got Osama bin Laden, but we got our own billionaire who's willing to fund a secret Christian battle against the Muslims, and I remember how proud I am to be part of it and how bad I want to pay them back for what they did." Burge searched Patterson's face. "Don't you remember how great it was to be recruited?"

Patterson remembered how intriguing the concept had seemed when he'd been part of the secret society at Freedom Christian University and how a few of the professors had recruited him by reminding him of 9/11 and the holy cause of fighting for Jesus. In the face of reality, however, the concept now seemed far too hollow. Reality was seeing so many young Muslims, barely more than boys, tortured in gruesome ways that no human should face, left dead, hanging upside down, a cross stapled to their backs. Serial killing was what it had amounted to back in the States before they'd shipped out.

And here? It bothered him more and more that the guys of the unit could go from prayers and hymns to bloodlust and then back to hymns and prayers again.

"Yeah," Patterson said. "I remember how great it was to be recruited."

"Good." Burge slapped Patterson on the back. "It's a crusade, man. Don't forget that. You ready for action now?"

Patterson forced himself to nod.

Burge gave him a grin. "Then let's send this next batch of heathens straight to hell."

CCTI HEADQUARTERS, TEL AVIV • 8:34 GMT

Major General Jack Hamer had left the office. Quinn was leaning back in his expensive ergonomic chair, eyes closed, feet on desk, earbuds of an iPod plugged in.

Kate picked up the iPod from the desk. If Quinn felt her presence, nothing on his face gave any indication. She glanced at the song displayed—The Who's "Baba O'Riley."

She cranked the volume, still staring at Quinn's face. What she wanted was a jump forward, his feet off the desk, or at the least a startled flinch.

What she got was the opening of his eyes and a slightly raised eyebrow. He glanced at the iPod in her hand, then back at her. He didn't even ask her to turn the volume down, even though the pounding beat of the song reached her clearly from his earbuds.

Kate turned down the volume.

Quinn closed his eyes again. Did he know how much it irritated her to pretend she wasn't there?

She yanked on the earbuds, popping them loose.

"You lied to Hamer about the beacon," Kate told Quinn, moving to sit on the desk. "You can't locate Safady that way. You can't locate anyone that way."

Quinn lowered his feet. "That was a private conversation with Hamer. Did he volunteer that information about the beacon, or did you make it a point to ask him what was happening?"

"Does it matter?"

"Wondering about the politics of our forced triangle," Quinn said. "We'll be in close quarters until this is finished. My impression was that you were a neutral prison guard here."

"Politics don't matter. The point is you lied to him about beacons."

"Web beacons are common. Safady went to our Web site last night to hook up the videoconference. We tagged him there." He leaned forward in his chair.

Kate was conscious of him in her body space, and she felt like squirming because of her heightened awareness of him, but she thought that moving away from the desk might show weakness. "You got Hamer to believe it's like a homing signal, but you'll be lucky if you were able to get Safady's IP address. Even so, that doesn't tell you the physical location of his computer."

That earned another slight raise of Quinn's eyebrows as he studied her face.

She'd been at a few cop seminars on cybercrime. She expected a smart-mouthed comment from Quinn about her computer knowledge. But he surprised her.

"Let me ask you something. Are you in or out?" he asked.

"Of what?" she snapped.

"Do you want to help the hostages? That's in. Or do want to play these little games and be an obstacle? That's out."

"You should be landing in Chicago right now to face indictment. I'm the one risking a career by lying about why you're not on that plane. Is that enough of an answer?"

"No. If you're not going to be a neutral observer, take the next step. Give your allegiance to me. Not Hamer."

"Weren't you the one who made a beautiful little speech about teamwork?" Kate tapped her front tooth with the fingernail of her index finger, as if she really were trying to recall something. "That's right. Just this morning. You know, when you were putting that little social engineering move on Brad Silver and making him your lapdog."

Social engineering. Another phrase she'd learned in the cybercrime seminars. A way of manipulating people. If hackers couldn't get into a site with computer skills, they finessed people working for the site.

"Hamer's IDF," Quinn said. "That means he has more on his agenda than saving hostages. He's got to juggle politics and hide whatever he's going to think needs hiding from me. Which means he is hiding a lot."

"You'll trust me instead?"

"Your agenda is simple and straightforward. You want me facing a jury on murder charges. Better the evil that I know than the evil I don't."

She didn't want to admit there was logic in Quinn's argument. She reminded herself of what she knew about him.

Social engineering. He was playing her against Hamer. Divide, then conquer. Then escape and murder another Muslim.

Kate hesitated just a moment. "In," she said, thinking that in the worst case, if Quinn was playing games, the best way to compete was to pretend that he'd succeeded in manipulating her, too. Best case, if he wasn't playing a game, she'd be helping the kidnap victims.

Quinn stared at her for a long moment, then finally said, "Good."

We do it again," Safady told Silver from behind the tripod and video camera. "Only this time I will be less forgiving of insubordination."

Silver drew a breath, audible across the room. He sat on a stool. Its legs had been sawed off. He knew the camera was pointing down at him, and he knew how it would appear in the video footage—that Silver was smaller. He knew this because he was so aware of the opposite; he had always demanded a slightly upward camera angle for all his television appearances. It made him look larger, more dominating.

"Do you believe and preach that the Dome of the Rock stands where the Jewish Temple once stood?" Safady asked.

This was public record. Silver saw no sense in denying it, especially because he believed it was true. "I preach that," Silver said, looking straight ahead.

"Look at the camera," Safady said pleasantly. "I like the posture that presents. Then repeat my question in the affirmative and plural. 'We believe and preach that the Dome of the Rock stands where the Jewish Temple once stood.'"

Silver closed his eyes. He hated this man. But he was on camera. He would project himself, show that he would not lose pride to a man like this. He spoke firmly. "We believe and preach that the Dome of the Rock stands where the Jewish Temple once stood."

"And do you believe and preach that the Jewish Temple must be rebuilt before God can return?"

"We believe and preach that the Jewish Temple must be rebuilt before Jesus can return."

"Do you believe and preach that Temple sacrifices will resume?"

"We believe and preach that Temple sacrifices will resume."

"This would mean tearing down the Dome of the Rock?"

"In theory, of course," Silver said. The Dome of the Rock was a holy site for the man in front of him, a man who held the power of life and death over all the hostages. "When God is ready for the Dome of the Rock to be destroyed, then the Temple can be rebuilt."

"Because the Jews are divinely promised the Temple Mount?"

Silver nodded.

"Repeat it," Safady said. "'Because the Jews are divinely promised the Temple Mount.'"

Silver repeated it.

"When will the Temple be rebuilt for God's return?"

"In the last days," Silver answered.

"How do you know this?"

"The Bible, specifically the books of Ezekiel and Daniel, tells us."

"You don't care that Muslims—millions upon millions—will be devastated and outraged when it happens?"

"Knowing the timetable of biblical prophecy allows any of us to become Christians in anticipation of Christ's return." Silver kept his wince internal, wondering if Safady would explode in his usual rage.

Instead, Safady retained his pleasant smile. "Just one last question, then we are finished. And I will let you answer any way that you like. You won't have to repeat anything I tell you. Fair enough?"

"Certainly," Silver said. Speaking what he'd been preaching for decades about Revelation had given him a degree of confidence.

"If your Christ died on the cross to cover all your sins as you frequently preach, why are the sacrifices necessary? Are you suggesting that the atonement wasn't complete? that your Christ only covers some of your sins?"

Silver opened his mouth to speak but could think of no immediate reply.

Safady laughed. "As I thought." He shut off the video camera. "We're finished. What a shame you can't watch this interview and see the look on your face as you struggled for that final answer."

CCTI HEADQUARTERS, TEL AVIV • 9:09 GMT

The office door opened, and Hamer walked in, waving his cell phone like a pistol. "I just got off the phone with some Mossad tech guys. They told me you can't plant some lighthouse thing sending signals that let you home in on Safady's computer. I don't care how badly Safady wants you as negotiator, you're gone if I know you're telling me lies."

"The Mossad tech guys would be right," Quinn answered, "if we had used a lighthouse. It's unfortunate that they got the wrong impression from you."

"No," Hamer said. "What's unfortunate is that you gave me that impression."

"Unfortunate," Kate said in a flat voice.

"Try to follow," Quinn said. "This is about to get technical, but I'll draw it out for you." He glanced at Kate. "*Both* of you."

Quinn grabbed another sheet of paper and a pen. He spent thirty seconds making a rough sketch. "It's like this," Quinn said, handing the paper to Hamer. "Internet access reaches users through ISPs—Internet service providers. That triangle I just drew? The tip of it is the Internet. Just below are gateway ISPs that flow traffic into the Internet. Below each gateway are a number of T1 circuits that give up to five hundred users access. At the bottom are all the residences or businesses hooked up to each T1. Got it so far?"

Hamer grunted.

"So Kevin—"

"Kevin?" Hamer interrupted.

"Our best IT guy. Better than anyone working for the IDF or the Mossad."

Another grunt from Hamer.

"Kevin ran a specialized trace route to help us find Safady's gateway provider. It lists each Internet router that's handled his traffic. According to IT, Safady was seven Internet hops away from us. I expect by now, IT has found the gateway provider. The gateway provider has the information on the physical location of Safady's computer."

"The gateway provider will give you that?" Hamer asked.

"Not without a warrant," Quinn said.

Hamer groaned. Kate groaned. Both had enough law experience to realize the potential difficulties of that, along with the certain time delays, especially when it came to computer crime.

"By the time the warrant is issued," Hamer said, "the Americans will be dead and none of this will even matter."

"Sure," Quinn said, "if you want the gateway provider to *give* it to you. You didn't ask if there was a way to *get* it from the providers."

"Legally?" Kate asked.

"If that's a concern for you," Quinn told her, "you might want to step outside of the room while this conversation continues."

"You're in custody. That would be dereliction of duty."

"What's his name . . . ? Kevin, your IT guy, is going to hack the gateway provider?" Hamer said.

"Not as easy as hacking Safady's computer. But yes. I'll let you know when."

"Fair enough," Hamer said. "I'll go back out there and call—"

Hamer's cell phone rang. He looked at it in disbelief, then looked at Quinn. "What about the buffering? the hidden scrambling device or whatever you called it? the reason you knew I hadn't called the prime minister?"

"Rule number one in negotiating: know when to bluff. You were talking on it when you first walked into my office. Not my fault you forgot."

"What if I had called your bluff?" Hamer asked. "Or remembered that my cell phone worked before? Then you'd look stupid."

"No," Quinn said. "Then I'd have told you I forgot to turn on the scrambler."

Hamer scowled and flipped open the cell phone. Almost immediately he lost his scowl. When he hung up, he spoke to Quinn and Kate in a quiet voice. "Television. CNN. They're playing a new video showing Jonathan Silver."

Brad Silver burst into the office. Hamer, Quinn, and Kate were still watching CNN.

"Did you guys release the new video?" Brad shouted. "I didn't make it back to my hotel before my cell phone went crazy with calls. I want to know exactly what's happening!"

Quinn paused the satellite feed, freezing the image on the screen.

"Then shut up and watch," Hamer said. "You'll know as much as we do."

Brad's mouth opened and closed as if he'd considered then rejected the notion of protesting Hamer's lack of manners. It was either that, Quinn thought, or instant curiosity. The plasma screen showed a CNN talking head with a background photo of Jonathan Silver standing in front of a Freedom Christian University banner.

Brad took a spot beside Quinn.

Quinn used the remote to start the video, and the CNN talking head went through the breaking news, yada, yada spiel, explaining that they had an update on the bus tour of American tourists in Israel.

The clip cut to Jonathan Silver, looking haggard and dispirited, speaking into a video camera in short sound bites. The editing was poor, with quick shifting from one declaration to another. This clip had already been shown a half dozen times in the half hour that Quinn had been watching with Kate and Hamer.

"It is true I am a Christian." *Shift.* "I have raised money to support Israel, a land with a vibrant economy and a high standard of living." *Shift.* "I have not raised any money to help Palestinians badly in need of hospitals or schools." *Shift.* The background changed. Now Silver was in front of a podium. Unafraid. The clip was obviously from one of his television sermons. "The Palestinians are a tainted and brainwashed people."

Brad screamed at the television. "Enough!"

The television didn't listen.

The video cut to a hooded man who spoke directly into the camera. "The Americans are hostages of Red September. It is time for America to make up for decades of injustice and help the Palestinian people. We want $650 million to release them. The same amount evangelicals have raised for Israel."

The news clip cut back to the talking head. "It was a difficult decision to air this, but as we said at the beginning of this segment, Brad Silver, son of the prominent evangelical Jonathan Silver, confirmed that his father and a busload of tourists were captured and have gone missing. This video clip is from a Web site apparently set up by the kidnappers."

A Web address appeared on the screen.

"Keep in mind this is from a terrorist group that claims to be Muslim," the announcer said. "Among other things, it accuses American right-wing evangelicals of being the X factor in U.S.-Mideast policy. In the time since this story broke, we've had a chance to ask American Christian theologians to review some of the points on the Web site, and they all agree the depth of the apparently Muslim kidnappers' knowledge of evangelical Rapture theology is surprising. We'll be back with more on these startling accusations against Jonathan Silver and his followers after the break."

Quinn muted the television.

Hamer snorted. "It'll be a media frenzy. Whoever is behind this knows media. Controversy sells. The talking heads will get all points of view going here. And isn't Rapture theology some kind of sacred cow with evangelicals?"

"Misplaced metaphor," Quinn said with the barest hint of a smile. "Cows are sacred to Hindus. But point taken. There is a large force of evangelical believers in the U.S. who won't take kindly to this. It's a viewpoint on the end times called dispensationalism, and—"

"Won't take kindly?" Brad exploded. "Questioning dispensationalism is heresy!"

"Case in point," Quinn said to Hamer. Then he addressed Brad. "This isn't the time to go into it. Get Kevin, our tech guy, to help you download all the Web site information, then review it with us so that we can understand more about Safady's motivation."

"Who's got time for that?" Brad pulled out his cell phone. "You saw how much the liberal media loved the story. Any excuse to attack Christians. I need to do some serious damage control."

"Good media spin is better than a dead father?" Kate asked him.

"Spin I can control," Brad snapped. "At least I'm taking action, unlike the rest of you." He began to dial a number.

"Hamer," Quinn said, "tell him about the scrambling device in my office."

"Shut the power off," Hamer said. "He's got some high-tech thing that blocks cell reception. He hits a button, and you can't make or take calls."

Brad glanced back and forth between them. Quinn shrugged. Brad powered down the cell. He missed the small grin on Hamer's face.

Quinn stood. "Can you get someone in Mossad to find out how CNN was alerted to the Web site?" he asked Hamer. "After Kevin has downloaded everything, my advice is to shut down the server immediately. It's probably already had a million hits, but Safady would like another ten million, I'm sure."

Hamer nodded.

"Brad," Quinn said, "the sooner you do this the better. We're going to need your help reviewing it."

"See?" Brad's voice rose. "One minute of CNN coverage and you're ready to believe all those accusations. I need to get out of here and make some calls, get our people started on a countercampaign."

"Take a deep breath," Quinn said. "Those accusations are coming from a Muslim terrorist. Our first reaction is skepticism. What we really need to know is how Safady thinks the Web site is going to help him. And if it is helping him, we need to know the best way to counter that."

Brad stopped pacing.

"Besides," Quinn said, "if you want to defend the accusations, you need to know exactly what they are. I'll go to the Web site, and you walk me through it and tell me where it's wrong."

"Half an hour," Brad said. "Then give me an office down the hall where I can make some outgoing calls. Or shut off that scrambling thing and let me make some calls in here from my cell."

"Sure," Quinn said. "I can shut off the scrambler. No problem."

KHAN YUNIS, GAZA STRIP • 9:25 GMT

"You're trying to make a point by forcing us to eat with the children," Silver said to Esther. "I find it childish."

He stood in front of her, a dull and warped plate in one hand, a cup of milk in the other. He'd just stood in line cafeteria-style with the other Americans, who'd been forced to wait until all the Palestinian orphans had received lunch.

Silver's plate held what looked like rice, but he wasn't sure. There were dark spots and lighter spots in the mixture, and he wasn't about to taste to see which were meat and which weren't. He'd glanced at the kitchen and half suspected the protein in the rice might be flies or the shelled insects that seemed clustered everywhere in the orphanage.

"Remind me what that point might be," Esther said. "I suspect we have different perspectives on the definition of *childish*."

"Surely you have good food that you save for the administrators here. A place you eat privately. That's where we should be."

"I'm the only administrator," she said. "We're not much into upper management here."

"You can't get me to believe you eat like this every day. That you don't give yourself better treatment than what you want us to endure."

"I eat like this every day."

"Sure, Miss High-and-Mighty," he said, "like you'd drink this milk. I tried some in line. It tastes off. It's obviously been warm too long and has gone so bad it has little lumps in it."

Esther looked closely. "Those lumps are bits of powder. Sometimes the children don't stir it long enough before we serve."

"Powder?"

"Mr. Silver, you may take refrigeration for granted, but it's a luxury here. So is real milk. Powder is much less expensive and keeps indefinitely. Even so, we have to strictly ration the powder. Each child only gets two cups a day. It's the only kind of milk they've tasted, and it breaks my heart how much they love it."

"It's obvious to me that you enjoy lording this poverty thing over me like a badge of honor. As if it makes you a better person to be stuck in this miserable little prison."

"I hate this poverty with a depth you'll never understand," she said.

"You're an American citizen, right? No one forces you to stay here."

"I hate this poverty for these children. I remember my childhood—Christmas gifts, first bicycle, Fourth of July parades . . . My biggest security concern was what might happen if I turned in an overdue library book. They can't comprehend such a carefree, idyllic life. Don't you feel any compassion for them?"

"I founded and built a Christian ministry," he said. "You're helping twenty or thirty kids from month to month. That's nice, of course, but I've used my time and gifts to help thousands, if not hundreds of thousands."

"How many of them do you know?"

"My office gets bags of letters every day from grateful people."

"How many of them do you *know*?"

"The body of Christ has many members serving different capacities," Silver said, feeling heat. "Some visit the sick and feed the hungry. Me—I make it possible for others to do that. For that matter, I'm in a position to make sure that funds reach your little orphanage. If you were smart enough to realize that, you'd give better treatment to me and the rest of us."

"The Jesus I serve," she said, "cares for all His children and commands His followers to do the same."

"What's that supposed to mean?"

"When you figure it out, you tell me."

"What I've figured out is that your attitude makes this place more miserable than the food you serve. Here's what I think of both." Silver dropped his plate and glass. Made of plastic, neither shattered, but the rice mixture scattered across the tile floor and the milk spread in rivulets.

Esther knelt and scooped as much rice as possible onto the plate. From the floor, looking upward, she stared at him hard. "To make sure that you and your friends don't go hungry, we've had to cut in half what we normally give these children. The least you could have done was give that glass of milk to one of them."

Jonathan Silver stared back just as hard. Although he knew she was right and he felt shame for his impulsiveness, pride stopped him from apologizing.

The silence was broken by Alyiah's voice.

"*Seel-ver,*" she said. She was moving awkwardly toward them on one crutch, more slowly than usual because she was using her free hand to carry a glass of milk.

Alyiah spoke Arabic to Esther, then looked at Silver again.

"She asks me," Esther translated, "if it is all right for her to give you her milk. She feels horrible that you have lost yours."

Brad and Kate and Quinn sat in the conference chairs in the corner of Quinn's office. Kevin had created a mirror of Safady's Web site on a CCTI server so they could thoroughly review it, then had worked his magic to disable the live Web site. Quinn had printed off the first several pages so that all of them could have copies. It was easier than standing in front of the monitor. But Quinn didn't want them distracted by the Web site material yet.

"Brad," Quinn said, "for expediency, let me give Kate the quick overview of a dispensational viewpoint, and you tell me if I'm wrong or missed anything of importance."

Brad squinted. "Why would you know about this?"

"It's been rough since I lost my family," Quinn answered. "I'm not sure I could have made it without faith. But it's been rough on my faith, too. I've had lots of questions. I've spent lots of time in the Bible. And I've done plenty of digging to understand if everything I was taught as a child is accurate. Including dispensational eschatology. You're not going to like to hear this, but some nights I wonder how different the Middle East would be without it. Wonder if my wife and girl might still be alive."

"Outrageous!" Brad said. "It's a theology that—"

"—has led to skewed geopolitics," Quinn interrupted. "It's a theology that's become a huge backroom player in the Arab-Israeli conflict. Not many people are aware of its influence."

He smiled, almost apologetically. "Given the tribal hierarchy of the Palestinians and the security issues faced by our firm, you'd be surprised how often it's been helpful to have a grounding in the history of the Israeli-Palestinian conflict.

I've become the in-house guru. So, aside from personal faith issues, profession-
ally I'm well aware of the huge impact that money and lobbying by American
evangelicals have had on the geopolitics here. Frankly, I'm surprised it's taken so
long for terrorists to pick a target like your father."

"This isn't about geopolitics," Brad said. "God has chosen this land for Israel.
They have a divine right to it."

"Hence the term *dispensationalism*," Quinn said to Kate. "It's a method of
biblical interpretation that says God's plan for mankind is divided into eras—
dispensations—that will progress to the final end-times era. One of the foundations
of this theology is that God will fulfill His promises to two peoples: the church
of Christ and ethnic Israel."

"You can plainly see that the promise came to fruition when Israel became
a nation-state in 1948," Brad interjected. "That's evidence enough. Anyone who
tries to divide Israel is going against God's will."

"A view held by roughly seventy million evangelical Americans," Quinn said.
"And it's partially why CCTI is in business—Middle Eastern conflict. By definition,
anyone for a one-state solution is against a two-state solution. Moderate Palestinians and moderate Israelis want a two-state solution. Hard-line Israelis and hard-
line Palestinians each want the other state destroyed. For the most part, evangelical
Americans have aligned themselves with hard-line Israel."

"God blesses those who bless Israel," Brad said. "God curses those who curse
Israel. So be careful of what you say here."

"Are you getting the point here, Kate?" Quinn asked. "Politics determined by
theological interpretations. The X factor that gets very little attention."

"Your father has how many million supporters in his television audience?"
Kate asked Brad.

"Enough that Congress and the White House pay attention to him," Brad
answered proudly.

Kate nodded at Quinn. "Yeah, I'm getting the point. Tell me about the Rapture stuff. People getting sucked into thin air—something like that—others getting
left behind?"

"Well," Brad said, "if you look at some key verses in Revelation and the rest
of the Bible, you'll see that—"

"Nutshell," Quinn said. "This theology teaches that believers in Jesus will be
'raptured' to heaven during a secret coming of Christ, while nonbelievers will be
left behind to face a seven-year global Tribulation, ending with another return
of Christ to lead a victorious bloodbath against all His enemies at the Battle of
Armageddon; then finally, after a thousand-year reign, Christ will in effect have
another return to judge all the living and the dead of all mankind."

"Not only that," Brad said, "but all the indications are that the end of time is upon us. Wars, tribulations, earthquakes, and the return of the land to Israel. It could happen any day."

"Let me get this straight," Kate said. "A secret coming of Christ, a return of Christ at Armageddon seven years later, and a third one at the end of a thousand years. I should have paid more attention in Sunday school when I was a kid. It says in the New Testament that Jesus is coming back *three* different times?"

"Not specifically," Brad said quickly. "You need to study the Bible and especially Revelation and see how verses in one part of the Bible point to verses in another. This allows you to construct the time lines. Look, even seminary-trained preachers study for years before they fully understand it all. Sometimes it's best to rely on the experts."

Quinn looked past Brad at the open doorway of his office. A kid had appeared, maybe twenty years old, holding a can of Diet Coke. He was skinny, with stringy dark hair and a white pallor against his black jeans and black T-shirt. He looked like he'd been kidnapped from a suburban bedroom, where he spent all his daylight hours on a computer. Which was close to the truth.

Quinn stood. "Sorry for the interruption. Looks like Kevin, our IT genius, wants me for a second."

"You're not going anywhere," Kate told him.

"The doorway," Quinn said. "No farther."

"If you step into the hallway, I'll shoot you."

"Fair enough." It was difficult to decide if she was joking. Quinn handed the papers to Kate and Brad. "Can you guys start going through this?" He glanced at the clock on his wall. "If Safady contacts us when promised, we have half an hour."

They took the papers.

As Quinn moved to the doorway, he casually reached into his pocket for a folded note. He palmed it and, as he shook hands and greeted Kevin, gave him the note. "Any word on Roz?" he asked Kevin in a low voice.

"Nothing. No hospitals. No police reports."

Quinn let out a breath. Too much stuff all coming at him at once. Best thing to do was keep priorities in mind and focus. Whatever was happening with Roz was out of his control; there were thirty Americans depending on negotiations going well. That was priority.

"Tell me about your progress with Safady's computer."

"I went back into his system, crawled around. There was nothing to show he knew he'd been hacked. To be safe, I went into the logs and deleted all activity that could point to me. And I added a screen grabber program and something to record all his activity. It shouldn't eat up too much of his processing speed."

Screen grabber. Quinn would get the other side of Safady's next chat room conversation.

Kevin was grinning broadly now.

"Saving the best for last?" Quinn asked.

"Cracked the gateway provider," Kevin said. "We now have the physical address of his account."

KHAN YUNIS, GAZA STRIP • 9:39 GMT

Ray Klein was halfway through the window, getting help from Abe Williams, when Safady and three men armed with machine guns dragged him back inside.

"Don't look so surprised," Safady told them. "All the windows are wired to a silent alarm system." He raised his right hand and pointed his index finger at them.

The soldiers lifted their machine guns to point the barrels directly at the chests of the two men.

"No need to shoot," Klein said frantically. "We'll go back in with the others, no problem. There's no harm done, right?"

"It won't be that simple," Safady answered. A fly landed on the back of his hand. He brushed it away. "In about two hours, I'm going to need some dead hostages anyway."

Klein held up his hands, palm outward. "We can talk, can't we? Whatever you think you're going to get, I can add to it from my personal fortune. Same with Williams here. Right, Abe?"

Abe was licking his lips, eyes fixed on the barrels of the machine guns. "All of it. I have a great deal of money to offer you."

"Did it occur to either of you that this operation took some planning?" Safady asked.

"Sure," Klein said. "I'm a businessman. I know all about planning. Overhead, too. Like I said, we can help out."

"Do you think it was an accident you ended up in this building?"

"No," Klein said, shaking his head with exaggerated sincerity. "Your planning was good."

"Better than you realize," Safady said. "Satellite setup, alarm system, and electronic listening devices everywhere." He gave a regretful sigh. "What was it you called us repeatedly? Oh yes, stupid camel jockeys."

"I can explain," Klein said.

"You don't have a lot of time left. I'd use it in prayer instead." Safady gave a mocking smile and lifted his hand again as if he were holding an imaginary pistol. He pointed it at Klein and pulled the trigger.

CCTI HEADQUARTERS, TEL AVIV • 9:51 GMT

"Don't get too excited about the physical address," Quinn told Hamer.

Hamer was holding a cup of coffee, just taken from the gourmet espresso machine in the kitchen of Quinn's office suite, where he and Quinn stood.

"Come on. It's his physical address. We can get men there, surround it. Me—I get excited about a break like this."

"Putting IDF operatives in play would change this from a kidnapping situation to a hostage situation. More pressure."

"You won't have any say in this. I've got to pass this on to Zvi. He'll make the decision to contain the terrorists."

Quinn knew the politics well enough to know this was true. "You won't find the Americans there anyway."

"You've got the address. He's been using his computer."

"The address is an apartment in Jerusalem."

Hamer frowned.

"Exactly," Quinn said. "You don't hold thirty people captive in an apartment."

"He's not in the apartment, but his computer is. That means we can wait till he goes back to use his computer and take him then."

"All we can get from the gateway provider is the address of the account. Probably where he keeps his desktop computer. Say he jumps to it from a laptop via remote access."

Hamer glared. "Keep piling on the optimism."

"It's not a dead end," Quinn said. "Maybe there's something in his apartment that will give you an idea. If you're lucky, his desktop computer is there. Something on the hard drive might point you toward him. This was an organized operation. There's got to be a trail."

Hamer set his coffee down on a nearby counter. He hadn't taken a sip. "If there is, we'll find it. That's a promise."

Patterson stood with his back to the wall beside a window. He held a small mirror at arm's length, angled to let him watch the compound without showing his body at the window. The Palestinians approached the trucks with the wariness and silence of jackals skirting a wildebeest mired in mud. Fifteen, Patterson counted. Some held ground-to-air missile launchers, watching the sky in all directions. Patterson understood their caution. If this weapons cache had been tipped to IDF, for example, Israeli jets could swoop in. Thirty seconds from the first appearance of the jets on the horizon until the bombs cratered them.

The Palestinian leader waved them forward, and they advanced inside the compound. Half the men walked in backward, machine guns waist high, alert for danger.

Because of the briefing earlier, Patterson knew this was something Saxon had anticipated. Watching the Palestinians, it struck Patterson that Saxon's intel was extraordinarily good. Since leaving Afghanistan, every part of this operation had proceeded without flaw. In a way, it seemed wrong. No combat mission was perfect.

Patterson dismissed the thought. It was not the time to wonder. He kept watching the Palestinians in the compound.

This was a tricky moment. While the unit essentially had the compound surrounded from hidden vantage points, Saxon didn't want a protracted firefight. Nor did he want any of the Freedom Crusaders exposed unless it was necessary. If any of the Palestinians fled the compound too soon, the gunfire would have to begin too early.

Patterson found himself holding his breath, waiting for all the Palestinians to step inside an invisible perimeter.

Any second now . . .

CCTI HEADQUARTERS, TEL AVIV • 18:82 GMT

"CNN is reporting that Safady's Web site was also posted in Arabic for the Muslim world to read," Kate told Quinn. "It got millions of hits before it was shut down."

"Public relations is part of any terrorist's bag of weapons," Quinn said. "They do a better job than a lot of American PR firms. What did you learn from Brad about the Web site content?"

"Not much," Kate said. "We didn't get too far into it before he went ballistic."

"I'm not surprised." Quinn glanced through the printout from the Web site, noting the boldfaced points. "Freedom Christian University. The television ministry. All that money and power. Men in those kinds of positions in ministry have a lot to lose by allowing an open debate on the merits of their theology."

"Especially when that theology is based on racism," Kate said. "On principle, I hate to agree with a terrorist. What do you think?"

"If this man is Safady, as he claims, he's the one behind the bombing that destroyed my family," Quinn said. "You can't comprehend how strongly I believe the means to his end are utterly without justification. The fact that he's a terrorist will smear whatever truth there might be in his accusations."

She nodded. "Which implies you think there is a degree of truth in this."

Quinn was very still, pulling his emotions together before replying. "I think Americans want to believe this is an irrelevant theology battle that basically doesn't matter outside of church circles."

"Except?"

"First, there's a terrorist holding thirty Americans prisoner, and he's obviously motivated by this, so by definition it's not irrelevant to the situation. Second, Brad's reaction is telling me that the accusations cut close to the bone. And third, as I told Brad, this has been a concern to us at CCTI for years."

"Look at the headlines on the printout. They say this theology makes God a racist and a land broker and that evangelicals need to acknowledge their role in the oppression of Palestinians and the consequent reaction of terrorism."

"Kate, a lot of Americans support Israel without understanding those implications. How much money do you think evangelicals have raised for Israel in the last twenty years?"

"Safady says 650 million. That staggers me."

"Safady is wrong. Double it and you're much closer. Christian groups have helped impoverished nations all across the world, with the major exception of Palestine. American Christians have given $1.5 billion to aid Israel—one of the richest nations in the world—billions more to other nations all across the world, and barely more than pennies to ease the wretched conditions in Palestine. Think Arabs don't know this? Sends a clear message: God loves all people except them."

"But suggesting this theology might be responsible for 9/11?"

"Perhaps in part. Remember what I said earlier. I have an interest in this because it affects Mideast geopolitics."

"Hard to believe that theology would be more than, well, theology."

"Tell that to extremists in the Muslim world who misinterpret the Koran to justify acts of terrorism."

"Okay, I get what you're saying. But Christian theology?"

"Remember when Brad said that those who bless Israel will be blessed and those who curse Israel will be cursed?"

"Yes."

"That's the dispensationalists' viewpoint, and it reaches into the White House," Quinn said. "Since Reagan, every American president has had to deal with it. Even for those who don't believe it personally, it's a major influence."

"The hidden X factor."

"Right or wrong, plenty of stuff has been written blaming a Jewish lobby for influencing the White House, and there's hardly any public discussion about a far larger constituency—Christian Zionists. Think about the polarization of U.S. politics. Red states and blue states; secular liberals versus conservatives who are largely Christian with a very fundamental, literal approach to reading the Bible. Jonathan Silver is right at the head of the pack. I doubt many politicians care personally about the theology, but they listen to voters. A Republican president will be very aware of a constituency of seventy million right-wing Christians who believe Israel has a divine right to the land. Even a Democrat like Clinton couldn't escape the pressure."

"Clinton?"

"In 1998," Quinn said, "evangelical leaders threatened to mobilize thousands of pastors if President Clinton continued to pressure Israel into peace efforts. Clinton backed down. That's when I first decided I needed to know as much as possible about this theology, long before I had reasons to reflect on my personal faith. By backing away from a two-state solution, Clinton essentially did nothing to stop both sides fighting for a one-state solution."

"But to say that evangelicals are partially responsible for terrorism attacks . . . ?"

Quinn gave her a tight grin. "Keep in mind, that accusation comes from a terrorist's Web site."

"You're saying I should discount it."

"I'm saying, time and again you'll read of angry young Muslim men all across the Arab world who cite that their main reason for hatred of the U.S. is American support for Israel, beginning a half century ago, when hundreds of thousands of Palestinians were forcibly removed from this land. They believe Israel would not exist in the middle of the Arab world without help from the world's super-power. For them, Jewish occupation of land that once belonged to Palestinians is a continued reminder to a very proud people that the West has defeated them and humiliated them. To the Muslims, this perception is their truth, and men like Jonathan Silver don't help when they declare God is punishing an Israeli prime minister with health problems for trying to divide the land. You and I may understand Jonathan Silver doesn't represent all Christians or all Americans, but that's not so easy for Arabs to understand."

"If the Israelis had a divine right to the land, then what?"

"Is that argument relevant to what the angry young Arabs think?"

"No," Kate said, "but it obviously is to the seventy million Americans who are very pro-Israel because of this theology."

"Fair enough," Quinn said. "Just for the record then, evangelicals disagree markedly among themselves on Israel's divine right to the land. During His time on earth, Christ refused to help the Jews of His day overthrow the Romans. His stated mission was to establish a heavenly kingdom, not an earthly one. Furthermore, the apostle Paul wrote that the true Israel includes all of those with faith in the divine Christ—Jews or non-Jews. In short, according to many Christians, God is neither a racist nor a land broker."

"You sound anti-Jewish," Kate said. "Pro-Palestinian."

"That's the first accusation someone like Jonathan Silver would throw at anyone who argues with him, which is not only a successful bully distraction from the examination of his theology but highly ironic. Evangelicals like Jonathan Silver have raised literally millions and millions of dollars to help gather the Jews of the world in a small geographic location, expecting fulfilled prophecies will shortly lead to the bloodbath of Armageddon, where two-thirds of these Jews will be slaughtered. Jonathan Silver says God gives Christians all of eternal paradise but promises Jews only a slice of land beside the Mediterranean. You tell me who is anti-Semitic."

"You've ducked my question about your personal feelings toward Jews. Or Palestinians."

"My wife was Jewish, and my daughter because of it," Quinn said quietly. "I love this land and this people. I'm not pro-Jew or pro-Palestine. I'm pro-people and pro-peace. And pro-children."

Kate cocked her head slightly, listening with intensity.

"In the Gaza Strip, 13 percent of Palestinian children under age five have severe malnutrition," Quinn said. "This where half the population is under age eighteen and over two-thirds of Palestinians live on two dollars a day. That puts conditions on par with Somalia. Nothing is going to change for these children until there is peace."

"Point taken," Kate said, just as quietly.

"In terms of American policy, I don't think crucial geopolitical decisions should be affected by a popular theology that is rarely examined for its validity." Quinn was talking with some heat now. "The past can't be changed, and both sides can argue all they want whether Israel has a right to exist. What matters is that regardless of the events over a half century ago that started the division, now the majority of the people in this land—Palestinians and Jews—simply want to coexist in peace. Israel must fight the way it has to protect its people and, I think, has practiced remarkable restraint in some ways, given its military advantage in this conflict. For the Jews, it's not an ideological battle but one of necessity. Theology? That's a battle between some Christians and some Muslims—extremists on both sides. Radical Islam is extremely anti-Semitic in nature."

"How generous," Kate said sarcastically, "suggesting that perhaps Palestinians bear some guilt here. I haven't read reports about Jews or Christians strapping on bombs and walking into crowded markets."

Quinn put up a hand. "The real horror to me is that it's not about ideology for the majority of Palestinians either. They're mothers and fathers who just want a place to raise their children. They're helpless against the radical Muslim ideology that keeps the conflict going. It's no accident that terrorists are young, single males who have nothing more important in their lives than hatred-centered theology based on a misinterpretation of the Koran. Perhaps there is a case to be made, then, that Jonathan Silver's Rapture ideology is like throwing gas on the fire started by Muslim extremists. If so, it's doubly important for this theology to be examined, especially if it has the blind support of seventy million or more Americans."

Quinn closed his eyes for a few moments, then looked directly at Kate. "Keep in mind that I have a bias too. I'm not sitting in a comfortable pew somewhere on the other side of the Atlantic putting money in a collection plate for Israel. I'm among those who have lost family to the bombings. Over there, it's an abstraction. Here . . ."

He paced away, then paced back. "I'll do my best to keep those emotions out of this. Aside from that, did I manage to give you a sense of how theology has had an impact on the conflict between the Muslim world and the West?"

Kate nodded. It was an awkward silence, the baring of Quinn's grief all the more poignant because of how much effort he was putting into pretending it didn't exist.

Quinn shuffled through the papers. "Let's set aside the theology. Is there anything you find remarkable about the Web site as a cop wondering about the kidnapper?"

Kate thought for a moment. "If the kidnapping was only for money, it's strange that all this effort has been put into the Web site. But if the kidnapping was driven by emotional motivation, it's strange that the Web site arguments are not rants but laid out in relatively unemotional language to present a compelling case. Either way, this material doesn't seem like it belongs here."

"I agree," Quinn said. "Go a step further. Is this Web site a defense of the Palestinian cause?"

Kate gave a puzzled look.

"At the 1972 Olympics in Munich, Palestinian terrorists used the hostage taking to draw worldwide attention to the plight of Palestinians. Terrorists nearly always justify their actions by arguing their cause. Back then, I'm sure they would have used a Web site in the same way Safady's doing now."

"You're saying this Web site doesn't argue *for* a cause or ideology but *against* one."

"You've seen CNN's feeding frenzy. Al Jazeera is covering it just as much. A kidnapping like this guarantees full-scale media attention. Setting up the Web site and releasing the video show media savvy. Cynical as it sounds, the airtime the media will give this until it is resolved is the equivalent of getting a string of Super Bowl ads for no charge. Maybe even the halftime show. A media savvy person or organization knows the smart move would be to position your product, not use the opportunity to draw attention to the obscure product of a competitor. I have to assume we're dealing with a smart group. The logistics behind a successful kidnapping of thirty Americans from a guarded tour bus is proof of it. So that leaves the important question: why is this terrorist or terrorist cell choosing to highlight a theology that's largely been ignored in this conflict instead of showcasing injustice against the Palestinians?"

"You have an answer?" Kate asked.

"Just that for some reason Silver is being set up here," Quinn said. "And a gut feeling that we don't know half of what's happening."

DAYR AL-BALAH, GAZA STRIP • 18:03 GMT

The ground around the Palestinians seemed to burst with a muted pop where demolitions had buried a large circle of smoke and tear gas canisters in the sand. Instantly, billowing clouds hid the Palestinians. But Patterson knew, of course, what was happening inside the cloud. The Palestinians would be on their knees, fighting for air, each desperate breath filling their lungs with more paralyzing gas.

There was no need for Patterson to hide any longer. He stepped to the window. Burge joined him, lifting his machine gun and pointing it at the cloud in the compound, maybe fifty yards away.

One man stumbled out of the smoke, falling on the ground, convulsing.

Burge snapped off a burst of shots, stitching the sand around the prostrate

Palestinian. The dust danced as more bullets rained in from other buildings, and within a couple of heartbeats, the man's body had been shredded.

Other Palestinians emerged from the wall of smoke in the same disoriented panic as the first. Bullets lifted and flung them as if they were marionettes jerked by strings.

"Like rats from a burning building," chortled Burge. "Come on!" He fired another burst from his machine gun. By then, maybe seven Palestinians were on the ground, bodies heaped as if thrown from a ladder.

Return gunfire came from inside the smoke.

Patterson guessed the ones inside were finally realizing what was happening and were firing at random at their unseen enemy. But it wouldn't matter. The Freedom Crusaders were protected by the buildings and could afford to wait to pick them off one by one, even if it took until the smoke and tear gas dispersed. Saxon wouldn't call off the firefight until the body count in the compound reached fifteen—100 percent enemy casualties.

Patterson was supposed to contribute to the slaughter. He knew that Burge would find it odd if he didn't. So he fired bursts from his position at the window into areas he knew would not hit the men hidden in the cloud of tear gas, enough bursts to make it look like he was taking the same joy in this death and destruction.

Then he tapped Burge on the shoulder and pointed at the red and black heifer.

Burge nodded and Patterson took advantage of the excuse to retreat from the window.

He reached the heifer and patted it. If Burge happened to look back, it would appear as if Patterson were trying to calm it in the chaos of the gunfire.

But Burge didn't seem interested in Patterson. He was too intent on picking off escaping enemies and yahooing each time a new one fell.

For a temporary office, Safady had set up his laptop in a small, dark storage room, with cables running from the computer under the door to a satellite hookup.

Safady sat in front of his laptop and watched a video clip of the execution of the two Americans who had tried to escape the orphanage. A shame he couldn't put that on his Web site, but as expected, it had been shut down. Didn't matter. The media had served him well to promote it, and it had accomplished what was necessary. Praise Allah for the greed of Western media. Terror only worked because of it. Forget whether a falling tree made noise in an empty forest; the relevant question was whether a bomb would make any sound if it went off and no media reported it. Safady knew the answer. If bombings didn't make headlines, how could terrorists inflict terror on the rest of the population?

As for the latest execution clip, he'd send it out via e-mail to a few contacts, and within hours it would spread across the world. In the short term, he needed his computer for something else.

Safady watched the computer clock until it was the precise moment to enter his password. Moments later, his Mossad contact initiated the chat, and words appeared on the screen.

> **Host:** When it rains in the park, who is happiest?
>
> **Guest:** A parched pigeon.
>
> **Host:** Your computer has been found in the Jerusalem apartment.

There would be crowing at the Mossad over that, Safady thought. Fools. If Safady had wanted to be traceless, it would have happened. He clicked his response.

> **Guest:** Took long enough. Do they need guidance to find
> me too?

> **Host:** They have the hard drive now. I expect they will
> learn your location immediately. The son will leak it to
> the media immediately after that. Watch CNN.

Only because Safady had practically drawn a map and left it on his hard drive. He keyboarded his next question as an order and took satisfaction in it.

> **Guest:** Report to me the gun shipment into Gaza. Was
> the operation a success?

> **Host:** Total casualties.

The Mossad was so easy to manipulate. Imagine that—helping Safady set up gun battles that killed his tribal rivals in Gaza. When he was ready, Safady would emerge to lead all of Palestine, revered like Arafat but feared like the Red Prince at Munich. The only difference was that Safady would become a figurehead for the entire Muslim world.

Safady responded with a change of direction in the chat room conversation.

> **Guest:** It is not enough that you have placed Quinn as
> negotiator. I will demand that he be sent into Gaza. Con-
> firm that you understand and will make adequate prepara-
> tions.

> **Host:** Confirmed. All you need to do is ask, and we
> will permit it.

Safady was tempted to spend more time in the chat room to debase the Mossad mole. But there were more immediate and more satisfying actions to be accomplished. Safady cut off the power to his laptop without acknowledging the confirmation or bothering to make arrangements for their next communication. He stood, planning out the next few minutes.

Next he needed one of the orphans.

An image sprang to his mind. Yes, he thought, it would not be difficult to choose.

CCII HEADQUARTERS, TEL AVIV • 18:26 GMT

"Let me read off a list of terrorists who were executed," Kate said. "The ones on a list as belonging to Red September."

Quinn was on his back on the leather couch, staring at the ceiling. He wanted sleep, but caffeine and adrenaline were pounding him with equal force, and he knew it would be useless to try. He'd been thinking about Roz, wondering how and why Roz had disappeared and who had taken him, when Kate had pulled up a chair to sit beside him.

"Don't bother," he said. He kept his eyes on the ceiling. "You'll mangle the pronunciations."

"An American prosecutor probably would too," she answered. "But I don't think a jury would find that relevant. Not when they discover that all those men were murdered after you tracked them down. If you're ever going to persuade a jury you didn't kill them, first you need to persuade me."

"I didn't kill them," he said.

"Then tell me what happened in Vegas. You were there. You can't deny you were there."

"Are you going to believe me?"

"I'll find a way to either confirm or disprove whatever you tell me. But I'd be hoping the whole time to find out you're telling the truth. Give me something I can go on."

"And here I'd almost forgotten that you were guarding me with the sole purpose of taking me back to the U.S. for a trial and execution. Funny how worrying about the lives of thirty other terrified people seems more important right now. Instead, you're right in the middle of cop work."

She leaned forward and put her hand on his arm. It startled him, but he didn't pull away. "I think I understand."

Quinn closed his eyes. He couldn't help a small smile. "Impressive," he said. Her hand was still there. It had been how long since he'd experienced even a small intimacy like this? He didn't want it to end, but at Acco Harbor, she'd already fooled him once.

"Impressive?" she repeated.

"The soft touch. Your empathy sounds real enough to encourage a person to share. But by not specifying what it is you understand, you're leaving the door open to learn the unexpected. Like pulling on a string to see what unravels."

She pulled her hand away. "I'm not that calculating."

"Right. Yesterday, how clear was it that you were inviting me to dinner to ask me questions about murder and extradition?"

"That *was* cop work," she said. "Black-and-white. Good guy, bad guy. Me the good guy."

"And catch the bad guy by any method possible."

"Back in Vegas, you are the main suspect in a brutal murder. Back in Vegas, terrorist attacks and bombings are abstract. Just part of the daily media filler. Here it's real. Somebody is holding thirty people and, for all we know, getting ready to kill them. Maybe I'm beginning to understand what would motivate a person to fight outside the law."

"Make sure to write a letter to the editor of the local paper," Quinn said. "Help others develop sympathy too."

"Classic male tactic," she said. "Avoidance and pretend cynicism, with just enough sarcasm to bully a woman into silence."

"I doubt you bully easy, but I can hope."

"What I'm trying to say is that suddenly this whole situation is not so black-and-white to me. I like black-and-white. Gray is not good in my job. Gray makes decisions difficult. Black-and-white is much easier."

"What a shame, living in a world without color."

"Black-and-white to me is that it's against the law to murder someone, even if the motives can be justified. Being here, so close to what's happening, is showing me the gray. Maybe I can understand why a man would cold-bloodedly track down other men and eliminate them one by one."

Quinn swung his legs off the couch and sat up. They faced each other, within reaching distance of one another. It made him aware of her attractiveness all over again.

"What I'm saying," she continued, "is regardless of the evidence against you, it might not matter if you could get a jury to fully understand how this fanaticism has no regard for the destruction of lives, how a man would want to revenge the death of his wife and daughter against this fanaticism."

"You're suggesting justification for murder is all a jury would need to hear," Quinn said, his throat so tight he could hardly speak above a whisper. "Convince them that revenge is not black-and-white but gray? Even for a man who says his faith in Jesus as a man of love is the only thing keeping him together? That revenge is something Jesus would applaud?"

She nodded.

He needed to take a breath, to hold back the rush of horror and pain and sadness that came with the memories. Time hadn't healed his wounds, only buried them, and when something brought them back to the surface, the vividness was like a blow.

"You have no idea," he said. "People would say, 'I'm so sorry for you. We know what you must be going through. You're in our prayers.' Sympathy, yes; prayers, yes; but don't dare tell me that you know what it must be like. Not even a parent who has lost a child can explain it well enough to another parent who has lost a child. It is so searingly devastating that nothing—absolutely nothing—can take away that pain."

Kate put her hands together in her lap and had the sense not to nod as if she understood.

"Revenge?" Quinn said. "If you don't understand the pain of losing a child, you can believe that looking for revenge is a way to deal with it. But if you did understand—which you can't—you'd know how futile revenge is as a reason to stay alive and hang on through the pain to track them down. How about hope instead, that as each terrorist is arrested, it means one less who can harm another child. One less animal who can put another mother or father into a place of hell that no other human can understand."

Quinn's need for catharsis ended in that rush of words.

"So," Kate said after a long silence, "gray is discovering maybe the law needs to be set aside if it saves innocent lives."

"You discover what you need to," Quinn said. "I've already discovered more than what I want."

It hurt just talking about how much it hurt. He could feel his little girl's arms around his neck as if he'd just set her down and she'd just giggled and run from the office. And in the same moment, he could hear the wailing of sirens and smell the cordite and the burned wreckage that had torn the breath from his lungs as he wandered through the devastation of the exploded bus.

Abruptly Quinn stood and walked out of the office and into the kitchen. Kate didn't follow.

Quinn was staring sightlessly at the far wall, waiting for his frustration to dissolve, when the door to the kitchen area opened. He didn't turn.

"Quinn."

It was Hamer.

"Yeah." Quinn's voice was flat.

"We found the hard drive in that Jerusalem apartment," Hamer said. "It was a gold mine. We've located Safady and the Americans."

"You don't look happy about it."

"It's about to become a hostage situation."

"I thought we were going to keep it from becoming a hostage situation for as long as possible."

"IDF won't have a choice," Hamer said. "Someone leaked it already. CNN is updating the entire world on this."

22

afady marched toward Jonathan Silver, flanked by a half dozen Palestinian men carrying machine guns. The children playing around the beds looked up, then continued playing. Silver, sitting on the edge of his own bed, remained in place.

"Last night," Safady said, "did I make it clear that there would be consequences if anyone tried to escape?"

Silver nodded. His focus was on Safady's hands. The Black Prince carried a grenade in his right hand, duct tape in his left.

"You heard those shots?" Safady snarled.

Silver closed his eyes and nodded again. Klein and Williams. He didn't need to be told. His gut told him that they'd failed.

"Two of your men were just executed. One was caught trying to help the other through a window." Safady didn't wait for a response. He pointed at Silver. Two of the Palestinian men stepped forward. One jabbed the barrel of his machine gun in Silver's belly.

All noise ended in the dorm. The children became still.

"Stand," Safady ordered Silver. "Remove your shirt."

"You can't shoot me," Silver said, fighting the urge to blubber. "I didn't tell them to try it. I'm not responsible."

Safady tucked the roll of duct tape under his opposite arm to give himself a free hand. He reached over the machine gun still pushed against Silver's belly and pinched Silver's nostrils shut. "You've forgotten that I control the air you breathe. Stand. Strip to your waist. Or the tape will go around your face instead of your chest."

Silver found the strength to stand. With trembling arms, he lifted his shirt over his head. He was acutely aware of his nakedness. Although he still wore pants and shoes, he was ashamed of his flab and his wrinkled, old skin, especially with the eyes of the children and of all the other Americans on him.

"Turn around," Safady said.

Was this how it would happen? A bullet in the back of the skull?

Silver turned. He forced himself to find some pride. A few tears escaped his eyes, but he managed to keep any sound from escaping.

Dear God, he prayed silently, hoping he'd be given enough time to finish his prayer, *please take me home to You. Please forgive all the wrongs I have done. I pray in Jesus' name. Amen.*

Would he even hear the sound, he wondered. Feel the impact of the bullet against his skull? Or would he die without realizing it?

The sensation he felt next was of something cold against his spine, halfway up his back. Something round. It took a moment to comprehend.

It was the grenade.

There was a ripping sound. Duct tape, peeled back from the roll, pressed against his skin. There was movement at his chest. Silver glanced down and saw a pair of hands. Again, another flash of comprehension. Safady was taping the grenade to his back!

Safady was thorough. He wrapped the tape four times around Silver, saying nothing. Then he spun Silver around again.

One of Safady's men carried a spool of thin cable and a pair of pliers.

Safady gave a quick order in Arabic. The man knelt at the side of the bunk bed and wrapped one end of the cable around one of the bed's support struts. He fumbled in his pocket and brought out a small piece of metal, obviously designed to be crimped. He used the pliers to attach the loose end to the main strand of the cable and crimped the loop together.

"Are you starting to understand?" Safady asked Silver.

"You are going to use the cable to tie me to the bunk."

"No," Safady said. His smiled showed cold pleasure. "The end that you see around the bed cannot be removed, of course. The loop at the other end you won't be able to see, but trust me, it will be equally impossible to pull apart."

Safady placed a hand on Silver's shoulder and spun him around one more time. "Hold still," he warned. "This is the delicate part. You see, I'm attaching the end of this cable to the pin on the grenade strapped to your back."

Silver froze and held his breath.

"Ah. I can see that you are beginning to understand the concept." Safady's fingers brushed against Silver's back repeatedly as he hooked the cable to the grenade's pin. "Don't move yet." He wrapped one more round of tape around Silver's chest and back, securing the grenade, then stepped back and admired his work.

He gave a couple of slight nods with a hint of a smile at the corners of his mouth. "Think of it as a leash. If you pull too hard or try to go any farther than the length of the cable, you'll pull the pin loose. That will give you about five seconds until the grenade blows you apart."

"Wait," Silver croaked. "When I have to go to the bathroom . . . ?"

"Interesting, don't you think? A man of your wealth, power, and means, yet in the end, it always comes down to the elemental human needs."

Safady pulled on the blanket that covered the mattress. "These men are going to make sure every one of you is wired like this. We're going to nail these blankets to the beds—" he tapped the top of the frame—"and tent each of you in place. No communications. If we hear noise, we shoot first, no questions asked."

"Bathroom." Silver already felt pressure on his bladder.

"Every hour the child that is assigned to you will appear with a plastic bucket. If you can't wait that long, too bad."

Safady tapped his teeth as he studied Silver. He opened his eyes wide, theatrically. "I almost forgot," he said in a tone that implied the opposite. "I did promise that if anyone tried to escape, I would execute a child as well."

CANNE TAL, GAZA STRIP • 18:27 GMT

Patterson and Orphan Annie were well to the side of the two trucks when a couple of the Freedom Crusaders opened a crate Saxon had specified for unloading.

Twenty minutes earlier, the unit had driven the trucks away from the scene of the slaughter in Dayr al-Balah. As Saxon had promised, the five minutes of machine-gun fire hadn't drawn the attention of authorities; it was a common sound in Gaza, and most residents ignored it.

Now, after a slow drive through the chaos of roads crowded with ancient vehicles, the men and the trucks were in a dusty orchard just outside a village that looked as depressing and dreary as the other villages and towns in the area.

Patterson didn't know what the plan was; none of the other soldiers did either. Saxon was playing this one step at a time.

The soldiers naturally indulged their curiosity as the crate was opened. Patterson saw an odd mixture of drab, olive-colored uniforms and luxurious, extravagantly colored capes.

"Shut the lid," Saxon barked.

The two soldiers who had just jimmied it open gave him a quizzical look.

"Now!" Saxon was furious.

The soldiers complied.

"What was the number on that box?" Saxon asked.

"Five."

Saxon pulled a piece of paper from his shirt pocket and consulted it. He shook his head in disgust. "Number seven—that's the one we want."

It took a few minutes of grunting and pushing to put the first crate back in place and find the other one. The soldiers in charge remained on top of the flatbed with the crate. Saxon hopped up and supervised the opening of this one. Once he saw the contents, he gave approval for it to be lifted down.

The lid was pulled off completely. Patterson saw small canisters, similar to the smoke and tear gas containers that had been used in the compound. The crate also contained gas masks. Saxon gave an order for the masks to be distributed, then commanded the men to hide them inside their shirts as well as possible.

The process took only minutes.

Saxon motioned for the men to get back onto the farm trucks. Whatever the next step was, Patterson had no doubt it involved another overwhelming advantage for the Freedom Crusaders.

KHAN YUNIS, GAZA STRIP • 18:34 GMT

In front of Safady, Alyiah stood motionless on her crutches. She had a tentative smile on her face. Two men behind Safady pointed machine guns at Silver.

"Up," Safady said.

Silver glanced at the thin cable that connected the bunk to the release pin of the grenade duct-taped to his back.

"If you think blowing yourself up in the next few seconds will kill me," Safady said, "you are wrong. I can clear the room before the grenade goes off. But this girl will die with you. She is not as fast on her crutches."

Silver had not thought of a suicide bombing. He wasn't that brave. Slowly he stood and inched away from the bed.

Safady nodded at his men. One of them placed the barrel of his machine gun against Alyiah's temple.

Is she going to be executed because of the failed escape attempt by Klein and Williams?

"When I tell you," Safady said, "you will state your name and confirm for me that there is a girl here and that I am able to have her killed. Do you understand?"

"Don't shoot her," Silver began to plead but was cut short when Safady punched him in the stomach. Silver gagged, swallowed, and stiffly fell back on the mattress, terrified that too much movement would jerk the pin loose from the grenade.

"Stand up," Safady said calmly. "When I tell you, you will state your name and confirm for me that there is a girl here and that I am able to have her killed. Yes?"

"Yes," Silver gasped.

Safady punched some buttons on his cell phone and put it on speaker-phone.

"Quinn," a voice answered.

Safady nodded at Silver. "Now."

"This is Jonathan Silver. I am confirming for Khaled Safady that he has a girl in front of him and is ready to kill her."

Safady took the phone off speaker and smiled at Silver as if the man were a dog that had performed a good trick.

Then Safady transformed himself into rage.

"Two Americans tried to escape!" he screamed into the phone. "I will kill two people for this. Before we end this call, two people—one American, one child."

Slow down," Quinn said into the phone.

"What don't you understand?" Safady screamed. "Now the hostages pay the price!"

"We need to talk about this," Quinn said. "If you keep them alive, we can negotiate."

"And maybe I will kill four people instead of two." Safady's breathing was ragged.

Slow it down, Quinn thought. *Get him talking conversationally.*

"I want trust between us," Quinn answered. "I want you to trust me. I want to be able to trust you."

"Trust? It's all over CNN. The Mossad has located me. You tell me if this is true or if the media has a bad source. Then I'll trust you."

"Let me speak to the Mossad. I don't have that answer."

"Did you hear what Silver said? Do you want the girl killed?"

"I will do what I can," Quinn said. "But I can't do the impossible. If you want to accomplish your goals, you need to keep that in mind. If you kill the girl over something that I have no control over, how can we negotiate long enough for you to get what you want?"

"If the report on CNN is true," Safady said, "what does the Mossad have planned? Let's talk about that. I swear if I see any soldiers, every American and every orphan will die in here with me."

"All I can do is pass on your request and respond as soon as I hear." Quinn wrote on a pad. *Let me confirm Mossad knows his location. Telling truth now helps in negotiations later.*

"Do not lie to me," Safady said. "I'm holding a machine gun to the head of a little girl."

Quinn knew his orders—to reveal nothing about any Mossad or IDF plans. He pushed the pad toward Hamer.

Hamer glanced at it, then shook his head to emphasize the order. *No!*

"You don't need to hurt anyone," Quinn said to Safady. "If you do, there's no turning back. It will change everything."

"So will lying to me. Listen to this."

Quinn heard a click on the other end. The release of the safety on the machine gun? Then a muted whimper.

"That's the girl. And here's someone else."

A moment's silence. Then, "This is Jonathan Silver again. I promise he is serious about his threat. Please—" Silver gurgled as if struck.

"There," Safady said. "I have one American in front of me. And one girl. Tell me you know where we are. If I don't believe your answer, she dies. If I don't believe your answer after that, Silver dies."

Hamer shook his head no again, writing on the pad, *Don't reveal what Mossad knows.*

"Yes," Quinn said to Safady. "Mossad knows where you are."

Hamer slammed his fist on the desk.

Quinn stared back at Hamer and spoke calmly into the phone. "If you kill the girl now, then I'll have no reason to continue telling the truth. Understand?"

"What does Mossad plan next?"

"I can't answer an open-ended question like that. How can I know from my office in Tel Aviv?"

"You must know what the Israeli government has decided to do next. Is a special-operations team surrounding us?"

"That's another question I can't answer. Don't hold me responsible for what the government might keep secret from me."

"But you knew we had been located. You didn't tell me that."

"There were some who felt I should tell you immediately. Some disagreed. I am not a decision maker, only a go-between."

"Yet you did make a decision." Safady's voice was deadly. "I think you just told me another lie. Lying to me has severe consequences."

"What do you think was the lie?" But Quinn knew what his mistake had been.

"You made a decision without them. You had a choice between the girl's death or telling me the truth. The fact that you answered tells me you are not the go-between you try to pretend to be. I think I will kill her now for the lie."

"Let me read to you what I wrote about you on a pad at the beginning of our conversation." Now Quinn was improvising, but he didn't change the calm tone of his voice. "He is willing to use a landline or cell phone to call instead of using Internet video because he already knows you have found him and has no need to try to hide his location from a landline trace or GPS."

Quinn paused. "I passed that note to the official in charge as our conversation continued. Because of it, I was allowed to tell you that we know of your location."

Quinn had long ago learned not to hold his breath during tense moments in negotiating. It was a signal to the person on the other end. But it took effort to breathe evenly over the next five seconds of silence.

"You have one half hour to wire $10 million to my account. I have e-mailed the account number to Mossad," Safady said.

Quinn felt some relief. This wasn't ideology. Safady wanted money. That meant he was likely to continue negotiations instead of killing people.

"No one dies yet," Safady finally said, confirming Quinn's hunch. "You have half an hour to find out and report back to me what military operation the Israelis have planned."

"I'm not sure I will be given that information. Even if I am, I'm not sure it will do you any good."

"That is for me to decide. Half an hour. Or the first dead American will be thrown onto the streets. Maybe I'll call CNN and let them film it."

KHAN YUNIS, GAZA STRIP • 18:38 GMT

"Patterson, you're worth more to me alive than dead," Saxon said.

"Glad to hear it, sir," Patterson said dryly. "Is that because there's no one else to handle the heifer?"

Saxon had motioned for Patterson to step away from the Freedom Crusaders for a private conversation. The trucks were parked in an alley in a poverty-stricken residential section of Khan Yunis, which to Patterson looked like all the other areas of the city that he'd seen so far. Patterson had a grip on the halter, and Orphan Annie stood placidly beside them. Given that they had just passed an open-air market where butchers were slaughtering chickens on blocks, the presence of a heifer did not make them look out of place. Saxon had informed the soldiers it would be a while before the next phase of the operation.

"Don't think your duty guarding that heifer is a joke," Saxon said, moving his face to within inches of Patterson's. "Understand?"

Patterson didn't understand. So far, this was a lot of work for a red and black heifer. What could be so important about it? Now was not the time to ask, Patterson wisely decided.

Saxon nodded in satisfaction at Patterson's silence. "You're worth more to me alive than dead because this is a unit of twenty highly trained men. I can't afford to lose even one for this final operation."

Saxon's jaw tightened when he stopped speaking. He began again after a pause that indicated he was grappling for the way to proceed with whatever he had decided Patterson needed to be told. "Seems to me that I'm on the verge of losing you anyway."

"Sir?"

"I'm not stupid, Patterson," Saxon snapped.

"No, sir."

"Burge told me you weren't exactly contributing to our last conflict."

Patterson bit off his reply. It had been too one-sided to be called a conflict.

"You might wonder why I'd even ask Burge such a thing," Saxon went on. "But you're not the committed solider you were when you left our training camp. I can see it. So can the others in our unit." Saxon stared him down, daring Patterson to disagree.

Patterson stared back. It struck him how odd this was, hearing the American accent come from the face of a man with dyed black hair and beard, dark contact lenses, skin colored with dark bronze tanning lotion—a man in clothing that would allow him to walk the streets of this poverty-stricken Arab village and not attract a second glance. Even odder for Patterson was knowing that he appeared the same to Saxon.

"This mission is so important," Saxon said, "that there is no way in the world I can let you walk away from it. What little you know about it is already too much. If you did try to walk, as you threatened me a few months ago, I'd have you shot. And there isn't a man in this unit that wouldn't do it. They believe in our cause."

The implication was unspoken but there. *You don't.*

"I'm going to tell you more about what's ahead just so you understand what's at stake. There's an orphanage up the street. See it? An old army barracks, once a school, now set up to hold the kids. I know every wall, every door, and every window. Not because I've been in it, but because I've studied the floor plan for the last two weeks so that I could walk it blindfolded if I needed to."

Saxon pointed.

The low, square building overlooked the alley and the squalid, mud-walled houses on the other side.

"Jonathan Silver is in there," Saxon said.

Patterson blinked.

"I thought that would get your attention." Saxon's teeth flashed in his dark beard. The tight smile, however, was gone as quickly as it had appeared. "Yeah. Jonathan Silver. And a busload of American hostages. Held by Muslim terrorists.

The Americans were kidnapped yesterday. It's our job to get them out alive. Does that motivate you?"

Patterson nodded, but he was thinking about the significance of Saxon's having studied the floor plan of the orphanage for two weeks. That a lot of planning had obviously gone into getting the men into Gaza with weapons. That one of the crates held clothing that made no sense at all, especially in terms of a hostage rescue. And that the Americans had been kidnapped only a day ago. Something bigger was going on. And why was Saxon telling him this and letting him realize it?

"We need you," Saxon said. "A lot of money and time went into training you because every single man in this unit matters to our goal. I can't afford to have you with us if you aren't committed. I can't afford to not have you with us. Understood?"

"Understood," Patterson said.

"Good. Unfortunately, it's not quite that simple. I haven't forgotten how you forced me to let you phone your wife. Call it what you want, but it was an act of insubordination and I haven't trusted you since. Fact is, no matter what you might say to me right now, I still won't trust you. That's why we're having this talk. Because it's what I'm going to say to you next that will allow me to trust you."

"Sir, you can—"

"Shut up, Patterson. You don't have any idea how big this is. So I'm going to tell you. You know our military unit is only a small part of a secret network of Christians dedicated to striking back at the network established by Islamic terrorists. All across America, men of influence and power are helping fight the war. All of them Freedom Crusaders, though not all of them soldiers. But you might not know exactly how far the reach is. Except if you were back in Georgia, you would, because you would have heard that your wife has disappeared."

"What?"

"We are not men to be pushed around," Saxon said. "You may have believed you won with your little stunt when you called her, but that was only because it served me best for you to keep that illusion. Your wife is gone, and she won't be returned to you until this operation is completed successfully. So if you want her to live, from here on you obey me without question."

CCTI HEADQUARTERS, TEL AVIV • 18:42 GMT

"You defied a direct order from me," Hamer said. "Let me guess. Rule one in negotiating is to follow orders unless you don't feel like following orders."

"How was his location leaked to the news?" Quinn asked. "That information could only have come from one of two sources. Either Brad Silver clued them in, or someone inside the Mossad did. Either way, you have a major security breach."

"Are you listening to me?" Hamer moved in on Quinn. He was shorter and older but broad enough to be a substantial physical menace. "*You're* the security breach. You have just compromised a national security operation."

"So arrest me," Quinn said. "It will keep me from getting on a plane and facing a murder indictment. You deal with the next call from Safady."

"Hey!" Kate protested from a conference chair in the corner of the office.

"While you're calling Mossad to get the arrest papers signed," Quinn said to Hamer, "tell them you are going to tell Safady how many men IDF plans to move into the area and where they are."

"Not a chance. You can't give up that information."

"You can. You'll be talking to him. Not me."

"Shut up," Hamer said. "You know he's demanded that you handle this."

"So if I'm handling this, I want to know how his location was leaked to the news within minutes of you and the Mossad finding out. If we don't stop the source, how much damage will the next leak do?"

"You don't think I'm furious too?" Hamer asked.

"And at the same time, I want the IDF special-ops plans."

"Not a chance. I just saw how you defied my direct order."

"Then you and I decide how much information we can give him. We're going to have to earn as much trust from Safady as possible."

Hamer glared.

Before he could reply, Brad Silver stepped into the office. "Did I miss anything?"

Quinn stepped away from Hamer. He knelt beside Kate and spoke in a low voice. "Lend me your pistol."

"No way," she whispered. "Are you nuts?"

"Trust me on this. We need to know Brad Silver's involvement here, and this is the most expedient way to find out. Besides, there are IDF agents all over the building. Do you really think I'm going to try to escape?"

"What's going on?" Brad asked loudly. "What are you two whispering about?"

"Come on," Quinn whispered.

Still Kate hesitated. He could see distrust in her eyes.

"Trust me."

Finally she relented. "Safety's on," she whispered. She unbuckled the firearm from her holster.

Quinn accepted the pistol, then turned and pointed it at Brad Silver's chest. "Give me your cell phone," Quinn said.

"What?" It was a near shriek from Brad.

"Quinn!" Hamer said.

"Cell phone." Quinn released the safety. "Drop it and kick it to me."

"You're threatening me at gunpoint," Brad said. "That's illegal."

"So's this," Quinn pulled the trigger, aiming wide.

Still, the explosion staggered Brad. He dropped to his knees and felt his body as if searching for the bullet entry point.

Quinn spoke calmly. "I want the phone."

Brad tossed it at Quinn's feet.

Quinn picked up the phone, turned his back on Brad and Hamer, and moved to the far side of the office. He dropped the cell phone again and pointed the pistol.

"Speed dial this," he said to Brad. Quinn fired again. The phone exploded. He kicked the jumbled, smoking remains under the couch.

The door to the office was kicked open. IDF security men. But they didn't stand in the doorway to present a target.

"Major General Hamer?" came a voice from the hallway.

"It's nothing," Hamer said, almost weary. "We're fine."

"Go out there if you want," Quinn said. "I doubt they're going to take your word for it."

Hamer shrugged. He stepped to the doorway and spoke to his security men, then returned.

Brad Silver was sitting now, his face pale.

"Any more dramatics planned?" Hamer asked Quinn.

"Only if necessary. Do you realize how much worse the kidnapping situation has become?" Quinn answered his own question. "Because it's no longer a kidnapping. It's a hostage situation. Now it's a win-lose situation. And if we don't win, people start dying."

24

his was my promise," Safady said. He stood at the far end of the room. The children had been moved to another area. All the blankets had been temporarily lifted so that the hostages could see him from the bunk beds. "That for each one of you who tried to escape, one of the children would be killed."

The silence that followed was as dense and pressing as the heat inside the room.

"Two tried to escape," Safady continued. "So, as you Americans are fond of saying, you do the math." He began to walk toward Jonathan Silver. "It is a difficult decision. Which two should die? After all, none of those children are responsible for your group's actions."

A couple of the women hostages had begun to weep. The men were staring at the floor.

Safady stopped in front of Silver. "You're the leader. I hold you most responsible."

Silver felt as if his entire body was trembling.

"Yesterday you made the choice between beheading and bullet for the two men who had to die," Safady told Silver, smiling. "Today you choose which two children pay the price. I'll have them walk past you, and you point out which ones."

"How can you hate us like this?" Silver asked, his voice a croak.

"The fact that you don't understand the reasons for my hatred is reason enough," Safady answered. "You give no thought as to how your actions affect the Arab world. Tell me again how much money you have raised in the United States to help Palestinians. Then tell me how much support you've given to the people who have taken our land."

"These children are innocent."

"It is only now that you are concerned for them?" Safady's tone was light and mocking. "What are two more lives compared to the suffering of all the other Palestinian children over the years?"

Silver was conscious of the line attached to the grenade on his back, conscious that sudden movement could blow his body apart. He wanted to bow with this emotional pain but had to sit straight, staring at Safady's chest. "Killing children now doesn't erase the past," he said.

"Think of it as your atonement," Safady responded, obviously enjoying Silver's pain. "That's a concept you're familiar with, correct? Let me recall from your New Testament stories. Ah yes. Wasn't it said that better one should die than a nation perish? That was atonement, the reason for a man to be sacrificed on the cross by the Romans. So let's try that concept of sacrifice here. I'll reduce it to the death of one child as punishment for allowing two of you Americans to attempt escape. Understand? You only need to choose one child for death. And the others will live. Fair enough?"

Silver put his hands over his face.

"Fair enough?" Safady repeated. "And I won't even bring them in here for you to choose. How about the little one with the burn scars? Let her die to save the others. She's disfigured. What does she have to look forward to as an adult? Men will look away from her; women will mock her for not having a child. Israeli bombs ensured a worthless life for her. Why not end her misery now and spare the other children?"

An image of Alyiah's smile flashed through Silver's mind, and he was seared by a sudden depth of compassion for the child. He kept his face buried. *Our Father who art in heaven,* he began to pray silently, *hallowed be Thy name. Thy Kingdom come. Thy will be done on earth as it is in heaven. . . .*

"Who will it be?" Safady demanded.

Deliver us from evil. Silver prayed. *Oh, my Father, please deliver us from this evil.*

"Make your choice, coward," Safady said.

Oh Lord, give me strength and peace to do what only I can do. Silver lifted his hands away from his face. For the first time, he met Safady's stare without flinching.

"Who will it be?" Safady said, that hateful mocking in his voice. "The crippled one with the burns?"

Silver felt resolve and strength given to him. "It will be you." Without hesitating, he dove forward and tackled Safady. Silver felt the cord attached to the grenade pull loose.

Safady flailed as he fell backward. Silver clung to the man and waited for death to take them both.

CCTI HEADQUARTERS, TEL AVIV • 18:46 GMT

"So," Kate said to Quinn, "are you going to tell me why you shot the wrong phone?"

"I thought you'd catch the switch." Quinn was sitting at his desk. He opened a drawer to his left, pulled out Brad's phone, and handed it to Kate.

"This is a fascinating process," Kate said. "Step by step, you're making me an accomplice. Social engineering at its best."

"It's not social engineering. Reverse Stockholm syndrome, maybe."

Stockholm syndrome, as cops knew, happened when kidnapping victims bonded with their captors. The term was coined after employees at a Stockhom bank were held captive for six days in 1973; a few hostages resisted rescue attempts and later refused to testify against the kidnappers.

"Jury's still out on whether you're playing me," Kate said. It was best to stick to the subject of her professional feelings toward Quinn and ignore discussion of her personal feelings. "If I get a whiff that this feels like it's about you and not helping those hostages, I go straight to Hamer. In other words, you'd better have a good reason for this." She tapped the cell phone.

"Call history," Quinn said. "The numbers and times of the calls should tell us if he was the one who leaked to the media the fact that the Mossad had Safady's location. It would be very helpful if you checked it out."

Kate looked down at the phone. "Only one thing here is making me happy."

Quinn raised an eyebrow.

"I know I don't have to worry about reverse Stockholm syndrome. You're not that easy to like."

KHAN YUNIS, GAZA STRIP • 18:49 GMT

In the seconds that passed as Jonathan Silver wrestled with Safady, none of the men with machine guns moved in to pull Silver away.

Safady tried to shove Silver off but failed. Silver had him pinned with his full body weight, and his anger gave him a temporary strength that belied his years.

Silver braced himself for the explosion that would rip them into shreds, amazed at the joy and peace that filled him instead of fear. In those seconds, there was a timelessness that confirmed for him that his faith was truly worth more than his life.

Then, dimly, the noise and physical sensations of his struggle with Safady intruded on the amazing grace that he knew was God's gift in his dying moments. And as he realized this, he began to understand that too much time had passed. He'd felt grace and peace, but this wasn't his time to die.

The grenade taped to his upper body had not exploded.

Hands pulled at Silver. A rifle butt hit his cheekbone, cutting a gash into his skin.

Moments later, he was standing, breathing hard, almost hyperventilating, blood pouring from his face.

Safady, incredibly, showed amusement. "Impressive dramatics. I would never have expected such courage from you."

Silver glanced at the end of the cord lying over the side of the bed.

"You're much more valuable to me alive than dead," Safady said in answer to Silver's unspoken question. "The others are wired to live grenades; not you."

Silver's legs began to give way. The tension and forced willpower and that moment of peace beyond all understanding had drained his emotional reserves. He let himself fall back into a sitting position on the edge of the bed. Tears mingled with his blood.

"A child still dies," Safady said. "I will make the choice for you. The burned one."

"No." Silver was reaching as deep as he could for this last strength.

"Another one, then," Safady said. "I don't care."

"No."

Safady just snorted. "You have no power here." He turned to walk away.

"You get no cooperation," Silver said, still trying to find oxygen between words. "No money."

Safady kept walking.

"Electronic funds transfer," Silver went on. "I have to provide someone in my organization with a password for money to be released. I won't do it." Saying it, he realized he wouldn't do it. Not even with the threat of death. He'd just faced that.

Slowly, Safady turned.

"You save these children, you have the money," Silver said. "That's the deal."

Blood dripped onto his knee, forming large splotches that soaked into the fabric.

"You're negotiating with me?" Safady asked scornfully.

"Harm one of these children, you receive no money."

"You are trying to negotiate with me."

"I'm the only one with the power to release the money. You're the only one with the power to harm or save the children. Send them back in," Silver demanded. "All of them. How many millions is that worth to you for each child? You do the math." He was touched again by the supernatural sense of grace. What a paradox. He'd never felt more broken yet more whole.

Amazing grace, he thought. *This is what it means.*

He couldn't help but begin to quietly sing as an act of worship, tears flowing again. "Amazing grace! how sweet the sound . . ."

Safady began walking again.

Before Silver had begun the next line, the women in the bunk beds started to sing with him. ". . . that saved a wretch like me!"

Safady made no indication that he'd heard.

The song spread like a windblown flame over dry grass. Before Safady reached the doorway, all the hostages were singing the glorious hymn, taking strength from the strength that had been given to Jonathan Silver.

Safady and his men left the room, but the hostages kept singing.

"'Tis grace hath brought me safe thus far, and grace will lead me home. . . . Yes, when this flesh and heart shall fail, and mortal life shall cease, I shall possess within the veil a life of joy and peace. . . ."

Movement at the door lifted Silver's head.

The first of the children had entered. As the hostages continued to sing, the children poured through the doorway, looking around in astonishment at the men and women and their joy in singing.

"When we've been there ten thousand years, bright shining as the sun, we've no less days to sing God's praise than when we'd first begun."

Silver had been watching the doorway as he sang, anxious to see the one face most precious to him. As the last of the children trickled in, he still had not seen Alyiah.

Surely Safady had not taken her aside or held her back.

No!

Finally, she appeared in the doorway on her crutches, unable to keep up with the others.

Silver closed his eyes in relief and began to sing softly again.

"Amazing grace! how sweet the sound . . ."

25

Quinn's phone rang. He glanced at the caller ID. "Safady," he announced.

Hamer nodded. Kate and Brad looked up too.

Quinn picked up the phone and spoke into the mouthpiece. "Quinn."

"What does the Mossad have planned?" Safady demanded.

"I've asked," Quinn said. "There are discussions at the top level. They promised an answer within the hour."

"And the first ten million in funds?"

"All I need is an account number," Quinn said. "I trust you'll have a way of verifying it has arrived?"

"Not good enough," Safady said. "You have ninety minutes to get here; otherwise two Americans die."

"Explain."

"I will shoot them."

"I should have asked that differently," Quinn said. "Where am I supposed to be in an hour and a half?"

"Here. If the IDF has my location, you know where it is. If the IDF doesn't have my location, I'll find out that you are bluffing me."

Safady hung up and left Quinn with dial tone.

Quinn replayed the conversation and didn't hesitate in his announcement. "I go. There's no choice, no downside from a negotiating point of view."

"Unless Safady kills you," Hamer said.

"That's a downside only from my point of view," Quinn said. "Rule one: don't let personal issues get in the way of negotiating." The cruel irony that he was likely dealing with the man who'd killed his wife and daughter did not escape him. And now he had to help this man and pretend it didn't matter to him.

"Rule one," Hamer said, "dead negotiators are lousy negotiators. Safady wants you dead."

"I go," Quinn repeated. "No choice. Safady is only going to indulge in trying to kill me after he's gotten what he wants from his hostages. But by then I'll be protected by military. He can't get me."

"You have no guarantee of that," Hamer countered.

"I can guarantee you hostages die if you don't send me in."

Hamer studied Quinn. "You want to get closer to Safady, don't you?"

"Yes. I want to learn everything I can about him. After this is over, it's going to help me hunt him down."

"I don't want a negotiator blinded by hate."

"It's not hate. Someone needs to stop him. And even if it were hate, you have no choice. I go."

"*We* go," Kate told Quinn. "No choice. Downside or not."

"No. Too much of a risk," Quinn said.

"Bad argument right after telling Hamer you'd be protected by military. I go too. Or you don't go."

Each glared at the other.

"Neither one of you is going without me," Hamer said, "but there's another problem. Think logistics. This is a small country, but the only way you can get there in time is by chopper."

"So the Israeli government won't foot the bill?" Kate asked. "How much is a chopper? In the States—"

"In the States," Quinn said, "you have budget and politics. Here, that's a little farther down the list."

Kate looked puzzled.

"Ground fire," Hamer explained. "Even teenagers in Gaza can get Soviet ground-to-air missiles. They might not be able to read, but they know how to use them."

"We go in fast," Quinn said. "Get someone in logistics to choose the safest area to land as close as possible to the site. Have a ground vehicle waiting there for us, and we drive the rest of the way."

"It's still a risk," Hamer said.

"How much is it worth to the prime minister to protect a friend of Israel like Jonathan Silver?" Quinn asked. "And do you want a full-blown military operation that will likely fail with the entire world watching? Or to just put me in for a behind-the-scenes effort that looks like our only chance?"

Hamer gave a heavy sigh and let that hang as he thought it over. "You'll get your chopper," he finally said. "To the Gaza border. No closer. I'll arrange for a vehicle to be waiting, and I can get us through the border crossing at high speed. You should have enough time then."

"Good," Quinn said. He moved to his desk, pulled open a drawer, and found his laptop. "Give me five minutes to pack. I want a flak jacket and helmet."

Quinn faced Brad. "You in for the ride? If not, I need a way to be in immediate contact, 24-7."

"I've got to deal with things here," Brad said, squirming slightly. "I'll go back to the hotel and make sure you can get through anytime."

"What about you, Kate?" Quinn asked. "Sure you still want to babysit me?"

"Maybe sissy-boy here is afraid—" Kate set her mouth—"but you can't scare me away."

KHAN YUNIS, GAZA STRIP • 14:27 GMT

Like each of the other Americans, Silver was again confined to a small, isolated prison behind blankets draped down both ends and the side from the top of his bunk bed, in silence and dimness and the stifling heat of the unmoving air. He felt like a child, remembering nights he'd lain beneath the sheets, pretending if he didn't move, the monsters in the dark could not find him.

Now, however, the monsters had him trapped.

He couldn't lie on his back, because the new live grenade taped to him would press against his spine. He was afraid to sit on the edge of his bed with his feet on the floor, for Safady had promised to interpret any movement shown outside the blankets as an attempt to communicate. He was too old and too inflexible to sit cross-legged. All that left him was to lie on his stomach, head turned sideways on his pillow.

His left wrist was tucked beneath the pillow, and his entire world had been reduced to the sound of the ticking of his watch beneath his ear.

This was a new concept of eternity. Not an abstract concept about joy and pleasure in the presence of God that he had often preached was the reward for good Christians in the life beyond but the passing of time boiled down to the essence, with no distractions to fool him into thinking his life would last forever. Just the tick, tick, tick of a force so unstoppable in this universe that only God, standing outside of it, was unaffected by it—time.

That was one of the devil's greatest tricks, he realized. Finding delightful ways to make humans forget about the tick, tick, tick of impending death and the consequences of where eternity would take their souls.

Silver wondered what he would have changed about his life if he could have lived every moment like this, hearing the tick, tick, tick, allowing urgency to galvanize him while he had the chance, as if he were hearing himself knock, knock, knock at the door to God's presence.

Tick. Tick. Tick.

Silver felt as if his soul were as stripped down as his tired body. That he could in this moment hide nothing from God or even from himself. If he were to enter God's presence today, he would have to confess that his preaching of the gospel had been much more about his own comfort than comforting others.

He could argue before God as he had in front of Esther—that his work in raising money for the ministry had empowered others like Esther to dispense comfort. But it would be a hollow argument.

Shortly, a little girl on crutches would appear with a plastic bucket for him to use to empty his bodily wastes. Without complaint, despite the difficulty of holding the bucket and using crutches, she would then take that bucket away. This was the same little girl who had offered to give up her precious milk because she believed he had lost his, unaware of his vast wealth and power.

Whose efforts would God smile over more?

Silver groaned.

He struggled to his knees, clasped his hands together, closed his eyes, and began to pray.

CCTI HEADQUARTERS, TEL AVIV • 14:36 GMT

Quinn spoke to Kevin from the doorway of the office; it was as far as Kate would string out the invisible leash.

Kevin held the perpetual Diet Coke in hand. Quinn had read about the dangers of artificial sweeteners and often joked that a biopsy of Kevin's liver would confirm or deny those dangers.

"I want 24-7 satellite and Internet connection," Quinn said. "That's priority number one."

"You've got a laptop, backup, and extra batteries?"

Quinn nodded.

"Then I'll take care of things on this end," Kevin said.

"Anything on Roz?"

Kevin shook his head.

"Let me know when you hear anything. Instantly."

"And I'll make sure you can access it via satellite."

"Thanks for taking care of me."

"Hey—" Kevin grinned—"if you can't trust me, who can you trust?"

26

eird." Kate's voice reached Quinn through his headset.

They were in the chopper, racing over the countryside, heading to an area east of Khan Yunis in Israeli territory. Hamer had agreed with Quinn; it was better to come in from a point directly east, stopping just short of the border and completing the last few miles on the ground. This minimized the chances of ground fire from Palestinians.

"Weird," Quinn repeated. Was she describing him? Or was this some kind of thing he was supposed to understand by reading between the lines?

Once, before his wife had died, they'd gone to a party where people had started playing Pictionary, the men against the women. The men got slaughtered. When it was their turn, the drawing would have to be almost photographic in detail before the team guessed correctly—a process that might take minutes. The women, Quinn remembered, had been uncanny. Five lines into a sketch that had no semblance to reality, some woman would always blurt out the answer. It was so consistent the men had accused the women of cheating. But Quinn had come to understand that women had an undercurrent of communication that defied logic.

"Yeah, weird," Kate said. "Can't you see it?"

We're in a chopper, Quinn thought, *racing to beat a deadline, and I'm wondering if a ground-to-air missile is going to blow us out of the air any second.*

"Not quite in the sightseeing frame of mind," he answered.

"It's like a line," Kate said, reaching across and pointing west. "Green and cultivated on one side. Brown on the other. Those funny circle things—I don't know what they're called, but that's irrigated land, right?"

Quinn followed her line of sight. She'd described it accurately. On the Israeli side of the border, irrigated crops looked like giant green circles from the air. The Gaza side, however, had none of the lushness.

"Yeah," Quinn said, conscious that the helicopter pilot and Jack Hamer could hear their conversation on the open channel. "Irrigated land."

A frown line appeared across her forehead. She was about to ask the obvious: why was it brown on one side of the border and green on the other?

Quinn touched her knee. In a way, it was a startling act, and it brought her eyes instantly to his with, he decided, a touch of anger in her glance.

He shook his head to silence her.

The frown line deepened.

Again, he shook his head.

Kate blinked a few times, then shrugged.

If he could find a time and place later, he would explain.

KHAN YUNIS, GAZA STRIP • 15:12 GMT

Safady pointed at the table in front of the backdrop. The video camera and tripod were set in the previous position. "You know why we are here," he told Jonathan Silver. "Another video session for you to speak to the world. Sit."

"No." The skin of Silver's chest stung in a narrow, horizontal band where moments before Safady had ripped the duct tape loose from the grenade and pulled away strips of hair. The muscles in his lower back were sore from sleeping on the thin mattress. He was emotionally worn and could not keep his weariness out of his voice. "It's not going to happen."

"Don't you dare defy me!"

"I'm finished taking orders from you," Silver said. It was more effective than if he'd walked over and slapped Safady. Silver took advantage of the silence. "Here's where you and I discuss terms. None of your men are here to listen, so you don't have to worry about saving face."

Safady's speechlessness continued. His eyeballs bulged, and his mouth contorted. Silver doubted the man was acting. He realized he actually found enjoyment in angering him, then felt guilt at this. Not enough guilt, probably. Jesus might have been compassionate enough to truly love His enemies, but Silver wasn't going to pretend to himself that he was capable of this with Safady.

"We understand that the children will suffer consequences if we try to escape," Silver said. "You have my word that no one in the group will attempt it again. Other than that, we refuse to serve your cause. Including this."

Silver's epiphany had come amid the joy of holding Alyiah upon her return. Was his faith in God real and worth anything? Yes. He'd been willing to give his life in order to save another, and that realization in itself was transforming. With this, Silver had been released from the fear of the tyranny of death. He felt he was finally beginning to understand and believe on a deep, emotional level that he was a child of God, that life beyond the shell of his body on earth would be joyful and eternal in the presence of God. Death was the worst that the enemy could deal, whether this enemy was Satan stalking humankind or Safady trying to inflict monstrosities on his captives. Once the fear of death had been shed, the enemy had no power; this was something the martyrs had understood, the men and women who'd bravely faced every antichrist through the ages, from Nero to Hitler.

"Do I have to remind you that I have your life or death in my hands?" Safady threatened, so filled with rage that he was hardly able to spit out the words.

"You don't," Silver said. "God decides when I die."

"I am god to you while you are in my power!"

"I believed that for too long. Now I don't. If you kill me, it's only because God has decided it should happen."

Silver had realized something else while lying in his bunk bed praying. Bowing to Safady's will was literally serving Safady instead of God. All that Safady had to offer was a reprieve from death. But death would arrive sooner or later regardless of the outcome over the next days. Weighed against the glorious hope that came through the resurrection of Jesus, Safady's power over the group of hostages was nothing. Understanding this had given Silver incredible new insight into stories of the Bible that had, until then, slowly become crusted with triteness until they were go-to clichés for him, handy when it came to preparing sermons for television broadcasts. Suddenly the Bible was real to him again. Time and again in the Old and New Testaments, God's people had trusted in Him, despite the overwhelming threats against them. And those people had not just used that trust for platitudes; they had acted on it.

If Silver died today, this renewed faith more than made up for the price he was paying for it. Especially because his faith gave him so much more than hope beyond life on earth. It gave him dignity. And power against Safady.

"The group is united," Silver said. "Every one of us is willing to die if needed. We are your prisoners, but you will no longer bully us."

Safady stared at him as if trying to measure whether Silver was bluffing. "The children . . ." With the back of his hand, Safady wiped a trace of spittle from his lips. "I hold their lives in my hands. If you defy me, you are responsible for their deaths. I sent them back to you. I can just as easily take them away again."

"They live or die according to God's will." Silver spoke calmly. "And you get the ransom money according to my will."

Safady spit into Silver's face.

"Just so you know," Silver said, ignoring the spittle, "you won't get a penny of it until the children are released first."

"You're prepared to give up your life to save them? That's insane."

"No," Silver said. "Making a sacrifice to save others is the way of the Cross. What's insane is asking young Muslims to give up their lives to destroy others."

Safady's first question to me will be about the IDF military plans," Quinn told Hamer. "It won't be smart for me to lie to him. I doubt you'll be able to disguise your commandos well enough to fool the locals. And you can bet Safady will have spies everywhere. He'll be like a smart trial lawyer, asking questions when he already knows the answers."

Just under twenty minutes to the deadline.

They were driving in a dusty panel van now, a cargo vehicle so ancient it would not draw any attention. The chopper had landed without incident. They'd been whisked away in a Mercedes, then taken into an orange grove and transferred to this vehicle. The switch had taken an extra five minutes but was a precaution to make up for the fact that the IDF had not had time to find them a bulletproof means of transportation. Anonymity would have to serve as protection instead.

"Stall him," Hamer said. The van had already made it through the Gaza border crossing. The soldiers inside the van were a token protection. They didn't have much time to talk last-minute details.

"This man is not stupid."

"Neither is the Mossad or IDF or the Israeli government. We don't make a habit of telling terrorists our plan of attack."

"This isn't flight 572 sitting on a runway," Quinn said. He was referring to the famous Black September hijacking attempt in 1972; Israeli commandos disguised as airline technicians had stormed the plane and successfully gained control of the aircraft.

"You're a negotiator, Quinn, not a military adviser."

Along with one driver, there were three young soldiers in olive green uni forms that marked them as general corps. They grinned at Hamer's comment, not hiding their amusement from Quinn. He'd noticed they'd done a bad job of hiding their admiration for Kate, too.

"Here's a question," Quinn said. "As a negotiator, not a military adviser."

The van hit a rut and bounced him in the air.

"What is it?" Hamer was sweating. The van didn't have air-conditioning.

"What do you think Safady really wants?" Quinn asked.

"I thought negotiators were good listeners."

"So you think it's the money. The hostage demand. That's it?"

"It's a well-planned operation. Almost American in its efficiency."

"What about media attention?" Quinn asked.

"That's obvious. Too obvious to even mention. That, and the fact that he's already getting it."

"All this time in the IDF, and still you don't think like an Arab."

The van turned hard as the driver swerved to miss a goat.

"I don't need you to lecture me," Hamer said. "Wasn't rule one something about teamwork?"

"Rule one is to understand the person on the other side of the table," Quinn said. "If this were a typical hostage situation—say a bank robbery gone wrong—the hostage taker's biggest motivation would be to get out alive. More often than not, the solution is to find a way to give the hostage taker a way to save face as he gives up. I don't think we have that in our favor here."

Hamer nodded. "Because if I thought like a radical Islamic terrorist, my life wouldn't be the most important thing in this hostage taking."

"Exactly," Quinn said. "Safady is a radical Islamic terrorist. If it's him."

"You're saying it's not Safady?"

"I'm saying let's not make an assumption that prevents us from considering all possibilities. So let's consider a broad generalization about the Arab world and one of the reasons it hates Israel."

"We win . . . all the time."

"Right. Palestinians are humiliated that Israel has managed to defy the Arabs for decades, despite repeated attacks from all sides." Quinn said, conscious that Kate was listening as closely as the soldiers in the van. "Humiliation that, from their point of view, the Palestinian land was stolen from them, and that they are helpless to do anything about it. You know as well as I do that Palestinian terrorist organizations brag endlessly about the tiniest of victories against Israelis."

"Brag?" Hamer snorted. "Exaggerate and lie. They wound one Israeli civilian and report on Al Jazeera that five soldiers died. What's your point?"

"A big part of the strategy of the war on terrorism—on both sides—is positioning in the media," Quinn said. "There would be a lot of prestige in this if one of Safady's motives is to use the hostages to lure an Israeli military contingent into an unmanageable situation."

"Our special forces are highly trained," Hamer said.

"Bring in tanks and surround the orphanage. Safady will love it. You'll have riots and more footage of boys with rocks defying Israeli soldiers with machine guns. And your soldiers will be helpless anyway. They'd never dare fire at an orphanage with children inside, not with the television cameras rolling. Because once the tanks get there, you know the media will be right behind."

Hamer was silent.

"Safady will like the alternative just as much," Quinn said. "If you don't bring in enough military force, the Israelis risk losing men in a pitched battle to Palestinian terrorists waiting and primed for the chance to fight you on their terms and their territory."

"Ah, so the best military strategy is none at all." Hamer spoke dryly. "Let's stop the van so I can call Zvi and tell him not to bother planning anything in support of the hostages."

"You think you're funny, but you're not. Has it occurred to anyone at the Mossad that Safady was relatively easy to find? Someone who has been invisible for five years. Who managed to kidnap thirty Americans and move them into the heart of the Gaza Strip in a way that the Mossad still hasn't figured out."

"It hasn't escaped me that maybe he wanted us to find him."

"So what if he's hoping you'll bring in the military? If so, he's made plans for it."

"The time and place to have this discussion was back in Tel Aviv."

"Then we'd still be back in Tel Aviv, still discussing options, with Safady about to begin shooting hostages and throwing them on the street. There's a reason I've waited until now to bring this up."

— "What are you suggesting?" Hamer asked.

"Exactly what you already suggested. Something Safady hasn't planned for. No military at all."

Hamer laughed, then stopped. He saw the look on Quinn's face. "You're serious? In your office, you talked me into this because you said you'd have military protection."

"Would you have let us into Gaza otherwise?"

"Not a chance," Hamer answered.

"Then it would have been stupid to make this argument there. But we're here now. There's no turning back. And our best shot is no military."

"Unbelievable," Hamer said. "To think that I once believed you were lousy at this."

15:27 GMT

"I have wronged you," Esther said to Jonathan Silver. "I've been angry with you, and I want to ask your forgiveness."

She'd just stepped away from her twenty minutes of daily solitude. Today, she'd been uneasy all through her prayer time, feeling separated from God. When she'd realized why, she'd argued with God, trying to justify her anger and her actions. But in His unyielding silence God had spoken to her.

Reach out to the man. He is one of My children too.

She'd kept fighting her pride, but after watching Silver risk his life to save Alyiah, it was easier to humble herself.

So here she was, apologizing.

"You told me last night that our presence here puts your children in danger." Silver's attempt at a brave smile pierced her. "I understand better now. You shouldn't blame yourself for being angry with me."

"There's more for you to forgive," Esther answered. There *was* more. She'd been carrying a secret satisfaction seeing Silver in this position, as if God had found this ironic way to punish the man. But if it was God's punishment, that was between God and Jonathan Silver. Her task was to care for him as well as possible.

"How can there be more? We don't know each other."

"True, you don't know me." She hesitated. Was the door she was about to walk through a selfish one? By revealing what she was about to reveal, would she be confessing a wrong or sinfully setting aside her remorse and attacking the man she wanted to attack? "But I've known about you for a long time. And I've been battling you for years."

There. It was said. Out in the open.

His shoulders straightened slightly. "Here. In Gaza. You've been fighting me?"

"I've been fighting your ministry, your end-times prophecies, your entire dispensational theology. I need to set that aside right now."

"*My* dispensational theology?"

"The whole idea that God has two peoples—the church and Israel. That this land has been promised to the Jews. That there must be a rebuilt Temple before God can return."

"That's not *my* theology. I teach it, but it's not mine."

"Who else in the evangelical world has a higher profile? If there is a single person who represents it best, it is you. 'God will bless those who bless Israel,' you say every week to your millions of followers. 'God will curse those who curse Israel.'"

"But fighting me from here? I don't understand. How?"

"Twice a year, I return to the United States to raise money and awareness to help children here in Gaza. I try to get Christians to donate their money to my cause. Many churches won't even let me speak. At other churches, I face those who call me a sinner for speaking against Israel. The truth is I'm very sympathetic toward Israel. I just want an equal voice given to the Palestinians. They have nowhere to go, and they are God's children too. What I hear time and again, however, is that it's God's plan to give all of this land to Israel. That as a Christian, I shouldn't be helping the Palestinians."

She waited for his reply. He gave none but glared at her, all his listlessness gone.

"See?" she said. "Your silence tells me enough."

"The Bible says—"

"The Bible says what you want it to say," she snapped. "I've seen your hateful television rants against those who disagree with you and your biblical interpretations. You call them replacement theologians. You call them anti-Semites, say that they have Hitler's anointing. That would be me, then. Does the orphanage look like Hitler's anointing?"

"The Bible is God's literal truth. I will defend those fundamentals with my last breath."

"Your passion I admire. But saying every word in the Bible is true in a literal sense is nonsense. There's poetry in the Bible, metaphors. God, the ultimate creator, uses words in a beautiful, creative way."

"To suggest the Bible contains fiction is a sin."

"And you're not listening to me. You're suggesting that I'm not a good Christian if I want to try to discern the truth."

"The truth is there, plain to see. All you need to do is pick up the Bible and read it."

All her good intentions at humility were long gone. "How arrogant, believing you can understand the Bible completely by reading twenty-first-century events into its pages, ignoring the historical and cultural context of those to whom the books of the Bible were originally written. You would do well to remember that while the Bible was written and divinely preserved *for* believers throughout the ages, it was not written *to* our generation."

"When you question the Bible, you are questioning God." Silver's anger was beginning to match Esther's.

"Have you heard of radical Islam?" she asked. "If not, look around. You'll discover you have been kidnapped because of it."

"Of course I have," he snapped back.

"Let me tell you what's been happening in the Arab world. Islamic terrorists are well versed in the Koran. They pick and choose verses for their purposes. Because Muslims are rarely given permission to try to interpret the Koran themselves, they are denounced if they question the radicals."

Esther paused. "It's like a pyramid. The radicals are reshaping the Koran to justify their worldview. Below them are Muslims who actively support them. And the wide base of the pyramid is the rest of them, those who remain silent, either out of ignorance or fear of reprisals. More and more, these radicals are convincing the rest of the Muslims that if you are not a radical Muslim, you are not a good Muslim."

"You," Silver thundered with surprising energy, "are comparing me to a fundamentalist Muslim?"

"You bully those who question your end-times interpretations. And you sit at the top of a large pyramid that prospers because of your theology."

"Nonsense!"

"I've been rejected for fund-raisers at colleges that share your interpretation of the end times. I've spoken to professors who must sign a statement that they believe dispensationalism or they wouldn't be employed. Many say they wish they could teach a different interpretation, but if they did, they would lose their jobs. And the colleges would lose alumni support."

She held up a hand to stop his protest. "Institutions from colleges to large churches to television ministries have put so much energy over so many decades into pushing this evangelical viewpoint that they would lose a huge power base to suggest that there might be another interpretation."

"Israel is God's chosen people."

"And you define Israel as ethnic Jews?"

"Of course. What else could the Bible mean?"

"Have you ever given that question serious consideration? Have you ever asked yourself what Paul meant when he wrote that all of us are Jews through faith?"

Silver glared at her again. "I suppose you have a theology degree."

"That's what it takes for anyone to discuss this? How convenient. Then none of your followers can even question what you teach."

"You came here to apologize to me," Silver reminded her. "Attacking my teaching doesn't sound like an apology."

"Answer this," Esther challenged him. "How much have you personally gained through your empire? And how much would you personally lose if you told the world there was a chance you might actually be wrong?"

Silver opened his mouth to retort but said nothing.

"That's what I thought," she said.

15:38 GMT

The platoon was ready for action again. Saxon was staying behind with the heifer. Patterson was part of the next phase of operations.

These were Patterson's new orders: shoot to kill if anyone tried to interfere with the two-man mission. Man or woman or child, regardless of age. Nothing was to stop Patterson and Burge from dropping the canisters at the time specified by Saxon. Patterson didn't know why or what was expected afterward, just that it was crucial to make it happen.

They were one of six two-man teams in motion, roaming the streets and alleys in their disguises as Arab farm laborers. Each man carried a hidden pistol. Here, even though it was common for men to carry machine guns, Saxon had specified he wanted as little attention as possible drawn to the teams.

Patterson walked alongside Burge, who carried what looked like a cell phone to anyone giving them a second glance. But it was a GPS locator preprogrammed with coordinates. It had been beeping every five seconds, but as the two of them neared the coordinates, the beeping grew more frequent—a sophisticated game of warmer-colder.

The air was dry and hot. It seemed to suck up moisture but exuded such a variety of smells that Patterson couldn't identify any of them. None of the smells were pleasant.

The two men were silent. Burge was focusing on the tempo of beeping sounds coming from the GPS locator. Patterson was in no mood to talk. His intense fear about Sarah was like acid eating at his stomach walls.

"You don't have any idea how big this is. . . . Our military unit is only a small part of a secret network of Christians dedicated to striking back at the network established by Islamic terrorists. All across America, men of influence and power are helping fight the war. . . . If you were back in Georgia, you would have heard that your wife has disappeared."

Even if Patterson could identify any of the rest of the secret network, where would he start looking for her, and how could he possibly fight back?

Patterson wasn't so lost in his thoughts that he had stopped surveying the street. They were approaching the front of a beat-up white van, just as junky-looking as most of the vehicles in Gaza. What was different, however, was the fact that three non-Arabs, two men and a woman, were visible through the windshield. Americans? Tourists?

Whoever they were, they seemed out of place. Their eyes slid over him as he and Burge approached, more proof of how well the Freedom Crusaders had prepared for their role here. To observers, Patterson and Burge were just another couple of Arabs.

If that wasn't enough extra indication of the thoroughness of the secret network, Patterson didn't need to look any further than the GPS locator in Burge's right hand. The locators, one for each pair of soldiers, had been in one of the crates. Patterson had no idea, of course, who had supplied the crates or how long it had been since they had been filled. He couldn't even guess at the route the crates had taken to reach them. Most certainly it had been at least a week of travel, probably more.

While Burge and the others probably would have found comfort in this efficiency, the implications were frightening to Patterson. It spoke of the power of the men behind the network. It also told Patterson that this phase of the operation had been planned well in advance. Which led to that other question. Who knew and how had it been possible to know so far in advance that Jonathan Silver would be held hostage in this part of Gaza? This too suggested that Patterson had no chance against the network.

If he wanted to see Sarah again, he'd have to obey Saxon. Even then, he'd have to trust and pray that Saxon would uphold the bargain when all of this was over.

Whatever it was.

15:35 GMT

"What's this?" Kate said, staring at dark fabric that Quinn pulled from a plastic bag at the back of the van.

Just ten minutes remained before the ninety-minute deadline expired.

"A cultural experience," Quinn said. They were inside, windows closed. The van was getting hotter, and he was sweating. They'd parked on the street just down from the orphanage. Now that the engine was off, noise from the nearby marketplace punched through the walls of the van. The view through the windshield showed two Arabs walking toward them. One was intent on a cell phone in his hand. The other glanced at him and Hamer with some curiosity, then looked away.

Kate unfurled the fabric. "A dress. A face thing."

"Niqab," Quinn said. "Traditional Muslim head covering for a woman. It shouldn't be uncomfortable. Slip it over what you're wearing."

"It just happened to be in the van?" Kate asked.

Hamer cleared his throat. "Quinn insisted we find one. I agreed. It's a great disguise. You wear it or you don't stay."

"I don't need to hide to be able to protect myself," Kate said.

"You'll be protecting Quinn," Hamer said. "And the operation. An American woman around here will be a neon sign screaming for attention."

"Without military to protect us," Quinn added, "we need to keep a low profile. Look in the bag. You'll see clothes for me, too. I won't pass as a Palestinian with close inspection, but it will allow me to move on the streets if I have to."

Kate's mouth tightened. "Fine."

"I don't see a portable air conditioner for this van," Quinn said to Hamer.

"It's not like we had a lot of notice. Didn't seem high priority."

"This van will be my base of operations," Quinn told Hamer. "The fewer the distractions the better. Including heat."

"*Your* base? I'm sure you meant *our* base."

Quinn shook his head. "I need you to call for another car to take you and the soldiers away before the locals figure out what's happening. And quickly; the deadline's closing in."

"You expect me out of here too?"

"You're in more danger here than any of us," Quinn countered. "We're all as out of place here as cat droppings on a marble floor. But I'm just the negotiator. How much is a high-ranking IDF official worth dead or alive to these guys?"

Hamer didn't answer, so Quinn pressed his point. "If I'm killed or taken hostage, it works to Safady's disadvantage because it will take time to bring in a replacement. On the other hand, it serves him for me to stay alive. He picked the orphanage because this is his territory. I'm sure he'll be able to put the word out to keep me safe from the locals. That's why I don't need protection, at least until negotiations are over, and I'll take my chances then."

Hamer thumbed in Kate's direction. She was still crouched in the back with the soldiers. "And her? What if they take her hostage?"

"That would be the terrorists' biggest mistake," Quinn said. "They wouldn't gain much from one more American, and she'd drive them crazy."

"Ha, ha," Kate said.

"Still, she should go with you," Quinn told Hamer. "Niqab or no niqab. But I can't make the call. You have to."

"No," Kate said. "I'm in it this far. I'm not going to turn back. Try, and I'll blow this wide open."

"This is my operation," Hamer said. "I can't just leave."

"Sure you can. Whether you and I talk face to face or by cell phone doesn't make much difference," Quinn said. "Find a place to park on the Israeli side. Stay in contact from there."

"You're just going to sit in this van?"

"Like it's my office. That's why I want a portable air conditioner. Rule one in negotiating: never ask for more than you know you can get. Which is why I didn't order a couch or plasma television."

"First you strip the operation of military, and now I'm gone. It's like I close my eyes for a second and suddenly you're running things instead of me. Cohen won't agree to this."

"He won't have a choice," Quinn said. "He's in Tel Aviv. We're here."

"This strategy is absurd."

"I prefer to describe it as unexpected. Rule one in negotiating: tilt the playing field in your favor."

"Rule number one where I come from is a lot simpler: when you have guns, you use them. What's the world going to think when it gets out that the Israeli government has left the hostages unprotected?"

"The world doesn't have to know it. Especially if you can keep Brad Silver from finding out. Or stop him from leaking information. Lock him in his hotel room. Cut his phone lines and Internet access. We'll be fine."

"But the IDF can't just do nothing," Hamer protested.

"How long would it take for choppers with soldiers to get here from the border?"

"Two minutes. Less if we've got the choppers in the air and waiting."

"Keep them ready, then. Monitor the orphanage from surveillance airplanes. If this guy tries to move the hostages or starts shooting them, then use force. But until then, give the negotiating process a chance. Just don't give the terrorists a platform to make this a bigger situation than it is by pouring Israeli soldiers into this area."

"Sounds logical, coming from you. Maybe you should talk to Zvi."

"So it looks like I'm giving you orders? How long did you want to keep your job? It's better if all of this sounds like your idea and you had to talk me into staying. If it works, you'll have Zvi's job as soon as he steps down."

"If it works," Hamer said. "And if I ever believe the Mossad is a step up from IDF."

"Have a little faith," Quinn said. "Think of how my negotiating shifted your landscape and hope I can do the same with the other side."

"This is what you call it? Shifting my landscape?"

Quinn shrugged. "Sounds better than having you think I outsmarted you."

"Astounding how good I feel at this point. Does it come with a massage?"

"Ask Kate. Just remember to arrange for the portable air conditioner before you leave. And make sure Mossad e-mails me the intel on who is running this orphanage."

"Anything else?" Hamer asked sardonically.

"Yeah," Quinn said. "Cokes. On ice. Have some kid deliver it. Safady's going to call, and I'll need it by then."

A boy, maybe ten years old, stepped in front of Patterson and Burge, holding up oranges. The kid was obviously hawking the fruit. He had stringy hair and pockmarks on the skin of his cheekbones.

Both men shook their heads and tried to push past him.

With a fixed smile, the boy stepped backward. Then he frowned. The near-constant beeping of the GPS locator was far too audible. The kid fired a question at them in Arabic, pointing at the machine in Burge's hand.

Neither man answered. According to the GPS signals, they'd located the house Saxon had told them to find. It was one of dozens lining this street, each pressed hard against the next with sagging walls of whitewashed brick. Saxon had promised the house would be empty.

The kid asked more questions in animated Arabic. He moved forward to look closer at the GPS locator.

Burge reached under his shirt for his pistol.

Patterson grabbed Burge's arm, afraid to utter even the word *no* in English.

The alarm on Burge's watch began to beep, adding to the small cacophony of technology. The two-minute warning.

Burge glanced at Patterson.

Patterson could read his expression. The canisters had to be dropped in at the exact same moment as all the others. This kid would not be allowed to interfere.

Shoot to kill if necessary.

15:39 GMT

"Here's your explanation," Quinn said to Kate. Now that the two of them were alone in the van, her presence seemed magnified. He was looking for a distraction in the last few minutes before the next call from Safady.

"The irrigation thing?"

See, Quinn thought, *there it is.* It had been how long since the helicopter had landed? Yet Kate knew instantly that he was picking up the irrigation conversation from where he'd left it there. Uncanny.

"The irrigation thing."

"I thought it seemed strange that you didn't want Hamer to hear us talk about it," she said. "I figured you had a good reason for it."

"No sense antagonizing Hamer just before going into a tense situation where we have to work as a team."

"A discussion on irrigation would do that?"

"Not irrigation. Water quotas. A nasty little weapon that Israel uses on the Palestinians." Quinn gave an overview. Many of the low-income Palestinians collected rainwater in cisterns on their roofs. Israeli jets strafed the cisterns, leaving the Palestinians without water. Then water was sold back to them at high prices. Widespread government fraud siphoned off other water that was supposed to go to Palestinian farmers by quota. Again, this water was sold back to them at extortionate prices.

"I never knew that," Kate said. "But the results of using water as a weapon are obvious when you see it from above."

"It's obvious on a Google Earth map too," Quinn said. "Even from satellite images, it's easy to see the border with green on one side and brown on the other."

"It seems kind of unfair."

"And that's exactly the reaction that would have set Hamer's teeth on edge. The Israelis don't see it as wrong."

"You're defending this?"

"Of course not. I just didn't want to get into it with Hamer right at that moment."

"Funny," Kate said. "It seems like you'd be a little more pro-Israel after what the Palestinians did to your . . ." Her voice trailed off as if she'd realized that the next word would hurt him.

"After what the Palestinians did to my family?" Quinn quietly asked. If that's why she'd gone quiet, she was right. It did hurt. It always would.

She nodded.

"Palestinian terrorists killed my family. Not Palestinians. Do you have any idea what it's like for nearly one and a half million people living at poverty level in this ten-by-twenty-mile strip of land? In the shadow of one of the richest nations in the world?"

"That takes moral guts," she said. "To be pro-Palestinian."

He shook his head. "Pro-peace, remember? Pro-children. I'm pro-Palestine because Israel will never be secure without a viable Palestine. I'm pro-Israel because Palestine will never be viable without a secure Israel. You're doing what the rest of the world does too—trying to make simple judgments based on a complex situation. This conflict goes back generations, with inflicted injustices that have mounted from and against both sides for so long that looking for the wrongs and rights only fuels the fire."

"What do you look for, then?"

"I've got a saying for business conflicts," Quinn told her. "Don't get mad—"

"Get even."

"Wrong again. 'Don't get mad; get even' is what has escalated this for sixty years. Try this instead: don't get mad; spend the other person's money."

She thought about it. "Set aside your emotion and find a way to make it work in a way that benefits you."

"Exactly. This has gone so far beyond who deserves what that it needs to be reduced to finding a solution without looking for retributive justice." Quinn paused. "The practicality of this is very simple. The Palestinian situation is not going to go away. Right now, much of the rest of the Arab world has found a way to live with the fact that Israel can't be destroyed. Yet if Israel goes the final step of taking the remaining land or obliterating the Palestinians, this uneasy truce ends, and it will be Muslims against Israel and all her Western allies. In short, the one-state solution won't work. Most Israelis recognize that; so do most Palestinians."

"Most?"

"Extremists on both sides are fighting to prevent a two-state solution." Quinn shrugged. "And it doesn't help when those seventy million Americans are basically brainwashed into believing that solution is against God's will."

"Brainwashed? You're talking about Silver's end-times theology."

"Right. Too often, anyone who even questions it is called heretical. There needs to be dialogue on how much the religious right contributes to the Mideast problem because of misguided theology."

"Yet you're here—" Kate waved her hand in the direction of the orphanage— "trying to rescue one of the most vocal and prominent fundamentalist proponents of a one-state solution."

"His life—just like any life in Palestine or Israel—is far more important than ideology."

15:48 GMT

The Arab kid kept pushing them to buy.

Patterson growled and pointed for the kid to leave.

The boy had enough street sense to know he had some sort of leverage here, even if he didn't understand why they wanted him to leave. He held out the oranges, speaking rapidly.

Patterson figured the kid had just doubled the price of the oranges. He still had a restraining arm on Burge and felt Burge's bicep tighten.

Patterson glanced up and down the alley and saw three bigger kids ahead. He told himself that obeying orders and shooting this boy would only draw more attention than it would prevent. Maybe even bring down a street riot and blow the entire operation.

The alarm on Burge's watch beeped again. They had to get inside the building and locate the pipes. The drop had to be coordinated at exactly the same time as the other teams. How many seconds were left?

Burge tried pulling his arm loose.

Patterson stepped in front of Burge, blocking the kid from harm.

The boy grinned.

Patterson held out his hands for the oranges. The kid retreated slightly, still talking. Probably asking for money.

Patterson smiled and snatched one of the oranges. The kid doubled his rate of speech. Patterson looked ahead, judged his distance, and threw a fastball with the orange.

It zipped through the air and at the end of the shallow arc hit one of the three kids farther down the alley solidly in the back.

The bigger kid turned around, yelling in anger.

Patterson pointed at the boy in front of him, who was still holding the other orange.

The three bigger boys made the connection and started walking toward the little kid, yelling louder.

The kid with the orange didn't hesitate. He took off running. Seconds later, the three others swept past Patterson and Burge in full pursuit.

Patterson checked his watch. "Still got a minute," he said. "Let's go."

Patterson was unsurprised that the door to the abandoned house was unlocked as promised. Like everything else about this operation, even this detail had been thought out ahead of time.

The interior of the house was completely bare. Patterson followed Burge to the back of the house and up steps onto the flat roof. Two pipes protruded side by side. They were vents, but they didn't lead into the house.

"Thirty seconds," Burge said, looking at his watch.

Patterson pulled out the gas cylinders and waited. Burge counted down, one second at time. At the ten-second mark, Patterson punched a button on top to prime each canister.

Burge continued the countdown.

At zero, Patterson dropped a cylinder in each tube. Then he and Burge began the trek back to the safe house. The op plans gave them less than five minutes to get there.

You missed the deadline," came the familiar voice. "You're not here. Two Americans die."

Quinn had just answered his cell phone. He and Kate sat on orange crates in the back of the van. She was wearing traditional Muslim clothing and had the veil in her lap. Dressed this way, she would be invisible on the streets. Even better than a flak jacket.

The six Coke bottles Hamer had had delivered were sitting in a plastic sack of ice beside them. On another crate, Quinn's laptop was open, the screen dark.

"I'm here," Quinn said, cradling the phone to his ear.

"I don't believe you."

"Rule one in negotiating: never lie."

Kate was watching Quinn. He pointed at the bottles, holding up two fingers, indicating that Kate should open a couple.

"I've heard nothing about Israeli military from my people."

"Maybe I'm in front of the wrong place."

"You had the address."

"I did," Quinn agreed as Kate searched unsuccessfully for a bottle opener. "Here's my problem: I need to know you are who you say you are and that you are where you say you are."

"I think you need to prove to me you arrived by the deadline. Didn't you say you needed to establish trust with me?"

"Just like you need to establish trust with me. I'm the one in the middle. If I can trust you, I take that back to the other side. My job is to get both sides what they want."

"Prove you are here first."

"Look outside. You'll see a white van. I'm in it."

"Now I know you're lying," Safady said. "You expect me to believe you're here without the protection of soldiers?"

"Look outside."

"So that an Israeli sniper can take apart my head with a bullet?"

"How about this," Quinn said. "Stand beside Jonathan Silver. Hold up your fingers in a peace sign. You know what a peace sign looks like?"

"Why should I do this?"

"Have one of your men take a photo. Your cell phone takes photos, right?"

"Nobody sees my face in a photo."

Quinn hadn't expected the terrorist to make that mistake, but it had been worth a try. "Then get someone else to stand beside him. I just want to see someone walk out of the orphanage with a photo of Jonathan Silver and a peace sign. Delivered to me in my white van on the street."

"All that does is prove I'm where I say I am."

Quinn glanced at Kate. She'd given up on finding a bottle opener. She'd taken a knife out and was using the flat part of the blade to pop the cap.

"You send someone. I'll give him a bottle of Coke. Ice-cold, just opened. He can snap a photo of me with a Coke in my hand after he shows me the photo of you with Jonathan Silver. Then you know I am where I say I am. And I know you are where you say you are."

Kate opened the second bottle. She took a long drink and grinned.

Quinn grinned back.

"This is a joke, right?" the voice said in Quinn's cell. "You are not alone in a van in the Gaza Strip to negotiate with me. Let me warn you, there will be no humor when I shoot the first Americans."

"This is not a joke," Quinn said. "And the stupidest thing you could do right now would be to shoot a hostage."

"Do not speak to me like that."

"Those hostages are your leverage. I've managed to keep the military out of this. If you shoot someone, they'll be here in as little time as it takes to bring choppers from the border."

"I want a negotiator with brains," Safady said. "Not someone so idiotic he comes into Gaza with no protection and is willing to sit like a duck to be shot."

"Shoot me and there won't be more negotiations. There will be a military operation. Is that what you want now that you're trapped?"

"I'll tell you what I want."

"First the cell-phone photo of one of your men with Jonathan Silver. Then I'll believe you. And once you send someone out to the van, you'll believe me, too." Quinn hung up.

"Are you sure you know what you're doing?" Kate asked. "You treated him like a baby just now."

Quinn took a pull on his Coke. "Actually, I thought it went rather well."

"Are you kidding me? He's probably lining up a couple hostages right now."

"Maybe. But if I thought I was pushing him too far, I would have backed off."

"Why push him at all?"

"If he's determined to take all of them down in a dramatic suicide bloodbath, there's nothing I can do," he answered. "Nothing the Israeli government can do. Jack Hamer knows it too. That's why he allowed me to run this in an unorthodox way."

Kate drank some more of her cola. Quinn noticed her habit of closing her eyes as she tilted the bottle back. He found it attractive. But then, he found nearly everything about her attractive.

She opened her eyes and caught him staring. She raised an eyebrow but said only, "So you're testing this guy. If he sends someone out with the cell phone, you'll know that he probably intends to negotiate his way out of this."

"I'll know that he's in there, and I'll know that Jonathan Silver is alive. I'll have also established who is running the show here. Rule one: take control."

She tapped the bottle absently with a fingernail. "Hard to tell whether you're smug or confident or just bluffing the confidence."

"That's part of my job too," he answered.

"Let me guess. Rule one?"

"Nope. But close to the top."

"So what if no one comes out with a cell-phone photo?" Kate asked.

"I die," Quinn said. "You live."

"Care to make sense of that for me?"

"If he's not interested in negotiating," Quinn said, "he doesn't need me. And since I am a sitting duck, it won't be hard for him to kill me. You, on the other hand, will be leaving the van in the next thirty seconds and should be fine."

"I'm not leaving."

"It's important for his soldier to find me alone in here," Quinn said.

"What about alone and handcuffed?"

"That would probably raise a few questions." He shook his head. "You really think I'm going to run at this point?"

"No," she said. "It just seems that you are good at orchestrating things. I don't like being orchestrated."

"Probably don't like the submissive female thing either, do you?"

Kate's eyes narrowed. "I'll go. But if you think it's submissive, you're in more danger from me than the terrorist."

"As long as all the other men around here believe you're submissive."

"What?"

Quinn drained his bottle and grinned. "Keep your veil on. Be sure to keep your head down when you walk along the street. No one will bother you; I promise."

He opened the van door for her on the side away from the orphanage.

She put on her veil and stepped down. "I can't believe I'm doing this," she said. "I really can't believe it."

Quinn shrugged.

"One thing," she said, pausing with the door still open. She held out her hand. "Keys."

"We've already established I'm not going to run."

"No, you won't abandon the hostages. But I can see you moving the van to a place where I can't find you."

"Kate—"

"Keys. You're playing this like a chess game. You got rid of the military. You got rid of Hamer. And you'll want to get rid of me until this is over because you think that's going to move me out of danger."

"Kate—"

"Am I wrong?" she asked.

Quinn handed her the keys.

15:45 GMT

All the hostages were outside in a small courtyard, and Jonathan Silver stood apart from the others.

He was outdoors for the first time in what seemed like years. His gratitude for the simple joy of fresh air told him that if he somehow survived this, his life would not be the same. After living this poverty, brief as it had been, he'd view his luxuries with a degree of guilt. He knew he should learn to help in a way that seemed to matter—Esther's way. He wondered if he would have the strength to deliver on this good intention.

Thinking of Esther, he looked around and saw her kneeling beside Alyiah.

Silver walked to her and touched her shoulder lightly.

Esther looked up, then stood.

"Thank you," Silver said. "I've learned from you. If I ever have the chance, I'm going to do my best to make sure that you receive enough money to keep helping these children."

"I won't refuse money," she said. "If Americans can help this lost generation of Palestinian children, they will be reducing the amount of recruits for terrorism in the next generation. But we need more than that from you."

"More." Silver thought he understood. He saw himself in front of cameras and thought of the PR those cameras would generate, following him as he worked with Esther's orphans. "I would donate some time, too. I'll work it into my schedule." He smiled grimly. "If we're delivered from this."

"If you want to make a difference here," she said, "stop predicting the end of the world."

He began to bristle.

"Please," Ester pleaded, "just listen to me."

"Sure."

"With your arms crossed like that?"

He hadn't even realized it. He caught enough of a smile in her question to relax slightly. It took effort, however, to finally uncross his arms. "The events in the Middle East clearly follow Revelation's timeline. I can't lie to the world about it."

"Haven't you ever even considered a different viewpoint?"

"Like what?"

"Like if the Great Tribulation prophesied in Revelation to happen 'soon' was actually fulfilled in the first-century persecution of Christians under Nero Caesar," she said. "Like if some of the cosmic apocalyptic phrases you interpret literally are actually Old Testament judgment metaphors meant not to describe historical events in literal detail but to highlight the eternal truths revealed through God's judgment of the nations?"

"Metaphors," Silver said. "Trying to twist the words of the Bible. Taking what is literal and—"

"In the Old Testament, Joel uses apocalyptic language of the sun being darkened and the moon being turned to blood to describe God's then soon-coming judgment on the enemies of ancient Israel. Are you suggesting the moon will actually turn to blood?"

"It will look red."

"Metaphor then."

Silver had no reply.

She continued. "Joel's apocalyptic symbolism of the sun being darkened and the moon being turned to blood is also used by Jesus and subsequently by John in Revelation to describe the great and terrible judgment on Jerusalem and vindication of the righteous that took place in AD 70. You can't understand Jesus and John here unless you are literate in the Old Testament too and realize how they use Old Testament metaphors in the New Testament!"

"But to say it meant the judgment in AD 70—"

"You do realize that many intelligent and devout Christians have held this view of Revelation throughout church history? That the holocaust of the fall of the temple to the Romans in AD 70 was the judgment that Jesus prophesied would happen within his generation."

"Well . . ."

"But you don't acknowledge this to your followers. At least let them understand that Christian orthodoxy allows for other views of Revelation."

"God promised Israel to the Jews. That miracle happened in 1948."

"And the Temple must be rebuilt?"

"Yes." But Silver was thinking of how Safady had challenged him.

"We are all Jews under Christ," she said. "Palestinian believers included. It's not about ethnicity but relationship. Israel as a nation-state now, a geopolitical entity, is not the kingdom Christ came to establish. And the Temple? Christ told the Samaritan woman at the well that the day was coming soon when she wouldn't have to worship at a physical temple. Christ is the Temple. We don't need stone walls and sacrifices on altars to worship God anymore."

"But people need to understand that their souls are in peril," Silver said. "They turn to God when they learn to fear the Great Tribulation and Armageddon."

"And turn away when the prediction of the month fails. Do you have any idea how many times since 1948 prominent leaders like yourself have predicted the Christ's return? Dozens of times. And they've been proven wrong every time."

"Events continue to unfold," Silver said. "Believers understand that. They don't lose faith."

"How many evangelicals believe what you teach?" Esther asked quietly.

"Seventy million," he answered. "Some estimate a hundred million."

"All believing Armageddon is almost upon us."

"The signs of the times—"

She didn't let him finish. "You have a huge following. When they believe the world is about to end, they believe there is little sense in trying to improve it. On the other hand, if you went on television and pleaded for your millions of listeners to support a two-state solution for Israel and Palestine, pleaded for the peace that would come with it for families here, poured the next three years of your ministry into Palestine and sent workers here among the poor who need it, can you imagine how your example of love would begin to erase Arab hatred and suspicion for America? And how that could help in the war against terrorism?"

It was a passionate outpouring, and she had to stop for breath. She looked at him expectantly, waiting for an answer.

"You won't let this go, will you?" he said.

Esther held Alyiah's hand. "Not until these children can grow up with hope, not despair."

Before Silver could answer, Safady marched toward them.

"You," Safady said to Esther. "I have a task for you."

15:45 GMT

Patterson and Burge made it back to the safe house with twenty seconds to spare. They stepped inside to be greeted by machine guns trained on the door. Visual identification was made, and the machine guns lowered.

At first glance, the interior looked no different from that of the house they'd entered to drop the gas cylinders. But the door and walls had been reinforced to withstand even armor-piercing missiles. And this house held the crates that the remaining soldiers had unloaded from the trucks while the six teams had been roaming the nearby streets and alleys.

Saxon was leaning against the wall. The other soldiers were sitting on crates in the empty interior. Saxon pointed Patterson and Burge to the far wall, where Orphan Annie was munching on hay that had been spread on the dirt.

Nothing was said.

The silence was broken only by the sound of horns outside and the clatter of bartering voices from the market down the street.

Within seconds, there was another knock on the door. The men with machine guns went on alert, then relaxed again when the final team entered.

Saxon wordlessly pointed at the door; two of the soldiers stepped forward and slid a bar of heavy iron into place to bolt the door shut.

Two others hurried to the back of the room and grabbed spades. They began digging into the dirt floor, and within seconds, Patterson heard a clunk of spades against wood.

Patterson had expected this. Before sending the teams out, Saxon had briefed them on what they would be doing upon their return. Still, Patterson was impressed by the thoroughness of logistics here. How much planning had it taken to prepare the house like this? And it brought the question to his mind again: who had known that the hostage taking would be here, and how could they have known far enough in advance to get all of this ready?

But there was no time to think about it now.

With the dirt removed, a trapdoor was revealed. The soldiers with spades opened it, uncovering a wide set of stairs dropping into darkness.

"Okay, men," Saxon said. "Now's the time for your gas masks."

Patterson and the others removed the masks from where they had been concealed beneath their clothing. When Patterson slipped his mask across his face, his breathing immediately became an eerie Darth Vader sound, except shallower and higher-pitched, a conscious reminder that fear was putting his body into high alert. Along with the faster breathing, he felt the tingle of adrenaline. Patterson knew his part in this next phase of the operation was to go with the first half of the unit to clear the tunnels of hostiles.

Once they secured the tunnel, all but three men of the second half would be in charge of moving the crates below.

The final three men would then close the trapdoor and cover it with dirt. Their instructions were to remain in the house and guard it against entry. Saxon had not said for how long they needed to remain or if they would be rejoining the unit again. Nor had they asked.

Hostiles.

Men already in the tunnel. Men, like them, highly trained and highly armed.

If everything went as planned, not a shot would be fired.

If not, Patterson was in for his first real firefight of the mission.

hen he slid open the side door of the panel van, Quinn was surprised to find a woman instead of a soldier. An American woman in her midforties with a calm face and a plain dress.

"I'm required to ask you for a Coke—" the woman held up a cell phone—"in exchange for this."

Quinn invited her in and pointed to a crate as a seat. He slid the door shut and turned to her. "You're one of the hostages," he said, relieved at the thought. This was his first real indication that Safady truly wanted negotiations.

"In a sense, yes. I run the orphanage."

"Esther Weber," Quinn said.

She blinked.

"I learned as much as I could from the Mossad about the orphanage. I'm Mulvaney Quinn." He offered her a cold bottle.

Esther accepted it but did not open it. She shifted on the crate and looked around the interior. "It's true, isn't it? You have no military backup here. Not even weapons."

"I've got my laptop to keep me connected. Mainly, though, I rely on my charm and wit."

"So you're suicidal," she said. Then she smiled.

"I'm working on a simple premise here. Intel says your official fund-raising status in the United States is that of a Christian relief organization. You've made it your lifework to help Palestinian orphans. You've been here for more than a decade, and the locals respect you and your efforts a great deal. This despite your Christian status."

"I don't advertise that," Esther said. "Francis of Assisi said to preach the gospel at all times, using words if necessary. These children don't need words. They need love and help. I give them what I can."

"In a Muslim nation extremely hostile to the West. Yet you are protected."

"Who would want to hurt the children?"

"Exactly," Quinn said. "I'm sure Safady knew that when he picked your orphanage as the place to hold the Americans."

"Three months ago, the local council, for the first time, arranged for money to help with building repairs to make it modernized, including computer connections and security. I should have suspected something."

"You're suggesting it was long planned that this would be the location?"

"Or coincidence," she said. "What do you think?"

"Convenient, but not coincidence."

The Mossad either didn't know about the modernization or had decided not to tell him. Quinn made a mental note of this.

"Either way, you are protected," he said. "In effect, I too am relying on your reputation to protect me. If the locals know I'm here to negotiate, hurting me hurts you and the children. My only real danger is from Safady, and if he wants to negotiate, he'll keep me alive too."

"*Wants* to negotiate?"

"You've got a photo of Silver on the cell phone?"

She showed him.

Quinn nodded. "Now I know he wants to negotiate."

"Versus going out in a blaze of martyrdom glory," she said.

"Exactly." Quinn noticed she had not touched the Coke yet. "How much time before he expects you back?"

"Almost immediately."

"Forgive me then for asking what I need to in this situation. All the hostages are fine?"

"Except for two who tried to escape. They were executed. The rest have learned their lesson."

"How is morale?"

"You'd be surprised at how high it is. They have faith. It's become real for them."

"How many men does Safady have? What kind of weaponry? Where are they stationed?"

"No," Esther said.

"No?"

"That's the kind of information you need to consider a rescue operation. I refuse to help you with that. There are children in there; I do not want them to become casualties."

Quinn knew it would be useless to try to change her mind. Not with a woman strong enough and determined enough to accomplish what she'd done here in the Gaza Strip.

Esther continued. "Somewhere along the way, can you remind the other side that there are children in there? Life has already been harsh enough to them. They didn't deserve what has put them in there. Nor do they deserve to suffer more now."

Quinn caught her looking at the plastic bag with ice and the other bottles and decided he finally understood why she wasn't drinking the cold Coke in her hand. "Not many soft drinks inside the orphanage," he said.

"It's like Christmas for them when we have it."

"You're saving yours for one of them?"

"A little girl named Alyiah. She's had a rough day. Safady was going to execute her too as part of the punishment for the escape attempt." Esther pointed the cell phone at Quinn. "He said he wanted a photo too."

Quinn stared at the phone and held up his bottle as promised. He heard the simulated click from the cell phone.

Esther pushed herself off the crate. "One more thing." She handed Quinn a folded piece of newspaper. "Today's headlines. Jonathan Silver wrote a note on it so that you know the message is today's. He's authorizing the release of $20 million into a Palestinian bank account, but he doesn't want Safady to know about it. Or the media."

"I don't understand."

"A donation to the orphanage," she said. "Jonathan Silver is no longer convinced that Palestinians are tainted."

15:58 GMT

Patterson saw the first body about twenty steps from the bottom of the stairs. It threw a shallow black shadow from the flashlight attached to Patterson's machine-gun barrel. Patterson hesitated, half expecting the man to rise like a zombie in the harsh silence and cool air of the tunnel.

"You know the drill," Burge said in a voice muffled by the gas mask.

He and Patterson advanced, the other soldiers behind them, and pointed the barrels of their machine guns straight down at the man's chest.

The man was no older than any of them. Clean-shaven with dark hair. Muscled but not fat. And, as Patterson could tell by the gentle rise and fall of his chest, he was still breathing.

The flashlight showed crisp details of the uniform, buttons gleaming.

Israeli military.

Patterson was baffled. An Israeli soldier? Here in the heart of Gaza?
"Tape," Burge said.

A soldier behind him squatted and flipped the Israeli soldier over without even a groan from the unconscious man. As their companion duct-taped the Israeli's wrists and feet together, Patterson bit back his questions, knowing Burge would report anything and everything to Saxon.

They left the Israeli soldier on the ground where he was and advanced farther into the tunnel. Even though he knew they'd dropped canisters with paralyzing gas into the vents to these tunnels, Patterson's heart was pounding. He knew the target he was presenting by holding a flashlight.

He smelled a faint stench mixed with a chemical odor. The flashlight beam showed another body on the ground and, just beyond it at the side of the tunnel, five camping toilets. It looked like the Israeli soldiers had been here for days, not hours. This was confirmed when his flashlight beam showed canned goods and bottled water farther ahead.

After binding this Israeli—also unconscious—they rounded a slight bend, and the tunnel opened and became a wide room. Patterson estimated it was twice the square footage of his mobile home back in Georgia. Army cots had been set on the floor in orderly lines. Patterson flicked his flashlight beam and counted five lines five deep. Twenty-five men, then. Two they had already bound.

The paralyzing gas had caught these men in various stages of repose. Some had been napping. Others had been reading books, which had fallen on their chests or on the floor.

Something about the situation bothered Patterson.

Then it clicked. Without giving any warning to Burge, Patterson reached across and snapped off the man's flashlight. Then, quickly, his own, putting the room into instant darkness. "Scatter," he grunted. "Retreat! Now!"

Patterson pushed Burge away and stepped sideways himself, moving from the last position he'd been standing with his flashlight.

In that instant, a flash point seemed to erupt from the black of the room. No explosion, but the *thwoop* of a silenced pistol.

Patterson's suspicion had been confirmed. Men don't read in the dark. One of the Israeli soldiers must have found a way to remain conscious and had shut the lights off and waited.

There were a groan and a gurgle behind Patterson, and as he was moving backward, he tripped over one of his own soldiers.

More silenced shots, with bullets caroming over his head.

By then, the rest of the Freedom Crusaders had dashed back into the tunnel away from the open room.

Patterson groped in the darkness, finding a gas mask with his hand, which he used as a reference point. The fallen man groaned.

That drew another shot from the far end of the room. To Patterson, it seemed like an invisible man had pounded him in the left shoulder with a baseball bat. A bullet had slammed into his Kevlar. It spun him back on his heels and he toppled, which probably saved his life. Two more bullets whined past his ear.

With his right hand, he found one of the fallen man's ankles and gripped and pulled, doing a crab walk backward until he was in the tunnel again.

"Burge," Patterson said, not caring how loud his voice was. He dropped the soldier's ankle and gripped his machine gun. "Throw a canister."

"Already got it," Burge said.

"How about throwing it now instead of later. If—"

Patterson didn't finish. There were more flashes in the darkness. The Israeli must have known he'd be trapped and decided that offense was as good a defense as any.

Patterson squeezed off a couple rounds at the flashes. The explosion was too loud for him to know if he'd made a direct hit, but no return fire came.

Patterson set his machine gun down because his left shoulder was so numb he couldn't use his left hand to turn on the flashlight again. With the barrel on the ground, he reached it with his right hand and hit the switch, illuminating an Israeli on his side, knocked backward from the force of bullets. Two more flashlights came on from behind Patterson, and he scanned the situation.

Burge was down, a round hole near the top of his gas mask and red sprayed across the visor portion. Another Freedom Crusader had toppled over him. Both of them dead from head shots, a vulnerable area not protected by Kevlar.

The first soldier, the one Patterson had dragged from the room, had what looked like a gallon of red paint soaking the ground beneath his leg. He wasn't breathing any longer. Patterson was no medic but could make the easy conclusion. This bullet had found a major artery.

Three of them dead, then. And an Israeli.

Saxon wasn't going to like this. They'd had standing orders since the mission began to take any Israelis alive. Apparently Israelis were worth more than Palestinians, Patterson sourly concluded.

One of the remaining Freedom Crusaders moved back toward the room with the cots.

"No," Patterson said. This Israeli had been smart enough to surprise them. If there were two, one would have stayed back to complete the trap.

Patterson took the canister from Burge's open and still hand. He pushed the button to prime the explosive cap and threw it into the open room.

"Five minutes," he said. "Then we go back in."

K eys," Quinn said as soon as Kate stepped back into the van.

"Negotiations over? You *are* good."

He held out his hand. "Not a good time for bad humor."

She handed him the keys.

Quinn started the engine and shifted it into drive. Traffic was slow. The narrow street was clogged with equally ancient vehicles. Boys on scooters zoomed in and out.

He reached an intersection well past the orphanage, and Kate still hadn't said anything. He liked that. He'd expected a protest or at the least an immediate question demanding the reason for this.

Quinn was forced to jam on the brakes as a taxi cut in front of him. At the same time, his cell phone rang. He'd wondered how long that would take.

He flipped it open. "Hello."

"What are you doing?" Safady was almost screeching. "Who said you could leave?"

"I'm looking for a Starbucks," Quinn answered. "Any helpful directions?"

"You can't leave. You're the negotiator."

"Cell phones have a wider range than face-to-face," Quinn said. He made an unexpected turn into a narrow alley. "You want to come out and negotiate in person? Then I'll park where you can see me again."

Safady's obscene reply was loud enough to make Quinn wince.

"Listen," Quinn said, "there are some terms you can dictate and others you can't. One of the things you can't dictate is my location. I'll always pick up within two rings. How much closer do you need me?"

Safady hung up.

Quinn glanced in his rearview mirror and saw two motorcycles turn into the alley. A few hundred yards down, he found another street, where he turned left, stopped almost immediately, and shifted into park.

Kate finally spoke. "I've spent a lot of time in patrol cars with male partners. One thing I learned early is that, contrary to popular opinion, guys are sensitive to subtext."

"So it's not just women who always listen for subtext and read too much into it?"

"You'd think a guy would understand that no means no. As in 'No, I don't want you to buy me a drink' or 'No, I'm not interested in giving you my phone number.' How much extra do you think they choose to read into the word *no* when they keep coming back?"

Quinn glanced at the rearview mirror, waiting for the motorcycles to exit the alley. "There's a reason you're giving me a Mars and Venus seminar, right?"

The motorcycles reached the street, and both drivers stopped briefly. Quinn had been looking for that. If the drivers had a destination in mind, they would have immediately turned left or right.

"You offer a guy advice," Kate said, "and he doesn't hear that you want to help. What he hears is that you think he's doing a lousy job and you can do better. So early on, I stopped offering advice until I was asked for it."

"You're so much more than a pretty face," Quinn said, still watching the men on the motorcycles, who turned their heads, then gave a telltale pause as they noticed the van parked just down the street. "Who knows? Maybe we'll find a way to get along after all."

"Another thing I learned in the patrol car is that if you ask a guy what he's doing or why he's doing it, he'll think you're second-guessing him. Which, to a guy, is like questioning his judgment. On the other hand, if you keep your mouth shut, what he reads between the lines instead is that you trust him and therefore respect his judgment."

"Interesting theory," Quinn said. Behind them, the motorcyclists leaned their heads together to talk above the sound of the idling engines.

"Let's try it out in real life," Kate continued. "Say a woman marshal gets into the van of the prisoner she's supposed to take back to the U.S. Say it's in the Gaza Strip, which is not the safest of areas for an American. Say she's given the guy enough trust that she lets him be the driver. Say the driver takes off without a word of explanation, and say the driver is leaving behind the American hostages that he's been using as leverage to push around this woman marshal. Would you expect—hypothetically speaking of course—that this woman marshal should start asking questions?"

"Hmmm," Quinn said. The motorcyclists each turned in a different direction. One up the street, one down the street. Quinn wondered if there was a third in position still down the alley. He'd find out. "I'm guessing your subtext is that you're trying to ask without asking. If so, I'm insulted that you are second-guessing me."

"Listen," she snapped, "I gave my partners the respect they deserved, but they gave me respect in turn. None of them put me in a situation where I'd have to ask. They'd discuss a plan with me, and we'd make a decision together. It's implied in the term *partner.*"

"We're partners now?"

"I believe that happened when I agreed to help you with this, then agreed to choose your side over Hamer's."

Quinn was waiting long enough for the motorcyclists to get just out of sight. If they'd parked right behind the van, that would have sent one message. As it was, he'd learned something different. He was under surveillance but wasn't supposed to know it.

"All right then," he said to Kate. "I'm sorry. I should have discussed this with you before driving away."

"I'll believe it when you tell me why you left the location."

Quinn backed up and turned into the same alley that had led him to this street. "I've already established a power position by getting him to concede the photo on the cell phone. Now that I know he wants to negotiate and not kill the hostages, I decided we were safe to move. Keeping mobile is good. It protects us."

"And this Steve McQueen driving . . . ?"

"I wanted to find out if anyone was watching the van."

"Two guys on motorbikes. You split them up, and they're down the street in both directions waiting for us to pass them again. One will probably call the other on a cell phone as soon as they've learned which way you're headed."

"You *are* good."

He glanced over at her, and their eyes locked briefly. Each quickly looked away, as if they'd accidentally touched. How come he was bantering with her? Time to change subjects, to focus.

"Also, knowing he wants to negotiate, I wanted to establish the terms a little more solidly. I can't have Safady thinking he can push me around."

"Plus, you didn't like being a sitting duck," Kate said.

Quinn gave her a sideways look. "So if you knew all this, why ask?"

"I didn't ask. That would be second-guessing you. I posed a hypothetical situation."

"Of course," Quinn said. "Or maybe you wanted to establish the terms here."

"Now that we got that figured out, care to discuss what's next?"

"Sure. I want to find a place to buy a couple cases of Cokes."

All the unconscious Israelis had been bound and moved out of the way and all the crates moved into the large room at the end of the tunnels, which was bathed in full light now. Patterson couldn't see a generator and guessed the electricity came from ground wires.

All told, the room was no more uncomfortable than an army barrack. There were televisions with headsets, some video games, an assortment of books. Given the food and water supplies and the camping toilets, it was obvious that the Israelis had known they would be waiting here for a while.

Waiting for what? Patterson wondered.

Not an attack, that was certain. If they'd been expecting an attack, the Israelis would have left soldiers in the safe house to guard the trapdoor, just as Saxon had positioned Freedom Crusaders there.

Patterson had also casually inspected the walls of this underground room—concrete blocks. As if it had not been dug out from beneath whatever was above but laid first like a foundation for a basement. The blocks seemed aged and had scattered graffiti in Arabic. The graffiti didn't seem fresh either and only added to Patterson's questions about all this. The tunnel had been here awhile.

He was standing beside the wall when Saxon began to speak.

"Men, we've had our first casualties. They were your friends and brothers, and I share your grief. Let us take comfort in knowing God will receive them in the spirit that their sacrifice has been made and that they are now in the presence of Jesus, our Savior."

The three bodies had been moved to the base of the stairway beneath the safe house and, along with the dead Israeli, had been shrouded by blankets.

"There will be a time and place for proper burial," Saxon continued. "But this is not that time. You have about forty minutes until the next phase of this operation. First, shave and put on your Crusader uniforms. Then cover yourselves with Palestinian clothing. You'll put the scarves on before you assist the hostages. Under no circumstances will you reveal yourselves as Freedom Crusaders until I give the order to do so. Any questions about procedure here?"

None.

"Good," he said. "Then the lights in here will be dimmed, and I expect you to find a cot and catch some sleep. It's going to be a long night, and you need to be rested. There will be no questions until the next briefing."

At least no verbal questions, Patterson thought. But Saxon was still giving no explanation of the platoon's ultimate mission.

What was ahead?

"I had no idea," Kate said. "This is like a third-world country."

She'd been silent for minutes as Quinn maneuvered through the streets of Khan Yunis to make sure they'd lost the men tailing them. Now they were parked again, this time in the shade of a three-story building that looked as if it were about to crumble into dust.

"No," Quinn said, "a third-world country would be an improvement on this."

In the shimmering heat, everything seemed gray: old, gray blocks for building walls; old, gray, broken pavement; abandoned cars without tires or windshields, gray with dust; and tired, old people, walking with the weight of a gray world on their shoulders.

"What would world reaction be if the United States required people of African descent to carry special ID cards?" Quinn asked. "Or what if recent European arrivals to America were given homes taken away from people of African descent?"

"Obviously we would be condemned as racist," Kate said, "restricting human freedoms."

"And what if our reaction to the world was that it was justified for biblical reasons?"

"Unthinkable."

"Exactly. And yet that's the situation here. In most third-world countries, there would be more freedom and less injustice to hamper economic and social advancement. The Palestinians, however, are treated as second-class citizens in Israel. In some ways, they're treated worse than the blacks in South Africa at the height of apartheid, including the need to carry specially colored ID cards to identify them as Palestinians. Almost the way Jews were treated in Nazi Germany."

"But to compare it to Europeans moving to the United States and taking away homes from African-Americans?"

"First understand this is a racial or ethnic situation. People with Jewish ancestry versus Arabs. That's how it's divided. Then consider the numbers. Palestinians today are among the largest displaced peoples in the world. To make room for the Jewish immigrants, over four hundred Palestinian villages have been destroyed. Take the infamous story of Deir Yassin."

"Deir Yassin?" Kate asked.

"Your reaction confirms one of the points I'd like to make. There are two sides to this story. The problem is that one of the sides of the story is largely untold. To the Palestinians, the Deir Yassin massacre symbolizes the entire issue. You, on the other hand, know nothing about it."

"Tell me then."

"Three years after the Nazi Holocaust ended in 1945, the Israeli paramilitary moved into Deir Yassin, a village near Jerusalem, and brutally slaughtered somewhere in the neighborhood of two hundred fifty men, women, children, and even babies. The Israelis went so far as to drive some Palestinian men to other villages to tell the story, spreading panic. Entire villages emptied, which was the entire purpose of the massacre. Israeli immigrants took over the homes and villages."

Kate was shaking her head. "I won't deny that's horrible, but you can't imply it's on the magnitude of the Holocaust inflicted by the Nazis."

"Not the magnitude. But one of the justifications for it was the need to give Jews a place to shelter them from another Holocaust. I'd argue the injustice was no different. One race indiscriminately slaughtering another."

"Surely you aren't saying the injustices inflicted on Palestine condone how Palestinian terrorists fight the Israelis."

Quinn smiled sadly. "See how easily this becomes an intellectual debate? My wife and daughter died to a suicide bomber, remember."

Kate let out a breath. "You're right. I'm sorry."

"There are wrongs on both sides. It's gone far beyond the point where you can find the Hollywood resolution of who is clearly the bad guy and whom you should cheer for. You ask me if I can justify the terrorism attacks? Hardly. I can give you a list as long as my arm of the outrages that Palestinians have inflicted on peace-loving Jews. I won't, because you already have a sense of it through media exposure. From a practical stance, I sympathize with Israel. It has no choice but to impose harsh control just to survive the constant terror threats inflicted on its civilian population. Palestinian terrorist attacks can't be condoned in any manner. Not the least is the long-term futility of it."

He paused. "You and I weren't around in the fifties, before the civil rights movement began in the United States, but we're familiar enough with Rosa Parks, Martin Luther King, right? You'll agree with me that the situation was wrong and needed changing?"

"It's still not completely fixed," Kate said.

"So imagine if the militant Black Panther movement had grown to the point where the civil rights battle was fought by terrorist tactics. Would the movement have made the progress it did? Or would it have steeled the majority of Americans to dig in and fight?"

"Dig in and fight. Like Israel now."

"Exactly. Go back to the '72 Olympics in Munich. Erase that hostage-taking incident and all the terrorist attacks since, and change the Palestinian tactics to peaceful protests and an appeal to the world for help—the Gandhi way. Things would be much different here now. Terrorism against Israel justifies our sympathy for it."

"Your wife and daughter would still be alive."

"And the wives and daughters of thousands of families on both sides of the dispute. People get involved in the politics. They forget about the damage it does to children."

Kate was silent for a few minutes, thinking about it. She shifted. "What was that you said about biblical justification?"

"Yeah," Quinn said with a sigh. "That too."

"Explain."

He rubbed his face briefly. "Let's compare it again to the United States. What would world opinion be if fundamentalist Christians reverted to using the Bible to justify slavery, as happened a century ago?"

"That's a rhetorical question, right?"

"Genesis chapter twelve, verse three—the Lord speaking to Abram. 'I will bless those who bless you, and I will curse him who curses you; and in you all the families of the earth shall be blessed.' Countless Christian fundamentalists use this as a mantra to justify unqualified support for Israel."

"Hang on," Kate said. "As devil's advocate, I have to say that's a pretty clear directive from God. So if you're a Christian, how do you not apply it to Israel today?"

"Historically, Christianity has always believed in one people of God based on relationship rather than race. The apostle Paul spelled it out clearly when he declared, 'You are all sons of God through faith in Christ Jesus. If you belong to Christ, then you are Abraham's seed, and heirs according to the promise.' Even in the Old Testament, God-fearing foreigners were counted among the faithful and were treated as spiritual Israelites."

"So you're saying Americans shouldn't support Israel?"

"Not at all. It's a democracy and a stable ally in the Middle East. I'm saying both sides of the story need to be understood. But remember the seventy million fundamentalist Christians who give unqualified support for Israel's ethnic cleansing of this land based on bad theology. And remember the Palestinian children. Any theology that contributes to an entire lost generation of children needs to be examined."

Quinn gestured through the cracked windshield of the van. "You don't have to look any farther than this to see the consequences."

"Or the green land on one side of the border and the brown on the other," Kate said softly. "I never knew."

"Five minutes," Safady told Quinn over the cell phone. "That's how long I'm giving you to come back to me with an answer."

Quinn hadn't moved the van too far. It was only minutes from the orphanage in case he needed to get back there quickly. "What's the question?" he asked.

"No. First you understand that it is a deal breaker. You give me what I want, or I kill the first hostage in five minutes and then one every half hour after that. I will throw their bodies over the wall onto the streets. Do you think that will cause any rioting—to have the bodies of dead Americans where these Palestinians can rip them apart?"

"If you begin to kill—"

"You've already taken great pains to explain that I need them alive to negotiate. That means you need to understand the conclusion here. There will be no more negotiating of any kind. You get me what I want. Or the hostages are dead. Afterward, I'll simply disappear somewhere in Gaza. I'll be a hero to my people."

Quinn made a mental note that Safady was still interested in self-preservation not martyrdom. "I understand the seriousness of your request. But I can't make a promise. You know that."

"You can get me an answer. Five minutes."

"What is your request?"

"It's not a request. A demand."

"Tell me," Quinn said.

"Two choppers—big ones. For transport to Jordan."

Another indication that Safady wasn't interested in martyrdom. Quinn dared allow himself hope that this might be resolved. There was precedent, too. Israel had done this in other hostage negotiations.

Safady's request made sense. The Gaza Strip was in essence a large prison, patrolled by Israelis, with a certain amount of freedom inside the borders. Now that Safady's location was known to the Israelis, he'd need a country with equal sympathy to the Arab cause but much more power and autonomy than Gaza to protect him and his men.

"I can't get that answer in five minutes," Quinn said. "No one can. Shifting this to Jordan makes it an international incident. It's got to be cleared by the highest levels of government. Israel might clear it, but the officials in Jordan will spend hours deliberating the pros and cons."

"Five minutes. The hostages will be split into two groups, half in each helicopter. That guarantees we won't be shot down by Israeli jets. Once we're safely in Jordan and I confirm that $60 million has been deposited into a bank account in the United Arab Emirates, half the hostages will be released. Then another $60 million, and the other half will be released."

"You asked for over a half billion dollars earlier."

"That was just to get world attention. Silver's organization can find sixty million. I didn't choose that number by accident. It's enough to punish the organiza tion, but not enough to collapse it. They'll get the money."

"Even if it's true, the money is a big complication," Quinn said. But he was doing the math. Maybe it was possible. "Both the Israeli and U.S. governments have a policy not to pay ransom demands. You know that."

"Four million per person. I'm told every person in the group has a kidnapping policy that covers them for the amount. This is what you do, isn't it? Act as go-between for insurance companies? That covers the first payment. The insurance companies will agree. It saves them a lot more than they'd pay out in life insurance."

"But five minutes isn't enough time. If you demand something that's impossible, I can't do anything about it."

"Five minutes is enough time to get the decision about the transport into Jordan. While the hostages are in transport, you can come up with $60 million. You'll have another five hours after we arrive in Jordan to come up with the remainder."

"Listen—"

"You arrogant American, thinking you'd established control with all your little games. Now it is time for you to listen to me. Five minutes, or the first body is on the street."

Safady hung up.

16:25 GMT

"Hamer, you heard his request." Hamer had been tapped into Quinn's cell conversations. "I think we're down to the endgame."

"We're not going to supply them with two Black Hawks. For all you know, that's his ultimate goal. I could see him dropping hostages from ten thousand feet until the choppers are empty, then heading into Syria."

"So rig the choppers with explosive devices. We'll let him know that if anything goes wrong with the hostages, he's vaporized."

"I can't see it happening. And if we do get permission, it won't be within five minutes."

Quinn slammed the steering wheel of the van. Kate, who couldn't hear the other end of the conversation from the passenger seat, raised a questioning eyebrow at Quinn's burst of frustration.

"What's the hourly rate for two Israeli military choppers?" Quinn asked. He glanced at his watch. Less than three minutes before Safady expected a call back.

"The military doesn't hire out choppers."

"It does if you want to save face," Quinn said. "You hire them out to CCTI. That makes our company responsible for all of this. The insurance companies will pay for it and it won't be an Israeli military operation."

"Maybe," Hamer said after some hesitation.

"Maybe isn't good enough. I think he's finished with posturing."

"You going to be able to raise $120 million to cover the ransom demand?"

Quinn wasn't entirely sure. But Safady had been shrewd in choosing his number. The kidnapping policies would pay out; the card he'd play with Lloyd's and other insurance brokers was that the publicity would drive a lot of extra business their way. The remainder would depend on Silver's organization, and Quinn couldn't see them refusing.

"Getting the money is no problem," Quinn lied. The important thing here was to beat the five-minute deadline. He'd worry about the next deadline after that.

"I don't know if I can get a decision back to you in time," Hamer said.

Down to a shade over two minutes.

"Do it," Quinn snapped. "Call me back in ninety seconds."

16:26 GMT

Sixty-five seconds and counting. Hamer's caller ID showed up as Quinn's phone rang.

Quinn snapped his phone open halfway through the first ring. "Yes or no?"

"Still waiting," Hamer said.

Quinn snapped the phone shut. He wasn't going to waste a second expressing his anger or frustration. He punched in the numbers to reach Safady. He too answered in one ring.

"Do I kill the first one or not?" Safady said. "I've got a machine gun trained on her heart right now. The video camera is running."

"You don't kill hostages," Quinn said.

"I'm getting my choppers?"

"Yes."

"When?"

"Nightfall." That was about an hour away.

"Not soon enough."

"It has to be," Quinn said. "The Israeli military won't bring them down in daylight. I don't have to explain why."

Because every kid with a rifle would be taking potshots.

Safady was silent. Quinn held his breath. He'd just lied outrageously, but if Safady bought it, that left until nightfall to find a way to pressure Hamer into getting the choppers.

"What about the money?"

Quinn tried not to let his release of breath become audible. "Done."

"All of it?"

"All of it," Quinn answered.

"Then we have nothing left to discuss."

"Yes, we do." Quinn couldn't leave this bluff incomplete. "The choppers aren't going to arrive unless you do some work on your end."

"I told you—no more negotiations."

"You're going to have to put the word out that these two choppers need safe passage. That any ground-to-air missiles will be killing you and your men too."

Nothing could prevent kids with rifles from shooting at a low-flying Israeli helicopter, even with the relative safety of a night landing. The only Palestinians with more sophisticated weaponry, however, were men in organized cells. Safady should be able to reach them with the warning.

Safady answered with more silence.

"You don't have the power and connections to make this possible?" Quinn asked.

"Of course I do," Safady snapped.

"Then arrange it. Also, you and I are going to arrange a time, down to the second, for the arrival of the helicopters. They are going to be coming in fast and with no lights. Thirty seconds before arrival, you're going to need to set out a circle of lights in the compound to guide them in. Got it?" Quinn knew these instructions would add credibility to his bluff.

"I don't like the tone in your voice. I'm the one in control here."

"No more games," Quinn said. "Your demands have been met. That should be enough control."

"The lights will be on," Safady said after a pause.

"One more thing," Quinn said. "Put the hostages out in the compound right now and leave them there. You don't get the choppers unless we know they are all alive and unharmed."

"You will have to take my word for it."

"No. We'll trust satellite images instead. Tell them to look upward frequently so we can make positive identification of each of them."

It didn't hurt to remind Safady that the Israeli military had the orphanage under constant surveillance, even if tanks were not surrounding the building.

"Anything else?" Safady asked sarcastically.

"Yeah," Quinn said. "In about twenty minutes, I'm going to be walking up to the outside gates with a couple of cases of Cokes. I want you to make sure the kids inside get them."

JUST OUTSIDE GAZA • 16:28 GMT

"Hamer." It was Zvi Cohen, reaching Hamer via cell phone.

Hamer sat in an air-conditioned Mercedes on the Israeli side of the border with a transmitter that gave him all of Quinn's cell phone conversations. The three soldiers with him were outside in the heat. They would not be hearing any of Quinn's conversations. Or Hamer's.

"It's going as planned," Hamer told Cohen. "We don't have much time here. I have to call him back on the demand for choppers."

"He didn't suspect anything when you suggested we send him in alone?"

"Got lucky. He brought it up first. I fought him on it."

"Excellent. Keep playing his request for choppers the same way. Keep making him work for the demands."

Cohen could be irritating. They'd gone through this a dozen times. Not only that; Cohen was getting a feed from anything on Quinn's cell. So he knew from the conversation barely over a minute earlier how Hamer had resisted agreeing to choppers. Cohen just liked giving orders.

"Of course," Hamer said. "Confirm for me that Brad Silver is now in Gaza."

"Confirmed."

"Hang on," Hamer said as voices came over the transmitter. Quinn and Safady. What was going on? Quinn was supposed to talk to Hamer before getting back to Safady. "Got to hang up. Quinn is talking to Safady again."

Hamer knew Cohen would hear the voices too from his office in Tel Aviv.

Hamer listened as Quinn promised helicopters. And the soft drinks. A few seconds after the call ended, he dialed the number to Quinn's cell and began acting.

"Are you insane?" Hamer shouted into the cell phone. "You can't promise him choppers! All of this is still going through channels."

"You're wrong," Quinn said. "I can promise him choppers. That was the easy part. Getting them there is what's out of my control."

"And if the choppers don't show up?"

"Hostages die. Better the chance that he starts killing them in two hours than the certainty he starts now."

"There's no way anyone's going to authorize choppers," Hamer said. "I've got to tell you that."

"Don't you guys have any imagination?" Quinn answered. "Once they're up in the air, gas them all. Have the pilots throw on gas masks. You'll have two choppers with unconscious terrorists and Americans. When Safady wakes up, he'll be in handcuffs in Tel Aviv."

Hamer didn't say anything.

"You still there?"

"I'm thinking about that suggestion," Hamer said. "It could work."

"It justifies getting the choppers cleared," Quinn said. "If it doesn't work, at least it won't look like Israel has given in to the demands but instead was attempting a military op that had a good chance of success. Or failing that, lease the choppers to CCTI. I'll take responsibility."

"Let me get back to you," Hamer said.

"Not good enough."

"You're not easy to like."

"Promise me the choppers," Quinn said. "Right now. Otherwise I start calling media outlets and telling them the Israelis have refused to end this."

After a long silence, Hamer spoke. "You'll have your choppers."

"Good. I'll be in touch with the details."

"Let me repeat," Hamer said. "You're not easy to like."

"I wasn't interested in dating you at any time," Quinn said.

"Mutual," Hamer said. He liked this guy. He hoped Quinn would understand the need for deception when he found out about it. If he survived that long.

KHAN YUNIS, GAZA STRIP • 16:48 GMT

The outer gate to the orphanage opened. Quinn had put on clothing that would help him blend in with crowds and found a couple of cases of Coke. This was a personal delivery.

The man who opened the gate was slightly shorter than Quinn, maybe a decade younger, clean shaven, poised and confident, Palestinian in features and clothing.

"For the kids," Quinn said in Arabic, gesturing at the drinks. "I promised it to Esther."

"Speak English. You sound like a grunting camel in my language."

There was something challenging about the way the man stood. Quinn felt a prickling of adrenaline, as if a harsh, hot wind as old as mankind had briefly swept away from both of them the thin veneer of civility that covered every man's primal urges.

Something about his own posture must have changed too.

"Ah," the man said. "You do know, don't you? I am your enemy. But isn't this what you wanted? Man-to-man? Otherwise why tell me you were going to deliver it yourself?"

Khaled Safady. All of Quinn's muscles tensed.

"I wanted you to see me," Safady said. "I wanted to speak to you, so close to each other that you could reach for my throat with your bare hands. But you won't. Because even if you could kill me right now, you wouldn't. Behind me are too many other lives that matter. It also makes you a coward to come here now, before the choppers arrive. You know I cannot kill you. Yet."

Quinn trembled. His hatred was so deep, so vicious, that he felt as though he were on the edge of a precipice.

"Right now, I too would like to reach across and tear your windpipe from your throat." Safady pulled out a knife that he had tucked behind his back. "Or better yet, slit your throat and lap at your blood as it spills onto the ground." He dropped the knife on the ground between them. "But I won't. Too many other lives matter. Oppressed Muslims, living under the tyranny of America."

"So killing is the way to peace?" Quinn said.

"Oh, the self-righteousness of Americans. You want peace? We throw rocks at your tanks because we have no water, because our tables are bare and our houses have no roofs. You want peace? Stop arming Israel. Help transform Palestine so that every child has hope. Let every Arab here see that you care as much about them as you do the Jews."

"Deliver that message to the world instead of delivering explosives. Killing women and children of the enemy is cowardice."

"Our women and children die at the hands of the Jews."

"Only by accident. Or only when your soldiers hide behind them. Like now in the orphanage. Ironic—you depend on the Israeli sense of moral rightness to protect you. If it were reversed, you would slaughter every child inside to destroy Israeli soldiers."

"You speak of peace," Safady said. "But in your heart, you want to kill me. Don't you find that to be hypocritical?"

Quinn knew it was true. He couldn't help but glance at the knife on the ground.

Safady noticed and gave Quinn a chilling grin. "It would give me great pleasure if you reached for the knife." His smile became mocking. "Yet you wonder. Is it me? The man you have hunted for five years? The man who killed your wife and your daughter? Or am I just posing as the man to take advantage of the reputation of the Black Prince?"

Logic told Quinn he could not make any assumptions. The deepest fibers in his body knew otherwise. This was the man.

"Blue jeans and a red shirt," Safady said. "Her precious little shoes were red too. She was holding a small backpack with a Barbie doll patch on it."

The edge of the cliff began to crumble beneath Quinn. But it was worse than a nightmare because he was so frozen with the shock and horror of his memories that it seemed they were all that was holding him in place, keeping him from falling yet leaving him so helpless he was unable to flail.

"I was there," Safady said. "At that coffee stand on the side of the road that morning. It was my first bomber, strapped with explosives, and I'd walked him to the bus stop and prayed with him as we waited for the bus to arrive. I remember you, because just when the door opened for my bomber to step onto the bus to martyrdom, I saw you standing inside, holding hands with the little girl in the red shirt with the matching red shoes."

Safady's continued smile showed he knew the effect he was having on Quinn. "And the woman behind you. Laughing at something you'd said. Wrapping her arm around your waist as the door began to close. I remember because you pushed open the door to get out just before it closed, and I was thinking that you didn't know it, but you'd just saved your life. I watched you for a few seconds and saw why you left the bus. You wanted espresso and a pastry. I watched you order it, but I knew you wouldn't even take the first sip.

"I was right. The bus was only three hundred yards away when it exploded. I watched you drop the espresso and pastry that had saved your life. I watched you run toward the fire. That filled me with joy. That's when I knew I was doing what Allah had called me to do—destroy Americans."

Quinn was doing all he could to breathe, sucking in quick sips of air, fighting off vertigo.

"So?" Safady said. "Now do you know I am who I say I am? The man you've been hunting?"

It was happening again—the shock, disbelief, guilt. As if Quinn were right there in the wreckage in the moments after it happened, searching for his daughter, telling himself that by some miracle she'd survived, because God wouldn't allow a death like this to happen to someone so beautiful and so vulnerable and so loved. Until he found the one red shoe.

"The knife," Safady said. "It's right there. Pick it up. I'm here."

Quinn had spent five years hunting this man. But he'd also spent five years rigidly holding himself together.

All he could do was blink.

"I didn't think you were man enough," Safady said. "That's what I wanted to know. Someday I'll kill you."

He backed away and closed the door, sliding a bolt shut.

Quinn stared at the door sightlessly. He wept without tears. Finally he turned away too, leaving the Cokes on the dirt beside the knife. He was a dead man. Walking.

"Pats. Wake up. Time to move."

Sleep felt so good. Patterson wondered if it was from the relief of surviving the firefight in the tunnels—some kind of physical release that had put him into the deepest, darkest sleep of his life.

"Pats!" The voice was a whisper from the cot beside him.

Patterson dragged himself out of the depths and squinted. The lights were still soft, but he was the last one sleeping.

"Pats! Check it out." A soldier knelt beside him, now shaking his shoulder.

"*Unngh,*" Patterson managed to say.

"Look."

Patterson shifted and found the energy to prop himself up on an elbow.

"It's him," the soldier said. "Unbelievable."

Patterson's eyes were still clouded with sleep. He blinked a few times to clear them, then focused across the room. "You're making it sound like Jesus. Who is it?"

"You don't recognize him?" Still a whisper. "Come on. It's Silver."

"He was kidnapped," Patterson said. He was still sleepy, but the tall man across the room seemed younger than Jonathan Silver. "Someone freed him?"

"Not the old man. His son. Brad."

16:56 GMT

"Hamer told me about your hand," Kate said to Quinn. "How it happened. You went into Gaza because of that woman and her daughter."

"Good, then," Quinn said. "No need to discuss it."

"I'm just trying to get a complete picture here."

"Like you were when you invited me for dinner with an extradition paper in your pocket?"

Kate ignored the remark. "Hamer says you've walked into the lion's den more than once."

"If Hamer knows so much, you should have this discussion with him."

"I'll be taking you back to face a grand jury and a possible death sentence. Before all of this, the thought gave me satisfaction. Now . . ." Kate looked away, then back at him. "I like compartments. Less messy that way. But it's tough to keep you in one compartment when things I see put you in another."

"Once I'm back in the United States, you'll be done with me."

"Are you kidding? I'll be one of the key witnesses for the prosecution unless you can give me something to work on to clear you. I've seen who you are. I want to help."

"I did hunt down those men that were found dead," Quinn said. "I located them, identified them. But I did not kill them. My goal was to have them arrested so that they could provide information to have more of them arrested."

"Help me prove it."

"I'll deal with the future when I get there. In the present, I need to focus on the next phone call from Safady. To make sure the choppers get in and the hostages get out."

"Is that how you deal with the past, too? By staying in the present?"

"You have no business in my past," Quinn said steadily. He was far angrier than he was going to show. "Stay out of it."

"Yeah," Kate said with a small smile. "I should. But I don't want to. Maybe you were right; maybe this is some kind of reverse Stockholm syndrome. Being stuck with you in an intense situation makes me want to get to know you better."

Quinn said nothing.

Her smile tightened slightly. "Come on. Talk to me."

Quinn remained silent.

"You're trying to stone-face me until I walk away from this conversation, aren't you?"

"Exactly."

She didn't, however, make a move to leave.

Quinn put out his left hand and pulled off the bandage, showing the knife wound in the center of it and the neat stitches from the surgery just the day before. "I was on a trip in Canada once. Read a short newspaper article with a headline that said 'Man Dies Trying to Save Son.' His six-year-old had gone onto the ice and fallen through. He crawled out there to reach for his boy's hand and fell through the ice himself. His clothes and boots were too heavy for him to swim and hold the boy out of the water. But it was shallow enough that he could stand with the boy on his shoulders, his own head underwater, and keep the boy's head in the air. People nearby got to the boy in time. But not the dad."

Quinn looked Kate squarely in the eyes and spoke with no emotion. "Every night I sang songs to my little girl when I tucked her into bed. She was afraid of monsters. Every night I promised that her daddy would save her from all the monsters in the world. I would have crawled onto the ice to save her. But I didn't have that chance. I read that article and wept with envy for the father who was able to drown himself to save his little boy. I didn't have that chance. I lived. She didn't. I lived and found her shoe with her foot in it."

He kept his defiant stare on Kate. "Try to imagine what that feels like. You want to know why I go into the lion's den? Because every day I hope I don't get out."

She blinked back tears.

"Satisfied?" he said with quiet savageness. "Or is there anything else you want to suck out of my soul?"

"You've made your point," Kate said. "But let me tell you this: you fight dirty."

She opened the door.

"Where are you going?"

"Anywhere that's away from you."

She left the van without another word.

16:58 GMT

Patterson stood in a line near the back of all the Freedom Crusaders. All were armed with submachine guns. Brad Silver and Del Saxon faced them. They were at the base of another set of stairs that led up to a door in the ceiling.

Saxon spoke, with Silver nodding, as if Saxon would not be allowed to address the Freedom Crusaders without Brad Silver's permission.

"You know who this man is." Saxon gestured at Brad.

Most of the platoon applauded.

"Men," Brad said, "I expected to be here earlier. But I had to find a way to escape hotel surveillance and become just another tourist going into Gaza. It took me longer than I wanted."

Saxon got the nod from Brad to continue. "He's the general behind all of this. From the beginning. Today the world thinks he's holed up in a hotel. Tomorrow morning the world will see him in glory, and all of us will be hailed as heroes."

More applause.

"The time has come for me to tell you about the next phase of our operation." Saxon motioned to the door above them. "Through that door is the orphanage where thirty of our brothers and sisters are being held hostage. Once we pene-trate, there will be no shooting unless absolutely necessary to preserve life. We don't want to jeopardize the lives of the hostages or the children."

Saxon paused. "There are hostiles in the orphanage, but they should already be neutralized. We do not expect resistance during our deployment above. Maintain silence at all times. Those of you appointed for cleanup have five minutes from when the hostiles are secured to complete your task and rejoin the rest of us. There will be no communications between any of you as we guard the hostages. No indication that we are not Palestinians. Any questions?"

There were none.

"Good." Saxon scanned the Freedom Crusaders one final time, then nodded. The first man in line began to climb the stairs toward the orphanage that held terrorists and kidnapped Americans.

At the top, he pushed open the door and stepped into a brightly lit room. One by one, the members of the advance team joined him.

Patterson noticed that Brad Silver waited until nearly all of them were up the stairs before falling in line.

The guy was only a leader, he thought, when convenient.

KHAN YUNIS, GAZA STRIP • 17:01 GMT

Quinn was still alone in the van when his cell rang. He'd been thinking about Kate, remembering part of the background report that Hamer had supplied him as part of his earlier demand. He remembered most the psychological assessment, impressed that the Mossad could dig up something that confidential on such short notice. He was appalled at the circumstances that Kate had dealt with in her childhood. A father, often drunk and occasionally abusive in the most horrible ways possible. The assessment had suggested that her belligerence and bulldog determination to close police cases were part of an ambivalence toward authority.

Thinking of this and of how savagely he'd just treated her, Quinn let the cell phone ring twice before answering.

"The choppers will be there just after dusk," Hamer said. "Let's hope this works."

Quinn hung up without responding.

Yeah, he thought. *I'm helping him escape to Jordan. But when this is done, nothing is going to stop me from finding Safady again.*

17:02 GMT

"You are very close to freedom," Safady announced to Jonathan Silver and the rest of the hostages. "Listen."

When Safady interrupted, Silver had been on his bunk bed, meditating on the words of Jesus as if for the first time, thinking about what Esther had said about the true kingdom of Israel. It had always bothered him that modern Israel was such a secular society, with a minority of Jews of faith. By extension, it had bothered him that these unbelieving people should be rewarded with a divine promise of the land around them. But he'd answered these doubts by telling himself that the end justifies the means, that it didn't matter if the Jews had faith in the Old Testament God who'd promised the land as long as they regained it so that a Third Temple could be rebuilt to usher in Armageddon. But what if Esther was right? What if all who followed Jesus became spiritual descendants of Abraham by relationship with God, not by ethnic heritage?

"Helicopters are on the way," Safady continued. "If you want to live, you will follow instructions. No questions, no hesitation in obeying commands. When the lights go off, my men will have flashlights to guide you. Once we are all aboard the helicopters, our destination is Jordan. We have been promised safe passage. Once we are in Jordan, if the ransom money is released, so too will all of you."

Safady gave an encouraging smile. It was eerie after all of his previous threats. "You can trust this. I am telling you because I don't want any problems getting you on the helicopters. This is a military operation run by the Israelis. You should be encouraged by the fact that we are going to Jordan. It means that my men and I can escape—something we could not do from Gaza. And the fact that we can escape means that you are important to us alive. It guarantees our freedom when this hostage taking has ended."

Safady surveyed all the Americans. "You will see that my men are masked to hide their identity from the Mossad. Take that as encouragement too. They do not want to become martyrs. So neither will you."

17:88 GMT

In the hidden room beneath the orphanage, Joe Patterson led the red and black heifer to the bottom of the stairs. He was surprised to see Saxon with a bucket of soapy water and a towel.

"Hold the heifer," Saxon told Patterson. "I'll go slow with this."

With what? Patterson wondered. But he obeyed silently.

Saxon dipped the towel in the water, then used it to begin gently rubbing the black spots on the heifer's hide. Immediately the towel began to blacken.

Patterson was perplexed until he realized that Saxon was washing away the splotches that had given the red and black appearance to the heifer.

"Sir?" Patterson asked.

Saxon stopped and grinned. "A harmless dye. This is a red heifer, son. A pure red heifer."

Patterson blinked a few times as the implications hit him.

"I see you understand," Saxon said. "It's a miracle from God."

Patterson nodded. But getting the answer to one question just led to others, questions that would not be smart to ask. He watched and waited for Saxon to finish scrubbing away all the blotches.

"Without a blemish," Saxon said proudly.

"The heifer has come this far with no injuries, but if this animal doesn't want to go up, it isn't going to be easy to keep it that way," Patterson warned the lieutenant. The other Freedom Crusaders were standing back, waiting and watching. "It weighs a couple hundred pounds. I don't see how even five men could hold it still and carry it, unless we hog-tie it first."

"Find a way."

"I'll do my best," Patterson answered, regretting again that he'd been the one to first control the animal in the cargo shipping container. Why couldn't someone else be responsible? In that moment, it occurred to him. Saxon had known of Patterson's expertise. It wasn't an accident that Saxon had barked orders at Patterson as the container was swaying in the air between ship and truck.

Patterson tried coaxing the heifer. He tried pulling the heifer. It would have nothing to do with the stairs. He was surprised that Saxon didn't get angrier. All of them knew the time from now to boarding the helicopters was short—very short.

Saxon responded instead by speaking into his walkie-talkie, reaching one of the Freedom Crusaders already up in the orphanage. "We'll need the crate. I want it here in less than thirty seconds."

Crate? Patterson wondered.

Saxon motioned for Patterson to move away from the stairs. "Get the heifer back too. I don't want to risk it in any way."

Noise came from above and Patterson glanced upward.

At the top of the stairs, two Freedom Crusaders were wrestling with a long, high, narrow crate. They placed the bottom of it on the first step, then held it as they slowly slid it down toward Patterson.

There had been a box up there? Ready for this?

The crate was built perfectly for the heifer. The animal could fit in but not move.

"Get it in the crate," Saxon said. "We've got enough men to carry it."

The meticulous planning was almost a sure promise of the success of the operation. But Joe was frightened because it showed how futile it was to expect he could disobey Saxon and get away with it. Especially with Sarah's life at stake.

17:14 GMT

Safady faced all his men. He had gathered the fifteen of them in one of the schoolrooms near the back of the compound. The men had left their weapons at the door at his request. They were sitting on the desks with relaxed postures.

Safady, however, had left his machine gun on a sling on his shoulder. He lifted it and pointed it at them.

"All of you," he said in a pleasant voice, "must lie on the floor on your bellies. I will count to five. Any of you who refuse will be shot."

It was such an unusual and unexpected request that not one of the men moved.

Safady fired a burst of bullets into the three closest men. They cartwheeled backward, limbs flung in all directions. The shots were deafening.

Safady waited for the air to clear. "One." He paused. "Two."

The remaining men flung themselves to the floor.

Safady didn't have to get to three.

17:16 GMT

Joe Patterson and five other Freedom Crusaders stepped into the schoolroom. A Palestinian man stood with a machine gun trained on several other men who lay prone on the floor, hands on their heads.

A pool of blood was spreading slowly across the floor, evidently the result of the gunshots Joe and the others had heard a moment ago.

The Palestinian with the gun barely acknowledged the entry of the Freedom Crusaders. He set down his weapon. The men, following Del Saxon's lead, ignored him as he rushed out of the room.

The Americans stepped forward. Two of them kept machine guns pointed at the Palestinians. Patterson joined the other two as they briskly and efficiently bound the hands of each of the captives behind their backs with plastic ties.

Once this was completed, they kicked the Palestinians until all of them were on their feet, gesturing and pushing until the captives were in a single line.

One of the Palestinians began a verbal protest in broken English.

One of the Freedom Crusaders waved him to silence.

It didn't stop the man, who grew louder.

The soldier who had gestured him to be silent pulled out a knife and, without hesitation, cut through the man's windpipe. The man toppled slowly, disbelief in his eyes.

When the Crusaders gestured for the other captives to step forward, there was immediate compliance.

Patterson had to step over the dying Palestinian to keep pace with the other Freedom Crusaders. He told himself this was a holy war and followed all of them out of the room.

Time to play the part of these dead men.

17:16 GMT

"What I did was wrong," Quinn told Kate. After Hamer's call, he'd sat in the van, totally drained by the emotional roller coaster he'd endured, waiting to find some energy to let him apologize to Kate. The sound of gunfire had reached him, but there was so much shooting on the Strip he didn't give it much attention. Not in his state of mind.

He'd moved out of the passenger side of the van and found Kate at the corner, where she was standing silent and motionless. Just another forlorn woman in the desolation of Gaza. "I was lashing out and wanted to hurt someone. You were in my line of fire. I'm sorry."

He could sense her anger shifting as she reappraised him.

"Rule one in negotiating," she said, "never get emotionally involved."

"Yeah. Rule one. I'm fine now. Teflon."

"If you're fine *now*, that means something got to you *before*," Kate said. "What?"

"The situation's the same," Quinn answered. The image of his daughter's shoe flashed into his mind again. And of Safady at the orphanage gate, taunting him about it. "Negotiations finished. I want to be gone before you get in the line of fire."

"Line of fire?"

"Safady still wants me dead."

17:16 GMT

Safady had hurried away from the execution of his men to find a window that overlooked the white van. He wasn't leaving Gaza until he knew that Quinn was dead.

This far into the operation, he knew he could risk a cell-phone call. He hit a speed-dial button. The call was answered so quickly that it clipped off the first ring.

"I'm in position," Safady said. "I can see Quinn's van. If you want this to continue, deliver on your promise."

"You received my e-mail with the phone number for the Waqf and the security password you'll need later tonight?"

"Yes. But we won't get there unless you deliver Quinn. Now. Before the choppers arrive. I want to see it happen."

"I'll make sure he's inside the van," the voice answered. "Give me about thirty seconds."

17:17 GMT

Just as Quinn began to turn his back on Kate, his cell rang. He answered.

"It's Hamer. You're done there. Start driving back. I want you out of there as fast as possible. If Safady's going to try anything, now's the time."

"We're on our way," Quinn said. Quinn wasn't about to try explaining where they really were or why they were out of the van. This argument with Kate was personal. "In gear and bouncing down these miserable roads."

"Good. You'll get a high-priority clearance at the border crossing. They'll be looking for you."

Quinn hung up and completed his turn back to the van.

Kate grabbed his arm. "Don't do this to me. We're partners. Tell me what happened at the orphanage."

"The choppers are on the way," he answered, "and we're supposed to be on our way too. I'm your prisoner again."

"What messed you up?"

"I'm sorry. Can we leave it at that?"

"You're lousy at apologizing," she said.

"Sorry about that, too," Quinn replied, not even smiling. Overhead he could hear the sound of the helicopters drawing nearer.

Kate appraised him. She stepped closer, reached toward his face, and was about to speak.

A fireball erupted on the street, throwing a shock wave of superheated air that knocked Quinn into Kate and both of them onto the ground. The reverberations of the thunderous explosion rose and fell along with debris.

On his knees, Quinn shielded his face with his arm and looked toward the source of the blast.

Their van had been torn apart.

THE NIGHT OF COUNTDOWN

35

Safady carried a gym bag onto the helicopter. Inside the bag were C-4, wires and a timer, a pistol, a machine gun, and two uniforms: Palestinian and one matching the uniform worn by the Freedom Crusaders.

As further protection, Safady wore Kevlar and an Israeli uniform beneath his traditional garb. The plan was going as expected. He'd watched the van until it exploded. While he'd enjoyed the irony that Quinn died in the same way his wife and daughter had, he regretted it could not be as originally planned—Quinn captive, Safady looking into his eyes and savoring the man's pain as he killed Quinn himself.

But Quinn was dead. Funds were on the way—funds that would enable Safady to have more influence than anyone else in the Muslim world. The Freedom Crusaders were now posing as Palestinian terrorists and were in position to board the choppers with the hostages.

Yes. All was according to plan.

17:38 GMT

Quinn stood in the crowd, staring at the smoking ruins of the van. The sun had set, and in the darkness, dressed the way he was, Quinn wasn't worried that anyone would see him closely enough to wonder what an American was doing here. The smoke, the sounds of approaching sirens, the wails of anguish coming from survivors—all of it brought back unbearable memories, now haunted by the specter of Safady's laughter at the gate.

Then he heard a voice from his right. English, tinged with an Israeli accent, speaking softly. "You'd be smart not to fight this."

The man was a few inches taller than Quinn. Dark hair, dark complexion.

He wore jeans, a blue T-shirt, and a dusty sports coat and was built like a body-guard.

"Who are you?" Quinn demanded.

"Sure," the man said, "I'll wave my IDF badge and give these camel jockeys a reason to rip us apart."

Quinn became aware of another man to his left, pressing in too closely to be casual crowd contact.

They hadn't asked about Kate, which confirmed Quinn's suspicions. Safady wasn't behind the explosion.

The first agent was patting Quinn down. He found the cell phone Quinn had been using to talk to Hamer when the van exploded. The man pocketed the phone, then kept patting until he was satisfied Quinn didn't have a weapon.

"We're going," the agent said. "Slow and easy. Last thing we need is attention here."

They steered Quinn through the crowd back toward the orphanage.

"Hope your car has air-conditioning," Quinn said, wondering where they had parked. "It's been a long, hot day."

"No car. We're going to a safe house for debriefing."

"I'm done with this," Quinn said. "If you guys aren't taking me out of Gaza, I'll find my own way."

Unsmiling, the agent reached inside his jacket and pulled a pistol. He punched the barrel into Quinn's ribs and used his body to screen this from any observers. "That's not happening."

17:38 GMT

In the darkness, the compound was full of the movements of men and flashlights. As ordered, Joe Patterson, like the other Freedom Crusaders, wore a face scarf to hide his features from the American hostages and the orphans. He was supervising the boarding process by standing hunched at the base of the chopper and helping them climb aboard.

Joe did not know who the hostages were, beyond that they were Americans about to be released from a hostage situation. But he was impressed. He had expected fear and exhaustion across their faces. Instead, he saw resolve and felt a shared calmness among them. More startling was the kindness and courtesy that each showed to him to the point where he wondered if they saw behind the face scarf and knew his true identity. Disguised in a way that had fooled every-one on the streets in Gaza, surely in their eyes he was one of their Palestinian captors; why would these people be so gracious to the men who had inflicted terror upon them?

He had other questions too—ones that needed to remain silent. What was the next phase of the operation? How had Saxon known to bring the Freedom Crusaders here to help the hostages? If the choppers were supposed to be bringing the hostages to safety, why was his platoon necessary? Why couldn't the Freedom Crusaders announce themselves as friends instead of maintaining this elaborate disguise? And what was Brad Silver doing among them now?

Patterson tried to concentrate on his task. All the American hostages had to be loaded onto the choppers along with the Freedom Crusaders.

He then saw a child on crutches, led by a middle-aged woman with straight hair and an angry, determined look. The child, a girl, was boarding the chopper. Why?

Walking with them, guiding the little girl moving forward on her crutches, was the man Patterson had been watching on television since his childhood, the founder of Freedom Christian University, and the most prominent proponent of Zionism among all fundamentalists.

Jonathan Silver.

The man leaned down as they approached the chopper, treating the crippled girl with tenderness.

Silently, knowing the strictness of orders, Patterson helped the two of them climb aboard the chopper.

Jonathan Silver.

It hit Patterson.

If Brad Silver was here, then of course his father knew about the presence of the Freedom Crusaders. All of the previous planning had been so meticulous; it was impossible that this wasn't part of it too. For that matter, it could easily be Jonathan Silver behind all of this. He had the resources and had used his university to recruit the Freedom Crusaders.

Jonathan Silver had set up his own kidnapping and all of this?

Patterson thought of the red heifer. It could be here for only one reason. Silver had preached about its importance numerous times. But to get the red heifer where it belonged would be impossible, right?

If the old man had been able to arrange this much so far, maybe it wasn't impossible after all.

Patterson climbed aboard the helicopter. He knew the approximate range of a Black Hawk—about three hundred miles. A radius that big gave a wide range of destinations. He'd discover it when they landed, so at this point, he had no choice but to trust Saxon. No choice, because Sarah had been kidnapped back home and was being used as leverage against him.

He shut his flashlight off and settled into the chopper, strapping himself in place.

The roar of the engines increased, and the chopper wobbled a little as it rose. Then it steadied and the compound dropped away. Seconds later, the lights of the Gaza Strip dominated the skyline.

The chopper tilted into a turn, then increased height and speed.

Patterson closed his eyes. Yes, at this point, there was nothing to do except wait.

T he IDF agents had taken Quinn to a room inside an apparently abandoned building across the street from the orphanage. A lightbulb dangled from a wire in the center of the room. The glare from it showed a few battered chairs. Quinn saw two things distinctive about the room. Both alarmed him. The first was a car battery. It had wires and clips running from both terminals. Crude but effective, and perfect when interrogators had to jury-rig something on short notice. The second was a trapdoor in the center of the dirt floor. The small piles of dirt on each side, a darker color than the rest, indicated that the door had been hidden until recently.

Quinn could guess what was below that door. His own death.

But he didn't see how he could prevent it. Just after pushing him into the room, the agents had cuffed his hands behind his back with plastic restraints.

"This Hamer's idea?" Quinn asked. It was a weak move to stall, but what else did he have? If they took him below with the car battery, it would get a lot more unpleasant.

"Shut up and sit down."

To Quinn's surprise, neither agent opened the trapdoor.

With the second agent holding the pistol on Quinn, agent one pushed a chair toward Quinn and motioned for him to sit. Quinn didn't need a second invitation. Anything not to be taken below the trapdoor.

"We're going to have a discussion about the call you made to Hamer," agent one said. "It can be an easy and painless discussion. Or not." He used another set of plastic cuffs to secure Quinn's ankles to the chair legs.

"Hamer," Quinn repeated. "He sent you here?"

Agent one stood over Quinn. "We have all the time we need. All the justification. After that last call, you're a proven threat to national security. An escaped murder suspect. And frankly, there's no one to miss you even if you were a political liability. To the world, you died in that van just like the American cop."

Agent two moved to the corner and lifted the car battery. He set it beside Quinn.

"You threatened Hamer," agent one said. "Not a good idea. Where did you store it?"

So the phone call he had made after the initial shock of the van's explosion had worked. Maybe too well. Quinn had realized the timing was no accident. The explosion had come moments after Hamer had called to tell him to begin driving, ensuring that Quinn was in the van. If Hamer had tried to have Quinn killed, he knew he'd have to make his next moves very carefully. So Quinn had called Hamer back on his cell phone to feed the general a story that would throw him off guard.

"Hamer," he'd said, *"That was stupid. I'm alive. Kate's dead. My computer was in the van, but once I get on the Internet, all I need to do is reach my server. Then the e-mail draft I had as backup with all the information on this goes straight to the media."*

"It's helpful to both sides if it's clear exactly what you're looking for," Quinn said now. *Stall. Stall. Stall.* "Assumptions in a situation like this can have bad consequences."

"Only for you." Agent two pulled aside Quinn's robe and attached one clip to his left nipple. He held the second clip ready for the right nipple.

"All right then," agent one said. "You told Hamer that you'd put together a draft of an e-mail and stored it on your server. We want the location of that server and access to it."

"Be more specific," Quinn said.

Agent one nodded at agent two. When the second clip touched Quinn's nipple, the electricity jolted through him and arched his back in an unnatural spasm that felt as if it had broken his spine.

"Is that specific enough?" agent one said.

"Hang on," Quinn gasped. *Stall. Stall. Stall.* "I was lying to Hamer. There's nothing about this negotiation process that can blow back on IDF. Nothing in an e-mail draft. I told him that so he wouldn't try anything else to kill me."

"Wish I could believe you," agent one said. "Server and password."

Quinn saw the clip coming again. He closed his eyes as if that would diminish the shock. It didn't. This time it lasted longer. It left Quinn panting, tears streaming down his cheeks.

"Server and password," the agent said. "We've got plenty of juice left otherwise."

SOMEWHERE OVER GAZA • 17:43 GMT

Shooting stars, Jonathan Silver thought, realizing in the same instant that the streaks of light were going in the wrong direction to be meteorite debris streaking past the front of the helicopter.

Cause and effect is so ingrained in human thinking that he strained for an answer as the next flash shot upward.

Fireworks.

But the chopper swerved with the violence of a bus careening over an embankment. A military phrase shot through Silver's mind, staying at the front of his awareness, even as screams rose in the chopper: *evasive action.* Then he knew without conscious articulation of the words in his mind.

Ground fire.

Someone was shooting at the helicopter!

Another flash sliced through the black of the night sky. More hideous dipping and swerving, like giant hands tossing the chopper back and forth.

Two more flashes.

The sound and the explosion registered at the same time, and the helicopter seemed to lurch in midair.

Dear Lord, Silver prayed, *preserve our souls.*

He expected next to feel the horrifying drop of the chopper spinning out of control, tumbling like a duck punched with lead shot. But the helicopter leveled.

Another flash of ground fire.

Then darkness again. Silver blinked to get his vision back.

The helicopter remained level.

But Jonathan Silver noticed a new glow outside. Not the lights of the countryside below but an eerie glow.

Fire.

KHAN YUNIS, GAZA STRIP • 17:44 GMT

A knock at the door interrupted the interrogation. Both agents flinched.

Agent one shouted at the door, telling the person on the other side to leave.

More knocking. Followed by the voice of a boy speaking Arabic, offering to sell oranges.

Agent one slipped his pistol beneath his sports coat and opened the door. There was the boy. And a woman beside him in traditional Muslim clothing.

The boy stepped inside, jabbering. The woman was holding oranges too, offering them with outstretched hands.

The agent stepped forward, grabbed the boy, and threw him back out on the street. He made a threatening move toward the woman. But she held something else among the oranges. A pistol.

She dropped the oranges as she raised the pistol and aimed directly at the man's forehead. He froze.

Agent two began to lift his weapon but not fast enough. Quinn pushed with his feet, driving into the man's chest with his body and the chair that was attached to his ankles. The clips raked loose from Quinn's nipples. They fell together, with the second agent trying to roll clear.

The woman didn't hesitate. She kicked the man in front of her directly in the groin. He doubled over, and she spun him around and grabbed him by the hair. Using him as a screen, she looked over the man's shoulder at the second agent, who was just rising to his knees, still holding his pistol.

"Drop it," she said to the second agent.

Without a clear shot, the man hesitated. The woman snapped off a shot, hitting him in the foot. He looked down in disbelief, then dropped his weapon.

She released the hair of the man she held and shoved him forward. "Both of you, on your bellies. Hands on your heads."

Both agents assumed the posture, the first groaning, the second moving gingerly with his injured foot.

"Who are these guys?" the woman said to Quinn. "IDF?" She pulled the veil away from her face, breathing hard.

"Kate," Quinn said, still on his side, still cuffed to the chair. "Glad you could come to the party. Yes, they're IDF."

"You were right about the explosion then," Kate said.

"Is that why you took so much time? Thought I'd called this wrong?"

"Had to check my makeup. In Vegas, it's about appearance. Nobody on *CSI* looks bad making a bust. It's something real-life cops live up to there."

"In Vegas, is it also about working hard to sound cool?"

"Better than sounding scared," she said. "Which I am. IDF blows our van, then sends killers in to make sure the job's done right. I don't like our chances."

"Me neither."

"What next?" Kate asked. Her pistol didn't waver from the two prone men. "Aside from cutting you loose from the chair."

"Hope they have a couple more sets of cuffs," Quinn answered. "We take their car keys, identification, and money. Beyond that, I don't have much of a plan. Except maybe find some aspirin."

"Aspirin?"

"Another Vegas thing." He pointed at the car battery and the clips. "While you were checking your makeup, I was the entertainment that kept them here."

Quinn couldn't walk away from the trapdoor in the floor. That's where the agents should have taken him for interrogation. They hadn't chosen this old building at random; there would be too much risk in it. They knew the building, knew the room, had confidence in it as a safe house. That meant they knew where the trapdoor led. So why not take him down there?

Neither man had answered Quinn's questions about it. Nor about the location of their vehicle. Both had refused to speak at all. They were still on their bellies on the floor, stripped down to their underwear. Kate had found a knife and used it to cut Quinn loose. Quinn hadn't found more plastic restraints, so they'd used laces from the agents' shoes to bind their wrists behind their backs.

The pain from the clips and electrical jolts was fading, and Quinn was still going on an adrenaline rush. "I've got to look," he told Kate, pointing at the door in the floor. He explained why, uncaring that the agents could overhear their conversation.

"I'd rather be looking for their car," she said. The keys were dangling in her hand. By the stamp of the ignition key, they knew it was a Mercedes, which would help. The only choice they saw was to search the nearby streets, clicking on the remote access to set off the flashing lights and the car horn.

"Give me ten minutes," he said. "I'll go alone. We can't both go down there."

"You don't have a flashlight."

But he had a cell phone. And a pistol.

The helicopter appeared to have stabilized, but the lights below were growing closer as the chopper seemed to sag downward each minute. Safady was not worried. He had expected this. And he knew the pilot had expected it too.

Because the Freedom Crusaders wore face scarves as if they were Palestinian terrorists, the pilot had no clue to their real identity. Safady knew the pilot
believed these were IDF commandos in disguise—the soldiers who had been
hiding in a tunnel below the orphanage. And because the pilot did not know
how badly the IDF operation had been betrayed, Safady needed to act as if this
were a legitimate emergency.

Safady scrambled forward, holding a pistol. He pressed the barrel into the
base of the pilot's neck. "Keep the radio open."

He didn't need to shout to be heard above the chopper engines. Safady was
wearing a headset and had insisted on being part of all communications between
the helicopters and the land-based operations.

"Get the pistol out of my neck," the pilot grunted. "We've taken ground fire.
I don't need any distractions."

Safady pressed harder.

"Unless you back off," the pilot said, "I'm going to stand and turn around and
punch you in the face. You'll have to shoot me to stop me. Good luck keeping
this thing in the air."

All of this conversation was being transmitted to the land-based operations.
Safady knew it. He also knew it would be leaked to the media almost immediately.
The emergency needed to seem real.

Safady eased off. "Tell me your name."

"Billy Orellana."

"Very good. Billy. You will not land this in Israeli territory," Safady said.

"If I don't land it, it's going down. Your only choice is whether it's a controlled
landing or a crash landing."

"Turn this back to Gaza."

"To get shot again? Not a chance."

"You will not land this in Israeli territory."

A radio voice broke into their conversation. "Orellana, this is Major General
Jack Hamer. What's the situation?"

"The starboard engine took a hit. I've put the fire out, but we're crippled. At
best, we can be in the air for twenty minutes."

"Not in Israeli territory!" Safady screamed, very conscious of how the media
would play this conversation again and again. "I know what you want—a place
to surround us."

Hamer's voice remained calm. "Orellana, can you get the chopper to Jordan?"

"Not at this airspeed."

The helicopter lurched.

"Let me revise my estimate," Orellana said. "We might have fifteen minutes.
I'm at thirty-five hundred feet and losing altitude at two hundred feet a minute."

"Not in Israeli territory," Safady repeated. "This is an Israeli plot to take us."

"Where else?" Hamer asked. "You can't make it to Jordan. Going back to Gaza is suicide."

"Listen to me," Safady said. "If your pilot doesn't do as I say, I'm going to shoot hostages, one per minute."

"I am listening," Hamer said. "I just don't see how to fix this. You can't stay in the air."

The helicopter lurched once more. Orellana fought the controls and managed to keep it upright.

"How far to Jerusalem?" Safady asked Orellana.

"Ten minutes. If we can keep this airspeed."

"Jerusalem," Safady told Hamer. "Both helicopters land. Together. In Jerusalem. Or there will be slaughter."

"Jerusalem?" Hamer repeated. "That's Israeli territory."

"Not all of it."

Radio silence. A long radio silence.

Safady broke it. "You understand, don't you?"

"You can't be serious," Hamer said.

"Clear it," Safady said. "It's flat, under Palestinian control, heavily walled for our protection, and it's the one spot you won't dare try any military operation against us."

"You *are* serious," Hamer said.

"Clear the airspace for both choppers." With media help, Safady was about to shock the world. "You know where I want us to land—the top of Mount Moriah."

KHAN YUNIS, GAZA STRIP • 17:58 GMT

Quinn moved down the steps slowly, knowing that he was framed by the light above him if anyone was in the darkness below. He didn't know how far the darkness would extend but held his cell phone open in his left hand, intending to use its light for guidance if needed. In his other hand, he held the pistol taken from one of the agents.

At the bottom of the steps, there was enough light from the trapdoor opening for him to see several steps in all directions. He waited for his eyes to adjust, then moved deeper into the room.

Slowly he began to realize the complexity and size of the underground cavern.

Then he saw the row of men seated against the wall. They were alive and bound, their mouths sealed by duct tape. He did a quick count. Twenty-five. He stepped closer and saw the uniforms. Israeli military.

It was eerie—their silence, their eyes, all focused on his movements. Twenty-five men watching and waiting. Twenty-five men helpless if Quinn decided to hurt them.

Quinn squatted beside the nearest man and whispered in his ear, pointing down the dark corridor. "Help me here. Is there anyone farther down guarding you?"

The man shook his head.

Quinn pulled away the duct tape. "What happened?" he asked, keeping his voice low.

Another soldier farther down the line grunted from behind his duct tape.

"That's my commanding officer," this soldier explained. "I don't have authorization to answer any questions."

Quinn shuffled farther down and repeated the process with the commanding officer, a bulky man with short, thinning hair and two days' worth of dark growth on his face.

"What's going on?" Quinn asked, still in a low voice.

"Where's your identification?" The man had an Israeli accent.

This question was a form of answer for Quinn. This was the Gaza Strip. If these were Israeli soldiers, they were on a covert mission. The question also told him that he wasn't going to get any other answers unless he played this like a poker game.

"I'm IDF," Quinn said. First bluff. If the two upstairs had already been down here, he'd have to come up with an excuse why he was now asking questions. But he was betting that if the two IDF men had already been here, the soldiers would no longer be bound and gagged.

"Identification," the commander said.

Quinn shrugged. The light was bad—bad enough, he hoped, to run the bluff further. He took out the ID taken from the agent upstairs and used his cell phone to illuminate it but not too closely.

"What went wrong?" Quinn needed to play this as if he knew about the mission.

"This isn't the time for a debriefing," the CO said, looking away from the ID and back to Quinn, obviously satisfied by Quinn's bluff. "You've got to call someone to stop the helicopters from getting to Jerusalem."

Jerusalem? Quinn's mind raced over the possibilities. If this man knew about the helicopters and hostage transfer, then these soldiers were part of a rescue operation. Quinn would not have been surprised to find out that Hamer had kept the presence of soldiers secret from him. But how could the soldiers have been put into position so quickly? And who had captured them before they could begin the rescue attempt?

Much as he wanted these answers, he knew asking the questions would reveal too much ignorance.

"If I make a call," Quinn said, "the person on the other end is going to need some answers before they stop the choppers. What went wrong?"

"Figure it out," the CO snapped. "We're not on the helicopters. Some other unit took our place. Americans is my guess by how they spoke. Disguised as Palestinians."

"How? Why?"

"Look, the how of it doesn't matter at this point. I think we were gassed, but I'm not sure. When the dust settles, I'm sure you guys will figure out who to blame for how the Americans knew how to find us. It was a well-planned op, and only a handful of people knew about it. I didn't even tell my own men our purpose until we were in position here."

If this was a rescue mission, why had Hamer agreed to the helicopters, Quinn wondered. At the least, Hamer would have negotiated a delay to give the soldiers time to move in on the Palestinians. Unless, of course, he expected these soldiers on the choppers. But how could Hamer expect that if Safady was the one who had made the demand for the helicopter transfer?

"You want me to get on the phone and say the wrong soldiers are on the helicopters?" Quinn said. "How long do you think we can keep that under wraps?"

"Listen." The CO lowered his voice. Quinn leaned closer but kept out of range of a possible head butt. "I also had orders not to tell my men why we were going to land on the Temple Mount until we were there."

"Land on the Temple Mount."

"Yeah. There's going to be ground fire around the helicopter. One engine's been rigged for a small detonation charge. It's supposed to look like an emergency landing for the Palestinian terrorists. Nobody would know we were on the helicopters instead. Those choppers need to be shot down, hostages or not. If this goes wrong, we're talking World War III—Muslims against the West."

The Temple Mount. Al-Aqsa. Where stood the Dome of the Rock. The third most holy place in Islam. It was inconceivable that IDF had intended to land there. Because the CO was right. If Mount Moriah was blasphemed in Muslim eyes, it would lead to a global war.

"I don't have clearance on this," Quinn said. His heart was racing. "But I'm not going to put my career on the line and make the call unless I know the importance of this."

"It's a national security issue. If you don't have clearance—"

Quinn interrupted. "You want me responsible for ordering the hostages shot from the air based on your promise that it's important enough to kill civilians. I don't think so."

"They had crates to load with them. Didn't see what was inside. They had a small cow, too. Light was bad in here, but it looked red. Does that mean anything to you?"

"Small cow . . . a red heifer on the Temple Mount." Quinn let out a deep breath. "You're kidding me, right?"

"No. Shoot the choppers down. It doesn't matter if the hostages die now. Not compared to that."

"You guys get thrown together for a hostage rescue and somehow in less than forty-eight hours some other group gets here with a small, red cow?"

"This wasn't thrown together; this was planned by IDF." The CO blinked a few times, then stared thoughtfully at Quinn. "Let me see that identification again."

Quinn had blown cover but still tried for more information. "This had been planned before the hostage taking?"

The CO just stared at him.

This was planned before the hostage taking? The implications were staggering to Quinn. But he knew he wasn't going to get any answers from this man. Maybe the answers were ahead. These soldiers wouldn't be going anywhere, and he needed to know what else was down here.

He replaced the duct tape on the CO's mouth. It struck Quinn that it might be helpful to have proof of this situation. He took a minute to pat the man down, hoping to find any kind of identification. He found none and assumed the rest of the men would be equally secure. It told him how extremely covert this mission was.

He left the men behind and took twenty slow steps toward the glow of a light. It was still silent. He was trying to hold his breath, tiptoeing and feeling slightly ridiculous about it. All of this was so perplexing; he wasn't even going to try to come to a conclusion.

The light was coming from behind a closed door. Quinn opened it and found another large room, scattered with cots. But that wasn't what drew his eyes. On the floor were the bodies of men. Another quick count totaled fifteen bodies. The clothing wasn't military. These were Palestinians.

No conclusions. Only questions. Had the Palestinians been executed by the Israeli military? But if the men behind him were Israeli military, who had disarmed and bound them? If someone else had done this, why leave the Israelis alive but not the Palestinians?

Beyond the cots, Quinn saw another set of steps leading up with an open trapdoor similar to the one he had left behind. He knew he had no choice but to see where it led.

He was cautious going up the steps and grateful that the trapdoor was open.

He would have dreaded the sitting-duck sensation of opening the door not knowing if the Palestinians' executioners were nearby.

When he reached the top of the stairs, the mystery deepened. It took only a minute of exploration to realize he was in the orphanage across the street from the safe house.

He returned to the trapdoor in the orphanage atop the stairs that led to the tunnel.

He smelled something that should have made no sense to him, especially amid executed Palestinians and captive Israeli soldiers.

But when he looked closely, his eyes confirmed what his nostrils told him. And what the CO had told him too.

On the floor was fresh cow manure.

Still, he didn't want to believe that a red heifer was on one of the helicopters. Not if the helicopter was on the way to the Temple Mount.

The lights of the city appeared on the horizon, at first a glow, then the spots of white broken up by the dark folds of small hills.

"We've got five minutes max before the engine gives out completely," Orellana told Safady. "We might not be able to make it to Mount Moriah. There are a handful of safe places to take this down. A few hospitals have landing pads. The rooftops of a couple of hotels . . ."

"And have the Israelis surround this chopper?" Safady said. "I don't think so."

"But . . . the Temple Mount?"

"Except for you and the hostages, all of us are Muslim," Safady said. Again, he knew this conversation would be recorded and broadcast to the world. "We will be protected by our brothers."

"IDF and Israeli soldiers," Kate said to Quinn. "I would not have believed it unless I'd seen it myself."

They were back on the streets now.

After Quinn had returned to Kate in the safe house, leaving the men in Israeli uniforms in place, he'd taken her back down the tunnel, then spent a few unsuccessful minutes trying to get the two IDF agents to explain this bizarre situation. Kate had remained silent during Quinn's quick interrogation. Then she'd helped him drag the IDF men down with the soldiers, and they'd left them there.

"Or IDF agents dressed as soldiers," Quinn answered her. "Or anything else you'd like to guess. The only thing I know for sure is that whatever it is, we're right in the middle of it. You saw the executed Palestinians."

She looked at the car battery and wires and clips. "Maybe go back down there and start doing it the IDF way."

"Aside from setting up dinner dates to arrest someone, are you any good at torturing men?"

Kate shook her head.

"Me either. Let's go."

"What about these guys?"

"Not my worry. They're hidden pretty well and not going anywhere."

"Quinn," Kate said, "that might be like leaving all those men there to die."

"Whoever sent the two agents to get me is going to send more when the first two don't report back. Our biggest worry is how long that's going to take. I just hope it's enough time to give us a good head start."

"We haven't done anything wrong," she said. "We don't need to run. Let's make some calls. Media. Law enforcement. Someone who can help."

"Here's a quick recap. Our van explodes right after Hamer tells me to start driving. Had to be a remote signal—not a problem for IDF. I put myself up for bait, call Hamer back. His guys show up. I know they're his guys because they don't ask about you; and they don't ask about you because I just finished telling Hamer you're dead. Hamer wants me as dead as you. I know this because the van exploded, but instead of putting me down as soon as I'm in the safe house, his guys first try starting me like a car. Why? Because Hamer believes I have something of value to give up. How long would they have let me live once they learned it? And how long are we going to live once IDF knows we're on the loose? They can get to us anywhere, Kate."

"The explosives had to be in place before we picked up the van." Kate looked past Quinn, blinking as she thought it through. She turned her eyes on him again. "What is it you know that makes them want you dead?"

He shook his head. "We didn't know anything before the van blew. Two questions then: What does Hamer gain if we're dead? Why had he decided to kill us early enough to rig the van with explosives before we picked it up? That was then. Now he's really motivated to make sure we are dead. Because we've learned a lot more since the van blew."

"I know where you're going with this."

"Yeah. When someone comes back for those agents, Hamer will know we know about a safe house that leads to the orphanage through a tunnel beneath the street. And that we know about the failed IDF op to land on the Temple Mount. This operation was in place long before the hostages were taken here. Tell me if that suggests something to you."

"This is big. A setup like this doesn't happen unless it gets sanctioned by the top."

"It is big. One of the things it means is that someone knew what Safady had planned. We're in the middle of it and have no idea what's going on."

That was a partial lie. Quinn had some idea. The heifer. Soon enough, he'd have to tell her about it. And he hoped she would understand too.

IN THE AIR OVER JERUSALEM • 18:09 GMT

The helicopter tilted dangerously as it made a turn.

Jonathan Silver found it strange that he wasn't terrified. Instead, he was enjoying a sense of peace. He had his arm around Alyiah and was whispering comforting words. The little girl couldn't understand, of course, but he knew she was able to absorb his calmness. She had one hand across her chest to reach upward and touch his arm where it rested on her shoulder.

Would the helicopter crash? Silver had been praying it wouldn't. But he was also content to let the future be in God's hands.

As he looked out, the helicopter's floodlight showed high stone walls. Then, briefly, a bell-shaped gold dome.

Impossible, he told himself. *We couldn't be at the—*

The helicopter leveled, then began to fall. Slowly.

It wobbled precariously a few times. But one side of the landing bar touched down; then the other banged the ground.

It was on land.

No explosions.

The inside of the helicopter became a chaos of movement as the engines shut down. Noise of human yelling replaced the throb of the motors.

Silver found himself pushed up. He made sure he had the little girl's hand and tried to protect her as people moved all around them. Silver looked in disbelief through the open door of the chopper and saw the dome outlined against the night sky.

Impossible, he told himself again. Yet if his eyes weren't deceiving him, they were at the Dome of the Rock. Almost in the night shadows of the shrine.

With security guards rushing toward them, armed with machine guns.

KHAN YUNIS, GAZA STRIP • 18:14 GMT

"Let's make some phone calls for help," Kate suggested again. They had taken a few minutes to shake any followers, then had returned back to the area near the safe house, clicking on the Mercedes key, hoping to identify the car by seeing blinking lights. "I think the chances of surviving protective custody are better than finding out what this is all about. And once we're on an airplane headed for the United States, we're fine."

"We're in Gaza," Quinn said, "not Chicago or New York. Protective custody will make us sitting ducks. Whoever is capable of organizing something like this is easily capable of finding a way to get rid of us and cover it up."

"You want me to bet my life that you're right, but from my point of view, you're going to argue against anything that gets you on the airplane, headed for prison."

"I'm not the one betting your life. The dice have already been thrown." Quinn handed her a cell phone taken from the IDF agents, along with a pistol. "But if you think the reason I want us on the run is to avoid extradition, go ahead; make your first call. Just think of where we are and how easy it is for something to happen between here and two coach seats out of Ben-Gurion. And remember that even when we got in the air the first time, we didn't get very much farther."

Kate took the phone and flipped it open. Then she studied Quinn's face and snapped the cell shut again. "Here's the deal. We play it your way for twenty-four hours. Then I make my calls. If it turns out you're doing this to get away from me, I'll spend the rest of my life tracking you down."

They'd stopped. They stood not far apart. In the darkness, along with the rush of surviving attempts on their lives and the chemistry that lingered from their first conversation in Acco, it seemed even closer, almost intimate. Quinn had the feeling all he had to do was move a little nearer. He wanted a touch. Any touch. A kiss on her forehead. A hand on her shoulder.

"Deal," he said, mentally pushing away the danger of intimacy. He took a step farther down the street. "Now give me your cell phone. I have an idea."

Safady stepped down from the helicopter, arms raised high.

Both choppers had landed easily in a wide area on the Temple Mount, well away from the Dome of the Rock. The engines had been immediately shut down, and the choppers' blades were slowly thumping into silence.

It was dark except for flashlights trained on the helicopters by the Waqf security—Muslim guards armed with machine guns. There were twenty-two, Safady noted with satisfaction and relief. Based on intelligence reports, this was the entire unit. The Waqf security had fanned out in a wide oval that surrounded both helicopters.

"Who is in charge here?" Safady called loudly in Arabic.

"Keep your hands raised," a voice to his left said. "Walk toward me slowly."

Flashlight beams blinded Safady as he obeyed the command.

"No," barked the commander. "All flashlights on the choppers!"

The beams moved back to illuminate the sides of the choppers, except for one, trained squarely on his eyes to reduce his vision.

"Nobody steps off the choppers," the commander shouted.

Arabic, Safady noticed. This was good. It meant the commander assumed there were more Palestinians aboard the helicopters.

"Any sign of weapons and we open fire."

Safady had no doubt the guards were filled with adrenaline. Fingers on triggers. Eyes intent on the first sign of danger from the choppers.

Safady was only a couple of steps away, unable to see past the flashlight beam in his face. "We will disembark in whatever way you order us," Safady said. "We praise Allah that we were able to reach this refuge."

"How many of you?" the commander asked. "Are the media reports accurate?"

"Only because I made sure the world was watching," Safady answered. "You know the situation. We had safe passage to Jordan until rocket fire disabled the helicopter."

"You still have the American hostages."

"Our only leverage. Much as I wished to throw them overboard."

This remark was met with a grunt. "You know the walls of the mount are surrounded by Israeli military already."

"I do," Safady said. "They don't dare take us. Not on sacred ground."

"You've made this difficult for us."

"You would release us to the Israelis?"

"That will be their demand."

"And mine will be for another helicopter. In one hour, we will be gone from here. You will have served Allah by allowing this." Safady paused. "It would be helpful if you allowed me to put my arms down. And the light on my eyes is painful."

"Keep your distance then."

"You don't trust a brother?"

"A brother who brings us trouble. Choppers. Wanted by the Israelis. Hostages. The entire Israeli army will be against us tonight."

"One hour," Safady said. "I may put my arms down?"

"I want you to return to the choppers and order everyone to stay on board. Understand?"

"My arms," Safady said. "Give me some dignity."

"Put them down," came the grudging answer. "Slowly."

Safady felt like a conductor as he began to lower his arms, knowing his movement had already triggered two countdowns.

As his hands hit his sides, he lifted them again and plugged his ears and shut his eyes hard for the first round of grenades.

The choppers burst into supernovas of blinding, searing light as stun grenades thrown from both helicopters detonated in perfect synchronization, sending shock waves of noise outward.

M84 stun grenades—*flashbangs*—had one million candela of flash each. Designed to overwhelm the photosensitive cells of the retina, making vision impossible for several seconds. With their eyes intent on the choppers, these security guards were rendered blind.

The flashbangs also blasted the Muslim guards with 180 decibels of explosion, disturbing the fluid in the ear canals so badly that they staggered with dizziness. Even with ears plugged and eyes shut, facing away from the choppers, Safady barely maintained his orientation.

This was the first countdown, giving a five- to seven-second window of opportunity as the Muslim guards tried to reorient themselves.

Safady dove to his side and landed on his belly, curling into a ball with his back to the choppers, knowing a round of sting grenades was already in the air, thrown by soldiers ready at the chopper doors.

Hornets' nests, enclosed not with metal casing but with two hard spheres of rubber. The inner sphere held the primer, explosive charge, and primer pin. Between the wall of the inner sphere and the outer wall of each were dozens of BB-size hard rubber balls.

The sting grenades bounced toward the Muslim guards, who were flailing to keep their balance, unable to hear the thud of the grenades' impact on the stone of the courtyard. Safady knew another couple dozen sting grenades would follow the first wave.

The explosions of these grenades were much more muffled, far less dramatic than the flashbangs. Safady had gritted his teeth, knowing some of the pellets would hit his body no matter how he protected himself. He was deluged; most of the projectiles ricocheted off his Kevlar, but a few slammed his thighs and the back of his skull. He bit off a scream of pain.

Around him, however, the hornets' nests had done far more damage, sending the Muslim guards to their knees in agony, knocking some unconscious. The second wave detonated a few seconds later, again hitting Safady with a barrage of pellets.

Then came the thumping of army boots. Safady rolled onto his side, seeing the bobbing beams of flashlights as Saxon's platoon rushed from the choppers.

Half were armed with machine guns and stopped a few yards short of the incapacitated Muslim guards. The other half continued to rush forward with cans of Mace.

Safady rolled onto his back, one hand over his eyes, the other over his mouth and nose. This was not only a visual clue to the soldiers to leave him alone but also protection in case one of them mistook him for a Muslim guard anyway.

Feet rushed around him.

The Mace was directed at the ring of dazed security guards, who were on their knees or bellies or staggering in small circles. Coldly and efficiently, the Freedom Crusaders blasted the Muslims and, when the Mace had cleared, began kicking the helpless security guards until all were on their stomachs.

As this happened, Safady slowly found his feet. Above the screaming and moaning, he called out clearly in Arabic to the downed security guards. "Hands behind your backs. Any resistance as you are put in cuffs and you will be shot in the head."

Then Safady moved to the commander, and knelt beside him. "I want your cell phone," he said.

No answer.

Safady nodded at one of Saxon's men, who stepped forward and put a machine-gun barrel against the back of the Muslim's head.

"I'll get it myself," Safady said, taking the phone from a belt clip.

He dialed a number and, when the call was answered, spoke in rapid-fire sentences, supplied the correct passwords to the Waqf security man on the other side, then hung up, knowing that this security man believed everything was still under Waqf control on the Temple Mount.

Amazing, Safady thought. *How could this mission fail?*

KHAN YUNIS, GAZA STRIP • 18:22 GMT

In a way, Quinn was grateful that night had descended. He and Kate had a better chance of blending in with the people still crowding the streets. This was the Gaza Strip. Few streets weren't crowded.

It took them only a few minutes to find the Mercedes two blocks away, parked in front of a café that had high, wailing music coming from cheap speakers above tables set on the sidewalk. The car was dusty and black and a few years old—not something that would get a lot of attention.

"What are the odds this thing is carrying a GPS transmitter?" Kate said.

"I'd say 100 percent. It's an IDF vehicle. That's why I wanted to find it. To make sure someone starts driving it."

"But not us."

"Not us."

"Right," Kate said. "We sell it. At the dealership back there between the butcher's block and the booth selling pirated CDs."

"Sarcasm diminishes you," Quinn said.

"Can't help it. Fear brings it on. I'm a victim here."

"What kind of fearful victim kicks a man in the groin and jams a pistol against his head?"

"If that's a thank-you for stopping the shock treatment, then you're welcome."

"If you could have been there a minute earlier, I wouldn't need aspirin."

"The Mercedes is right here. How long are we going to stand here trying to impress each other with light conversation?"

Quinn grinned. He stood at the driver's side and clicked open the door locks.

Kate made a move to get in on the passenger side, but Quinn shook her off with a head gesture.

Instead of getting in, he reached inside and started the engine, then stepped away from the Mercedes. "I saw a car at the orphanage," he said. "An old Fiat.

The keys were in it. It's not much, but it should be enough to get us where we need to go." He started walking and motioned for Kate to follow.

"Changed your mind about selling it?" she asked.

"Anyone with street smarts would be too suspicious," he answered. "Especially because I speak Arabic with an obvious accent. It's easier this way."

He was right. Before they'd reached the next corner, the black Mercedes blasted past them with two teenaged boys in the front seat, heads bobbing up and down to music from the radio.

TEMPLE MOUNT, JERUSALEM • 18:25 GMT

Jonathan Silver was still dazed as he began to lower himself from the helicopter to the ground. The noise from the explosions had disoriented him.

Esther, already on the ground, had told Alyiah to wait in the helicopter. Esther reached up and provided balance for Silver as his feet touched the ground, then they helped Alyiah.

Searchlights from the choppers were on again, throwing the scene into harsh whiteness. No guards were in place to monitor their movements, and already some of the hostages were walking confidently toward the fallen Muslims, where the first wave of men who had leaped from the helicopter were stripping off layers of clothing to reveal uniforms.

What was going on? Had the grenades stunned him so badly that he was losing his eyesight?

"What is this?" Silver asked Esther.

She didn't answer but gripped his elbow and pulled him forward until they reached one of the soldiers. "Ask now," Esther said.

The soldier turned his head. He straightened and saluted. "Sir!"

Silver couldn't deny that this recognition bolstered his spirits. "We're free now?" Silver asked.

"Yes, sir," the soldier said. "We've got the situation contained." He kicked the bound man beside him, who was still groaning from the Mace attack. "We've got orders to move all of these dogs, and then the real work begins."

"Dogs?" Esther bristled. She put a hand on Silver's forearm. Her other arm was around Alyiah's shoulder.

The soldier ignored her and grinned at Silver. "No sense shooting them. We could be here a week. Dead meat spoils. Easier to feed them than it is to refrigerate them."

"A week," Silver echoed. "I thought we were free."

"Of course you are, Mr. Silver. Anywhere you want to go, you can. This is God's house, and it's been returned to us."

Silver cocked his head and was about to ask more questions, but a shout farther down interrupted. All attention was drawn to the soldier who had shouted and the machine gun he'd lifted to his shoulder. A Muslim security guard was on his feet and running.

"Stop!" The shout was repeated.

But the Muslim, hands still behind his back, ignored the command. He didn't get five more steps before a single shot snapped through the night air and he tumbled forward.

Esther's intake of horror was audible.

"Just a Palestinian," the soldier said with a shrug. "They're going to die anyway."

Esther's grip on Silver's forearm became tighter.

"Can you tell me what is going on here?" Silver asked.

"I thought you would know," the soldier said.

"I don't," Silver snapped. "You tell me."

"No, sir," the soldier said pleasantly. "I can't do that."

"You don't know?" This was as surreal to Silver as the initial hostage taking. He wished he could think more clearly, but the rapid and unexpected unfolding of events had disoriented him as much as the stun grenades had.

"We were fully briefed on the helicopter," the soldier continued. "But I don't have the authority to tell anyone." He pointed down the line. "Ask one of them."

"Don't leave," Esther said. "That man is still alive."

She meant the Waqf guard who'd been shot. The man was slowly turning from side to side, calling out in Arabic, ignored by all of the soldiers.

Esther pulled Silver's arm, taking his attention away from where the soldier had directed it. "We're going to help him."

Silver managed to nod.

Esther faced the soldier squarely. "You're going to give Mr. Silver your flashlight."

"I can't," he said.

Esther squeezed Silver's arm. "That man needs us."

Silver found some strength and spoke with as much authority as he could muster. "The flashlight, young man. You don't want to disobey me."

He didn't expect the soldier to listen, but with a nod of respect, the soldier handed it over.

Esther pulled Silver forward to the wounded man.

"Stop!" a voice called out when they were within a few steps of the guard.

Silver instantly pictured a machine gun pointed at their backs and froze.

"A wounded man is begging for help," Esther said. "Shine the light on your face. Tell them who you are."

Everything in Silver told him to retreat.

"Go back, then," Esther said when she saw Silver hesitate. "If they want to stop me, they'll have to shoot." She let go of his arm and took another step toward the dying man.

"Stop!"

Silver turned toward the voice and held the flashlight in a way that the beam played across his face. "I'm Jonathan Silver," he called out as loudly as he could. His own flashlight beam blinded him from seeing how the soldier was reacting. "You will not shoot!"

He took a breath, waiting for an answer. When it didn't come, he lowered the flashlight and turned back to Esther.

She was already kneeling on the ground beside the wounded man.

The flashlight showed blood thickening on his back. Esther rolled him over gently. More blood poured from the exit wound in his belly.

He gurgled words that Silver couldn't understand.

Esther whispered back in Arabic.

"How do we stop the bleeding?" Silver said.

"We don't," she answered. "Take off your jacket. Make a pillow for him."

"But the bleeding. If we don't do something—"

"You've never seen someone die, have you?" Her voice was as terse with Silver as it had been gentle with the Arab. "These wounds can't be patched. All we can offer is compassion and to keep him from dying alone."

She raised the man's head. He put one arm upward around her neck. He was weeping.

"The pillow," she repeated.

Silver felt shame for worrying about the blood that would stain. He closed his eyes and asked God to forgive him for that weakness, then slipped out of his jacket, wadded it into a pillow, and placed it beneath the man's head.

The guard croaked another plea.

"Find his wallet," Esther said.

Slight surprise kept Silver from moving.

"His wallet," she said, adding urgency. "He is asking to see his children."

Silver reached beneath the man, feeling the slime of blood, and found the wallet. He wiped his fingers against his pants before digging into the wallet for two small photos.

The light showed head shots of a boy and a girl, not yet teenagers, with smiles that seemed alive in their dark eyes. Silver held them above the Arab's face with one hand and with his other shone the flashlight on the photos.

It brought a smile to the Arab's contorted face. He stared at the photos, tears in his eyes, and spoke again.

"He thanks you," Esther told Silver. "He wants to know your name."

"Jonathan," Silver answered, keeping eye contact with the man. He sensed it wasn't enough. "Ask him their names," he whispered to Esther.

She did.

The man's eyes shifted to Silver. "Aban. Boy. Hafa. Girl."

"Aban," Silver repeated. "Hafa. They are beautiful."

Esther translated.

The Arab managed to nod as he smiled again. He mumbled something. It took him great effort, and when he was finished, his eyes fluttered.

"He says he is not afraid of dying," Esther said, "but afraid for them when he is gone. And so sad that he won't be able to watch them grow up."

"Tell him that I promise to find them," Silver said. "Tell him I promise they will be cared for."

"Do not make this promise lightly," Esther said.

"Tell him," Silver said.

Esther leaned down farther and whispered to the man. His arm fell away from her shoulder, and he reached toward Silver. Silver gave Esther the flashlight, and she trained the beam on the photos he kept above the man's face. With his free hand, Silver accepted the Arab's fingers, and the dying man squeezed hard. His eyes, however, were on the photos, and he spoke a few more words. The man's grip faded and his eyes closed.

Esther kissed the man's forehead, then stood. "Alyiah. Where is she? We can't leave her alone."

Silver nodded. He took his jacket from beneath the dead man's head and draped it over the man's face and shoulders. He put the two photos back in the wallet and put the wallet in his pocket. That would give him the man's address. With Esther's help, he would find the boy and the girl.

If he was ever able to escape whatever was happening around him.

Small floodlights mounted on the helicopters threw crisp shadows on the courtyard stones. Jonathan Silver stepped away from Esther to join four of the uniformed men, who stood holding hands, heads bowed in prayer.

Silver bowed his head as well and listened.

"Lord, our heavenly Father," one of them was praying, "please bless our work so that it may advance Your Kingdom. Give us the strength and wisdom to complete the duties that You have honored us with by placing on our shoulders, Lord. And may Your Kingdom come before our eyes. In the blessed name of Jesus, we pray this. Amen."

The men moved away from one another with the slight awkwardness that often came after holding hands in public.

One of the men stopped at Jonathan Silver's side. "It's amazing how God has supplied the needed technology at the moment that His prophecies are about to be fulfilled," he said. "Of course, it's always easier to understand this looking back in time, isn't it?"

Silver was confused. "Technology?"

"GPS," the soldier said, waving an arm upward at the night sky. "Satellites circling the world. I believe God allowed man to invent these specifically for tonight, that all the other uses for satellites that He gave to humans were just icing on the cake."

"Tonight," Silver repeated.

"To mark the borders of the walls of the original Temple. I've got the points programmed into a GPS locator. With a flashlight and about half an hour's time, I'll be able to mark exactly where the Holy of Holies stood."

Before Silver could ask anything more, the uniformed man pointed at the helicopter, where other men were unloading boxes in the glare of the floodlights.

"That looks like my gear," he said. He shook his head and spoke in admiring tones. "This is like reconquering Israel. And God has given us the honor."

SOMEWHERE IN GAZA • 18:42 GMT

"You've been with me since we were in the tunnel below the orphanage," Quinn said. "You know I've had no chance to listen to radio, watch television, or reach the Internet for news."

Quinn was driving the Fiat they'd stolen from the orphanage, and the car bounced on bad springs every couple of seconds.

"I assume you're pointing out that obvious fact for a reason," Kate said.

"If I'm right, things are going to get a lot more complicated. And you're going to have to really begin to trust me."

"Twenty-four hours," she said, a warning note in her voice. "Don't even try to shift my landscape. It might have worked on Hamer, but it won't on me."

"We're going to listen to the news. Together. Right now. I'm going to predict what we hear. If I don't, you might later think I'm playing you."

"Playing me?"

"Coming up with a plan that's in reaction to the news. Trying to take advantage of the situation. I won't be. There's something else I learned down in the tunnel. Let me tell you now. Then let's hope it's not on the news. That means it didn't happen."

"What if it did happen but isn't being reported on the news?"

"If it happened," Quinn said, "it will be on every major media network in the world, 24-7. All languages."

"Don't build this up or anything," she said.

"Choppers taking the hostages to Jordan. Ground fire cripples a chopper. No way to get to Jordan. Choppers land on the one spot in Jerusalem where Palestinian terrorists will be protected—the Temple Mount."

"You're right," Kate said. "If we turn on the radio and hear that, you've got some credibility in your favor."

"Go to 1323 AM," Quinn suggested. "BBC out of Jerusalem. The signal should be strong enough to reach us here. I'd rather be wrong than credible."

Kate reached for the dial. The interior was dark until soft light glowed from the radio when she turned it on. It hissed as she adjusted the amplitude. She stopped when a clear English voice came out of the speaker. They both listened.

Quinn kept his eyes on the road, tempted as he was to glance at her face in the soft light. In Gaza, you never knew what might appear—from goats to bandits armed with machine guns.

"Wow." Kate turned off the radio. "Ground fire from Gaza, chopper in trouble, hostage standoff now on the Temple Mount instead of Gaza. Listening to the news, it doesn't seem real that . . ." Her voice trailed off. As if she still couldn't believe it.

Quinn took an attempt at completing her thought. ". . . that some IDF guy in the tunnel knew it was going to happen?"

"It's hard to believe."

"Yeah. It's equally hard to believe in any left-behind explanation."

"Huh?" she said.

"If it was IDF special ops, it's hard to believe their men aren't on the choppers and actually got left behind. Then you'd have to believe the IDF set this up and someone knew about it and had the resources to double-cross IDF. But who? And why?"

"It sounds legitimate. You think Hamer wanted us dead so we wouldn't be able to contradict the news?"

"Maybe, but I don't know. Once the choppers were in the air, we'd believe what the BBC and entire world believes—that Safady and his terrorists are on the Temple Mount. Why kill us for that?"

"I just want to get this straight," Kate said. "Those soldiers in the tunnel were supposed to replace Safady's terrorists. IDF or Mossad or whoever they are were supposed to land on the Temple Mount instead."

"Yes." Quinn nodded.

"But that switch didn't happen. Someone else did what IDF was supposed to do. A different switch took place."

"Yes."

"Who?"

"I don't know," Quinn said. "What frightens me is that Hamer doesn't know either. He's listening to the news, believing the operation is successful and his guys are there in a way that's fooled the world."

"Why does that frighten you?"

"Because Mossad and IDF at least have Israel's safety in mind."

"Not *our* safety. Obviously we're expendable."

"Something huge must be happening for IDF to have planned a hostage situation with a known terrorist just for the chance to do this. And it went wrong. If it went wrong for IDF, it's obviously not good for Israel's national interest. Especially if Safady found a way to double-cross them."

"I think I understand so far. We're the only ones who know a switch has been pulled on a planned IDF switch. But how bad can it be? It's only two choppers. Safady couldn't get much of an army on two choppers."

"It's not the army or lack of an army that's dangerous."

Kate put her hand on his arm with a small gasp, just audible above the car noise. "Not something nuclear."

"No," Quinn said. "If it's what I think, it's a lot more explosive than that."

TEMPLE MOUNT, JERUSALEM • 18:47 GMT

Esther stood beside Jonathan Silver. "We're safe here," she said. "I think you can take consolation in that."

The night air was chilly. Balancing a crutch, Alyiah kept her tiny hand in Silver's, and it made him feel stronger.

"Safe," he repeated. "This is the Dome of the Rock. Non-Muslims would be executed for this."

"We're permitted here," she said, "just not in the worship area itself. But what I mean is that there will be no gunfire, no rescue operations by IDF that will endanger us. The Israelis wouldn't dare. There would be months of rioting."

Silver was looking at the Dome again. This was thought to be the site where Abraham had offered to sacrifice Isaac, where Solomon had built the first Temple, where Herod had expanded the second Temple, where the Ark of the Covenant had been guarded for centuries.

Esther was still speaking. "That must be why the helicopters landed here. As far as the Israeli government knows, we were brought here by Palestinian terrorists, who would be protected here."

"I suppose you're right." Silver was only half listening. "The problem is it's not Palestinians who brought us here. They seem to be Americans, and no one will tell us what's going on." Movement near the helicopters caught his eye. Four men were unloading a large wooden crate. "Esther," he said in a low voice. "Look."

Her eyes followed where he had pointed. A small floodlight framed the scene.

Again Jonathan Silver wondered if he could believe his eyes as the men opened the crate.

Standing in the center of the crate was a small cow. A red heifer.

SOMEWHERE IN GAZA • 18:47 GMT

"A red heifer? Is that all?" Kate scoffed. "For a second, you really had me worried."

"Do you have any idea how close it could bring the world to an Armageddon of global holy war?"

"By the tone of your voice," she answered, "I guess I don't."

"Well, here it is in a nutshell: if whoever is on those choppers is planning to bring a red heifer onto the Temple Mount, it almost certainly means they're planning to destroy the Dome of the Rock in preparation for rebuilding the Jewish Temple."

"And you know this how?"

"I'll get to that in a second. But bear with me. It's important that you understand exactly what the implications are if the Dome of the Rock were to be destroyed. Do you remember the Danish cartoons depicting the prophet Muhammad?"

"Riots in the Arab world," Kate said. She remembered standing beside the cube van near the Hoover Dam, having a similar conversation with her partner, Frank. Neither of them had been tuned in to Middle Eastern politics, but even so, both had a sense of what was happening outside of the cocoon of America. "Death threats. Burning of embassies."

"Those were cartoons. In a newspaper. Imagine desecrating Islam's third most holy site."

"A heifer will do that?"

"Stay with me. Soon enough you're going to need to trust me on something. The most holy site is the Great Mosque in Mecca, Muhammad's birthplace. The second is the Mosque of the Prophet in Medina, which contains his tomb. The third place, the Dome of the Rock, is where Muhammad is believed to have ascended into heaven to receive God's commandments. Remember how you said you like making things real in your head?"

She nodded.

"Here's some perspective. The entire city of Mecca is barred to non-Muslims. Roadblocks and all. Same with Medina."

She nodded again.

"Rumor has it that holy water from Mecca is imported to the Dome of the Rock. The Israelis have no control over this."

"Didn't you say that Israel controls nearly every aspect of Palestinian life?"

"That should give you some idea of the political importance of the Dome of the Rock. It's the only exception. Thirty-five acres under total control—I mean *total* control—of the Waqf. Which in itself is a tinder point in a field of dry grass."

"I can imagine."

"Not unless you know some ancient and recent history. Ancient history first. Mount Moriah is the site where it is believed Abraham brought his son to be sacrificed. How familiar are you with this?"

"I think I know the basics, but why don't you remind me?"

"Abraham was obeying God's command to offer his son as a sacrifice. But just as he was about to kill Isaac, a ram appeared. God gave Abraham the ram to sacrifice instead. You can imagine how much significance Mount Moriah has to the Jews. Solomon built the first Temple on the site. That Temple was destroyed by the Babylonians at the time of the Exile. The second Temple was built by the returning exiles and expanded by Herod shortly before the time of Christ, then torn down by the Romans in AD 70, within the generation predicted by Christ."

"Still with you."

"Six centuries later, according to Muslim tradition as I already mentioned, the prophet Muhammad visited Mount Moriah. A shrine was later built there in his honor—the Dome of the Rock. It's the one still standing today."

"And it's located exactly where the two temples of the Jews once stood?"

"More than likely, although there is some scholarly and not-so-scholarly debate on this. But all agree the Temple was somewhere on the mount."

"Scholarly means academic papers. Not-so-scholarly I understand too."

"Do you?"

"I'm a cop," she said. "Not-so-scholarly involves fists, clubs, knives, and guns."

"But I'm not sure you understand what's at stake here in comparison to the crimes you've seen on the streets," Quinn said. "The Dome of the Rock is the flash point for three major world religions."

"Three?"

"To the Muslims, of course, it's a holy site. To right-wing Zionist Jews, it's the place where the Temple once stood, a place that rightfully belongs to them. Today, the Wailing Wall is the only remnant of their Temple, and to say there is deep resentment that the Waqf controls the Temple Mount is a serious understatement."

"You said three."

"Fundamentalist Christians." Quinn let out a sigh. "To them, the book of Revelation can only be fulfilled with the rebuilding of the Temple that was destroyed by the Romans."

"A Third Temple."

"Fundamentalists teach that the Temple must be rebuilt before they can expect the second coming of Christ. To them, when Israel regained control of the land in 1948, it was certain confirmation of God's timeline, that the end times are almost upon us. Here's what's scary: a battle over the Temple Mount could really trigger it. A clash of civilizations and war all across the world. Muslims against Jews and Christians."

"Why?"

"Think about it. I can't emphasize this enough. To rebuild the Temple of the Jews on the same site as the first two, the Dome of the Rock must be destroyed."

"And if Danish cartoons led to riots and burnings . . ."

"Remember the Israel-Lebanon conflict in the summer of 2006? Bomb after bomb shelled Lebanon, but not a single Arab country stepped up to the plate to help. It was a geopolitical battle. On the other hand, Danish cartoons that reportedly mocked Muhammad united the Muslim world in outrage. As did comments the pope made at an obscure German university, taken out of context. But if that's not enough to convince you, let me tell you about 1967."

"You mean the Six-Day War?"

"Right. When the war was over and Israel had regained control of Jerusalem for the first time in nearly two thousand years, the advancing Israeli army was on the verge of driving the Muslims from the Temple Mount until it was commanded to stop. Even then, Israelis recognized that profaning the site would lead to disaster."

Quinn watched Kate think about the implications. "Israel doesn't dare move a single soldier onto the site?" she asked.

"Not in 1967, and not for even a minute's duration since. Not a single soldier. Not a single bullet. Not a single surveillance camera. Any attack or operation would trigger global jihad. Safady couldn't be in a safer place in the entire world. To me, that's the reason that the Israeli government has released so much information to the press about the situation. It's absolutely crucial that the Arab world understand that the landing of the helicopters was demanded by a Muslim and that it is a group of Muslim warriors behind the walls on those thirty-five acres."

"Except that it's *not* a group of Muslims, because the Palestinians who were supposed to be on the chopper are dead in a tunnel beneath Gaza."

"Right," Quinn said. "And whatever else is going on here is big enough that the IDF thought it was worth risking an awful lot to sneak their agents onto the Temple Mount. If it leaks out that it wasn't Palestinians on those choppers, at dawn a half billion Muslims will be starting a holy war all across the world."

"But the IDF agents are tied up in the same tunnel. So whom does Safady have with him on those choppers? And why?"

Quinn was grim. "That's what we desperately need to find out."

TEMPLE MOUNT, JERUSALEM • 18:49 GMT

Silver had never felt more in a daze. So much had happened since the sniper shooting in Megiddo—hostage taking, death threats, the promise of escape, a near crash of the helicopter—all of it an emotional roller coaster that had stressed his system so badly he simply wanted to lie down on the inlaid stonework of the courtyard and sleep there for a week.

Now this. Total confusion. The men he'd thought were Palestinian terrorists had stripped down to unfamiliar uniforms and now virtually ignored him and the other hostages, who were wandering throughout the courtyard in small groups.

Silver was watching the soldiers unpack another crate. On one level—an abstract, intellectual level—he was able to put things together. He prayed he was wrong, but he feared he wasn't. He'd seen the red heifer.

In front of him, soldiers were pulling out what at first appeared to be costumes with glass jewelry. Silver knew better. He'd once visited an evangelical group seeking funds to re-create all the priests' clothing from the Temple days in Jerusalem. The group had impressed him with their evangelical fervor, and he had believed there was publicity value to gain from a few subsequent sermons about the glory of a rebuilt Temple, holding the work of these evangelicals up as an example of God's work.

Silver gasped. *An ephod?* An intellectual understanding was one thing. But to comprehend this emotionally was something else.

Priestly garments. A red heifer. Did these soldiers actually have the audacity to go ahead with a Jewish ceremony on the Temple Mount? Especially this—the one that involved a red heifer?

Silver had preached sermons on this, too. He'd even donated ministry money—and done television appeals based on this publicity—to American ranchers for a breeding program to attempt to produce a red heifer without blemish.

Silver knew he could occasionally seem buffoonish, but he wasn't stupid. A man able to build an empire like his was definitely not stupid. He was beginning to understand that the hostage taking had been a setup. All for what he was seeing from the crates. Priestly garments. Ephod. Red heifer.

Now the questions whirling through Silver's head turned in a different direction. Not why this was being done but who was behind it.

Then he saw a man he never expected he'd see.

His own son.

Brad Silver.

"Tell me more about this red heifer," Kate said.

"The border is about five minutes ahead." Quinn slowed the car.

"It'll take a lot longer than that if you don't pick up the pace."

"I'm slowing down because we need to stop for a minute before we get to the border."

"Stop for what?"

"You're going in the trunk," he said. "After I tie you up."

"I can see why you've worked hard to set me up to trust you. Because you knew what the answer to that would be."

"I don't expect you to like it. But I've been thinking about it, and it's our only chance to get across the border. I've got to run a bluff and hope IDF doesn't realize the shock-jockey specialists they sent to find us are MIA. If we don't make it past the border, we're dead. I don't mean that metaphorically."

"You're asking for a lot of trust here."

"You can keep your gun."

"Still a lot of trust."

"Let me explain the red heifer." They were stopped now. Quinn turned and faced her. "Then you'll know why this is so important. If I'm right—and I pray I'm not—it might as well have been that nuclear bomb you mentioned."

"You sound scared."

"I am."

"All right," Kate said. Headlights of an approaching car swept over her face. "I'm ready to listen."

"I know about it because of security alerts within the CIA, the Mossad. For these agencies, the possibility of a pure red heifer being born is like a dormant volcano—one that nearly erupted in the 1990s but has been quiet for so long everyone else has forgotten it."

"What happened in the nineties?"

"Hang on. Remember what I said about the Temple. It's more than that. For some Jews and Christians, the birth of Israel as a nation was a divine marker proclaiming that the end times are upon the world. Though they disagree about whether it will be Christ's first or second coming, fundamentalist Christians and Orthodox Jews believe that rebuilding a Temple is essential for the coming of the Messiah. But the Temple can't be rebuilt unless the shrines on the Temple Mount are destroyed."

"Even I can understand the political fallout there. We just covered that."

"Right. From a political perspective, it's obvious. Ownership of the Temple Mount is one of the biggest difficulties to resolve in the Mideast peace talks. From a religious perspective, it's less obvious but even more profound. For many Muslims, any attempt to destroy their shrines is also a sign that the end of time has arrived."

"How does a red heifer fit into this? And why should it matter enough to allow you to tie me and throw me in a trunk when I'm the U.S. marshal who is supposed to take you back to the States to face murder charges?"

"Because in the Bible, in the book of Numbers, God told Moses that in order for the high priest and the site of the Tabernacle, the precursor to the Temple, to be purified, they had to be sprinkled with the blood of a pure red heifer. Afterward, the heifer had to be burned, and its ashes were used in another ritual that cleansed the entire Jewish nation of sin."

"You're losing me."

"It's this simple: if someone has brought a red heifer onto the Temple Mount, it can only mean they're preparing to kill it in order to perform an ancient purification ritual that will cleanse the site and allow the Jews to be purified so that they can rebuild the Temple."

Kate let out a breath. "Now *I'm* getting scared."

"I mentioned the 1990s. In 1996, a calf named Melody was born in the Jezreel Valley to a black and white Holstein, artificially impregnated by semen from a brown beef cow. Melody was entirely red, almost a freak of nature considering the breeding line. News about this red heifer began to spread, and within months, busloads of American fundamentalists and devout Jews were stopping by to see it. Fundamentalist leaders proclaimed it as one of the final pieces of prophecy with the approaching millennium. Orthodox Jews rejoiced too. Finally a heifer had been born that would allow the national purification necessary for rebuilding the Temple. All they had to do was remember the words found in the Mishneh Torah."

"Don't lose me here," Kate said.

"A twelfth-century code of Jewish law."

"I'll never play you in Trivial Pursuit."

"I agree it's arcane, but not if you're in the security business in the Middle East. The Mishneh Torah records that only nine cows in all of history qualified for the requirements of a sacred red heifer. It states that the tenth cow will arrive in the time of the Jewish Messiah, a time tradition foresees the Temple being rebuilt on the Temple Mount. A time that, not coincidentally, also signifies the end of time."

"So if Melody was the tenth red heifer in all of history, then it would signal the time of the Jewish Messiah and the Third Temple. A red heifer is this important?"

"It's that important. Imagine how much it infuriated religious Jews in 1967 to finally have control of Jerusalem after nearly two thousand years but then to have Israeli authorities leave the Temple Mount in Muslim hands."

"I can."

"To appease the religious Jews, the civil government needed help from the rabbis, who provided a religious excuse to dictate why the Jews could not and should not enter the gates of the mount. In the end, it was this religious mandate that prevented right-wing Jews from storming the Temple Mount and starting that holy war."

"The excuse was . . ."

"Lack of a red heifer. According to Jewish religious law, anyone who comes in contact with the dead by touching a corpse or a bone, by entering a grave, or even by being in a place where the dead have been is rendered impure and cannot go through the gates of the Temple Mount. That basically means all Jews."

"But—"

"During the era of the second Temple," Quinn said, "priests purified themselves with a sprinkle of water mixed with the ashes of a sacrificed red heifer. There hasn't been a red heifer since AD 70, when the Temple was torn down by the Romans. When Israel's leading rabbis ruled that Jews cannot enter the mount without the same purification, the Temple crisis in 1967 was averted. Until Melody. Fortunately the heifer sprouted a few white hairs and became disqualified. The volcano stopped rumbling."

"White hairs?"

"According to the Old Testament, the red heifer has to be absolutely pure. That's why there have only been nine in recorded history."

"You think the cow on the helicopter is the tenth?"

"I can't think of any other reason it would be on there," Quinn answered. "Think about it. If it is the tenth red heifer, all that remains is getting the animal to the Temple Mount, which is impossible because you can't do that without provoking war, since the Temple Mount is under Muslim control."

Kate looked at him. "Unless someone found a way to get men and weapons and a red heifer onto the Temple Mount without Muslims discovering it until it's too late."

Quinn looked back at her. "Like now. With the entire world believing that Palestinian holy warriors are the ones taking refuge on the Temple Mount. Think somewhere in those two helicopters there's enough explosives to destroy the Dome and clear the way for a Third Temple? Because if they've got a red heifer and the ashes are produced, it's no longer Muslim holy ground."

"We're talking about World War III starting tonight. In Jerusalem."

"Worse. The previous two world wars were caused by political problems and ultimately had political solutions. But destroying the Dome would fulfill the end-times prophecies of all three religions. This would be a religious war. And religious wars never end. We're not just talking about World War III; we're talking Armageddon."

Kate opened her door and stepped outside.

Quinn did the same, looking at her across the roof of the Fiat.

"You said five minutes to the border?" she asked.

"Five minutes."

"Make it less if you can. I've never been tied up and thrown in a trunk before. I don't expect it will be any better than it sounds."

I didn't want to put you in a position where you would be accountable if this leaked before it was successful," Brad said to his father. "Your worldwide ministry is too important."

"This was funded by money diverted from my ministry. Without my knowledge." Jonathan Silver was sitting on a crate, exhausted again, looking up at Brad, who paced back and forth in excitement, the proud son showing off for his father.

"I couldn't let you know. That gave you deniability. It was my head on the chopping block the entire time. I did it because something had to be done."

"A secret organization of Freedom Crusaders, you said. Recruited at my university."

"A crusade!"

"From what you've described, it sounds more like a network of terrorist cells."

"We used those principles," Brad said defensively, "only because it's an organizational structure that's extremely effective. We're serving God using terrorist tools against terrorists."

"The ends justify the means."

"Osama bin Laden formed a secret organization of Muslim warriors to fight the Western world. This is the organization that can fight back against him, using his methods. War is war."

"With ministry money. By working with a Muslim terrorist."

"He's not a terrorist," Brad said. "He's an actor, paid to do this."

"Actors don't execute people." On familiar ground as leader, Silver was finding his strength. "Four men from the tour are dead."

"I was promised he was an actor pretending to be Safady. Promised no one would get hurt. I'm sure the executions were staged."

"Who promised you this?" Silver asked.

"Sorry. I have to protect my source."

"You've met this source?"

"Via Internet chat rooms. For his safety and mine. We're protected. The intel that this source gave me was far more risky for him to give than for me to receive." Brad was becoming impatient. "You have no idea how big this is. It involves U.S. and Israeli personnel. Men of power in various places. All of them dedicated to this cause."

"You know that for certain?"

"My source delivered me information from different places. Wheels were greased when I needed it. I was like a general, served by some of the most influential people in the world." Brad paused. "But let me emphasize: we're protected. It's a cell-group structure. I have only one link. That's to my source."

"Son, Safady is no actor. If your source lied to you about that, where else have you been deceived?"

"Deceived?" Brad gestured at the activity around them. "Look at the results. We're about to reclaim the Temple Mount from the Muslims and rightfully place it in the hands of God again. The prophecies will be fulfilled. When the Temple is rebuilt, Christ will return."

"This entire hostage taking was a setup?"

"I wanted to tell you beforehand, but it had to be absolutely secret. I was told I'd be directly involved in negotiations, and I hoped I'd have a chance to step in earlier and tell you."

"The red heifer," Silver said. "It's truly without blemish?"

"The result of a breeding program in the United States. Seven years. Isn't that a significant number? Doesn't the fact that God made the program successful tell you that all of this has His blessing? And that we made it here to the Temple Mount? If all of this wasn't ordained by His will, surely it would have failed."

"You're going to sacrifice the heifer? Tonight?"

"And sprinkle the ashes and reclaim the Temple Mount."

"You don't expect you'll be able to keep the Temple Mount, do you?" Silver asked.

"You're not listening," Brad responded. "This is about men in very high places, including the Israeli government. Once we've accomplished this, Israeli military will remove control of the Temple Mount from the Arabs. It will finally be under Jewish jurisdiction for the first time in nearly two thousand years. The Temple will be rebuilt." Brad's expression showed that he could see his father wasn't convinced. "Don't you get it? It's everything you've been preaching. All the money you've raised and sent here—it's all for Zionism. We're about to reach your dream."

Jonathan Silver remained silent.

"When this is over," Brad said, "we will be heroes to Americans and Jews. And especially to all the Christians across the world who have supported your ministry. This is a night to celebrate!"

GAZA/ISRAELI BORDER • 19:01 GMT

Quinn stopped just short of the border and unlatched the trunk of the car. He drove the remainder of the distance with the trunk lid swinging high.

At the crossing, large concrete blocks were set in staggered formation so that cars had to weave between them at a slow pace to get into Israel. On this side, the equivalent of a third-world country, the average daily wage was five dollars. On the other side, sharing the same land and geography, the prosperity of an economic and military machine ranked fifteenth in the world.

By design, there were only a few border crossings, and all were severe bottlenecks. It was a military necessity to prevent terrorists from penetrating Israel. Yet it was more than that. If Israel wanted Gaza to suffer, the soldiers didn't let produce trucks through for days, until the produce was rotting and useless. If Israel didn't want gasoline to reach the Gaza Strip, it squeezed the Palestinians by the neck here.

If Palestinians in Gaza wanted to reach relatives in the West Bank, they first had to pass through here. Some had not seen sons or daughters, brothers or sisters for decades.

The lights above threw a harsh glare onto the line of vehicles, and when Quinn arrived, it was apparent he would be forced to wait for hours. So he pulled out into the opposite lane, forcing cars into the ditch to avoid a head-on collision.

He knew if he drove too fast, soldiers at the checkpoint would decide he was a suicide bomber, and the tank at the crossing would destroy him before he got within a hundred yards. Instead, he drove deliberately to give approaching vehicles enough time to avoid him and flashed his headlights and blew his own horn, drawing maximum attention. This was an all-or-nothing gamble anyway.

As he closed in on the final barricades, a tank swung toward the vehicle, turret trained on the car. Quinn stopped immediately. He put the car in park, eased open the door, and stood with his hands high. He wasn't wearing any bulky clothing, and that was in his favor. It would appear unlikely that he was wearing explosives.

Five soldiers advanced cautiously, machine guns trained on Quinn.

Quinn threw his wallet on the ground, then put himself in the brace position feet spread apart to prevent him from making a sudden movement, hands
on the hood of the car, head down. "Check my identification," he called out. "IDF.
I have a prisoner in the trunk."

If the lid had not been open, the soldiers might have suspected a bomb that
would trigger when one of them opened it. Even with the trunk lid open and the
IDF identification, they were going to be supremely cautious.

"Step away from the vehicle, take your shirt off, and walk backward toward
us," came the reply.

Quinn would have made the same request if he were among the soldiers.
They needed to reassure themselves that Quinn wasn't baiting them into range
of a suicide explosion.

He did as directed.

"On your belly."

Again, he moved slowly. Pebbles bit into his skin.

One of the soldiers stepped on the back of Quinn's neck. "Talk."

"No," Quinn said. "All you need to know is that I've got a prisoner, and this
was the best and fastest way to transport. Anything else is a matter of national
security."

"Not good enough."

"I'm not even going to ask you your names." Quinn's face was pressed against
the pavement. Which was good. He'd chosen the ID from the IDF interrogator
that most resembled him, but under bright lights and close examination, it would
be a stretch. "If you make a stupid decision and slow me down, I'll have your
schedules pulled and get your names later. I'm not going to waste time right now
making threats either. Send a soldier to the trunk. You'll see a woman. I need her
in a place where she can be interrogated immediately." Quinn paused. "It also has
to be invisible. No trail. You don't even want to make record of this."

"Listen—"

"No, you listen. This isn't about pulling rank, even though that will happen
if you're stupid about this. This is about what's good for Israel. Let me through,
no questions asked, and I'll still have your names pulled. Only it will be to make
sure you're no longer guarding the border. It will be for a promotion."

"Give me a reason to believe. Without compromising security."

"Two choppers," Quinn said. "Diverted to the Temple Mount. I'm sure you
know that by now."

"Who doesn't?"

"You may think the choppers held a ragtag team of Palestinian terrorists,"
Quinn said. "They don't."

"Our guys?" Just enough belief to give Quinn hope.

"Shut up," Quinn said. "Do you have any idea of the massive riots that will begin if any Arabs discover the Dome of the Rock is part of an IDF operation?"

Muttering.

"We've got until daylight," Quinn said. It was a strain holding this conversation with only the pavement in front of his eyes. He wished he could read the body language of the soldier in charge. "If we're not out of the Temple Mount by then, you can expect another war. Only this one will spread to every Arab country in the Middle East."

Quinn didn't have to explain much more than that. Every Israeli citizen understood the tinderbox that was the Temple Mount.

"We'll give you an escort."

Quinn restrained himself from a breath of relief. They'd bought the story.

"Don't be stupid," Quinn said. "Don't you think there's a reason I'm driving the car I am, with Palestinian plates?"

"His ID looks good," a voice said. "I'll call it in."

"Do that, and suddenly you've started a chain of accountability that the media could sniff out someday. It was difficult enough to take care of the Munich terrorists over twenty years ago without the world spotlight on us."

Another reference understood by Israeli citizens, especially soldiers. The Mossad had covertly tracked down and assassinated every Palestinian responsible for the murder of the athletes and coaches taken hostage at the Munich Olympics in 1972. The Red Prince had died to a Mossad bomb planted in his car. The Israeli government had steadfastly denied the hunt, knowing it would provoke world outrage. And when it was finally leaked to the world, the predictable outcry occurred.

"Go," the soldier said. "We didn't see you."

42

hat's happening?" Esther asked quietly. "Those look like propane tanks."

She stood beside Silver, watching with him as soldiers began to assemble parts from crates.

"I'm afraid to tell you."

"It's not weaponry," Esther said. "Propane isn't efficient enough."

"An incinerator," Silver said. "More specifically, a crematorium."

She drew back.

"Not for humans," he said.

"How do you know this?"

"That's what I'm afraid to tell you."

"Tell me."

Silver pointed at Brad, a little distance away, supervising the soldiers. "That's my son. He planned this."

Esther waited for the explanation, and he gave it to her. When he finished, she took several moments to absorb it.

"Incinerator," she said. "For the ashes of a red heifer. To allow for the Temple to be rebuilt."

"When you put it like that, it sounds so crazy and bizarre." Silver stopped; then he spoke more quietly. "Yet here we are."

"Bizarre? It's what you've preached your entire life."

"Not a military takeover of the Temple Mount," he protested.

"If what you told me about Brad is true, all the Freedom Crusaders are here because of what you've taught about the Bible and Revelation."

"Yes, but—"

"So you were just preaching abstractions?"

"I was preaching what the Bible teaches about the end times."

Esther looked at him. "Jonathan, you have to stop this."

"I don't know if I can."

"Think about Alyiah. Imagine what will happen to her. She's no different from the thousands and thousands of children in families that will be torn apart in riots and war if the Freedom Crusaders succeed in permanently taking the Temple Mount out of Muslim control." She gripped his shoulder. "You can stop this. He's your son."

Silver kept staring at the soldiers busy with their tasks. "Maybe Brad was right. If this is succeeding, perhaps it is God's will. Perhaps that's why my ministry has been blessed for all these years. God had this planned for me and is finally revealing it. A rebuilt Temple!"

Esther took a breath. "Would you agree it's heresy to say that Jesus atoned for some but not all of our sins when He died on the cross?"

"Of course. His atonement was complete and perfect."

"Yet you preach the need for a rebuilt Temple and priestly sacrifices. Why are those sacrifices necessary if Jesus was the complete and final sacrifice?"

"Ceremonial sacrifices," Silver snapped.

"Think through the implications. It's a ceremony that represents the need for further atonement. To me, that's heretical."

He didn't respond.

"Jonathan," she said, softening her voice, "remember what I said before about Jesus and the Samaritan woman at the well. 'A time is coming when you will worship the Father neither on this mountain nor in Jerusalem.' He explained to her that God is spirit, and His worshippers must worship in spirit and truth. Jonathan, because of Christ we no longer need a physical Temple."

"God made a promise to His people. This land belongs to the Jews. And the Temple."

"Jesus promises a new heaven and a new earth to those who follow Him. But you want to restrict the surviving Jews to a piece of land by the Mediterranean."

"Surviving?"

"You've raised millions and millions to help Jews gather in one spot on earth, where your prophecies say two-thirds of them will be slaughtered. That makes you not only anti-Semitic but, in theory, a proponent of genocide. If you don't stop this, tomorrow the bloodbath will make it genocide for real."

"How . . . how . . . ?" Silver was sputtering mad. "How dare you take something I've been preaching all my life and twist it into something evil!"

"There *is* evil here," Esther insisted. "And if your son and his men succeed in their plans, that evil will be unleashed upon the whole world. This is your chance. If you don't do something to stop it now, it will be too late."

"If you're finished thinking," Kate said, "I'm finished with my courtesy silence. It'd be nice if you told me where we were going."

They were twenty minutes down the road now, past the border on the Israeli side.

"This is where it gets more complicated."

"I'm guessing that translates to me trusting you even further."

"With your permission, your next destination is the U.S. embassy."

"That's a safe place for us."

"*Your* next destination," Quinn said. "Not *our* next destination."

"We separate? No deal. I climbed into the trunk because I knew you couldn't leave the car behind without the border soldiers chasing you down. But no separation."

"We may be the only ones at this point—outside of the men in the helicopter and whoever planned all of this who know that there's a military squadron on the Temple Mount. It's crucial that we keep this from going public at all costs; the Muslim world can't know about it."

"That puts us out of the frying pan and into the fire," Kate said. "If we don't tell anyone, the outcome will be just as bad. Right? If what you said about the red heifer on the Temple Mount is true . . ."

She ran her fingers through her hair. "Options: we stop it ourselves, we tell someone else who can stop it, or we get as far away as possible and let the war begin. That about sum it up?"

"We can't stop it ourselves."

"We find the right someone who can. There has to be a government agency able to keep this from going public. CIA?"

"No," Quinn said. "The CIA doesn't have enough jurisdiction or manpower in this country. Has to be Israeli."

"Wonderful. Would these be the same Israelis who want us dead to keep all of this a secret?"

Quinn grinned at her spunk. "Remember rule number one."

"Of course. And what's rule number one this hour?"

"We leverage them."

"Right. Rule one."

"You go to a safe place. I apply the leverage. Remember? I'm a negotiator."

"What I wonder is how far a man might go to escape a murder indictment."

In his silence, the wind noise of the Fiat seemed magnified.

"No," Quinn said a couple hundred yards down the highway. "What you wonder is how much you can trust me."

"Same thing." A pause. "Don't get me wrong. I want to trust you. I think I can trust you. But I'm also a cop."

"Don't think trust. Think risk assessment. Weigh the cost of the downside of my escape. Compare it to the downside of not trying to prevent the deaths of thousands, maybe hundreds of thousands, who will die in a holy war across the world if the Dome of the Rock is taken hostage or destroyed."

"Good argument. Say you run instead of trying to get the right people to stop this. Maybe the real rule one is save the negotiator from the electric chair."

Quinn held his hand out. "There's a knife wound in the center of my palm. That was for one little girl. You really think I'm going to run with this much more at stake?"

The silence was Kate's this time until she finally answered, "Like I said, I'm a cop. Still, what if you get in touch with the right people, leverage them to get this stopped, and then run while I'm in the safe place?"

"You found me once."

"You weren't trying to hide. All I had to do was follow you from your office to Acco. But that was a century ago, when my biggest concern was a killer hunting down Muslims. Say you're lying to me right now about all of this risk—the red heifer, Armageddon. In theory, the way you've explained it, all of it makes sense. But where's the evidence I file away to protect myself when I have to write a report?"

"Here's what you confirm with the U.S. ambassador when you get him on the phone," Quinn answered. "In 1982, a group sponsored by Jerusalem rabbis is tunneling along the Temple Mount's Western Wall and begins to clear out chambers beneath the mount. Palestinian workmen hear the noise, open up a cistern, and find the Jews. To stop Palestinian rioting, the Israeli government prohibits the work and seals the entrance."

"Rioting. But not Armageddon."

"September 1996—an archaeological tunnel is opened for tourists. Even though it's three hundred yards from Al-Aqsa and the Dome of the Rock, rumors begin that the Israelis are tunneling beneath the Dome. Violent protests, seventy-five dead."

"Still not Armageddon."

"Pay attention," Quinn said. "Each new incident shows escalating tension. September 28, 2000—Israeli opposition leader Ariel Sharon and hundreds of Israeli police visit the Temple Mount under the pretext that he's checking for archaeological vandalism by Muslim religious authorities. He was warned that riots might occur. Riots begin and within six days, fifty-five Palestinians are dead, nearly two thousand injured."

"Escalating, sure. But—"

"The riots end, but the Arabs declare the Al-Aqsa Intifada as a result."

"*Intifada,*" Kate repeated.

"Arabic for 'uprising.' It lasted five years. Palestinians fought it mainly with rocks and suicide bombers. Israelis used their tanks and jets. Nearly four thousand Israelis and Palestinians dead and countless injured. All of this simply at a hint that Al-Aqsa and the Temple Mount were being profaned. Then there was the failed plot to blow up the Dome of the Rock by a radical Jewish group. If you need a copy of the Shin-Bet report, I'll get it to you. Conclusion was simple: had it been successful, it would have united the entire Muslim world in a religious cause against Israel."

Quinn paused and pointed at a road sign coming up in the headlights. "We're almost to Jerusalem. I've got a CIA connection there. I don't want to call ahead because they probably monitor his phone as a general policy. I doubt the Mossad knows yet we're in Israel, so I should be safe to stop by his apartment and call in a favor without telling him why I need it. Let me run it past you and tell me if you see any flaws in it."

They discussed what he had in mind. When both were satisfied, Quinn said, "How about we stop at a phone booth? I don't want to use the cell phone we took from IDF. Too easy to track. I want to make two calls. The first call is to Kevin, our IT guy. He'll meet you at a drop point and take you from Jerusalem to Tel Aviv."

"Tel Aviv?"

"To the U.S. embassy," Quinn answered. "That's the second call. To the American ambassador. I've got a direct number to him, day or night. He will get you inside, no questions asked. I want you to get on the line with him and verify all the historical facts I've just told you. Then you make your decision."

Kate spoke quietly. "I've made it already. The last Temple uprising—the Intifada that lasted for five years—I just realized how much it cost you. The suicide bomber that killed your—"

"You don't need to go there."

"Quinn," she said, "do whatever it takes to stop this."

TEMPLE MOUNT, JERUSALEM • 19:18 GMT

Silver had walked away from Esther in rage, refusing to turn at her call to come back. He now sat near some shrubs, away from the activities at the helicopters. Any other evening, it would have been pleasant in the soft night air.

He'd written best-selling books; he'd built his church and his television ministry; he'd founded a university. All on the dispensational view, which promised that current events showed the end of time was about to deliver punishment to nonbelievers and escape for believers. He knew critics called it a theology of despair, but it was a successful and appealing theology. In uncertain times, those who despaired because they felt little control wanted a certain leader. So certain that Silver did not allow students at his university to graduate unless they literally signed agreement forms to confirm his end-times teachings. Many of these students went on to be preachers, insisting on the same views within their own congregations.

Over forty years, he'd built the ministry. Wasn't it obvious that God had blessed it by the revenue He directed toward it? What did Esther expect, that after forty years he would stand at the pulpit and say he was wrong? that he'd changed his mind?

He thought of Alyiah—how she'd offered her precious milk to him. Thought of her hesitant smile and the slow way she moved on her crutches without any self-pity. Thought of the Muslim guard dying in his arms and of the photos of the two Palestinian children who would hear the news that their father had been killed guarding the Muslim sanctuary. Thought of Esther's warning about the consequences of taking the Temple Mount, the riots and wars that would follow.

Yes, he could try to ignore what Esther had said about Christ and the Temple, ignore her questions about the atonement. But ten hours earlier, he had been willing to give up his life for Alyiah. Now couldn't he at least question his own certainty on his end-times teachings enough to follow the teachings of Christ and save countless thousands of little girls like her?

Quinn stood on top of the rampart that surrounded the Old City of Jerusalem. It was a fortified wall about as wide as an alley, some forty feet above the ground. It had been built by the Ottoman Turks in the sixteenth century, some two miles of imposing stone barrier. Now tourists accessed the top of the wall from one of the gates.

Quinn had chosen a spot near the citadel, and from it he saw car traffic passing below. He was in a position to see two men approaching exactly at the time he'd set up via his CIA contact.

"Hamer," Quinn said in greeting. He kept his hands out of his pockets. He did not want to appear threatening.

"Quinn?"

Quinn watched the other man, who was easily a head taller than Hamer, dressed in a black jacket and black pants. Quinn knew he was Hamer's bodyguard; the CIA guy had warned that Hamer wouldn't go anywhere in Jerusalem without security.

"Surprised?" Quinn asked Hamer in return. Quinn stayed away from the wall's railing, only waist high. Then a forty-foot drop to the pavement.

"Surprised?" Hamer repeated. "Let me think about it. Our last conversation ends with you blaming me for blowing up your van and then threatening to go to the media. Then silence, which makes you my biggest worry until the choppers got diverted and I had to deal with hostages stuck on the Temple Mount with Palestinian terrorists. Then I get a call from the CIA demanding I come to a clandestine meeting about a national security issue more important than all of that. Now I show up, and you're here. Nope, not surprised at all."

The bodyguard had drawn a pistol and made no secret of it.

"Tell your bodyguard to relax," Quinn told Hamer. "Much as I'd like to shoot you, all I have is a cell phone."

"Would that be the same cell phone you decided not to use to call me over the last few hours? Any reason you couldn't have done something that simple?"

"Like letting you track me via GPS and giving you a third chance to kill me?"

"My wife does this a lot," Hamer said. "Answers a question with a question. Expects me to read between the lines."

"So read between these lines. I wouldn't be here unless I had insurance."

"Any chance you could explain enough to make me feel like I'm part of this conversation?"

"Probability tells me you want me dead," Quinn said. "I've ensured it won't happen. Kate's in a safe place, sitting in front of a computer."

"Kate? You said she was dead."

"Nice try, Hamer. If I don't get back to her, she hits a Send button with everything we know. It reaches the media outlets. They'll dig up the rest. You can't muzzle the media. Not enough explosives or IDF for that."

"Back up. You think I knew she was alive. You think I want you dead."

"I'm a slow learner, but the two IDF agents you sent in after the van exploded were a helpful hint. Just in case I didn't figure out that you set me up for the explosion with your phone call to tell me to start driving back."

"Two agents. I've got operatives in Gaza looking for you."

"Exactly. Backup for missing me in the van."

"I sent operatives in to rescue you after your call to me."

"Can you get your guy to put his gun down?" Quinn asked. "I'm in a bad mood here."

The bodyguard didn't shift.

"Humor me," Hamer said. "Pretend for a minute that I really don't know what's going on. I don't have to pretend, but you go ahead."

"What's the point in trying to drag this out? I'm not here to run from you. Like I said, Kate's in a safe place. You'd be stupid to kill me or arrest me now. Remind your bodyguard of this. The Rottweiler-at-the-end-of-a-leash routine is getting old."

Hamer shook his head, puzzled. Or pretending to be puzzled. "I already got the part about me trying to kill you. If you believe it, why are you here?"

"On the chance that I'm protected enough that I can force you to stop whatever you have planned on the Temple Mount."

The night was quiet. In the morning, from where they stood, they'd be able to plainly hear the call to worship from the Al-Aqsa. It was barely two hundred yards away, down cobblestone streets barely wide enough for loaded camels to move.

"You're scaring me, Quinn. I'm serious."

"I'm serious too. And scared. By this time tomorrow night, a thousand people in Jerusalem might be dead. Maybe ten thousand. Jews and Palestinians. Innocent people. Kids. Tourists. Multiply that by a hundred across the world a week from now."

"No," Hamer said. "What scares me is how your little world of delusion seems so real to you."

"The entire hostage situation was a setup. IDF had a special-forces team in place at the orphanage. IDF wanted it to look like choppers were sent into Gaza to load up with Palestinian terrorists. Except those terrorists didn't get on the choppers like the world thinks. They were replaced. And it wasn't random ground fire that forced the choppers to be diverted to the Temple Mount. It was just supposed to look that way. You had a nice little transcript of an emergency call from the pilot to prove it to the media."

Hamer said nothing for so long that Quinn wondered if he was considering an execution order right there. Quinn noticed Hamer had yet to ask the bodyguard to put down the pistol.

"Sooner, rather than later," Hamer said, "I'd like to know how you learned this."

"So you're confirming it was an IDF special op?"

"What's more important is that if Kate leaks this to the media, it will cause the very thing you say you want us to stop."

"Like maybe the Muslim world will riot, burn, and kill once it learns that IDF has violated holy ground? Very astute, Hamer."

"The political fallout terrifies us. But in about five hours, the choppers will be out of there. Unless you and Kate do something stupid, the sun will rise on a world that has no idea any of this happened."

Quinn sighed. "I see it one of two ways. First, you're lying to me and you know how badly the operation's gone wrong. If that's the case, I didn't need to risk this meeting, and Kate's going to make sure the blame falls on the right people."

"The operation will be complete by dawn. If you don't get in the way."

"The second way, you're actually telling me the truth and have no idea the operation's gone wrong." Quinn gave a tight grin. "Either way, Hamer, you'd better do something about the situation, or Kate lets the terrible little birdie out of the cage."

"You're telling me our special unit didn't get on the helicopters."

"The two agents you sent in to take me out haven't reported back yet, have they? Otherwise you'd know that."

Hamer shook his head. "My operatives have been calling every half hour with negative results on their search for you."

"You're a good liar, Hamer. I'd prefer to deal with what's really important. The operation has gone wrong."

"Convince me our special unit didn't get on the choppers and I'll find a way to convince you I'm as blind to this as you are."

Quinn stepped toward Hamer, then immediately stepped away when the bodyguard growled. Literally growled. Now didn't seem like the time to make another smart Rottweiler comment.

"I'm going to toss you a cell phone from one of the IDF agents who tried to take me out after the explosion. I used it to take photos and video of the Israeli special-unit soldiers who were left behind in Gaza. Keep the phone. Kate's got some photos on her cell phone too. If that's not enough, I have the badges of the agents."

Hamer studied the open phone. His shoulders sagged. "Where did you find these guys?"

"A tunnel under the street, accessed from a safe house across from the orphanage. Same safe house where the two IDF agents took me and tried to barbecue me right after I threatened you by phone. That threat was bait, and you took it."

Air exploded from Hamer's lungs in frustration. "I sent in men to rescue you. They didn't get into Gaza for at least a half hour after your van exploded. From my end, I'm thinking Safady blew it up. I was glad he didn't get you. I knew you needed help."

"If I can believe that," Quinn said, "there's only one alternative. Someone else was in on both operations—the negotiation *and* the special op to put choppers on the Temple Mount."

More silence. Quinn waited for Hamer to realize it. And say it.

"Cohen," Hamer said. "He called me just before your van blew. Told me to confirm you were safe. He was set up to listen to any calls you made, including the threat to me."

"That's the other reason I'm here," Quinn said. "In case it wasn't you. In case those were Mossad with IDF badges. Mossad sent by Cohen. So find a way to prove it."

Quinn started to turn his head toward the bodyguard as he caught a glimpse of movement. The bodyguard was lifting his arm, pointing the pistol. Before Quinn could react, there was the tremendously loud sound and the flash from the muzzle.

The bullet punched Quinn in the center of his chest. He fell to his knees, then onto his stomach.

From there, he heard Hamer speak to his bodyguard. "Are you crazy?"

Quinn saw the bodyguard spin and coldly lift the pistol again, pointing it at Hamer's chest.

Hamer's voice was filled with sad comprehension. "You're going to do this? We're friends. I'm godfather to your first son."

Quinn had managed to push himself up onto his knees, unnoticed by the bodyguard, who was totally focused on Hamer.

"I've got to do this," the bodyguard said. "Sorry."

"Why?"

"I take my orders from Zvi Cohen. That's all I know and all you get."

Quinn dove into the large man, managing to lock his arms around the bodyguard's upper thigh. In that same upward push, he shoved, toppling the man over the wall and down to the unforgiving pavement below. Quinn's momentum sent him sprawling on his belly. Even from his prone position, the sound of flesh and bone on the pavement was horrible, cutting short a scream, leaving Quinn the kind of memory no sane person ever wanted.

Hamer looked at Quinn, frozen by disbelief.

"Don't need much more proof than that to clear you," Quinn said, struggling to his hands and knees.

"He shot you. Point-blank."

"Rule one in negotiating." Quinn's voice was a wheeze; the impact of the bullet in the center of his chest had left him struggling for air. "Make sure your CIA buddy lends you Kevlar."

TEMPLE MOUNT, JERUSALEM • 28:21 GMT

"Brad," Jonathan Silver said, "we need to speak. Privately."

Brad was in conversation with one of the soldiers, touching the priestly garment as he inspected it. He showed impatience but stepped away, his face thrown in shadow. "I don't have much time, Father."

"A wedding day seems like a terrible day to cancel," Silver said.

"Like I said, I don't have a lot of time. Especially for riddles."

"There's only one thing worse than leaving a bride or groom at the altar. That's getting married when all your last-minute instincts tell you it's wrong. Sure, you leave a church full of people buzzing about it. But that's better than a lifetime of misery."

"Father—"

"Brad, I know this operation, as you called it, has taken a lot of planning."

"A lot?" Brad nearly laughed. "Do you have any idea of the difficulty of getting armed men on the Temple Mount? And all the equipment? Right in the heart of Israeli-protected airspace? All of this verges on genius."

"You can still walk away from it."

"What?" Brad squinted. "You're serious. You expect me to—"

"You're in command."

"I'm on the verge of fulfilling the prophecies that have waited two thousand years. That's what I command."

"I'm thinking about the riots and deaths that will follow. Do you want to be responsible for it? Women and children. Innocents."

"God's people will be protected. Revelation tells us that."

"But what if it isn't prophecy?"

"My whole life you've been teaching me these prophecies. Now you're saying you've been wrong?"

"I'm saying I'm not sure enough to believe it justifies turning Muslims against Christians all across the globe."

"You're telling me that the Temple doesn't need to be rebuilt for God. That a red heifer isn't necessary for sacrificial pureness. That the end times aren't upon us."

"If I've been right about all that, God will make it happen. In His own time. But if I've been wrong, what's happening tonight is—"

"Don't you think God *is* making this happen? The existence of the red heifer. Our success in landing on the Temple Mount. It's just like when David conquered Jerusalem from the Jebusites. God led him into the heart of the enemy's stronghold. God has led us here."

"This will change world history. Doesn't that scare you, Son?"

"Scare me? It exhilarates me. I'm a Freedom Crusader for our almighty God."

"I'm afraid, Son. I keep hearing the words of Jesus when He said His Kingdom was not of this world. He didn't lead warriors into battle against the Romans."

Brad walked back and forth. Slowly. Silver gave him the time to think.

Finally, Brad moved in, his face barely inches from his father's. "I think this discussion is about power," Brad said quietly. "You've never treated me like I was an equal. You've always made it clear that your ministry grew as it did because of you and that I'm simply stepping in to maintain what you've built. Now, tonight, you see what I'm capable of, and you can't handle it."

"Son, I—"

"Don't worry about not getting enough credit for this. Trust me; I've taken care of it." Brad turned away.

"Son, please, let's keep talking."

Brad spun around. "No." He was almost savage in his anger. "Tonight, stay out of my way. Tomorrow, it's going to be a whole new world."

SOMEWHERE IN JERUSALEM • 28:21 GMT

Since picking Kate up at a drop point, Kevin had been driving a circuitous route, saying little and checking the rearview mirror frequently enough to put Kate on edge.

Kevin's car was an older model four-door Mercedes—blue, maybe purple; she hadn't been able to decide in the streetlights when Kevin had driven up to the meeting place Quinn had designated. It was more vintage than restored with a sputtering exhaust system and diesel smoke that she smelled whenever the car stopped at a traffic light. She was sitting up front on the passenger side, where a spring from the seat pushed hard against her thigh. She had a wry thought, imagining terrorists chasing them, needing nothing more than scooters to keep pace.

"Quick stop for fuel," Kevin said, pointing ahead, a can of Diet Coke in his hand. "I didn't expect all this driving tonight."

"Yeah," Kate said. Kevin had made enough turns to lose anyone tailing them, unlikely as that possibility was. Maybe she'd run in and get a Coke for herself while Kevin was pumping gas. He hadn't offered any from his stash.

She didn't get the chance.

Kevin stopped at the pump. A man who had been fueling a white Peugeot on the opposite side of the island stepped across and opened the back door of Kevin's Mercedes, sliding in directly behind Kevin.

Kate's first reaction was escape. She yanked at the door handle, but it popped loose in her hand. At the same time, Kevin accelerated, leaving behind the Peugeot with the fuel line still in its gas tank.

Kate half turned, lifting the door handle to swing it as a weapon.

"It's okay," Kevin said. "Really."

"No," Kate snarled. This had been a setup. It wasn't an accident that the door handle had been loose. "You're about five seconds away from needing a big set of stitches. Tell me what's happening."

"I will," the man in the back said. "Just don't do anything stupid. Kevin had his orders. Don't blame him for this."

Kate caught a glimpse of the man's face as the Mercedes passed under a streetlight. She knew the face instantly but faltered with the name. She'd met him at the Ben-Gurion airport and later at CCTI with Quinn.

Dapper, arrogant, held himself like his presence was a gift to all women

Cohen. That was it. *Zvi Cohen.* Head of the Mossad.

"Start talking," Kate said. She wasn't going to let her anger fade.

"Kevin works for the Mossad," Cohen said. "That should tell you a lot."

"Mossad—or IDF working for Mossad—blew up the van that we were using for a command post in Gaza. Sent in two men to take out Quinn. That tells me a lot too."

"Told me a lot too," Cohen answered. "Hamer wants you both dead. He's got something going. I don't know what yet."

Kevin was turning again. Kate saw a road sign pointing to Tel Aviv. Kevin had taken the opposite direction.

"Hamer," Kate repeated. "Kevin, you let Quinn go meet Hamer."

"No," Cohen said. "I did. All that Kevin is responsible for is calling me after Quinn made the arrangements for Kevin to take you to the embassy."

"I expect that's where we're going," Kate said. If Cohen said yes, she'd know he was lying. And she'd take appropriate action. Like clawing his eyes out after hitting him with the broken door handle.

"No," Cohen answered. "Kevin's taking us back to the Old City of Jerusalem. To Mount Moriah."

"Quinn's got a cell phone. Let me make a call and warn him."

"I don't like that."

"Hamer won't hear my end of the conversation," Kate said.

"Still I don't like that. I can't give Hamer the slightest opportunity to suspect he's being watched."

"That's why you let Quinn meet with him? To set Hamer up?"

"As a cop, I'm sure you'd understand."

"As a cop, I would have let Quinn know what was happening." Then Kate understood, and her anger swelled more. "You've been using Quinn all along. Because you knew he'd be tethered to Kevin and everything would be reported back to you."

"Hamer is playing Russian roulette with a gun called Armageddon," Cohen said. "Your opinion on ethics doesn't bother me. Too much is at stake."

"I'm calling Quinn. He deserves better than this."

"Although you didn't mind setting him up at the harbor?"

"Go spit," Kate said, not allowing her outside voice to match what her inside voice wanted to say. "Quinn's good. He won't give anything away to Hamer."

"I don't trust Quinn," Cohen said.

"I do."

"Although he was supposed to be on an airplane with you to face a murder indictment?"

"He's meeting Hamer, and I'm going to call him."

Cohen's sigh was audible above the bad exhaust system of Kevin's old Mercedes. He leaned forward and put the barrel of a pistol against Kate's skull, just below her left ear. "I would rather have you helping me than have you dead. But you don't understand what's at stake here. So I will shoot if I have to. In the meantime, Kevin is going to pull over and put handcuffs on you."

Kevin slowed down as ordered and shrugged apologetically.

Another sigh from Cohen. "I'll take the handcuffs off you as soon as I can. But that won't be until we're under the Temple Mount."

"Under," Kate repeated. "As in underground. Below the Dome of the Rock."

"I'll say it for the third time," Cohen told her. "You have no idea of what's at stake here. You're going to find out anyway, so you might as well keep your mouth shut and show a little patience."

OLD CITY, JERUSALEM • 20:28 GMT

Quinn and Hamer walked at a brisk pace along the ramparts toward the nearest set of steps to take them down into the warren of alleys among the ancient buildings of the Old City. The dead body was behind them in the dry moat at David's Citadel; Hamer had called for police but wasn't going to wait.

"About four months ago," Hamer said, "your partner brought us some information that the Mossad confirmed for IDF."

"Rossett?" Quinn wasn't surprised. Rossett kept secrets. Plenty of them.

"He's got as many connections in the Arab world as we do. I don't have to tell you about Iran's hatred for Israel and America."

Except for occasional couples, they were alone. The Old City was frenzied during the day, but at night it rolled up like the awnings over the street bazaars.

"Rossett had a source that discovered a lot of Iranian oil money was going to Khaled Safady. We had the resources to go from there and trace the money trail from both ends. We confirmed Iran. Here's the irony: Safady was able to stay invisible for years. But when a lot of money begins to flow, it's impossible to hide the flow. So we followed the money, and it led us to Safady. Just as important, we found out he was using the money to plan this hostage-taking event to humiliate Israel and the United States. His idea. Fully supported by Iranian sources."

"What? You knew about this? You could have stopped it?"

"You'll understand soon enough why Rossett couldn't tell you. By following the money, the Mossad also found substantial evidence that, over the last few years, Iran's been able to smuggle binary chemicals into Arab hands in Israel—sarin."

Quinn couldn't help a sharp intake of breath. Sarin had a short shelf life when mixed but lasted much longer when stored in binary chemical weapons, with methylphosphonyl difluoride on one side of a portioned chamber and a mixture of isopropyl alcohol and isopropyl amine on the other.

"Yeah," Hamer said flatly. "Can you think of anything worse?"

As a weapon of mass destruction, sarin was a security nightmare. It was colorless, odorless at room temperature, and an extremely potent organophosphate compound that disrupted the nervous system, five hundred times as toxic as cyanide. Because it was invisible and undetectable by smell, victims had no idea they were about to die until they started bleeding from the mouth, nose, and eyes, then going into respiratory failure, convulsions, coma, and death.

"Bad news," Quinn said, wondering what this had to do with Safady. "Still, Israel's security is too tight to allow enough in to take out a major part of the population."

"But not tight enough to stop canisters in small quantities coming from cargo ships."

"That's my point. Small quantities means relatively small danger. Takes it out of the realm of weapons of mass destruction."

"Unless those small quantities accumulate." Hamer pointed at an upcoming corner to show Quinn they were going to turn. It seemed deathly quiet in the Old City. IDF had sealed off the traffic arteries around it. Many of the residents had fled earlier. It was hard to believe that only hundreds of yards away, across the Armenian and Jewish quarters, there were hundreds of IDF special forces in place, guarding a terrorist incident that was playing out on a world stage.

"This country is too small for a storage area that the Mossad wouldn't discover," Quinn said. "Wouldn't be any sense trying to find a place in Gaza or the West Bank to store it. If you release the binaries in any quantity there, you only kill Arabs. Not Jews. So it doesn't do the terrorists much good there."

"How about in the center of Jerusalem?"

"I don't buy it. Your intel is too good to let that happen."

"There are thirty-five acres we don't control. Thirty-five acres we can't even check."

Quinn stopped abruptly. "The Temple Mount."

"Right. With dump trucks going in and out that Israel is helpless to stop."

"Bulldozers, too," Quinn said. "The Temple excavations."

Once, despite protests by horrified Jewish archaeologists, the Waqf had brought in a bulldozer to clear a foundation. This, in retrospect, was nothing compared to the next project. To make an emergency exit for Solomon's Stables, an underground area sometimes used as a mosque, Waqf bulldozers had created a cavern the size of a soccer field. Six thousand tons of dirt, filled with archaeologi cal potential, were hauled away by heavy equipment and large trucks. Hundreds of truckloads were taken, often in the dead of night. Israeli authorities had been helpless to stop this, knowing the potential for riots if they interfered with Muslim control of the Temple Mount.

"I'd heard rumors that the Waqf was moving holy water there from Mecca to underground cisterns below the Temple Mount," Quinn said. "You're going to tell me that right in the middle of the one city where Jews and Palestinians barely managed to coexist without war, there's a hidden weapon that can kill all of them by the thousands?"

"Wrong breeze, or lack of a breeze, and you can make that hundreds of thousands. Surviving Palestinians would blame the Jews. Surviving Jews would blame the Palestinians."

Quinn was getting weary of making the same point. But such were the politics of Israel and Gaza and religion. "The war that would follow would make the riots over Israeli occupation of the Temple Mount seem like a pillow fight in comparison."

Hamer pointed at another turn into a small, cobblestoned parking lot almost beneath the rampart, lined with the small, square buildings of the Armenian Quarter. Quinn followed.

"That should tell you how bad we believe the worst-case scenario would be. That we were willing to risk the fallout of the operation going wrong just on the possibility the WMDs were there. The Mossad wanted to confirm the story, but politically, it would have been impossible to go in, let alone do anything to disarm the weapons."

"True. And you couldn't exactly ask the Waqf to confirm it."

They had reached Hamer's vehicle, a small, unmarked white truck. Hamer paused before unlocking the door, talking across the hood to Quinn, who stood on the passenger side.

"Consider our options," Hamer said. "One, we permanently evacuate the city, which really isn't an option. Two, we request the Waqf to allow us to search for it. They refuse, and all we've done is alert them to the fact that we know something's in there. Three, we do nothing, and someday, sooner or later, when the breeze is right and the terrorists are primed, it hits us, wiping out half a city. Four, we storm the place to search for it, and the political fallout is as disastrous. All it took was for Sharon to visit the place looking for archaeological damage and the result was a five-year uprising."

"So you went to option five," Quinn said. "Mossad and IDF work together to put men on the Temple Mount at night when the entire world believes your guys are Palestinian terrorists stuck until another chopper can move them to Jordan

Just bold enough to work. I mean, who is going to suspect anything but what the television shows them?"

"We needed night as a blanket of cover. By dawn, the weapons are either confirmed as a false story, or they've been found, disarmed, and moved onto the helicopters. The hostages are released through the gates, and the helicopters fly away with the Arab world believing that their terrorist heroes have succeeded in outwitting Israel."

They reached Hamer's truck in the parking lot. A small Toyota. Hamer opened his door and slid in behind the steering wheel. He waited for Quinn to get in on the passenger side.

"I'm with you so far," Quinn said. "But no matter what you do to try to convince me, I won't believe you turned Safady to help you with this op."

"We had someone buried deep in Iran—someone who could get close to Safady. We supplied funds to Safady through this contact. The condition was that our Iranian op worked with Safady to set this up. Our guy, the Iranian double agent, found Safady the orphanage as a base. It used to be army barracks. That gave us time to set up the tunnel into the orphanage. Our plan was to spring our men on Safady just before the choppers arrived. This would do three things: save the hostages, take out Safady, and get our guys on the Temple Mount."

"You didn't need a negotiator except for window dressing."

"The hostages were not supposed to be in danger. We had assurances. Our Iranian guy was supposed to make sure of that."

Quinn snorted. "Rule one in negotiating: never believe assurances."

"Still, you now understand why we had to take the risk." Hamer rubbed his face. "WMDs in the heart of the city. But we both know this was flipped. Someone replaced our special unit and landed a different army on the mount."

"Cohen was working you," Quinn said. "He got rid of Rossett, tried to get rid of me, and let you continue as if everything was good. So the big question is why."

"And who replaced the IDF soldiers. You and I don't have those answers. I don't like this."

"I told you the CO believed the replacement soldiers were Americans."

Hamer started the engine and put the truck into gear. "I can't see the CIA being behind it. No motivation. Even if somehow they knew what we'd intended to do."

"Not unless the CIA is into livestock."

That startled Hamer. He put the truck back into park and turned to stare at Quinn. "What?"

"There was a small cow on board one of the choppers. Your IDF CO down in the tunnel at the orphanage told me he'd seen it. I found fresh manure that seemed to confirm his story."

Hamer shook his head. "It wasn't red, was it? Tell me it wasn't red."

"It was red."

"Stick with me, Quinn. You and I may be the only two people able to stamp out the fuse of Armageddon."

"You're just figuring that out now?"

44

Cohen had switched Kate and Kevin from Kevin's car to his own, a gleaming black BMW. Kevin drove toward the Old City. At a security checkpoint, Cohen got out and spoke to the IDF soldiers and showed his ID; the soldiers waved them through after Cohen moved into the backseat again beside Kate.

He gave Kevin directions, navigating him through the streets before instructing him to park at the entrance to a narrow alley. Kate didn't know much about Jerusalem, but she realized they'd reached the Old City. To her, it seemed as if they had entered an Indiana Jones movie set of a market bazaar . . . without the crowds.

"Don't scream for help," Cohen told Kate as he helped her out of the BMW. "It won't do you any good, and it will only irritate me. The soldiers around here have better things to do, and if I tell them you're my prisoner, they won't help anyway."

Handcuffed, she didn't think there was much point in trying to escape. It was too dark for her to see where she could run. But she remained alert for any chance. She owed Quinn a call to warn him about Hamer.

"We're near the Temple Mount," she said.

"The Muslim Quarter of the Old City," Cohen answered. "This street is Via Dolorosa. The way of suffering. You might know it as the way of the cross."

The cobblestones were worn smooth, and in the quiet and the dark with the cramped buildings seeming to push in on her from both sides, Kate could easily imagine Jesus of Nazareth stumbling from step to step with the weight of the wooden cross on His back. She wasn't given much time to contemplate, however; Cohen turned her down an alley that seemed barely wide enough for a motorcycle to navigate.

"Not too far," Cohen said. "Bear with me. Then you'll get the answers."

He stopped at an ancient door of carved wood and opened the lock with a large key. The door was surprisingly quiet on its hinges, and the interior was dark. He took a small flashlight from his back pocket and clicked it on, then walked directly to a wooden bench on a small square of carpet. The scope of his beam didn't show much of the interior, but Kate had a sense it was simply a bare room.

Cohen dragged the bench off the carpet and onto the tile floor. In the almost eerie silence of a stone building centuries old, the scraping of the bench across the tiled floor was magnified. Cohen moved the carpet aside. His flashlight beam showed a nearly invisible latch. He pulled it up and revealed a trapdoor.

Kate thought of the trapdoor in Gaza, leading to a tunnel with captured and bound soldiers.

Cohen reached underneath the bench. A rope ladder had been hidden there. He attached the end of it to two prongs at the edge of the trapdoor opening and dropped the rope ladder down.

"Kevin," Cohen said, "you'll know where we are once you get down there. The Western Wall tunnel." He turned to Kate. "For centuries, houses here had openings like this to give them access. Residents simply lowered buckets to get water from the aqueduct below. The water flow is gone, of course, and now tourists go through the tunnel during the day when the lights are on."

"Don't quit your day job," Kate said, trying to read what was happening by the tone of his voice. It was dark except for his flashlight beam, and she couldn't take cues from his body language.

"Day job?"

"As a tour guide, it's pitiful when you have to handcuff someone to force her to go with you."

His answer sounded patient, not vexed. "You need to know what's down there so that you understand there's nothing to fear. It's going to be a lot more difficult to get you down the ladder if you decide to fight me. So I'm asking you not to fight."

Cohen surprised her by handing her the pistol. "I'm going to take off your cuffs because I don't want you falling off the ladder. It's about a twenty-foot drop. I'll stand up here shining the light. Kevin will go down first. I'm asking you to follow him. I'll go last."

"So you can slam the trapdoor on us and walk away." Still, Kate was thinking that when a guy gave you his weapon, there was a little more reason to trust.

"Kate," Cohen said, "a couple hundred yards down, the tunnel below us ends at a gate at the Wailing Wall. That's where Hamer has set up his base of operations. If I walked away, you could be there in minutes if the lights were on and you could see inside the tunnel."

"He's right," Kevin said. "I've been on the tour."

Cohen removed her cuffs. "You ready?"

"Ten minutes," Kate said. She backed away, giving herself a little room. She wasn't going to hold the gun on Cohen as she made her deal, but she wanted time to lift it if he tried to disagree. "You get ten minutes to make this clear. If not, I find Quinn."

"Give me fifteen," he answered. "You're going to have to see what's in one of the caverns to understand why I had to do it this way."

"Ten," Kate said firmly. After all, she now had the pistol.

TEMPLE MOUNT, JERUSALEM • 20:32 GMT

Joe Patterson had a small, high-powered flashlight on the top of his gun barrel and flicked it toward the approaching figure, catching just enough features to recognize the man. Jonathan Silver.

"It's him," Byron Davidson said to Patterson, speaking in a hushed tone. Davidson was the new Freedom Crusader assigned by Saxon to report anything unusual that Patterson might try. Davidson was a chunky, muscular man with the type of build doomed to middle-aged flab that would show no history of his former athleticism.

"Yeah," Patterson said without any of Davidson's enthusiasm.

Days earlier, Patterson wouldn't have made this remark with any degree of cynicism. But the Gaza events had taken away his blind allegiance to the cause even before he'd learned that the Freedom Crusaders were holding Sarah hostage to ensure his good behavior. The threat against her had been the tipping point. Now he doubted everything he'd been taught about the cause. Especially the leaders. They'd chosen to kidnap his wife and threatened to kill her.

"He's better than the pope to me," Davidson whispered. "Catholics ain't doing a thing to fight for God's Kingdom. But look at all Silver's done for Israel."

Patterson didn't answer. He put his hand on the back of the red heifer tethered beside him. His job was to keep guarding it until the sacrificial ceremonies were ready to begin.

Silver reached them seconds later and made a point of asking them their names and shaking their hands and congratulating them on doing God's work.

Patterson remained politely distant. Davidson, however, gushed praise for Silver. Patterson hated the thought that he might have once been like Davidson, remembering the days on campus at Freedom Christian University when a glimpse of the man sent students buzzing, Patterson and Sarah included.

"Praise the Lord," Jonathan Silver said, patting the red heifer on its back. "Here's the animal that God sent us to deliver the Temple unto Him."

"Yes, sir," Davidson said.

To Patterson, it sounded like Davidson was as proud as if he'd actually given birth to the heifer.

"It shouldn't give me any trouble, should it?" Silver asked.

"Sir?" Again it was Davidson speaking. Patterson's coldness toward Jonathan Silver and what the man stood for was the coldness he felt toward his own foolishness in signing up for the Freedom Crusaders.

"They want me to lead the heifer there now," Silver said like a kindly uncle. "It's not an honor I deserve. You boys are the ones who did everything to make this possible. But I don't want to let them down. You understand."

"Yes, sir; yes, sir," Davidson said. He turned to Patterson. "Need help untying it?"

Patterson was looking for any excuse to be insubordinate. He knew this feeling. It reminded him of his teenage years, when he had to sullenly listen and obey his own father. He'd eventually done what he was told, but in such a foot-dragging way that it vented his frustration and, better yet, consistently angered his father.

"I don't need help," Patterson said. "But we've got our orders from Lieutenant Saxon. This heifer doesn't move anywhere without Saxon's express permission."

"Joe!" Davidson said. Then he spoke to Silver. "Sorry, sir. He doesn't mean it as an insult."

Yes, I do, Patterson thought with juvenile satisfaction.

"No offense taken," Silver replied. Then he addressed Patterson. "I appreciate your concern for the heifer. But let's not delay things."

"Of course not, sir," Patterson said. "I'll just radio Saxon."

They didn't have walkie-talkies. Too few channels; too much chance that someone could listen in. Instead, they had cell phones. Patterson beeped his.

"Son," Silver said, "there's a lot of things happening right now, and my patience is wearing thin. I need to bring this animal as soon as possible."

Patterson's cell phone beeped back, giving him an excuse to ignore Silver. "Sir, just want confirmation that I'm to release . . ." Patterson stopped briefly. He'd almost said *Orphan Annie.* ". . . the red heifer to Jonathan Silver."

"Hang on," Saxon's voice came back. "I'm right here with Brad Silver. I'll clear it with him."

A few moments of silence.

Then came Saxon's terse order. "Hold the heifer there. And take Jonathan Silver prisoner."

WESTERN WALL TUNNEL • 20:38 GMT

"It's just ahead," Cohen said. "We're walking north along the Hasmonaean aqueduct. It parallels the Western Wall of the Temple Mount."

This portion of the shifting and turning tunnel had been so narrow that they'd been forced to walk single file, with Cohen at the back holding his flashlight high and shining it ahead for them. Occasionally, they'd pass a light fixture, and Kate thought this would be so much easier if the power had not been shut off for the night.

Without warning, the tunnel widened, and it seemed the air grew cooler. Cohen's flashlight played over a small pool. The dark water was still, filling the width of the tunnel ahead of them, with the pool ending at a brick wall that entirely blocked the tunnel to its arched ceiling.

"We're at the northwest corner of the Temple Mount," Cohen said. "In the time of the Temple of the Jews, this water was a moat for the fortress that held the Roman barrack overlooking the mount. After the Jews were defeated in their final revolt against the Romans, the emperor Hadrian covered the pool. This is one of two arches that support the foundation for the streets and buildings above us. The newer bricking at the end of the tunnel splits the pool. On the other side is an entrance into the basement of the Convent of the Sisters of Zion."

"Fascinating," Kate said, not fascinated at all. "Your ten minutes is down to about one minute."

"You mock me," Cohen said. "You have no understanding of how proud I am to be a Jew. Or of the injustice that we cannot fully reclaim our heritage. The Temple was ours centuries before the Muslims stole the mount from us."

Cohen squatted. His flashlight beam showed the end of a thin, nylon rope along one wall of the tunnel, disappearing into the water. He pulled on the rope, and like dragging a large, dead fish, he was able to retrieve a black backpack.

"Help me," he said to Kevin. Cohen held the flashlight and grabbed one side of the backpack. Kevin grabbed the other side. Water splashed as they dragged it onto the tunnel floor.

"There's a container in there," Cohen said to Kevin as he trained the beam on the backpack. "Pull it out and open it. Then you'll both see why we're here."

Kevin had to struggle to get a square, watertight container out of the main compartment of the backpack. He grunted as he set it on the tunnel floor, then hesitated.

"Go ahead," Cohen said. "Open it."

With the pistol in her right hand and pointing at the floor, Kate found herself leaning closer briefly. She stepped back a little. She was intensely curious but wanted to keep space around her.

Kevin unsnapped the container lid. He opened it to reveal dull metal in Cohen's flashlight beam. The object looked like a watermelon with fins at the rear. It had a U.S. military stamp on it.

"Not much to look at," Cohen said. "It's nearly fifty years old. Goes by the name of Davy Crockett. It's long been considered obsolete, and few outside of military buffs will remember it. Kate, even with your police background, I'd be surprised if you know anything about it."

"You could have explained back in your car without going to all this trouble."

"I needed you here where it would have a lot more impact on you," Cohen said. "But of course, maybe you don't even understand I just made a great pun. *Impact.*"

"This is a bomb," Kate said.

"Designed to be launched from soldiers in the field like grenade rockets," Cohen said. "With one big difference. This one has a nuclear payload."

OLD CITY, JERUSALEM • 28:38 GMT

Hamer had gone around the Old City by driving out through the Jaffa Gate near David's Citadel then going south and east around the perimeter to come back in through the Dung Gate near the Temple Mount. On the short trip, Hamer had been in constant contact with his subordinate officers via cell phone and walkie-talkie. Hamer had driven Quinn as close as possible to the Western Wall of the Temple Mount. They'd walked the remainder; the Old City had been in existence for centuries and was not set up for automobile convenience. It was also obvious that the military factors that had required months of siege for the Romans to conquer the Temple Mount in the first century AD imposed the same difficult logistics on the Israeli Defense Force.

The east and south sides of the mount faced the extreme drop of the Kidron Valley; soldiers were in place on both sides but merely for containment. It was just as impossible for soldiers under attack to scale the walls as it had been two millennia earlier.

Residences of the Muslim Quarter crowded against the wall to the north and northwest of the Temple Mount. Hamer was reluctant to move many soldiers into the nooks and warrens here. It was too easy for a riot to start and too difficult to contain it. Instead, he'd arranged for large spotlights on the ramparts to be trained on the Temple Mount in that direction with concentrations of troops in strategic areas nearby for more containment.

The entire Western Wall was about five hundred yards long, but it wasn't until the final portion along the south that there was an open plaza at the Wailing Wall, which was as close to the Temple as Jews were permitted to pray. From a military viewpoint, the best that could be said for the open plaza here was that it was in the Jewish Quarter and that the area was large enough to comfortably set up a base.

The downside was obvious to Quinn as he reached the communications center with Hamer. The wall loomed over them, forty feet high, made with some of the biggest stones produced by man before the machine age—stones as big as semitrailers. The base seemed open and vulnerable to attack from anyone on the wall above.

"It would feel safer with choppers giving support," Quinn said. Soldiers kept a respectful distance from the two of them. "But then I suppose the media would wonder why you have them in the air and open to ground fire from Palestinian terrorists on the Temple Mount."

"Exactly," Hamer said. "Of course, when I believed IDF was in there instead, I wasn't worried about getting shot here. And since we don't know who is inside . . ."

"And you've only got until dawn to clear them," Quinn said. "Less if they decide to broadcast to the world that they've taken over the mount and the Dome of the Rock."

"Don't need the reminder. I can't even consult with any of my generals on this. Nobody is supposed to know we were going to put IDF in there. I mean nobody."

"Your paradigm has shifted," Quinn said. "But I'm sure you've realized that."

"Keep talking."

"You've got the Temple Mount surrounded on the original premise that this was just for appearance, right? You didn't expect hostile fire, and you knew the IDF men on the mount would be gone in a few hours."

"Right."

"The world thinks you can't storm the place because there are Palestinians with hostages behind those walls."

"Right."

"What if they aren't hostages? It's not hard to make a link between Jonathan Silver and a red heifer and end-time prophecies. Not when it sounds like Americans replaced your IDF."

Hamer looked at the massive wall ahead of him, then back at Quinn. "That would mean, from my point of view, all of them are hostiles. I don't have to worry about hostage casualties."

"It's a theory."

"If it were more than theory, I could mount a military op. In and out before any Muslims even knew about it. There'd be a lot more casualties on their side than ours; I can promise you that."

"If," Quinn said.

"We might have to move in regardless. Think of the consequences otherwise."

Quinn nodded. "How much better would you feel if you could verify who was on the other side? maybe even negotiate a surrender?"

Another thoughtful stare from Hamer. "I can't send anybody in. I'd have to explain why I did. If that leaks, it's as bad as anything else that could happen."

Quinn stared back at him, waiting.

"I see," Hamer said. "You alrcady know about the situation."

"And I won't leak anything to the media, either." Quinn said. "You have nothing to lose."

TEMPLE MOUNT, JERUSALEM • 20:38 GMT

"Dementia," Brad snapped at his father. He was carrying a laptop and faced Silver. It was obvious that he didn't care that Patterson and Davidson were right there and easily able to overhear the conversation. "Can you come up with any other reason for what you tried to do? Or has Satan entered you the way he did with Judas?"

"I'm afraid for you," Silver said. "First you compare yourself to King David. Now to Jesus Himself."

"God has given me an important role. I will not let you or anyone else stop me from fulfilling it. Now tell me what you expected to do with the heifer."

Silver spoke truthfully. "I don't know."

He'd never been a man of action. Not real action. He'd built an empire based on his ability to speak passionately and sincerely, knowing his fundamentalist audience well enough to understand how to push emotional buttons that would give him the response he wanted.

Action?

Until he'd stepped in front of Safady to save the little girl's life, he hadn't realized he was capable of action instead of words. He'd chosen to try to take the red heifer because it seemed like the only way of stopping this. Without the ashes from the heifer, the Temple Mount could not be purified. Without the chance of purification, perhaps Brad would have abandoned the operation.

"You don't know?"

"Hide it from you, I suppose," Silver said. "Maybe find a way to let it escape."

"To stop the sacrifice."

"Don't do this. Muslims are God's children too. Their lives are as important to Him as ours."

"They can find their way to heaven?"

"We can show them. But not by destroying them. By helping them. We could take ministry money and help Palestinians in the name of Christ and—"

"This is a holy war!"

"War kills people."

"You've preached the doom of Armageddon your whole life. You've raised money to help Israel by telling everyone the end of time is upon us. I don't understand why you fear this."

"Because it's no longer about preaching. You're making it about action."

"Exactly."

"But it shouldn't be about destructive action," Silver said.

"Suddenly you're the voice of political correctness?" Brad laughed. "I brought this over to show you something." He opened his laptop, and the screen brightened. "You say Safady isn't an actor. I say he is. Paid to work for us. And look what else he delivered to me—his interview with you. Here's what he put together for me." Brad turned the laptop toward his father.

Jonathan Silver saw himself in the first image and immediately recognized the backdrop as the pulpit of his television ministry.

"Israel is the chosen people of God," he spoke in the video clip.

Then a blank spot in the video.

Back to a different shot of Silver, at a fund-raiser. "God will bless those who bless Israel. God will curse those who curse Israel."

Blank.

An image of Silver in the campus church, raising his hands in triumph. "The end times are unfolding in front of our eyes as Revelation has foretold. God will triumph over His enemies."

Blank.

Jonathan facing the camera and speaking directly to it. Here, he'd been facing Safady, answering questions. "The Temple must be rebuilt to fulfill the prophecies. Why else would God tell us to measure it in Revelation 11?"

Blank.

Again from when he faced Safady. "God's people will do what is necessary on earth to help God usher in His Kingdom."

A long shot of Silver behind his pulpit. "The Palestinians are a tainted and brainwashed people."

Blank.

A shot of Jonathan Silver during a daytime talk show. "Osama bin Laden will be repaid a hundredfold for daring to attack God's people."

Blank.

The Dome of the Rock, with floodlights directed on it.

A cut back to Silver. "What is God's will be returned to God."

Blank.

Silver at the pulpit. "Americans are God's people because America helps Israel."

Blank.

Jonathan Silver at the pulpit again, eyes closed in prayer. "Forever and ever; amen."

The video ended.

"Those things were taken out of context," Silver protested. "Some of it from my interviews with Safady. It looks like I'm totally in favor of the Temple takeover. You can't show that to the media."

"In about an hour," Brad answered, "this is exactly what we're going to deliver to the media, along with a press release stating that the Dome of the Rock has been conquered on behalf of God. Like it or not, you will get full credit. And millions of Americans who have always supported you will rise up in their pews and cheer."

"I'm begging you, father to son, please reconsider."

"Just so you know," Brad continued, "the video isn't quite complete."

The blank spots, Silver thought.

"We're going to insert other footage," Brad said in confirmation. "The world is going to see the red heifer and the sacrifice." He snapped the laptop shut. "God and America will triumph, and the world will know it by morning."

WESTERN WALL TUNNEL • 28:48 GMT

"The Davy Crockett was decommissioned because of its disadvantages in the field," Cohen said. "Its explosion radius is too small to do much damage to approaching tanks unless it was a direct hit. Of course, the explosive yield could be increased. But dialing up the yield made it impossible for troops to launch it without harming themselves. The Crockett's propulsion range was a little over a mile."

He still had his flashlight on the bomb. "Davy Crockett was essentially an incredibly expensive one-shot, one-kill weapon against tanks. It wasn't accurate and didn't have recall feature. Once in the air, it was committed to detonation. It couldn't even self-destruct. All in all, a bad military weapon. But perfect for what's above us."

Cohen flashed his beam at the arched ceiling. "The Muslim Quarter. This fat little thing has about three times the explosive power of the bomb that destroyed the federal building in Oklahoma City. Just enough to limit the damage to the Muslim population. Everyone else will clear out before the radiation harms them, but the radioactive fallout in the hours and days following will make the Temple Mount a place the Muslims can't visit anymore. Israel can clean it up, but then Israel will own the Temple Mount."

In the darkness, Kate raised her pistol slightly. Cohen sounded like he enjoyed the prospect.

"So we need to get it out of here," Kevin said. "Let's get it in the backpack."

"Kevin," Kate said, raising her pistol higher and stepping farther back from Cohen. "Maybe ask him first why he didn't get someone else to remove it. Or how he knew it was here in the first place."

"Very relevant questions," Cohen said. "But you missed the important question: why did I need both of you here?"

Cohen's flashlight beam settled on Kevin's chest.

"Hey," Kevin said. "You're creeping me out."

No warning. A silenced shot from the black shadows behind the flashlight. A bloom of red across Kevin's chest. He fell, gurgling.

Then the beam found Kate. She dove sideways, rolling.

Cohen crisscrossed the beam, trying to find her.

Kate had the pistol up as she made it to her knees, aiming at the flashlight beam and pulling the trigger.

Nothing but a dry click. Twice more.

The noise alerted Cohen to her location and the flashlight beam swung toward her. He fired two quick shots, and the bullets caromed with the whining noise of angry wasps.

Kate made another rolling dive and fired another shot from the pistol. Dry click. Still nothing.

"You were set up," Cohen said, chuckling lightly. "There's no ammunition."

Kate bit off her reply. Cohen just wanted the sound of her voice as a target.

She made another dive, and her shoulder collided with the wall. Her involuntary gasp drew another shot.

But this time she felt it instead of hearing it. The bullet was a baseball bat against her left shoulder, an epicenter of pain, riding outward in seismic waves. She dropped the pistol and clutched her shoulder.

Hunching, Kate ran. She collided again with the tunnel wall, but at an angle that bounced her forward.

Cohen's beam found her again, but it also gave her enough light to see a turn in the tunnel. She ducked into it as another shot smashed into the stone.

But she was blind. She let go of her shoulder with her right hand and placed her palm against the side of the tunnel. She used the wall as a guide, sliding her hand along it as she ran as fast as her pain would allow.

Brad Silver was gone.

Patterson and Davidson stood beside the heifer, waiting for the call from Saxon to bring it forward for sacrifice. Jonathan Silver had been sent with another soldier, who was ordered to watch the old man and the woman from the orphanage. Brad hadn't even had them tied up; evidently he didn't see them as much of a threat.

Almost losing the heifer to the old man had sure made Saxon jump, though.

In fact, it all came down to the red heifer. Patterson knew that. He had known it ever since seeing Saxon wash off the painted spots, and he had suspected it even before that. Overhearing the conversation between Brad and Jonathan Silver confirmed it.

Patterson was also at the point he'd been at that day in Afghanistan, when nothing mattered except talking to Sarah and he'd forced Lieutenant Saxon to allow him to make the phone call.

Except the stakes were higher now. Instead of letting Sarah know he was alive, her life depended on his actions.

Patterson couldn't imagine getting out of this alive. He was part of a group barricaded on the Temple Mount. Maybe the other Freedom Crusaders were willing to fool themselves into thinking that once the site was taken they would be welcomed back into the world as heroes. But Patterson couldn't see that happening. What he could see was some kind of pitched battle at the end of an indefinite standoff. Didn't matter if it was Muslims or Israelis swarming the grounds; it was going to be their own Alamo.

Some of the Freedom Crusaders might believe it would be worth their lives to be the ones freeing the Temple Mount for the Christian world to reclaim after this Alamo was finished. At one time, he would have believed it himself.

It was coming down to something else for him, though.

Sarah.

He had to save her. He didn't know where she was, and he didn't have the power to release her anyway. But Saxon did. Or Saxon would be able to make a call to the person or persons with the knowledge and power to free her.

It shouldn't be that difficult to get them to let her go, Patterson thought. After tonight, not much was left to keep secret. The whole world would know about the Freedom Crusaders. Sarah telling people that he was still alive and had called her wouldn't be a threat to the operation then.

So he just needed something to bargain with to get Saxon to let Sarah go.

This *something* was obvious.

How to do it didn't seem insurmountable either. Thirty-five acres was a lot of room to hide something.

But he didn't have much time to do it.

Patterson lifted his rifle and pointed it directly at Davidson's head.

"Huh?" Davidson said.

"I'm counting to five. You've got till then to get on your belly with your hands behind your back. Make any noise for help, and I'll belly-shoot you. That way I'll die a lot faster than you."

"You're kidding," Davidson said.

Patterson replied with a single word. "One . . ."

WESTERN WALL TUNNEL • 20:46 GMT

When Kate finally collapsed, she didn't hear footsteps, didn't see a flashlight beam. Adrenaline had kept her going; a screaming instinct to survive had propelled her. She knew she hadn't gone far. It was too dark in the tunnels. She couldn't guess how far she was from the tunnel entrance at the Wailing Wall. Only that she'd passed the rope that led up to the house in the Muslim Quarter and had kept going because she knew there was no way to climb it with a shattered shoulder.

She'd stumbled forward until she'd reached some sort of cavern.

She fought to rise again. Feeling along the wall, she found what seemed to be a pillar embedded in a stone wall, then a large, upright stone. She fought off thoughts about spiders and sat and leaned against the stone, trying to wedge herself between it and the wall. With the first reaction of unbridled fear dissipating into the beginning stages of shock, the futility of her situation became clearer.

Kate was lost in total darkness. Her body was incapacitated. Even if she could somehow stop the bleeding and begin to search for an exit, Cohen was behind her, tracking her down.

Then a thought exploded through the lethargy of shock.

Tracking her. All Cohen had to do was use his flashlight to follow the blood trail she'd left behind. He'd see that she'd been hit and that she hadn't used the rope.

She tried to think things through from Cohen's point of view. He couldn't know how badly she'd been injured. He'd have to find her to make sure she had not survived. He would keep looking. There was no way she was strong enough to fight back. Or even keep running, for that matter.

What did she have?

Maybe enough resolution and anger to push away the blanket of shock that beckoned with such comfort.

And she had her cell phone.

Her right hand was slick with blood from where she'd clutched her shoulder. She wiped it on her jeans, then fumbled to get the cell phone. She flipped it open one-handed and concentrated hard to see the screen, willing away the unconsciousness that was so tempting.

There was no signal. That didn't surprise her.

But maybe there was a way to beat Cohen. Even after she was dead.

Using her right thumb, she began pressing the keypad.

TEMPLE MOUNT, JERUSALEM • 28:52 GMT

"Sir." Patterson had stepped into the floodlights around the nearly constructed incinerator.

Saxon had been in conversation with one of his soldiers and broke away with a frown. "You're supposed to be guarding the heifer."

"That's why I'm here. It's gone."

Saxon's mouth opened, shut, and opened again. "Gone? Who took it? Why didn't you call for help? Give me a full report."

"I moved it," Patterson said. He set his rifle on the ground in front of him, then backed away slightly, making it clear he wasn't armed.

"Son, you better start making sense real soon."

"I disabled Davidson and moved the heifer myself."

Saxon had a sidearm. He unholstered it, cocked it, held it chest high, and aimed it squarely at Patterson. "You're still not making sense. But I do know insubordination when I hear it. Where is it?"

"Hidden about as good as a man can hide something like that in thirty-five acres in the dead of night. It's muzzled, too. Don't expect you'll find it by listening for it. You can shoot me, but if you do, you won't find it; I can promise you that."

Saxon lowered the sidearm.

"I need to speak to Sarah again," Patterson continued. "You arrange to get her somewhere safe where she can give me a call so I know she's alive and escaped. Then you'll get the heifer."

"I can't do that."

"You told me she'd be dead if I didn't obey orders. That tells me you know who to call."

"I lied," Saxon said. "She's already dead."

"That's not true."

"You killed her, Patterson. You broke silence and forced me to get you on the phone with her. She was dead the next morning."

"That's not true."

"You got nothing to bargain for, son. Tell me where the heifer is."

Patterson roared and charged Saxon, who easily sidestepped and tripped him. Patterson fell heavily, and Saxon was on top of him, pistol against his head.

"Now, son," Saxon said, "tell me where the heifer is."

"Not after what you've done to my Sarah. I'd rather be dead myself."

"I'll certainly arrange that," Saxon said. "But I promise you, it will be painful."

The sound of footsteps warned Kate of Cohen's approach. Then came the beam of light, moving slowly from side to side, searching for spatters of blood.

She was in a fetal position. She'd removed a sock and balled it and was pressing it against the entry wound to stem the bleeding. She couldn't tell if the bullet had exited and couldn't do anything about bleeding on the back of her shoulder anyway.

With Cohen's approach, she tapped into her anger and found the strength to roll into a sitting position and lean her back against the tunnel wall. She would face the next bullet, not turn away from it.

The light grew brighter. Slowly. And then it was trained on her face.

"Here you are," Cohen said. The light moved down her body. He was probably trying to determine how badly she was wounded.

"Back there you didn't monologue much," Kate said. Her mouth tasted coppery. She didn't think the bullet had pierced any part of her lung. The copper was from fear.

"Monologue?"

"It's a term from a great movie called *The Incredibles*. Bad guys monologue to gloat and to justify themselves. You spent a little time bragging about the Davy Crockett. But to do it right, you should have first told Kevin how stupid he'd been to trust you and how brilliant you'd been to fool him. That was cold—shooting with no warning."

"Ego is secondary to efficiency," he answered. "Now won't be any different. I don't need to monologue. I just need you dead."

He leaned in. Behind the flashlight came a click. He'd released the safety on his pistol.

Kate saw the outline of his hand and the gun. Ever cautious, he had not leaned in far enough to give her a chance to fight for it.

She was out of time.

"I was hoping you'd find me," Kate said. His curiosity would maybe buy her an extra few seconds.

Then she waited. Next would come a question. Or a bullet.

TEMPLE MOUNT, JERUSALEM • 20:54 GMT

Circles of flashlight beams and the distorted shadows added to the eeriness. Patterson stood on his tiptoes, his ankles held together by plastic cuffs, his back against the trunk of an olive tree. His arms were extended in opposite directions along low branches, his wrists wired to the branches.

"We've got to do this," Brad Silver said. Two Freedom Crusaders flanked him. One of them was Davidson. "Nobody stops us."

"You had my wife killed." Patterson doubted his body could feel any pain. He was deflated. "Nothing else matters anymore."

Brad nodded at Davidson.

"Can we give him a chance?" Davidson asked.

"No. Kick him. Make it matter."

"Sorry, man," Davidson said. He kicked Patterson solidly in the groin. The sound of the impact was like a foot striking a soccer ball.

Patterson bucked forward so hard that the wire cut the skin on his wrists. Moments later, he vomited, silencing his low moans of agony. He choked on his vomit for a few seconds, then found air.

"Here's what's next," Brad said. "Davidson's going to put spikes through your hands, nailing you to the tree. Three spikes in each hand. Tell us where to find the heifer, though, and we'll cut you down before any of this gets started."

Brad cocked his head, as if waiting for Patterson to speak. "All right then. Davidson . . ."

Davidson approached with a hammer. "It's dark," he said in a soft voice. "I'm going to put the first one in the tree. Not your hand. Okay? But if you don't tell him about the heifer, I got no choice for the other two."

"Don't feel bad," Patterson said. "I know you got no choice."

Davidson nailed the first spike.

"Tell us," Brad said.

Patterson remained silent. They'd killed his wife. Wouldn't tell him what they'd done to his wife and child. A spike wasn't going to hurt compared to that pain.

Davidson put the second spike in the center of Patterson's palm. He was crying. "Please, man, don't make me do this."

The spike hurt most with the first blow. Once it had gone through the front of his palm and the back of his hand, Patterson felt more shock than pain. There was mercy in the third spike because the pain from the second blurred with the next.

"We'll stop now," Brad said to Patterson. "Tell us where to find the heifer."

Tears streamed down Patterson's cheeks. He closed his eyes and remained silent.

"Kick him again," Brad said.

"Sir, I—"

"Do it!"

Davidson put a half stride of momentum into the next kick.

More bucking. More vomiting.

"Where is it?" Brad asked.

"Killing a man's wife," Patterson said in a hoarse whisper. "That's not freedom fighting."

"Other hand same way as the first," Brad told Davidson.

Davidson began crying again as he put two spikes through Patterson's other hand. The third spike he nailed into the branch just below Patterson's hand. "Come on. I can't stand doing this to you."

Brad pushed Davidson aside. "Given where we are," he said to Patterson, "I doubt you'll appreciate the irony as much as I do. This tree makes for a good enough cross, and you're about to be crucified. Where's the heifer?"

"Dear Jesus," Patterson mumbled, "I'm sorry for what I did wrong over the last months. Please take me to heaven and let me see Sarah."

Brad laughed. "You won't get there for a while. Let me explain why cruci-fixion was such an effective threat for the Romans. Suffocation, exhaustion, and dehydration. You're in pain right now, but you're nowhere near dead."

Patterson had his eyes closed, whispering his prayers.

Brad slapped his face. "You're standing on the ground right now. Your dia-phragm is working the way it should. But as soon as you start hanging from your wrists, you're going to slowly suffocate. You'll need weight on your feet for the diaphragm to push air into your lungs. Understand?"

Patterson opened his eyes and stared unflinchingly into Brad's face.

"What we're going to do next is exactly what Roman soldiers did to criminals on the cross. We're going to push your legs up and spike your ankles into the tree. Much as the leg cramps are going to hurt, they won't kill you. Neither will the bro-ken ankle bones. But you're going to let yourself hang from your wrists because it will hurt too much to place any weight on your shattered ankles. Got it?"

Brad continued without waiting for an answer. "Except as you hang from your wrists, you'll slowly suffocate. Then you'll put your weight down long enough to breathe. Until you can't bear the weight on the broken bones. And it will start all over again."

He slapped Patterson's face, gently this time. "Crucifixion won't kill you. You'll go back and forth between suffocation and agony on your broken ankles for a few days while you get thirstier and thirstier. In the end, dehydration is what's going to do it."

Brad stepped away. "We'll be on the Temple Mount long enough for that. The beauty of all this is that you'll be conscious the whole time. You can stop it whenever you want. Just tell us where to find the heifer."

Davidson stepped to the side. He vomited, then straightened.

"Patterson," Brad said, "spare yourself all of this."

"Jesus knew how bad this was," Patterson said. "Maybe when I get to heaven, that'll get me extra mercy."

The second soldier stepped up to the tree. He grabbed Patterson's ankles and lifted his feet until his knees were bent at a forty-five–degree angle. Patterson was too worn out to struggle.

Davidson lifted the hammer.

WESTERN WALL TUNNEL • 20:56 GMT

"I'll humor you and ask the obvious," Cohen said to Kate from behind his flashlight. "Why were you hoping I'd find you?"

"Gives *me* the chance to monologue." She was alive as long as she could keep him curious. "Except I'm the good guy."

"You find an extra thirty seconds of life that precious? Fascinating."

"I'm curious too." She coughed. "Why this?"

"Tedious and predictable question."

"You had to get me because I knew too much, right? And Kevin died because we told him what we knew. Why not take us out to the desert? Why go through this tunnel charade? Just to show off your bomb?"

"The desert leaves tracks. Your bodies would leave evidence trails. Down here, the evidence will be vaporized and buried under tons of rubble." He laughed. "Much easier to let you walk through the tunnels than kill you and drag you. Especially with time running short."

"How short?"

"At twenty-two hundred hours GMT. Midnight here. A symbolic time. Israel is ready for a new dawn."

"Midnight," she repeated. GMT meant nothing to her. But midnight did. Just over an hour away. "But why all this—the Temple operation?"

"Enough," he said. "Why were you hoping I'd find you?"

"I'm dying here. You know that. Why not indulge me? You tell me why you're doing this. Then I tell you how I know Quinn's going to stop you."

"No, you tell me now."

"You sounded very proud of that Davy Crockett," Kate said. "Probably not many people you can let in on your secret. Doing all this was impressive."

Cohen laughed softly. "When the bomb destroys the Muslim Quarter, the Palestinians will blame the American fanatics who took over their Temple Mount; the Israelis are going to blame the Palestinians for hiding a weapon of mass destruction. Either way, Israel's going to be able to reclaim the Muslim Quarter and the mount. Either way, the swamp will be drained."

Americans on the Temple Mount. Quinn's guess had been right.

"Swamp?" Another cough. More pain. She hoped it wasn't from blood in her lungs. Not that it mattered. She didn't have a lot of optimism about her life expectancy.

"You know why Palestinians get their children to throw rocks at our tanks? They know that we won't fire back at rocks. They push as far as they can but stop short of forcing us to unleash what we have." Cohen was talking faster now, his anger breaking through. "When this bomb goes, it's going to be war. A real war. And Israel will move in with everything we have and clear this land of every Palestinian on it. Finally, we'll be one land. One people. And we have no fear of being able to protect our borders from other Arabs. Because the West is going to have to unite with us and the United States as the holy war spreads. It's going to be a war that rids us of the Palestinian threat, the Iranian threat, and all other threats in the Middle East. When the political landscape settles, Israel is going to have a huge territory to administer. And no more suicide bombers and market explosions."

"Americans," she said. "You know who is on the Temple Mount too? You set that up—the switch?"

"We helped set up the Mossad-IDF operation and used it to get the Americans up there, then helped the Americans plan their op to get to Gaza."

"We?"

"I'm finished with answers. You don't get all your wishes before you die."

"But I get the important one—the satisfaction of letting you know that you've lost. Quinn's way ahead of you on this."

"Right." There was no concern in Cohen's voice. Not much interest, either. All it would take was a squeeze of his forefinger. The bullet would come without warning.

"See my smile?" Kate said, leaning against the wall. It took effort, but it was there. "I'm imagining your face when you discover all of it's exposed. That suicide will be your best option. That whatever the reason you have for the Davy Crockett, it's not going to succeed." A spasm of pain gripped her, and she grunted. Then grinned when it passed. "That's why you should monologue. So much better when you can rub your victory in."

"You've bought yourself another thirty seconds."

"Don't need it. I'm not leaving here alive. The extra thirty seconds doesn't matter anymore."

"Quinn doesn't know anything."

"Right," Kate said with yet another smile. She closed her eyes. "Check my voice mail. Listen to the message he left for me."

"What does he know?"

"Phone's in my pocket. Power it up, then press and hold 1. You don't need a password to access it. More fun for me if you hear it from Quinn, the way he explained it to me."

"Tell me or I shoot."

Kate had lost a lot of blood. She could feel it by the way she was getting cold. She wouldn't be leaving here, even if he didn't shoot her. A bullet in the skull now would be a mercy.

"There's no signal down here, stupid woman. I want to know what he knew."

"Plenty. I was looking for a way to stop you from the second you got into the car. Thought I had my chance when you gave me your gun. I didn't expect that it wasn't loaded. I wanted to see what else I could learn before I took you down and dragged you back to Quinn."

"What does he know?"

Kate managed to snort. "Are you going to threaten me with torture? Or tell me you'll kill me if I don't tell? A woman with nothing left to lose is a dangerous woman."

"Give me the phone."

"I'll bet you don't like getting blood on your hands anyway."

"Too bad you won't be around after midnight. Then you'd see how much blood I'm willing to spill. Give me the phone."

"Go spit." She doubted this guy even recognized the line from the original *Lethal Weapon* movie. Her favorite line of defiance. Danny Glover, playing Mel Gibson's partner, said it when he knew he was about to die. The difference was, Mel had shown up and rescued Danny. Because it was a movie. That wouldn't happen here. The best she could hope for was a chance to warn Quinn.

"I want the phone."

"No reception, remember? Guess you'll never know how much he's already figured out until it's too late. That makes me feel great."

She didn't see the blow coming. It took her an instant to realize he'd pistol-whipped her across the skull. She tumbled sideways, limp.

The flashlight moved across her face. But her eyes were closed. It wasn't difficult to fake unconsciousness. Now that she'd accomplished what she wanted, it was tempting her again.

Cohen's hands were on her, roughly searching. She wished she had the strength to make a move, to try to get the pistol. But she was out of reserve.

Cohen found the cell phone in her front pocket and worked it loose.

He stood back.

With no ceremony, he pulled the trigger.

She knew this because the bullet didn't come. His pistol dry clicked.

It made her want to laugh. The moron hadn't even counted shots as he'd fired at her earlier.

Cohen threw the gun at her feet and walked away without touching her.

He had the phone. That had been her goal.

Kate could take satisfaction in something else. She'd been right. Maybe he was willing to spill blood, but he didn't like getting it on his hands. Otherwise he would have used them to kill her instead of leaving her to die slowly.

47

"Enough," Quinn said from the shadows behind the flashlights. He'd arrived at this corner of the Temple Mount just after Davidson hammered Patterson's second hand to the tree. "Take the soldier down."

Brad's flashlight dipped, then turned toward Quinn, catching him square in the face. "You?"

There was only one way for Quinn to play this negotiation: as if he had all the cards. "Take the light out of my eyes. You'll see a cell phone in my hand. I've got it on speakerphone. This entire conversation is monitored."

This was a crucial moment. Quinn needed to establish power. If Brad refused to take the light out of his eyes, the negotiations would be a lot more difficult.

Brad lowered the flashlight to the cell phone in Quinn's hand.

Some of Quinn's vision returned. Enough to see that the two soldiers who had been about to hammer a spike into the ankle bones of the man were still kneeling, hesitant about what to do next.

"Take the man down from the tree," Quinn said. He hid his repugnance at the torture already inflicted on the nearly unconscious man pinned there. "This operation is over."

"I've got twenty soldiers across the Temple Mount," Brad said. "Explosives wired where I need them. You don't give the orders here."

I already have, Quinn thought. *The soldiers around you know it too.*

"Twice that many would only buy you about five minutes of fighting. Hamer, you explain."

Brad's flashlight beam darted in a few directions, searching for Quinn's companion. The answer came instead from the phone Quinn held.

"Brad Silver," the tinny voice said, "this is Major General Jack Hamer. Remember? The guy with the prime minister on speed dial. Time to put your toys away.

I've got a thousand soldiers surrounding the walls and enough body bags for all your men. Quinn's there to help you decide how you want the next half hour to go."

WESTERN WALL TUNNEL • 21:86 GMT

What did Kate have to write with? The pen she'd taken from Quinn.

But she had no paper. And it was pitch-dark.

Still, she had to try. Cohen had said midnight. That he was ready to spill the blood of thousands. She had to leave this message somewhere.

Kate couldn't move her left arm. It was numb. She used her right hand to twist it so that the fleshy part of her left forearm was facing her.

In the dark, she pressed her pen against her forearm. As slowly as possible, trying to visualize the letters, she wrote them on her skin.

The effort and pain exhausted her, but she refused to quit.

It was better than the alternative.

Dying.

OLD CITY, JERUSALEM • 21:88 GMT

Cohen hurried out through the Muslim Quarter. It was fortunate that he'd found Kate so close to his exit from the tunnels. With less than an hour to detonation, he needed as much time as possible to clear the area.

Except for Kate's threat about the voice mail, he was satisfied. Kate didn't know that Cohen had already ordered the deaths of Hamer and Quinn through Hamer's bodyguard. There would be some confusion after the blast; Cohen's man would take care of Hamer and Quinn.

The blast would also mean nobody would tie Cohen to Kate or Kevin.

Chances were he'd be able to remain head of the Mossad and deal with the aftermath of something he'd orchestrated over the last few months.

But was there something on the voice mail? Something he would need to counter with damage control? At the worst, if his cover was blown, he'd be out of the country in two hours.

He powered up her phone.

As instructed, he pressed and held the 1 key. Her voice mail came on.

No messages.

Stupid, lying woman. Thought she could fool him.

Cohen dropped the phone in a garbage can. He wasn't worried about his prints tying him to Kate. The phone would be destroyed in less than an hour. Along with the Muslim Quarter.

Yes, Cohen thought. *It's all coming together.*

He resumed walking.

From the garbage, when the phone beeped to indicate it had sent out a text message that had been waiting for the phone to get service, Cohen was too far away to hear it.

TEMPLE MOUNT, JERUSALEM • 21:18 GMT

"You're busted," Quinn said to Brad Silver. "Simple as that. The Israelis know you've left the IDF special ops soldiers behind with the dead Palestinians. They've got the walls here surrounded. You can't get out. And you've got ten minutes to surrender. Otherwise it will be a slaughter."

"No," Brad said. "It's another bluff."

"Hamer," Quinn said, "mind turning on the lights?"

Hamer didn't reply, but seconds later, the whistling began. High shrieks that made no sense until the first of the flares lit the sky a couple hundred feet above the Temple Mount. Then dozens, then hundreds—in arcs so painfully bright that it seemed a supernova had exploded directly above them.

Quinn didn't make the mistake of watching, awestruck. He stepped to Brad, knowing the man's night vision had fragmented. He jabbed a hypodermic needle into Brad's leg and pushed the plunger.

"Hey!" Brad staggered slightly.

"That was my life insurance." Quinn handed Brad the needle. "If I make it out alive, you get the antidote. It was something that the IDF suggested before I came in here."

"Antidote?"

"Try not to sound stupid," Quinn said. "Remember, every word between us is monitored and recorded."

"You're saying you just injected me with poison?"

"Not poison. A special flesh-eating bacteria. You won't feel the effects for about an hour. But if you don't get the antidote in two hours, nothing can stop it. Hands and feet go first, dissolved by gangrene. Works its way up the body. Takes about a week to die. Gruesome, actually. Ready to talk without ordering one of your soldiers to shoot me?"

The flares were just beginning to die, shrouding them in darkness again. Brad was shining the flashlight on his leg, thigh high, where Quinn had jabbed him.

"Fifty-nine minutes and thirty seconds until you run out of time," Quinn said. He found it encouraging that Silver wasn't hiding a reaction to pain. The man was essentially a sissy Quinn had banked on that. "You want to waste it looking for your owie?"

Quinn's cell phone beeped and lit up. A text message had arrived. He ignored it.

"We're not surrendering," Brad said. "What does it matter whether we die here or in jail?"

"For you, it matters. I don't think you're going to enjoy the smell of your body rotting."

"I'll trade your life for the antidote. That's it."

"How about a get-out-of-jail-free card? For all of your soldiers?"

"I don't believe you."

"Think about it," Quinn said curtly. His tone for the entire negotiation was going to reflect a power position. From what he guessed about Brad Silver, he'd spent his whole life answering to an authority figure. Quinn was taking that role here. "The Israelis will do just about anything to avoid a full-out firefight on the Temple Mount. In terms of political fallout with the Muslims, the only worse alternative is leaving you here. They want you off quietly and immediately so that the sun rises on the same Temple Mount it set on the night before."

"And if we fight you to the death," Brad said, "we still win. Muslim riots across the world."

"That's what you want?"

"At the least. Muslims are trying to take over the West, but no one is ready to believe it. If the war makes it into the open, the West will finally wake up. And win. We'll get this site back, one way or the other."

"I can hear the music," Quinn answered. "'Onward, Christian Soldiers.'"

Hamer's voice broke through. "The prime minister guarantees no jail, no courts. That's what he's willing to give if your soldiers walk out. We've got a jet at Ben-Gurion ready to take all of you to an island in the South Pacific."

"Right," Brad said sarcastically. "A jet that will explode halfway there."

"The prime minister will be on board with you as insurance," Hamer said.

"He's serious," Quinn said. "Once you're off the Temple Mount, you still have considerable leverage."

"In handcuffs?"

"Don't be stupid. Your biggest weapon was and is the media. If you or any of your soldiers go public with what happened tonight, it's still catastrophic for the Israeli government. They're going to want all of you in isolation until enough time passes that this can be leaked gradually."

Quinn didn't want Brad Silver thinking through the implications. He needed to apply pressure. Quinn turned the cell phone so that its glow showed his watch. "You've lost another couple of minutes. How's the leg feel?"

Brad rubbed his thigh. "They won't attack the Temple Mount. They're too afraid of the political fallout. Hamer's bluffing."

"Hamer?" Quinn asked into the cell phone.

"I've got a direct order from the prime minister to begin the assault at my discretion. We've put riot police on the Temple Mount before. We're not afraid of doing it again."

"You won't," Brad said, growing more confident. "Not when we take refuge in the Dome of the Rock. You fire a single bullet into the walls, and the Muslim riot will destroy this half of Jerusalem and bring every Arab country into war against Israel."

"Going to camp here until your food and water run out?" Quinn asked. "Watching your body parts rot?"

"Just until the heifer has been sacrificed and the Temple Mount purified. It won't take long to get that news out to the world. Or much longer for the Temple to be ready for Jesus' return."

"You think you can force God to follow your timetable?"

"He's laid that timetable out in His holy Word. And the time is now. All the signs point to it."

"You've got one problem," Quinn said. "The heifer is gone. I heard what you were trying to get from this guy. Maybe it's a sign from God. That and the fact that I'm standing here."

"We'll find it. Sooner than later."

"Not during a full-scale military assault. And not if you're hiding in the Dome. By the way, IDF has decided it's not going to worry about casualties. The media has been cleared out of the area. Not a breath of what happens in here will reach the world. All your soldiers will die. Or, if you cooperate, they won't. Either way, this is ending before midnight."

Brad kept rubbing his leg.

Quinn had borrowed the hypo from one of the paramedic teams. It had been filled with a saline solution. Quinn had guessed a direct physical threat would intimidate Brad enough to put him on edge. The fact that he couldn't leave his leg alone told Quinn a lot.

"Make the call, Brad. Get this poor man down from the tree. Save the lives of all your soldiers. Take the pass to freedom offered by the Israelis. And keep your hands and feet from rotting off your body."

Brad Silver didn't answer. He fell to his knees and bowed his head in prayer.

Quinn gave him the time and space. Innocuous sounds of the city filled the silence here in the garden. The sounds of people living through just another night, unaware of how close the next few minutes could bring all of them to unthinkable carnage.

Brad opened his eyes.

Quinn spoke softly. "If this really were God's time, He would have allowed you to be successful."

Brad stood. "I'll call in my men."

Quinn felt the knots in his shoulders dissolve. "You heard that, Hamer?"

"I heard it. Outline how we need to do it."

Quinn spoke to Brad. "Have your men put down their weapons and line up at the entrance to the western plaza. They will be supplied face scarves and Palestinian garb; then they'll be marched to a couple of waiting buses. The media is going to see that the Palestinians have been released."

Quinn would figure out how to deal with what the hostages knew later. All that Hamer needed to control right now were these soldiers. What was absolutely crucial was that the Arab world never learn that these Americans had replaced a Mossad-IDF attempt to control the Temple Mount. Quinn knew what was ahead for Brad Silver and his men—the prison terms they deserved for being criminals of war. The difference was that they would get no visitors. As far as the rest of the world knew, they would be dead men.

"Our men will be ready," Hamer said. He and Quinn would be inside the wall, supervising the surrender. None of the IDF soldiers would see the Americans before they were disguised as Palestinians.

"Good," Quinn said to Hamer. "A text message came in from Kate. If I cut you off while I read it, I'll call you right back."

"Sure."

Quinn opened the message and scanned it. He read it again, more slowly. Then he read it twice more.

"Hamer?"

"Still here."

"Get some paramedics ready at the entrance to the Western Wall tunnels. You're going to need to handle this alone while I go into the tunnel. Make sure the entrance is open, even if it takes C-4 to clear it."

Quinn looked at Brad. "You can try something stupid, but nothing's going to work, understand? Help me out here, and I'll make sure you get help later."

"What about the antidote?"

"That's another reason to make sure this goes smoothly. I can't stick around."

"What are you talking about?" Hamer asked. "You cannot leave them there to surrender themselves."

"The alternative is evacuating this half of Jerusalem in the next forty minutes," Quinn answered. He started running back to the entrance at the Western Wall, speaking into the phone as he ran. "And, Hamer, make sure you have some bomb squad guys waiting there with the paramedics too."

48

We're done. Drop your weapons and come in. Over."

Despite the hollow sound of a cell phone transmission, Jonathan Silver recognized his son's voice. He opened his eyes to squint at the flashlight beam that Smitty, a Freedom Crusader, had kept on him and Esther since the assignment to guard them after Silver tried to sabotage the operation.

"Repeat," Smitty said. "Over."

Against the dazzling brightness, Silver was able to see the outline of the submachine gun pointed at them. The soldier's vigilance didn't waver even now. As if Silver and Esther were actually going to attack him.

"I've negotiated terms of surrender. Drop your weapons and come in. Over."

"Need password verification," Smitty said.

"Armageddon," Brad's disembodied voice said through the cell phone. "Get moving. Israeli forces will be here any minute. We're supposed to be evacuating within a half hour. Over and out."

"And the prisoners?"

No answer.

"The prisoners," Smitty repeated. "What are my orders for the prisoners? Over."

"Bring them in with us. Meet at the Western Wall entrance."

Smitty shifted the flashlight away from Silver's eyes. "This is insane," he said. "I don't understand."

"It must be for your own good," Esther told the soldier softly.

"We need to find Alyiah," Silver told the soldier.

"Alyiah?"

"A little girl. We'll bring her to the entrance and meet you there."

"I thought we would win," Smitty said. "All this and now nothing?"

Silver took Esther's hand and helped her stand. He wasn't surprised when the soldier didn't protest. He sounded defeated.

Silver took his first step away from Smitty, then turned back to him. "I need your flashlight. We can't leave the girl behind."

WESTERN WALL TUNNEL • 21:17 GMT

Kate was getting even colder. She knew she couldn't deny it any longer. She was dying.

The lack of fear surprised her. She guessed maybe that was the shock kicking into a second gear. The loneliness didn't surprise her though. Her entire life had been a fight against loneliness, building a facade that didn't permit any hint of the ache it concealed.

Maybe it would have been better if she weren't a fighter. It would have been so much easier to give up on the battle. Turn to drugs. Alcohol. Aimless pursuit of a different man to hold her each night.

But she couldn't not fight.

Even now. Why not let go and slip into the eternal darkness?

Instead she'd taken off her belt and tightened it across her upper body to cinch the balled-up sock into place as tight against the wound as possible. She was deliberately breathing slowly, aware that the slower she could keep her heart rate, the less blood it would pump from the open wound.

Still, there was nothing else to do but wait for the inevitable.

She remembered the tightness and pain and resolution in Quinn's face when he'd described how he wished he could have died trying to save his daughter's life.

He wasn't a quitter either, she thought. No easy way out for him. No crutches of alcohol or drugs. Kate had no doubt that he could have found a lineup of women to occupy him, but she was certain he'd turned his back on that, too.

So he'd chosen the lion's den as a place of escape.

Kate was sad. Not necessarily thinking about herself and that she would die. But thinking about Quinn's fierceness and his determination to go into the lion's den, hoping someday he might not make it out.

No, she realized, that wasn't the root of her sadness as she lay dying in the tunnel. It was that Quinn had loved his little girl so much and that the little girl was gone but the love was still there.

A father's love.

All right, she told herself, *don't deny it. Especially now.* That was her yearning too: for memories of a father who loved and protected. Not a father who . . .

Kate snapped that thought off like a brittle twig from a rotting trunk. She wasn't going to die with those memories crawling around her mind like snakes.

Somehow remembering the pain in Quinn's eyes gave her comfort. That was love. The better it was, the more it hurt when it was taken away. Couldn't something like that last forever? Didn't it deserve to remain shining and pure until time ended? Should that be how a daddy always loved his girl?

Kate caught her breath as a spasm wracked her upper body.

Yeah, death was that much closer.

She wanted to pray.

She wanted to believe.

But how could she? All her life, she'd been told about God the Father. There was a cruelty in that. God, the loving Father, when every time she heard the word *father* she had an emotional recoil. How could she trust any father after her childhood?

She saw it again, as if the conversation were happening this instant. Quinn's pain and anger and resolution. And his deep, deep sorrow.

Yes, that was a father's love that could be trusted. If she could believe God held that same kind of love for her . . .

Maybe she could pray.

OUTSIDE JERUSALEM • 21:19 GMT

Cohen had taken advantage of his security clearance and the speed of his BMW to reach Highway 1 to Tel Aviv. His cell phone rang. His private cell. Not many knew the number.

Cohen turned down his music. Mozart. A majestic piece.

With no foreboding, he answered on the third ring.

"Zvi," the caller said. "It's your CIA friend. You might remember a conversation we had once. Over dinner and wine. At a seafood restaurant in Yafo."

Couldn't be, Cohen thought. What he said was, "This line isn't secure."

"Does it need to be? We're old friends."

Cohen realized he was pressing his cell phone hard against his head. "Are we old friends?"

"You mean maybe I'm using some kind of computer trick to re-create a voice pattern to fool you."

"Are we old friends?" Cohen repeated.

"June 1992," his caller said. "I find you in a hotel room, drunk and singing Elvis songs."

"I still owe you for keeping that from my wife. Correction, ex-wife."

"From the beginning," the CIA man said, "I've known that Kevin was feeding you information."

"Kevin . . . ?"

Traffic was sparse. The taillights of a few distant cars ahead. Headlights of another about a half mile back. With Mozart, in a BMW that kept highway noise to a hush, it would have been a peaceful drive. With this conversation, it was anything but.

"Don't play games," the caller said. "Think I don't have a pipeline into the Mossad, too? Only I wouldn't have used it to put Quinn on a platter."

"Spell it out, then." This was classic interrogation technique, the caller implying that he knew a lot, waiting to see what would be revealed. Cohen was essentially calling his bluff. Or assessing damage.

"Gaza Strip. The Iranian connection. Fawzi. Kevin fed you enough to pass on the time and location of the hostage exchange to Safady. And he fed it to you early enough that Safady could get to Zayat and try the botched attempt on Quinn."

Cohen didn't answer.

"Acco," the caller continued. "Same thing. You had intel early enough to set it up for Safady. Did Kevin also supply the coordinates for the GPS locator to make sure Safady's men could find him easier?"

A pipeline into the Mossad, too. This was big damage. If the CIA knew this much about Acco, then his source deep inside the Mossad wasn't a bluff.

"What do you want from me?" Cohen asked.

"You broke our deal," the caller said. "Quinn wasn't supposed to be part of this."

"Safady wouldn't do it any other way. We needed Safady to get IDF special forces to the Temple Mount. I did the math. It made Quinn expendable."

"Obviously the American cop and Kevin are expendable too."

"What do you mean?" But Cohen's scalp prickled.

"You drove them into the Old City. I noticed they weren't in your car on the way out. We both know what's going to happen to the Muslim Quarter. If you left them there, you left them there to die."

"What do you want from me?" Cohen said once again. He'd been under surveillance? Suddenly, the emptiness of the highway seemed dangerous.

"With all those connections to erase," the caller said, "isn't it too bad you missed one?"

"Look, you're the one who helped plan this. You're the one who connected me to Safady. There's just as much fallout on you if you take this public."

"You're Mossad. And you have a secret order from the prime minister. Who's going to suffer more damage if this gets out?"

"You've made your point," Cohen said. This would be a disaster for the

Mossad. For the entire government. That's why he'd needed to obliterate any connections to himself and, by extension, any connections to the Mossad. "Last time. What do you want from me?"

"Just wanted to call."

"You've got leverage on me," Cohen said. "You'll be safe."

"Like Quinn was?"

"That was different. Nearly everything is going as planned. Even after Quinn went to IDF. The operation is less than an hour away from success. You'll get what you promised your people. There's no reason to get you out of the way."

"No reason anymore. You tried once"

"Point made again," Cohen said. "But you would have played it the same way if you were in my position. It's not personal."

"Of course." A pause. "Look in your rearview mirror."

Cohen glanced back. The car behind him had moved closer. Now the headlights flicked to high beam, then back to low beam. His caller was behind him.

Instinctively, Cohen accelerated. His BMW was a 700 series. It would be hard to catch on this road.

"Just so you know," the caller said, "it wasn't personal to me, either. Until you made it personal. I've got a little payback headed your way."

Cohen checked his mirror again. The headlights were farther back.

"I'm going to call in support," Cohen said. He had the BMW at 120 miles per hour. He'd be able to maintain distance. "You'd be smart to leave this alone."

"My first choice would be to do this where I can see your face," the caller said. "Second choice is this. At least you're going to hear it directly from me."

"What's that?" In twenty minutes, Cohen would be in Tel Aviv. All he needed were a few security guys to meet him on the road. He'd be fine.

"Remember how you had the van rigged to explode on Quinn in Gaza?"

Cohen didn't answer.

"The bad thing from my perspective is that an explosion happens too fast," the caller said. "You're dead, but you don't know it and you don't know why. Much better that I could have this time on the phone with you and let you know that your lovely black BMW is rigged the same way. I've got my finger on the button here. It's not anything you can outrun."

"Let's talk," Cohen said, adrenaline washing through his body.

"Now that you know it's coming," his caller said, "I'll count it down. Five . . . four . . ."

Cohen threw his phone down and slammed his brakes, tires screeching. If he could get the BMW down to 10 or 15 miles per hour, he'd jump clear, roll from the explosion, run into the darkness of the hills, and hope for the best.

He fumbled to unsnap his seat belt. It was not easy. He had to fight the steering wheel with his other hand to keep the BMW centered. He glanced at his speedometer. Down to 40 mph.

Finally he got free of his seat belt. The car was shuddering to a standstill. At 20 mph, he threw his door open. An automatic warning alarm beeped from his dashboard, and for a split second, he thought that was the explosion.

But he was wrong.

It came a heartbeat later.

TEMPLE MOUNT, JERUSALEM • 21:19 GMT

Esther and Silver had decided to split up to cover as much ground as possible. The Temple Mount's thirty-five acres left a lot of room for a frightened little girl to hide from soldiers.

Silver used the flashlight beam to probe the gaps of an ornamental hedge. There was movement beyond the leaves. Thin, dark lines. Two. Then three. Then four.

He was transfixed but couldn't comprehend. The leaves rustled slightly. Small branches cracked.

He stepped back slightly, then relaxed. It was the heifer. Seconds later, he saw something else through the leaves.

"Alyiah?" Silver said. Then he heard a small cry. "Alyiah!" He squatted. With one hand, he pushed aside some branches. With his other hand, he trained the flashlight on his face.

"Seelver!" she uttered.

It took some maneuvering for Silver to get through a gap in the hedge and reach her. She hugged him, not saying a word. He felt profound relief that the girl was not hurt.

He let the moment continue, enjoying the relief and the sense of protection it gave him to wrap his arms around her frail back. He wasn't the first one to push away, either. Before, any physical intimacy had scared him; handshakes, hugs—they were meant to be endured only for as long as the publicity moment demanded.

Instead Alyiah broke loose and immediately spoke in rapid-fire Arabic. Soft but urgent.

He shook his head. "I don't understand."

More soft, urgent words. She pointed over his shoulder.

"Let's find Esther." Silver knew she'd recognize the sound of the name and repeated it. "Esther." He stood again and took one of her hands.

She tugged back, pulling him in the opposite direction.

"No," he said. "Not that way." The broad, high outline of the Dome blocked the starlight. He needed to get her off the mount.

Alyiah pulled her hand loose and moved a few steps away using only one crutch.

"Seelver!" She slipped through the hedge.

He had no choice but to work his way through the gap again, scratching his arms and face. When he broke through, she was waiting. But she moved away again.

"Seelver."

He tried to catch up to her, but she refused to wait, teasing him forward a few strides at time.

This continued until they reached the steps of the shrine.

"No," he said.

But Alyiah climbed up the steps.

The great doors were closed, but there was a side door. Open.

"Seelver," Alyiah said again. This time she waited for him to climb the steps and reach her. She took his flashlight and snapped it off. Then she took his hand and pulled him through the door, into the shrine that was the third most holy site in the Muslim world.

WESTERN WALL TUNNEL • 21:19 GMT

All Kate knew was the Lord's Prayer, the one that began with "Our Father, who art in heaven." Ever since she was a little girl, she'd hoped she never made it to heaven. One father on earth had been enough horror.

Again she snapped off that thought. She imagined Quinn leaning down to pick up his little girl, kiss her forehead, tell her stories.

It gave her the strength to begin.

Our Father, who art in heaven . . .

She let herself go, whispering to this Father that she was lost and alone and cold and very, very lonely and could He maybe find a way to take away the hurt of dying without someone to love her and hold her hand and gently stroke away the hair from her forehead the way she'd always wanted a father to do.

She wasn't ready for the hot tears that rolled down her cheeks.

She wasn't ready for the cold to disappear as it did. For the loneliness to fall away from her as she slipped into warmth and peace that made her forget that her body was pressed against a stone wall and that her blood was seeping from her body.

Kate told herself her mind was giving her the gift of a desperate delusion. But as she ended her prayer, it felt as though she was in the strong arms of a Father she could trust.

If this was dying, she thought, she was ready.

If this was dying, there was one last thing to do before giving up the fight.

Kate fumbled for her wristwatch and punched a button.

Then she closed her eyes.

Hamer was waiting for Quinn at the top of the steps that led from the western plaza through the gates to the Temple Mount.

"Are you nuts?" Hamer said. "You just left them there."

"They're either going to come in or they aren't," Quinn said. "If they don't come in, you send soldiers. Brad Silver knows that."

"But—"

"I don't have time for this." Quinn rarely snapped. But this was too urgent. "Are paramedics waiting at the tunnel entrance? Bomb squad?"

The Western Wall tunnels were accessed near the Wailing Wall, just off the plaza where Hamer had set up base of operations for IDF.

"Already had the power turned on in there," Hamer said. "Seemed smart, even though you sound crazy."

"Read this." Quinn scrolled the message so that the screen lit up and handed Hamer his cell phone. The message was burned into Quinn's memory.

```
     Am in wall tunnel. Nuke threat. Davy Crktt. Cohen shot
Kevin. Me 2. Losing blud.
```

Hamer waved Quinn toward the steps to the plaza. "I'll deal with the surrender. Keep running! If there's a nuclear bomb in there, find it!"

Alyiah held Silver's hand, step by quiet step, only five paces into the shrine. She was trembling when she stopped, and she was gripping his hand so hard that his knuckles hurt.

Silver knelt beside her, wishing he could speak words of comfort that she might understand. She pressed a finger against his lips.

This he could comprehend. She wanted silence.

His eyes began to adjust to the semidarkness. The air was so still with such absolute silence that Silver imagined he'd be able to hear and feel a butterfly if it passed within his reach. The slight scuffle to his right, however, was not his imagination.

Instinctively he stepped back, pulling Alyiah with him.

"Stop," a voice said from the darkness, maybe thirty paces to their right. "That's far enough."

Alyiah gave a small cry of fright and clutched harder on his hand. Silver inched back farther. He and Alyiah were only a few rushed steps away from the side door and the freedom outside.

"I thought the girl had seen me," the voice said. "Too bad for you she brought you back. I've got a machine gun. Any farther and you're both dead."

Silver froze. He knew that voice.

"Let's talk," the voice said. "We both want the same thing."

Silver switched on his flashlight and swept it in the direction of the voice.

"Enough!" the voice barked. "Take it out of my eyes!"

With more courage, Silver would have thrown the flashlight and bolted. It might have provided enough distraction to get those precious few steps to freedom. But Alyiah was with him. He didn't believe he could make it with her. So he obeyed and turned the beam downward. Then he realized how much easier a target it made him. He flicked off the flashlight beam. He'd seen the machine gun held waist high in the man's hands. And he'd seen enough of the man's face to confirm the owner of the voice.

The terrorist. Safady. Wearing the uniform of an Israeli soldier.

Silver was a prisoner again. With the life of this little girl to protect.

WESTERN WALL TUNNEL • 21:28 GMT

With the tunnels fully lit, Quinn, the two paramedics with a gurney, and two bomb squad technicians made fast progress. Quinn knew the tunnels; he had taken the tour before. After the Muslim general Saladin had taken Jerusalem from the crusaders in the twelfth century, he had raised the city to the level of the Temple Mount by constructing arches and vaults to support a foundation for the buildings above this tunnel. Archaeologists had discovered it all these centuries later and excavated.

From the entrance at the Western Wall, they moved through the Secret Passage, named because of an inaccurate legend that said King David had used it to move under the city. There was a turn, and the western plaza with the floodlights set up by IDF appeared through a grill above, then disappeared as Quinn hurried forward toward Wilson's Arch, part of an original bridge built by Herod.

Quinn wondered if he needed to explore any of the side rooms. Then he heard a sound from somewhere farther down the tunnel—a piercing sound above the noise of the gurney's wheels. Quinn didn't pause to explore nearby chambers. He knew that sound.

By the time he reached Warren's Gate, a filled-in entrance to the Temple Mount, Quinn was certain.

Kate had activated her wrist alarm.

The sound took his mind back to their first meeting at the harbor in Acco. The dress swirling around her legs in the breeze. The flat look on her face when she'd activated the alarm to call in Israeli police.

He moved as fast as he could, grateful that Hamer had had the foresight to power the lights in the tunnels. The sound drew him like a beacon. It took him through a narrowing called the Kotel Tunnel, past the Hasmonaean Water Cistern, and then into an ancient promenade with upright blocks of stone and walls built around ancient pillars.

Then he saw her.

Kate. Kate. Kate.

Her face and body were flooded with the bright halogen of the tunnel lights. She was still sitting upright against the wall. Her eyes were closed, her head fallen sideways. The blood soaked in her clothing seemed black. Like death.

Quinn knelt beside Kate and lifted her wrist. He remembered that she'd pushed a finger underneath the alarm watch. He did the same here and found a small button. The shrieking of the alarm ended.

Her wrist was clammy and cold. He couldn't tell if she was still alive. No time to guess. One of the medics was already pushing him aside. The other was moving the wheeled stretcher.

Within seconds, Kate was on the gurney.

"Quinn," one of the bomb squad men said. Stefan, if Quinn remembered correctly. Short and wide with lots of dark beard. Stefan focused his light on a nearby pistol. "Hers?"

"Don't think so."

"She's got a pulse!" One of the medics was applying a pressure bandage to Kate's wound. The other was inserting a needle into her arm to begin an intra-venous drip.

"The shooter was this close and she's still alive?" the other bomb squad guy said. Tall, thin. Easier name to remember. Paulie.

"She text-messaged me after she was shot," Quinn answered. Later he'd allow himself the emotions of relief and hope that she was alive. "He wouldn't just stand here and watch her do it. She'd have been shot first, then escaped long enough to use her phone."

"How did he find her?"

"Look to your left," Quinn said. There was a small, shallow pool of blood on the tunnel floor. "That's how he tracked her. A trail of blood."

Paulie focused up the tunnel and spotted the first small spatter. "Let's move. If there's a bomb, we should be able to follow the trail back too."

Again Quinn forced away an emotional response. There was nothing he could do for Kate. Not in this moment.

He had taken a step when one of the medics called out.

"Something on her other arm. Looks like writing."

Quinn hurried back and leaned in close. She'd used ballpoint pen, her writing barely legible. Three short, crooked lines of words.

> timer set for midnight
> mq, sorry dinner didn't work out
> Rember rule one. dont let lions get you too

"Lions?" Paulie said.

"Let's go," Quinn answered. The first line was for the bomb squad techs. The second two were for him, and he was going to keep it that way.

Kate had written the message thinking it might be her last communication to the world. Thinking of him. The memory flashed into his mind again—the first time he'd seen her by the harbor, that hint of allure.

Quinn glanced at his watch. *Push aside feelings and regrets,* he commanded himself. He could do it. He'd spent five years doing it. "That gives us less than forty minutes."

COUNTDOWN TO 22:00 GMT

Earlier, Safady had seen the girl at the entrance of the shrine. Crouched by his gym bag at the far end, he hadn't been able to follow her out. And he hadn't even been sure if she had seen or understood the significance of what he was doing. Her return meant she probably had, especially because she'd brought the old man. No matter. It was a complication, but nothing he couldn't handle.

Silver's voice trembled as he spoke. "It's done, Safady—this whole operation. My son said so. He's surrendered, and by now Israeli soldiers are on the Temple Mount."

Safady listened closely for another scuffle of footsteps to warn him if Silver was moving closer. With a machine gun, or even bare-handed, Safady wasn't afraid of Jonathan Silver. But if he had to fire the machine gun, it would draw attention from outside. Ten minutes from now, that attention wouldn't matter. He needed to stall the old man.

"Typical American cowardice," Safady sneered from the darkness that hid him. "But this can end in a way that both of us desire."

"We'll never want the same thing," Silver said.

"No?" Safady's voice was lightly mocking. "Your son, though a coward, would disagree. He went to a lot of trouble to get me here."

"Brad believed you're an actor. I don't."

"We needed him to believe that. Do you want to know the truth?"

"You are a terrorist. I know that already."

"There's more to it than that." Safady was happy to keep the conversation going, strange as it was to be talking to a man he hated in the near darkness. "Much more. I think you'll find it interesting."

The old man didn't answer. But there was no movement.

"The Mossad and IDF set this up," Safady continued. "It was pitched to me by an Iranian double agent who was going to turn on me. Mossad and IDF wanted soldiers on the Temple Mount to search for weapons of mass destruction. I was supposed to be killed just after taking you to the orphanage. Then the Mossad could pretend from there to negotiate your release and demand the choppers. The hostages would not be in any danger."

"You killed two of them right away."

"Along with the Iranian traitor," Safady said, glancing at the luminescent hands on his watch. Just a few minutes more. He had to time the old man's death perfectly and get out of the shrine. Not too late. Not too soon. "From the beginning, the Mossad had no idea how wrong the operation had gone. It all comes down to money. In this operation, there was some CIA involvement. I have a contact in the Mideast branch who has received a substantial amount of money to keep me informed about the hunt for the Black Prince. He knew enough about it to make a lot more money by feeding me the plans for this. Your son, it seems, was also paying him."

"What do you mean?"

So easy to string along the old man. "The CIA contact betrayed the Mossad operation twice. Once to your son. Once to me. Except Brad only knew about the Mossad, not that I would be coming along for a free ride. Brad believed he was on a mission from God. It was easy to fool him. I made sure to set up a Web site that focused on his theology to make sure the world would blame him for this."

"And your mission?"

"What does it matter?" Five minutes, Safady decided. He would shoot without warning. "You're going to get the credit for what happens next anyway. No one can stop what's next. A united Arab world, blessed by Allah."

"You want war?" Silver asked.

"You and I will be on different sides of the war, but at least it will have begun. Then we'll find out. Is your Bible the ultimate truth? Or the Koran?"

"This is what you want? A battle to test God?"

"Don't you? Isn't that what you've been preaching for the last decades? The end of time according to the timetable of Revelation? So now it's upon us. Embrace it. If you're right, you have nothing to fear." Safady laughed. "Nothing to fear except the combined will of millions and millions of Muslims united against your God because of the desecration that will take place here tonight."

"Too late," Silver said. "IDF forces have secured the Temple Mount."

"Brad and I wanted the same thing," Safady said. "The Dome of the Rock. It's the fuse of Armageddon. He wants a new Temple. I want a reason to lead my people against you. I'm betting my civilization wins. Not yours."

Another voice rang through the darkness. Higher pitched. Urgent. "Bumb. Bumb."

The girl. She *had* understood the significance of the gym bag. She was struggling to find the English word to explain.

"What?" Silver asked.

"Boom! Boom! Boom!" the little girl said.

Safady could work with this. "I blow up a portion of the shrine, old man. Just enough damage to enrage all Arabs against Israel and the West. Israel will be destroyed."

Silver's flashlight beam snapped on. Safady could tell he was looking for the explosives. The beam stopped first on the gym bag that Safady had carried onto the helicopter, then on the C-4 containers and the wires leading to them. A very simple timer was attached. That's why Safady needed the delay. IDF's bomb squad could defuse the explosives in seconds.

"Drop the flashlight," Safady said.

"You wanted us to keep talking until it blew," Silver said.

"Drop it. I'll shoot the girl first."

Silver dropped the flashlight.

Good, Safady thought.

Then he heard the old man and dimly saw that he'd lifted the girl and was carrying her out of the shrine.

"I can see you!" Safady shouted. "Stop! Or you're both dead!"

WESTERN WALL TUNNEL • 21:23 GMT

Three waves of death, Quinn thought. The first wave—an explosion that would wipe out the Muslim Quarter of the Old City. The second wave—radioactive fallout. And the tsunami wave—global jihad.

The bomb squad guys had gone into more detail for Quinn about the Davy Crockett as they'd followed the blood spatter trail. It had ended here, at the Struthian Pool. The dark water was motionless, glinting from the lights installed by the tourism bureau.

Kevin's crumpled form lay next to the pool, a single bullet hole in his forehead. Quinn glanced at the dark form, then looked away. There would be time for grieving later.

"I don't like this, Paulie," Stefan said.

"Maybe she had it wrong," Paulie said. "Really. What are the chances it really is an M-388?"

Both men were in black pants and gray T-shirts, with tool bags hanging from their belts. Quinn had asked them about the lack of protective gear at the tunnel entrance. The answer had been grim. They needed to move fast. And if they were going to defuse a nuke, it didn't matter how much protective gear they wore.

"She had to be right about the bomb," Quinn said. "Why else call it a Crockett in the text message?"

"That's what I don't like," Stefan said. "Too easy to hide."

"Her blood trail starts here," Quinn said. "It's got to be in the water."

"The thing doesn't even weigh eighty pounds," Stefan said. "Could it have been moved after she was shot?"

"One way to find out," Quinn answered. He waded into the water. His feet hit something. Bulky, easily moved. He reached down. It was a large backpack. Empty.

He tossed it on the stone floor. "Maybe that's good news. If Cohen moved it after Kate was shot, he would have used the backpack."

Paulie and Stefan waded in with him, spreading to each side.

Seconds later, Stefan called out. He had the end of a nylon rope and began to pull. "There's something on the end," Stefan said, backing out of the water. He reeled in the rope and was rewarded by a slight bumping sound. A watertight plastic container emerged.

Stefan lifted it and grunted. "About the right weight."

Paulie was already there and helped him set the container down. "Think the lid is rigged?"

"Maybe."

"Doesn't look like anyone expected it to be found," Paulie offered. "That's in favor of no booby trap."

"I don't like the odds," Stefan said. "Lots of bombs are hidden *and* booby-trapped."

"How'd she know it was a Crockett unless she saw it?" Paulie asked. "Which means the lid was open not too long ago."

"Or maybe the shooter told her it was a Crockett and left the lid closed. Really, how many people have even heard of a Crockett, let alone can identify it by looking at it?"

"Or he told her while it was open."

"Or he didn't," Stefan said. "Are we going to flip a coin on this?"

"Think of the time," Paulie countered. "If we're wrong about the booby trap and we waste too much playing around with the lid . . ."

"Just as bad as if it's rigged and we set it off early." Stefan looked up at the arched stone ceiling. "Even if this one is dialed down, it's still got a nuclear yield that's going to blow away the Muslim Quarter."

Quinn grabbed the empty backpack. "The bomb is stable, right? I mean, if it was going to blow because of movement, it would have happened already."

"Fair enough," Stefan said.

"So don't worry about trying to defuse it," Quinn said. "Let's get it out of here."

"It's ten minutes back to the plaza. That only leaves, what, a little over twenty more minutes after that till midnight? You know how densely populated it is around here. No way that gives us time to find a spot it can go off without hurting civilians, let alone somewhere that radiation fallout won't put ten square miles out of commission for a decade."

Quinn pushed the backpack into Stefan's hands. "Hold this open and help me load it."

"Why?"

"Because I hope to prove you wrong."

DOME OF THE ROCK • 21:35 GMT

Jonathan Silver had picked up Alyiah and cradled her in his arms. He turned his back to Safady, using his body to shield Alyiah. Silver left Alyiah's crutches behind and took a step away from Safady. A slow but steady step. Only a few more steps to the open door and the evening air on the Temple Mount.

"I can see you!" Safady shouted. "Stop! Or you're both dead!"

Silver stopped. "How much time left before the explosion?"

"Time enough for us to leave together," Safady answered.

"Liar," Silver said. He'd finally figured it out. Safady's hatred was real. He had not worked with Brad; he had used and betrayed Brad. Safady would gladly have killed Silver by now. Along with Alyiah. So what had been delaying him? Silver knew. "You don't want to shoot."

He took another step and braced himself for the roar of death that he doubted he would even hear or comprehend. But Safady didn't pull the trigger.

Another step. Alyiah shivered against his chest.

"You'll be dead before you reach the door," Safady said. His voice now sounded strained. "Stop!"

"You won't shoot," Silver said, his back still turned to Safady. "That will draw the Israelis. This entire conversation has been about delaying me longer, then shooting me just before the bomb goes off. That would give you time to get away but not enough time for the soldiers to come in and find it."

"This is your chance," Safady said. "If you believe your God will be the victor when the war is over, you'll have the Dome. You can rebuild the Temple. Isn't that your life goal?"

"Good-bye. You'd better start running now if you don't want the Israelis to find you here."

"You're bluffing," Safady said. "You won't give up your life, even to save the world."

Silver took another step. He was going to win one way or the other. If he made it outside, he'd find the Israelis. If not, the Israelis would find him, alerted by shots.

The silence stretched for Silver. Such a quiet night outside. He didn't want to die. But he was praying, and he felt the presence of more than just the pressing silence. He felt the promise of an eternity of peace.

"Oh, Lord," Silver breathed. "Please spare the child."

He was close enough to the door now.

He threw himself forward, making sure Alyiah was safely outside.

There was time enough for him to see the flash of gunfire reflected on the walls, hear the roar, and feel the impact of pain shredding his back.

51

They had made it back to the plaza in eight minutes. From the Struthian Pool, Quinn had taken the first shift of carrying the bomb out in the backpack. Paulie had stayed with Quinn, and they had alternated carrying the backpack, managing to maintain a half-jogging pace. Stefan had raced ahead, knowing he'd need to get closer to the tunnel entrance to make walkie-talkie contact. That had given Hamer enough notice to be waiting for Quinn at the western plaza outside the entrance to the tunnel.

"Tell me you had not yet cleared the choppers from the Temple Mount," Quinn said to Hamer. He still had on the backpack and didn't stop walking.

"Stefan got to me in time," Hamer said, staying with Quinn. "I put my senior pilot on standby up there with the engine running."

"Have you talked over the math with the pilot? How long to reach the Dead Sea?"

"Under forty miles to the Mediterranean," Hamer said. "A Black Hawk has top airspeed of two hundred miles an hour. There's a tailwind. Pilot says with liftoff and acceleration, twelve minutes could get him there, maybe eleven."

"There'll only be twenty-two minutes left once we're in the air," Quinn said. They were almost at the steps leading up to the Temple Mount. "Dead Sea's half the distance. Why not take a larger margin of time?"

"We want this bomb three or four hundred feet underwater when it goes. That's not going to happen in the Dead Sea. It'll float no different than a fat tourist."

Hamer pointed at two soldiers about twenty yards away and waved them close.

"Plenty of time to get well out over the Dead Sea. Drop it halfway across, and that explosion won't do any damage, even with the bomb floating. It's a low-yield nuclear device."

"A tailwind to the Med means an offshore breeze to take fallout away from land," Hamer said. "On the other hand, halfway across the Dead Sea puts the bomb directly on Jordan's border. Think IDF wants to explain why we dropped a nuclear device within even a couple miles of it? It's not like we can hide the explosion or deny it."

"But cutting the margin to ten minutes? What if the timer is not accurate?"

"No choice. At the least, the chopper will be somewhere over the water."

"You're putting this pilot on a possible suicide mission."

"No choice."

The soldiers reached them. From here, it was only a couple hundred yards up the steps and to the chopper on the Temple Mount.

"Take this man's backpack and hump it upstairs," Hamer told them. "Get it inside the chopper that's on standby. Don't drop it."

Quinn followed the soldiers.

"Where are you going?" Hamer asked. He had to hurry to catch Quinn.

"Someone's got to help the pilot throw the backpack out," Quinn said. "Especially since we're cutting it a lot closer to take it into the Mediterranean. When you asked the pilot about his margin of time, did you tell him why?"

"Wasn't going to say a word until you made it out of the tunnel. Then I'd see how much time was left and if I'd send him out."

"I'll be with him. I'll fly then if he has to bail."

"You keep playing Russian roulette with your life, sooner or later you're going to catch a full chamber."

Quinn gave him a flat stare. "I can always hope."

Hamer shook his head. "You need therapy."

That's when the sound of machine-gun fire up on the Temple Mount reached them. *At the Dome of the Rock.*

The gunfire was followed a second later by the sound of exploding grenades.

DOME OF THE ROCK • 21:37 GMT

Inside the shrine, Safady had carried his gym bag and dashed past Jonathan Silver's body, cursing him, wishing he could stop long enough to spit in his face. From there, Safady had moved away from the Dome, waited until the soldiers had swarmed the mount, then lobbed a couple of grenades away from the holy site hoping to keep them away from the shrine.

Because Silver had guessed right. Who would have expected the old man to be so smart? All Safady had needed was another five minutes. Then he could have killed Silver and the girl. In five minutes, the machine-gun fire would have been the perfect distraction. It would have drawn in the Israeli soldiers. The bodies would have distracted the soldiers for another crucial thirty seconds. Then the explosives would have killed the soldiers and provided the perfect cover for Safady to escape.

Now?

The Temple Mount seemed empty except for the two choppers. One of them had its engine running and blades turning slowly.

And directly in front of Safady was the crippled girl. Without her crutches.

He scooped her up and kept running.

He could only hope it would take too long for the Israelis to arrive. If they got there too soon, it would be simple to disarm the timer. The bomb was not sophisticated. There'd been no need for it.

Safady was looking for movement that would signal a convergence of soldiers on the Temple Mount. He needed to escape. He was not a martyr. He could have gone back and triggered the explosives himself, taking down the shrine in a final blaze of glory. Except none would have known he deserved the glory. Except he'd be dead, unable to use the events on the Temple Mount to transform himself into a leader able to unite Muslims across the world.

No, he was not a martyr. If the Dome was not blown up tonight, he would make sure the Muslim world heard about the events that had taken place. The media would broadcast everywhere that the hated Christians had taken their red heifer there for sacrifice, that they'd placed explosives inside the Dome of the Rock. Outrage would spread in waves of violence—violence that could only be answered with violence. When the war was over—when all the Muslims across the globe had united to defeat America and Israel and their allies—his people would have Palestine returned to them.

Yes. He needed to survive. He needed to escape.

He had his machine gun.

He had more grenades.

Safady stopped briefly. The girl was struggling, but it was ineffectual. He hit her once and got another grenade from the gym bag. He pulled the pin, throwing it hard and as far away as possible. Then another grenade. And another.

There was a five-second delay. He covered another dozen yards at a full run. Perfect timing.

The first grenade blew. After a short delay, the second followed. And the third. That would distract the soldiers when they arrived.

Still running hard, he made it to the open area near the helicopters.

The gunfire and the grenades had worked.

Except for two men running toward the chopper with a shared load, the Israeli soldiers at the top of the steps were headed where the grenades had exploded.

Safady grinned. Allah had blessed him with the foresight to wear an Israeli uniform.

There was one way to get off the Temple Mount, and the opening was there, right in front of him.

He boldly stepped toward the chopper. The girl was struggling again.

"Say a word," he hissed in Arabic, "and the pilot dies. Do you want to kill an innocent man?"

TEMPLE MOUNT, JERUSALEM • 21:37 GMT

Esther had reached Jonathan Silver's bleeding body when the Israeli soldiers cautiously approached the steps leading up to the shrine. She crouched.

He lay facedown. Blood soaked the back of his shirt.

Esther yelled at the soldiers. "I need medical help for this man."

"We've got orders to contain this situation," one soldier said. "Whatever it is."

"*Uunnngh.*" Silver's groan was barely audible to Esther. She knelt, her face close to his.

"Bomb inside," he muttered.

Bomb inside!

Esther was up again in a flash. "He says there are explosives inside."

She and the soldier locked eyes briefly, each knowing the implications of an explosion inside the Dome of the Rock. Then he lifted his walkie-talkie and barked orders into it. "We need a bomb squad. Now!"

Esther tried lifting Jonathan. "He's too heavy," she grunted. "Help me."

"Find a way," the soldier said. "No time."

21:38 GMT

Safady used perfect Hebrew speaking to the helicopter pilot. "This is the girl," he yelled. "She needs to be evacuated. Diabetic shock. Someone radioed you, right?"

Safady recognized the pilot. He'd been flying the other chopper, the one that supposedly took ground fire. Even though he'd put a pistol to this man's head earlier, Safady didn't worry about being recognized. On the way out of Gaza, he'd been dressed as a Palestinian terrorist, complete with face scarf. Now he was in an IDF uniform.

The pilot nodded. "I've been on standby."

Safady had expected he would have to bluff that the order had not reached the pilot. All he needed was to get close enough to catch the pilot unawares and hijack the chopper. This was a bonus.

The pilot reached down to help them up. When Safady and the girl were on the chopper, the pilot put up his hand and turned away from Safady, obviously taking another call.

Seconds later, the pilot turned around again. "What's going on?" he shouted to Safady. "I'm supposed to wait for two soldiers and a backpack."

Safady was about to reach for his machine gun, but the soldiers arrived. One jumped aboard. The other handed him the backpack. Both ignored the pilot and Safady. Then the soldier on the chopper jumped down.

Once again, the pilot turned to Safady to ask a question, and once again, he was interrupted as another passenger jumped onto the chopper.

A man Safady knew all too well.

A man Safady believed was dead.

Mulvaney Quinn.

As Quinn jumped on board, he pointed up and yelled at the pilot over the noise of the chopper. "Get this in the air. Now! Hamer's orders!"

"We've got a soldier back there with a girl! Says somebody radioed permission for them to board."

Quinn only half turned to see an IDF uniform in partial darkness, the soldier cradling a machine gun in his right elbow. With his left hand, he held the hand of a small Arab girl balancing on one leg. She looked frightened.

Quinn wondered if he could afford to waste another minute or two trying to sort this out. He decided against it. There was still time to get to open water and dump the bomb with a small margin of safety. If they left now and there were no complications, everyone would be fine. They'd deal with the soldier's mission after that.

"In the air!" Quinn said. "Now! I'll explain as we fly."

The pilot responded by placing a hand on the controls, and the chopper lifted. Simultaneously he tilted the chopper forward, gaining airspeed.

Quinn harnessed himself into the seat on the passenger side and put on his headset as the chopper moved. He turned again and gave a thumbs-up.

From the shadow, the soldier just stared back.

Quinn's smile didn't seem to reassure the girl much either. He turned forward again. He had bigger things to worry about.

Quinn glanced at the time. Twenty minutes left. Eight minutes of margin. If the timer didn't go early.

Had he been recognized?

With his adrenaline flowing, Safady's skin felt alive, as if it were crawling in ripples. The last man he'd expected to board the helicopter had been Mulvaney Quinn.

Should Safady hijack the chopper now?

Not in Israeli airspace. If the chopper didn't head directly where it had been ordered, it would alert the ground command that something was wrong. Within minutes—less time than that, even—Israeli jets would swoop in ready to launch missiles.

For that matter, did Quinn's presence complicate matters? Safady's machine gun was enough leverage against two men, especially with both strapped into their seats.

It didn't complicate things unless Quinn had recognized him.

Safady told himself no. He was in the Israeli uniform. Quinn had only glanced back, and Safady had been deep inside the helicopter, his face in the shadows. Quinn had turned away again, showing no reaction. Impossible that he could have guessed.

Yet Safady would not underestimate the man who had been hunting him for five years, getting closer as he eliminated each outer ring of men that Safady had used as protection. Maybe Quinn had hidden the recognition. Maybe he was merely waiting for the right moment.

Safady watched closely, almost enjoying the heightened sensations of a full adrenaline rush.

The chopper was moving in a straight line, and Safady decided he didn't want to make his move until he had a better sense of where they were headed and why the pilot had been waiting on standby for Quinn.

21:48 GMT

"I'm Billy Orellana." The pilot's voice came through Quinn's headset. "What's this about? All I was told was to get to open water as fast as possible."

"We've got a low-yield nuclear bomb, and the timer is down to less than twenty minutes."

To his credit, Orellana didn't flinch. "We should be a few miles offshore in twelve minutes. Maybe eleven."

He pointed ahead. The city lights below were thinning. Clear sky. Half-moon. Bright stars. Quinn could already see the glow of Tel Aviv.

"We'll be south of Tel Aviv," Orellana said. "That will keep us clear of commercial airspace. No worries."

"No worries," Quinn repeated, trying to put the image of a mushroom cloud out of his mind.

"I'm going to contact base and find out who was supposed to radio me about the soldier and where we need to take the girl. If it's a hospital, the more notice we can give the better."

Quinn nodded and listened through his headset to Orellana's communications with Hamer.

Then Quinn looked back at the soldier after Hamer reported with a negative. No IDF soldier had been ordered onto the chopper by any other commanding officer.

DOME OF THE ROCK • 21:48 GMT

Stefan and Paulie had reached the shrine. Both were breathing hard from the sprint up the steps from the western plaza and the dash across the Temple Mount.

Neither had put on protective gear. Yet. Other soldiers were carrying it behind them. What was more important right now was to assess the situation. If any part of the shrine was damaged, the consequences would be far too grave.

With no hesitation, they rushed to the entrance, ignoring a woman kneeling on the ground beside a man, cradling his head.

Both had flashlights, and they found the C-4 easily. There had been no effort put into hiding it. They rushed toward the explosives, knowing the C-4 could blow any second.

TEL AVIV AIRSPACE • 21:44 GMT

It didn't take long—the little girl frozen in fear beside him—for Safady to confirm the westward direction of the chopper. It was easy to identify Tel Aviv fast approaching, an irregular mass of lights with a jagged black edge where the sea stopped the city's growth. He saw the border of darkness, the line north and south, where the clusters of lights of different cities along the coast ended. To the right, he identified Haifa.

Was Tel Aviv the destination? If so, it was probably to take Quinn back to Mossad or IDF headquarters.

Safady had chosen the chopper as an escape route, knowing anything was better than remaining on the Temple Mount. Should he now divert the flight into the Gaza Strip?

No, he decided. Israel controlled airspace over Gaza. Escort jets would remain a threat. If Safady survived that threat, trying to get the chopper landed in Gaza was an almost certain suicide mission; it would draw ground fire from trigger-happy kids. Even if he did get down without injury, he'd essentially be imprisoning himself. Escaping Gaza would be an entirely new problem.

But the Lebanon border was only sixty miles north. Beyond Lebanon was Syria. How long would it take the chopper to get him there? But escort jets wouldn't let the chopper stay above land.

Safady did some rough calculations. What if he made the chopper go out into international waters before heading north? On this heading, it wouldn't take long to get out of Israeli territory. When the solution hit him, he realized that he'd been given a gift. With both men in their harnesses, they would be unable to do anything to stop him.

His choice was made easier by Quinn. The man had turned and was staring harder at him. There was enough light from the instrument panel for Safady to notice a sudden tightening of Quinn's features.

Recognition. Movement of his lips. Quinn was speaking to the pilot through the headset. Safady wrapped one arm around the girl's shoulders and dragged her forward.

He wasn't worried about the pilot. Orellana had to keep the chopper in the air. Safady could watch his hands easily enough. But he didn't know if Quinn was armed, able to come up with a pistol while Safady focused on the pilot. Safady knew he needed to prevent any communication between the two of them, prevent them from planning a surprise to stop him.

Safady swung the stock of his machine gun hard, smashing it flat against Quinn's head. It sent the man forward against his harness straps. Quinn hung limp briefly, then straightened.

Safady ripped off Quinn's headset and put it on his own head. Pressing the barrel of the machine gun against the base of Quinn's neck, he moved to the side so he was looking over Quinn's head at the pilot. Now he could watch both. The girl, struggling to keep her balance, was no threat.

"Do you hear me?" he asked the pilot. Safady almost pulled the trigger to blow apart Quinn's head. But he was too conscious that the bullet might do serious damage to the interior of the chopper. Quinn was more leverage alive than dead.

"I hear you," the pilot replied. "Just have no idea why you're doing this."

"Roll this or drop it to make me fall," Safady said, "and I'll hold the trigger on the machine gun until it runs dry. Think your chopper can sustain that kind of internal gunfire?"

"Whatever you want, give me time to—"

"I want to hear you tell air control that you're going to change your heading. We're going to Syria."

"You don't understand—"

"Get over the water; head into international waters. When the jets appear, don't give them any reason to think this chopper is going to be a threat to any civilian targets."

"Listen—"

"*You* listen," Safady said. "Or he dies. And the girl is next."

TEMPLE MOUNT, JERUSALEM • 21:44 GMT

Jonathan Silver was dying.

Esther was on her knees, cradling his head, just as she'd cradled the Waqf guard who had died earlier that evening. She could not get any soldiers to help her. Two men had rushed past her into the shrine. She couldn't lift Silver, nor did she dare leave him and search for help from anyone else.

Then she looked up and saw the red heifer. It wandered closer and closer until it was just above Esther and Silver. The end of its halter dragged on the ground.

Had it been sent by God?

It stood placidly, ignoring the sounds of soldiers moving.

Esther only had to move her right hand a couple of inches to reach the end of the halter. She remained cautious and slow, hoping she would not spook the miracle. Only when the rope was firmly in her palm did she gently set down Silver's head with her other hand.

Speaking in a low, soothing voice, she eased into a standing position and patted the heifer's back.

TEL AVIV AIRSPACE • 21:46 GMT

The shock of recognition had nearly the same impact on Quinn as the unexpected blow from the butt of the machine gun.

He'd been trying to tell Orellana to get the chopper over the water at all costs when Safady swung the gun without warning. It felt as though his upper cheekbone was shattered; the pain was a beacon of light keeping away the darkness of oblivion.

Quinn blinked hard, trying to keep his thoughts from dissolving into confusion. *Priority: get the nuclear device over the water. Then figure out a way to save the pilot and the girl.*

The urgency of the moment put his pain into the background. Quinn kept organizing his thoughts.

Safady did not want to die. That's why he'd hijacked the chopper. Safady would keep the passengers alive as long as possible. That was his leverage.

But Safady did not realize there was a nuclear device on board. If he did, he'd be trying to force the pilot to dump it over Tel Aviv. Not only to save his life but because of the destruction it could mean for Israeli citizens below.

Get the nuclear device over the water. Even if we all die when it explodes.

Quinn lifted his hand—the one nearest the pilot—and pointed straight ahead. Orellana nodded and kept the chopper flying toward the Mediterranean at two hundred miles per hour.

Quinn had expected another blow. When it didn't come, he again lifted his hand and motioned for the pilot's headset.

He was hoping, betting, praying that Safady would be curious enough to allow it. That would buy Quinn extra time to get the chopper away from Tel Aviv, now directly below them.

Again Quinn braced for another blow. It didn't come.

But the headset did.

It hurt badly to slip it over his head but was well worth the pain. Especially when he heard Safady's voice.

"Make this happen," Safady said. "You'll live. They'll live."

"Make what happen?" Quinn asked. The chopper had not changed direction. He needed as much conversation as possible until there was no chance the nuclear device would harm anyone but them.

"I want to reach Syria. You negotiate for me. You make sure Israeli jets allow us to get out of this airspace."

"How do you guarantee our safety?" By the digital readout on the chopper's instrument panel, Quinn knew down to the second how much time was left before the nuclear device detonated. It was crucial not to look at the device itself to confirm it. Safady must not find out what it was. "What's to stop you from killing your hostages when you get there?"

"You tell me," Safady said. "Isn't that your job? Negotiating?"

Just ahead was the black of the water, stretching out to the horizon. Quinn glanced at the altitude showing on a dial. Fifteen hundred feet. How low would it need to be for the girl to drop down safely?

Maybe there was a way to get the pilot and girl out of this alive. And a way to take out Safady.

"First we drop the pilot and girl into the water," Quinn said. "I fly this the rest of the way to Syria."

"Not good enough," Safady said. "I don't trust you."

"Just the two of us. Once we're over Syrian water, same thing. I drop you in the water just offshore, then fly back. In Syrian water, you're safe."

"Give me a reason to trust you."

"Here's why it works," Quinn said. "You won't shoot me while I'm flying, or it kills you. For that matter, if you try to kill me as you bail out, the chopper crash could easily land on you in the water."

"That's your leverage," Safady said. "What's mine?"

"You decide if I want you dead badly enough to commit suicide. Because short of crashing the helicopter, how else can I stop you?"

Now they were over the water. Maybe a half mile offshore. Not so far away that the girl and the pilot would be at risk in the water.

"I'm going to tell the pilot to go lower." Quinn didn't wait for Safady's answer. He motioned to Orellana, pointing downward. He pantomimed the rest of his plan. He pointed at Orellana and the girl, then pointed out of the chopper, making a diving motion with his hand, followed by swimming motions. Then Quinn pointed at himself, pantomiming that he would fly the chopper. He hoped Orellana would understand the implications and keep a poker face.

Orellana stared at him hard for a few seconds, then nodded, his face blank. He turned the chopper downward.

"Let me speak to the pilot and explain," Quinn said.

"No. You have no communication with him."

"Then when I give the pilot back the headset, you tell him our plan. You tell him I'm going to fly. Tell him he's dropping in the water, and he needs to make sure he keeps the girl safe in the water with him."

The chopper was down to a thousand feet. Moonlight dappled the water. It was calm. If Billy and the girl jumped from a low enough altitude, the girl would be fine.

"You can fly this?" Safady asked. Quinn knew he had the man. Safady wanted to live badly enough to take the deal.

"I can fly it," Quinn said. He'd been watching Orellana with the controls. He knew enough to lift the chopper again and move it forward. Out to sea. He didn't need to know anything more. Not with the nuclear device about to detonate within minutes.

Because Safady had guessed wrong. Quinn *was* willing to die.

If you weren't going to make it out of the lion's den, the next best thing was to make sure the lion would never get out again either.

53

nfidel, Safady thought. *He has no idea how much I hate him.*

The chopper was low enough now that the wash from the blades was beating the water below to a froth. Quinn's side of the chopper was open to the night air.

The girl stood in the opening, clutching the side because she had no crutches to help her stand, swaying with the movement of the chopper. She was wearing an inflated life jacket, far too large for her. Her eyes were closed tight. There was resignation on her face, not fear.

"The girl goes first," Safady said. He reached over, keeping his eyes on the pilot and his machine gun trained in place. With his other hand, he felt for the girl's fingers and pried them loose. Safady gave the girl a shove but didn't look to see if she'd fallen. Too much at stake.

Safady's eyes were still on the pilot. "Your turn."

Quinn's plan was sound, but Safady was about to change it. He only needed a pilot, and a pilot would be strongly motivated by self-preservation to keep the chopper safe.

But the pilot didn't need to be Quinn.

Safady was going to enjoy shooting Quinn and kicking his body out into the water.

Inside the shrine, Paulie grinned at Stefan. "It's about time we had an easy one."

Stefan grinned back. "No arguing this time."

It was an extremely simple setup. It had obviously been put together by someone with little sophistication and little time

The timer was down to sixty seconds. But Paulie had his wire cutters poised over a center wire. It was the only connection that mattered. Without a detonator, the C-4 was harmless. After snipping the connection to the timer, it would be easy to remove the explosives.

"Plug your ears," Paulie said. Old joke between the two of them.

Stefan obliged.

Paulie snipped through the wire. He winced some. Hard not to.

"That's it?" Stefan asked.

"That's it," Paulie answered. "All is well that ends well."

OVER THE MEDITERRANEAN • 21:54 GMT

Quinn watched the girl fall into the darkness. Time to get Orellana into the water to help her.

He glanced at the clock on the chopper controls. Six minutes. Still time to get the chopper farther out from shore after the pilot was gone.

Orellana handed Quinn the headset.

"When you unbuckle your harness," Safady told Quinn through the headset, "no sudden moves. After it's unharnessed, you put the headset down on the seat again. I'm going to stand back and give you plenty of room to take the controls. Again, no sudden moves."

Quinn nodded. He was conscious of blood running down his face. He unbuckled slowly and stood slowly. Orellana kept the chopper steady.

Quinn made his first step around the back of the seat.

Safady stepped in front of him and lifted the machine-gun barrel, pointing it at Quinn's chest.

Quinn was aware of the open chopper door behind him. He understood. Safady had a safe backdrop for a spray of bullets.

Safady grinned as if he realized that Quinn knew his intentions.

Quinn braced for impact.

And in the next second, he felt himself plunge backward.

TEMPLE MOUNT, JERUSALEM • 21:54 GMT

"Stay with me," Esther pleaded with Silver. "Don't give up now."

"Hurts," he said. "Ice."

The cold of shock. She prayed that God would spare his life.

"Arm around my shoulder," she said. "Hold on. Just a few more minutes."

She squatted beside him and did her best to help him stand. She tottered under his weight and nearly fell backward. Shifting slowly, Esther managed to put

Silver's upper body across the top of the red heifer. She expected it to bolt. But her prayers were answered. The heifer remained docile.

She lifted Silver's legs. "Hold the neck. Just a few more minutes."

With Silver's upper body in place, Esther grabbed his legs and swung them upward. Again she feared the heifer would bolt. And again her prayers were answered when it remained steady.

There was enough of Silver's weight on the heifer now that Esther was able to arrange his legs easily. When she was finished, he was straddling the heifer completely, the tips of his toes dangling near the ground.

"Hang on," she urged Silver. She meant it figuratively . . . and literally. "Please, just hang on." Then she urged the heifer forward.

Christ had ridden a donkey to His death in Jerusalem. She prayed that Jonathan Silver would be able to ride the red heifer of sacrifice to survival.

OVER THE MEDITERRANEAN • 21:54 GMT

Safady laughed.

Let the infidel die, he thought.

Safady started to squeeze his trigger finger, but his world tilted, a sudden roar filling his consciousness, and he lost all balance. It took him a moment to realize that the roar was the chopper engines—that the headset had ripped loose from his head.

And that he was falling toward the water.

54

Billy Orellana relaxed. He had plenty of time. He had seen Safady ready to shoot and, still at the controls, had turned the chopper violently on its side, flipping Safady and Quinn out the open door before Safady could fire the machine gun.

The chopper had swung back and forth, its blades seeming to almost touch the water, and Orellana had fought it back into horizontal position. As the craft settled into place again, Orellana had gunned it forward and had already put a few miles between the chopper and Quinn.

Quinn would be alive in the water. The girl had a life jacket. Safady had probably lost his machine gun. Orellana would give it another three minutes to dump the bomb farther out to sea, then turn around and find the girl by following the flashing beacon on her life jacket.

He didn't know what wave effect the bomb would cause, but he knew that Quinn and the girl would be fine. They'd just bob like corks as the wave passed beneath them.

Orellana glanced behind him to make sure of the backpack's position. It would be tricky to throw it out himself but not impossible.

Then he felt as if someone had jabbed amphetamine into his heart.

The backpack was gone.

Gone!

There was only one place it could be. It must have tumbled out of the chopper when Orellana tilted it on its side.

The bomb was in the water far enough offshore not to be a risk to anyone on land. That meant the safe choice for Orellana was to keep going and sacrifice Quinn and the girl.

MEDITERRANEAN SEA • 21:55 GMT

When Quinn surfaced, coughing for air, the chopper's roar was already fading.

In the air, he'd seen a blur of the chopper's lights—enough to figure out what had happened. He'd felt, rather than heard, the splash of another large object.

Dazed from the blow across his face, he tried to orient himself. His hand brushed against something, just beneath the surface and sinking slowly.

Kicking to keep his head above the water, Quinn grabbed it.

The backpack! It had enough air in it to offset some of the weight of the Davy Crockett.

Quinn fought the weight of the backpack briefly, not thinking clearly. What was he going to do? Grab the girl and outswim a nuclear blast?

The shore lights were barely visible above the gentle swell of the waves. He guessed they'd made it a couple of miles out. When the bomb exploded, the buildings and people on land were out of danger. The deeper the bomb sank before detonation, the better for civilians on the shore. Not that a couple hundred feet of water would protect Quinn and the girl from the blast and the shock and the geyser.

Quinn dropped the backpack, and it fell slowly from his hands.

Here he was, in a place where there was no sense fighting life or death any longer. Safady had escaped him, but no matter what Safady tried in terms of hijacking the chopper, time was running out for him, too.

The girl would die with Quinn. But instantly and without understanding what had happened. Quinn took what solace he could from that.

A minute passed as he waited for the bomb to detonate.

Then Quinn heard the girl scream.

TEMPLE MOUNT, JERUSALEM • 21:56 GMT

Esther and Silver and the red heifer stood at the exit to the Temple Mount. Below, at the plaza, she saw the swarm of soldiers and paramedics.

"Help," she said to a soldier guarding the exit. "This man's been shot."

"You need to be searched for weapons and explosives," he said. "I have orders not to let anyone leave the Temple Mount."

"This man just risked his life to save the Dome of the Rock from destruction," she snapped. "Do you have any idea of the war that would have broken out in Israel if he hadn't?"

The soldier blinked. The harsh, white floodlights showed him to be barely more than a boy.

"He's an American," Esther said more quietly. "If he dies because no one here would save him, it will be a great embarrassment to Israel. Save him. You will be serving your country just as much as he did."

Another few blinks. Then he reached for his walkie-talkie.

Seconds later, paramedics burst toward the stairs.

If Silver were conscious, Esther thought, she'd enjoy the chance to remind him of the irony that the sacrificial heifer had saved his life.

MEDITERRANEAN SEA • 21:56 GMT

Where is the girl?

Quinn kicked off his shoes. He dog-paddled, trying to lift his head as far out of the water as possible. He heard another scream to his left, twenty yards maybe. He saw movement in the water—dark, blurred objects. A flashing light.

Quinn could have gone into an overhand crawl, essentially sprinting through the water. But it would make too much noise.

He ducked his head into the water and began a stealthy breast stroke toward the noises. Even in the dark, it didn't take him long to understand what was happening. The life jacket had a flashing beacon that threw off enough light.

Safady was fighting the girl in the water, trying to take away her life jacket.

Safady? Had the man fallen from the chopper too?

Murderous heat surged through Quinn. Safady would drown the child to ensure his own safety. He swam harder, now keeping his head above the water. The girl's arms were above her head. Safady was pushing her under, and had managed to slide her out of the life jacket.

Quinn had no illusions. The girl was going to die in the nuclear blast. But he wasn't going to let her die in terror or with water filling her lungs as she desperately thrashed for air.

He reached the girl and, kicking hard with his feet, held her head above the water.

Safady ignored the life jacket and attacked.

Quinn held the girl in his left arm and threw a punch that bounced off Safady's skull, an ineffective blow because Quinn was hampered by the weight of the girl and had no way to brace himself to throw his weight into the punch.

It was enough, however, to move Safady away briefly. Quinn took advantage of it. He grabbed the life jacket and thrust it into the girl's arms.

Safady paddled away, and Quinn made the mistake of following, too eager in his lust for murder.

Safady's move, however, was just a feint. As Quinn closed in, Safady kicked hard, the heel of his boot bouncing off Quinn's forehead. It dazed Quinn, and he slipped under the water.

He fought for the surface, but Safady reached him just as his mouth reached the air. Safady rolled his full weight onto Quinn, pushing him under.

Quinn kicked and struggled but could not lift both of them out of the water. He was totally submerged, his mouth closed tight. His lungs fought for air, and the noise in his ears seemed like a train rumbling through his skull.

Then he felt Safady's hands around his throat. Quinn reached for Safady's wrists, but the man was too strong and Quinn couldn't pull them away. The rumbling of the train grew louder and louder. It was black, confusing, and still Quinn kicked with his last ounce of energy. It was futile, and he knew it.

So this was death.

Then, suddenly, something else was pounding against his back. The water roiled more, and Safady's grip released.

The weight fell off Quinn, and he kicked for the surface again, coughing and sputtering, drawing in lungfuls of air, and trying to orient himself.

The splashing nearby was frantic. He saw enough to understand.

It was the girl. She'd abandoned the life jacket to help Quinn. She was clinging with both arms to Safady's neck. Riding him.

That's what he'd felt on his back. Her foot.

She'd managed enough of a choke hold on Safady with her arms that he'd been forced to release Quinn. Now Safady was spinning and churning in the water, trying to shake the girl loose. But he had no leverage.

Quinn took in more gasping lungfuls of air and kicked, keeping his head out of the water. He reached down, unbuckled his belt, and pulled it loose. Then he moved toward Safady and the girl. Quinn slipped one end of the belt back through the buckle. It gave him a noose, and when Safady spun around again, Quinn dropped it down over Safady's head.

"Let go!" he told the girl. "I've got him."

She didn't listen.

He tried it in Arabic, and she released her grip, reaching for the nearby life jacket.

Now Quinn was able to brace against Safady's body. He pulled the belt tight against the man's neck with one hand and pushed off Safady's body with the other.

Quinn was filled with enough hate and rage to want to decapitate Safady, and the man's choked groans of agony fueled Quinn's efforts.

Safady's kicking became weak flutters, and still Quinn pulled at the noose.

He became aware that the little girl was crying. "No, no, no," she pleaded.

Her cries alone might not have stopped Quinn, but in that moment of awareness, the night lit up above him. He realized the roar of anger in his ears was more than that.

The chopper. A spotlight settled on them. Quinn saw that a cable with a hook on the end was swinging back and forth as the pilot began to lower it.

Quinn looked back. The girl with her life jacket was in easy reach. He grabbed her and pulled her in. She let go of the life jacket, and Safady grabbed it. Quinn pushed him away.

The end of the cable splashed into the water beside them.

Quinn checked to see if Safady was going to attack again. The man was swimming backward slowly with the life jacket and its flashing beacon. The spotlight showed a jeer on his face. It was a jeer of triumph. A man believing that he would be impossible to find in the darkness of the water once the chopper lifted Quinn and the girl to safety.

Quinn should have felt satisfaction, knowing Safady would die to a bomb. In the same way that Safady had destroyed so many others.

But unless Quinn managed to grab the cable, he and the pilot and the girl would die with Safady when the bomb detonated.

How much time remained?

TEMPLE MOUNT, JERUSALEM • 21:57 GMT

In the thirty seconds after he'd learned that the man who'd saved the shrine from destruction was Jonathan Silver, Hamer had turned the entire focus of everyone around him to saving the man.

Now he was focused on Esther. And the red heifer.

Esther had asked for white strips of cloth and a few bottles of water at the paramedics' station. She was using the cloth and water to wipe Jonathan Silver's blood off the heifer's hide. It didn't seem right for an innocent creature to carry a man's blood.

"You've got a dangerous animal there," Hamer said.

"Please listen," Esther said. "There's still a girl missing up on the Temple Mount. If you're not going to help, at least let me go back."

"I've already sent some men. There are other issues here. We're going to need you to spend time with IDF. Debriefing."

"I don't say a word until I know the girl is safe."

"Fair enough," he answered. "I understand your concern. The other issue is this heifer."

She stopped wiping it.

Hamer noticed. "I'm sorry. As long as it's alive, it's going to be a security concern for us. I don't have to explain why."

Esther noticed something strange about the top of the heifer's shoulder, where she had been wiping away some of Silver's blood. She looked at her cloth again. There were two shades of red. One was blood dark. Another shade held more copper.

"I think the children at my orphanage are going to grow very fond of this beautiful animal," she said. "I would be grateful if you helped arrange transportation for me and the animal back into Gaza when your debriefing is finished."

"Maybe you don't understand," Hamer said. "The heifer is a liability. We're going to have to destroy it."

"No, you don't understand." Esther poured water on the heifer's shoulder. She used a fresh white cloth to rub again, then held the cloth up for Hamer to see more copper color. "Look at that small patch of white hair. It's red everywhere else. Except for the patch. It was covered with dye."

Hamer touched the area on the shoulder of the heifer. It was only the size of a dime, but without doubt, it was white. "You're telling me this heifer is a fraud."

"Yes." Esther smiled. God had sent the heifer to save Jonathan Silver. Just as God had used Jonathan Silver to save the heifer. "The animal is blemished."

OVER THE MEDITERRANEAN • 21:57 GMT

Quinn's first few attempts to grab the cable failed.

It was wet. His hands were wet. And the girl clinging to his chest made it seem like Quinn was swimming in mud.

Finally, his fingers clawed enough of a grip to swing it toward him. But there was no way he had enough strength to hold the wet cable with one hand as the chopper pulled upward.

He was able to pull hard enough, however, to get a few feet of cable dangling below him in the water.

"Hold the cable," he shouted at the girl in Arabic.

She was afraid and clung harder to him. She didn't know the urgency.

How much time before the bomb detonated?

"Hold the cable!" he shouted again in Arabic. He needed both hands.

Quinn saw her eyes—wild, terrified. He leaned forward and kissed her forehead. That relaxed her, and she reached gingerly for the cable.

"Both hands!" he shouted. The chopper's noise added to the difficulty here.

Once she had a secure enough grip, he dropped his left arm away from her, reaching down into the water and fishing for the free end of the cable. He found the hook at the end and brought it back to the surface, making sure his left thigh was in the loop. He slid the hook around the cable in front of his chest. Immediately the loop tightened as his body weight pulled down on it.

It didn't matter. Now he could hold the cable in front of him with both hands, his arms around the girl, the cable secure around his thigh.

He gave a thumbs-up, trusting that the pilot could see it in the spotlight.

With a jerk, the chopper pulled Quinn from the water. With his entire weight on the cable, the pain on the bottom of his thigh was searing.

But they were in the air, moving.

The chopper gained forward speed, and the cable lost its vertical angle; Quinn and the girl trailed the helicopter as if they were a kite's tail. Fierce wind whipped at Quinn, and he closed his eyes.

His world was reduced to black, to the roar of the chopper, and to prayer and hope that they would clear the area far enough ahead of the detonation.

One minute? Two? How much longer?

It seemed like an eternity before an unnatural brightness snapped through the darkness of his shut eyes. Seconds later came the horrible thunder far louder than any chopper engine. And then the tremendous buffeting of a surge of air that seemed to tug, then throw the chopper.

Then Quinn realized that they were still safe, that the chopper was still flying, that the girl was still huddled against his chest.

Despite the pain of the cable cutting into his inner thigh, Quinn closed his eyes with a sense of peace. It had been a long, long time since he'd felt trusting little arms around his neck like this.

EPILOGUE

The catamaran was roped to the end of a wharf. It was a Hobie 16, the double hulls connected by framework and the taut nylon fabric that served as a deck. The sails were still furled. An elderly man began to untie the mooring ropes. He was wearing only shorts, his skin tanned, his build powerful despite his age.

The man glanced up at a tourist couple walking down the wharf toward him. His face registered no apparent alarm. The couple approached. A younger man in khaki pants and a white T-shirt. The woman, attractive in a summer dress, a little younger.

The couple stopped when they reached the tanned older man.

"Rossett," Quinn said.

"You found me," Rossett said, still squatting at the ropes.

"Mossad, IDF, and CIA did the work," Quinn said. "They had a lot of motivation. The money trail that led to Safady kept going. All the way to Jamaica. Brad Silver's cell phone had a call to a number that led to you. After you were supposed to be dead. His old man was tough enough to live through a half dozen bullets in the back."

"I heard Silver's had a conversion of sorts," Rossett said. "Started a big campaign to help the children of Palestine. I'm just as surprised he sent you my way."

"He told us how Safady explained a mystery CIA contact helped set up a double cross on the IDF Temple Mount op. After a month of digging around, turns out the mystery is over."

Rossett stood. A slight breeze ruffled his hair. "Who'd guess Safady would be a leak? He had a good thing going."

"You mean because you passed along everything I learned in five years of hunting him?"

"It let me know where he was all the time," Rossett said. "He was a good weapon, too. You'd identify someone close to him, and to protect himself, he'd make sure they died one way or another. Over the last year, the Freedom Crusaders took care of it."

"Safady paid you to tip him. Brad Silver did too."

"Think I did it for the money?"

"I wish I could believe you liked seeing Safady's circle get smaller," Quinn said. "To protect the free world and all."

"You were a bird dog, pointing them out one by one. Didn't hear you complain when your dirty work was done by others. Gave you the moral high ground. You know, as you protected the free world and all."

Quinn had no answer to that.

Rossett looked at the woman in the summer dress as he spoke to Quinn. "You brought a date?"

"Kate Penner," Quinn said. "She's got extradition papers to take you back to the States. Your retirement options have narrowed."

She didn't reach across to shake hands. Just nodded. She stood slightly behind Quinn and kept listening. Behind her, the sharp rise of the Jamaican hills was a lush backdrop of green, framed by the incredible blue of a Caribbean sky.

"Didn't expect retirement to last long."

Rossett turned his back on Quinn. "Extradition. Right. Who else is on the island?"

"The Mossad," Quinn said. "And IDF. Neither trusts the other right now to get any job done."

Over his shoulder, Rossett glanced at Kate. "You're naive or an optimist if you believe I'll make it to the airport alive."

"I'm good," she said. "The best choice you have right now."

Rossett faced Quinn. "You have any idea how deep this goes?"

"Zvi Cohen left a few more tracks than you did," Quinn answered. "Not many tracks. But enough. Apparently he didn't expect to be one of the casualties."

"Apparently not. I got the same impression during my last conversation with him."

"That would be in the last few seconds before his car blew up."

Rossett nodded. "Almost as hard to hide cell phone records as a money trail, isn't it?"

"Why did you do it?" Quinn asked.

"Cohen double-crossed me. And he put you on the block."

"No," Quinn said. "All of it. Why? Even now, I believe you have a code of honor. I believe you want to protect the free world and all. I'd like to keep believing that."

"You mean after I'm gone," Rossett said.

Quinn let that one hang for a second. "Why?" he asked again.

Rossett squatted and began to untie the ropes, making it look like it was going to be just another day on the waters. "It started at a seafood restaurant. Great place. You should try it. In Yafo. Look over the water and have a toast in my memory."

Rossett stood, then dropped the rope in his hand. "I'm there with Cohen. Just the two of us. CIA and Mossad. Friends. At first it was just an idea. A what-if. Between the two of us, we had enough connections to pull together the handful of real players in the world that could take the war against terrorism to the next level. If we gave them a way to do it that kept them protected—cell group structure. We started talking about a plan every time we got together. Until it looked good enough that we got serious. Then Cohen and I set up meetings in a way that protected both sides. We both had great British accents we'd use pulling together the links. Took about a year. After that, all Cohen had to do was sell the Mossad and the prime minister on a reason to go to the Temple Mount."

"Binary chemicals threat."

"The Mossad had to buy it." Rossett looked at the horizon, as if it offered freedom. "Don't need to tell you much more, do I?"

"You and Cohen used everybody. Even came up with a fake red heifer."

"Just had to understand their motivations to make them the fall guys," Rossett said. "Misguided evangelicals. A Muslim extremist."

"What was *your* motivation?" Quinn asked. "That's why I called in a favor from Hamer. So I could be here to hear it from you."

"Same one I sold to generals and politicians and money guys who gave intel and connections and funds to make it happen."

"They gave you a Davy Crockett, too," Kate said.

"From U.S. inventory. Easier to steal than you think. World's worried about a nuclear suitcase, forgetting that America's got a couple thousand Davy Crocketts in storage, no matter what the government tells you has happened to them."

"Roz," Quinn said, "I want to hear it from you. I trusted you. We were friends."

"Motivation? It wasn't money. But Safady needed to believe it, and I wasn't going to throw it away as he paid me. For me, it's never changed. Protect America."

Rossett had one rope left to untie before the Hobie would drift off. "Remember Rumsfeld? Drain the swamp. That was motivation for all of us. To start the kind of war we can win."

"No matter the cost in lives," Kate said bitterly. "You used people like pawns. Threw them away."

"You *are* naive," Rossett told her. "It's going there one way or another. Eventually a Davy Crockett is going to make it out there. Terrorists don't even have to worry about smuggling it onto American soil. If not, a suitcase bomb from Russia through one of our ports. Iran's got money, and Iran hates us. It's going to happen. This way, we've got the best chance of winning."

Rossett untied the last rope and held it in his hand. Now the Hobie was free to go.

"Rossett," Quinn said, "the American government is willing to hide you where you can't be found."

"Really." There was no inflection in Rossett's voice.

"There's a soldier," Quinn said, "hardly more than a kid. Joe Patterson. Thought his wife was dead, but Del Saxon lied to him about that. He's given the feds enough to unravel the Freedom Crusaders network. Feds delivered on a witness protection promise to unite the kid with his wife and new baby. They're probably living somewhere in Utah, their biggest worry whether they're going to run out of diapers."

"The kid only knows about the Freedom Crusaders. Not the real players. I do. They're in the same government you think wants to hide me."

"Had to let you know the offer was there," Quinn said. "And Kate's good. It wouldn't hurt to try to make it to the airport."

"I don't think so," Rossett said. "I'm not Cohen. I made promises to protect my sources. Win or lose, I keep those promises."

Kate asked, "What are you going to do? Sail away into the sunset?"

"If you let me." Rossett slapped the rope against his open palm.

"Have a pistol on that little sailboat?" Quinn asked.

"Nope. Never needed one here."

Quinn reached into his back pocket. "Take this. An IDF special. Hamer says if you want to end it on your terms, call him when you're ready. Just press the Send key." He handed Rossett a cell phone.

Rossett took it. No more words. He threw the rope down, and stepped onto the Hobie. Once he pushed off, Rossett began to raise one of the sails. The gap between the Hobie and the wharf widened to ten yards.

"That's it?" Kate said. "He's gone."

"You're good," Quinn said. "But you're up against Mossad, IDF, and CIA, plus all the players who know he's the only person who can link them to all this. Rossett knows nobody in the world is good enough now that he's been found."

"So he gets a few hours' sailing before he gives himself up?"

"Kate," Quinn said gently, "he's not coming off the water again."

"But . . ."

"The cell phone is loaded with C-4. An IDF special. Rossett knows that too. Hamer's giving him the choice. End it now, or run and wonder every minute when it's coming."

Kate paused. "Hamer gave you this chance. To let you hand Rossett the phone."

"For all he did wrong, Roz honored his code." Quinn tried to smile but couldn't quite manage it. Too much sadness in his eyes.

"You knew he'd take the phone."

"Rule one in negotiating: understand your opponent."

"Yeah," Kate said. "I'd almost forgotten. Rule one."

They stood there for a minute in silence. Like an ordinary tourist couple. Rossett was a hundred yards out now. Full sail.

"You all right?" Kate asked. She stepped closer to Quinn.

"Not really."

"In a couple of hours, we'll be back at the airport, headed different directions on different flights."

Quinn watched Rossett, the wind sending the Hobie out to the open waters. Alone.

Kate touched Quinn's cheek gently. She faced him squarely, put her arms around his shoulders, stood on her toes, and kissed his chin. Then she stepped back. "I won't apologize. I've wanted to do that for a while. Unless you want to miss your flight and walk the beach, I'm thinking that was my only chance."

Quinn studied Kate, who was waiting for a reaction, nibbling her lower lip. He was tired of being alone. He glanced back at the disappearing Hobie, thinking that this was over, that he'd never forget the past, but maybe, finally, he could leave it there and begin to think about the future. It was hard to forget how good it had felt over the Mediterranean, when the little girl had those trusting arms around his neck.

"You asked if I was all right," he said, turning away from that one last look at Rossett. Sunshine felt good on his shoulders. "Some hurt never leaves, but it's better than it has been for a long time."

Quinn took Kate's hands; he drew her forward and kissed her forehead with the same softness as she'd kissed his chin. He'd spent enough time alone. "It would be nice to walk the beach."

CHRISTIAN RESEARCH INSTITUTE

The Christian Research Institute (CRI) exists to provide Christians worldwide with carefully researched information and well-reasoned answers that encourage them in their faith and equip them to intelligently represent it to people influenced by ideas and teachings that assault or undermine orthodox, biblical Christianity. In carrying out this mission, CRI's strategy is expressed in the acronym EQUIP.

The E in EQUIP represents the word *essentials*. CRI is committed to the maxim "In essentials unity, in nonessentials liberty, and in all things charity."

The Q in EQUIP represents the word *questions*. In addition to focusing on essentials, CRI answers people's questions regarding cults, culture, and Christianity.

The U in EQUIP represents the word *user friendly*. As much as possible, CRI is committed to taking complex issues and making them understandable and accessible to the lay Christian.

The I in EQUIP represents the word *integrity*. Recall Paul's admonition: "Watch your life and doctrine closely. Persevere in them, because if you do, you will save both yourself and your hearers" (1 Timothy 4:16).

The P in EQUIP represents the word *para-church*. CRI is deeply committed to the local church as the God-ordained vehicle for equipping, evangelism, and education.

CONTACT CHRISTIAN RESEARCH INSTITUTE:

By Mail:
CRI International
P.O. Box 8500
Charlotte, NC 28271-8500

In Canada:
CRI Canada
56051 Airways P.O.
Calgary, Alberta T2E 8K5

By Phone:
24-hour Customer Service (U.S.): 704-887-8200
24-hour Toll-Free Credit Card Line: 888-7000-CRI

Fax:
704-887-8299

For information (Canada):
403-571-6363

24-hour Toll-Free Customer Service (Canada):
800-665-5851 (orders and donations only)

On the Internet:
www.equip.org

On the Broadcast:
To contact the *Bible Answer Man* broadcast with your questions, call toll-free in the U.S. and Canada, 888-ASK-HANK (275-4265), Monday–Friday, 5:30 p.m. to 7:00 p.m. Pacific Time.

For a list of stations airing the *Bible Answer Man* or to listen to the broadcast via the Internet, log on to our Web site at www.equip.org.

THE REAL
CODE BREAKER
FOR THE
APOCALYPSE

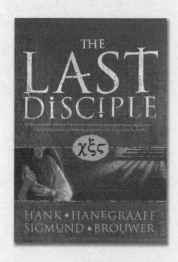

From Best-Selling Authors

HANK HANEGRAAFF
AND
SIGMUND BROUWER

✝ ✝ ✝

visit

www.decipherthecode.com

for more info